A Neighborly Affair

an erotic novel

Peter Mack

D1453875

ISBN-13: 9780977457564

ISBN-10:   0977457567

Cover Concept Design & Layout:
oddballdsgn.com
Typesetting & Interior Design:
Industrial Fonts & Graphix

Manufactured & Printed in the United States
09 10 11 12   BCT   10 9 8 7 6 5 4 3 2 1

A
Neighborly
Affair

TRU·LIFE·PUBLISHING

Brooklyn · New York

11202

Mack

JG

To
My Great Grandfather
Peter Mack Cooks
(1889 – 1954)

—I'ma ridah cuz I got ridin' in my bloodline/
I'ma shine cuz I got shinin' in my bloodline/
I get that dough cuz I got hustlin' in my bloodline/
I bleed concrete —

—Lil Wayne

Acknowledgements

In the pit of hell, stripped of everything I valued, I prayed. God, thank you for revealing in me a gift that would shield me from a lifestyle of sure destruction. Thank you for the will to struggle and the dedication to claim a glorious reward. Amen.

Mom. You said hold on until I could see my way through. Well, I can see clearly now. I love you 1000X.

Dad. It's true. All the ducks are flying in the wrong direction. And you were right about something else too— my swing gets better with every at-bat.

Christina Hunter. A love like yours is rare indeed. It's what poems and songs are written about. Nothing can compare. You've held me down when the winds got strong. You might stumble, but never fall. I love you truly.

Lisa Nichols. You carried my seed for nine months and gave birth to a beautiful replica of me. The bloodline continues. Thank you. I love you for the magnificent woman that you are.

Crys Rae. Hey, sis. We are the same spirit. The same breath. Live rich, die ready. XOXOX, bro.

Laine Laine. Hey, sis. We are the same grain of salt. We add flava to this muthafucka. I told you help was on the way. XOXOX, bro.

Coretta Haltom. Hey, you. I keep forgetting that I was your first love. I keep forgetting you don't love me anymore. I keep forgetting how you betrayed me. I keep forgetting that I should not love you still.

The Spears Family. Fred, my brother from another mother. It's just all the way real with you...all the time. Moms II, thank you for opening your home to me all those years ago.

Shouts out to: Ansar from Philly (already rich), Alley Cat from Richmond (freedom ain't free, ya heard?), Pooh from Oakland (she do all she can do like a Hindu), Cadillac Mike from South Park (keep you on her mind), King Dah from Boss Angeles (lean hard on a mark), and David Turner from Vegas (smile when it hurts). Live and direct, y'all served it raw and uncut to get my weight up and BOSS UP!

Glenda Brass and Mika Akim. Thanks for that scratch. Find me if you feel me.

Karen Mitchell. Beautiful. Magnificent. Believer. Sistren, when you invite a BOSS to the table of TRU LIFE, the meals get real rich and fantabulous. Let 'em know that this is only the first nail in the coffin of the competition. Let ''em know that if it ain't a Peter Mack novel, then it ain't TRU LIFE. Better yet, tell 'em to break their fingers and throw their laptops in the Jacuzzi behind the wet bar cuz they won't need them. TRU LIFE is taking over! Peter Mack said that!

Jah Love,
Peter Mack II

Part One

Chapter One

Sherrelle

The sun was rising earlier now that summer was approaching. It creased through the sheer curtains like a happy smile to welcome a new and exciting day. Sherrelle could feel the warmth on her face, massaging her forehead, eyelids, cheeks, and lips. It felt good. She stirred under the soft goose-feathered comforter, angling her head so that the moving sun would not escape her.

With this movement her entire body warmed and her fingers instinctively trailed down her soft thighs. There was heat coming from the spot she reached for, making her smile with her eyes closed. Her breasts swelled together as she turned onto her side, pushing her ass into her husband. She was hopeful that he would take the bait. She nudged against him harder, trying to feel any reaction. Softer this time, she ground her bare ass into the thin silk of his pajamas. She hated that he wore pajamas. Still he did not stir.

She creased her warm pussy with her delicate fingers, taking advantage of the warm feeling emanating from within her; the sun moving over a bit, forcing her to disengage

1

her ass from her husband's groin to follow its warmth. She rubbed herself slowly, rubbing her legs together at the knees with the pleasurable feeling. Dipping one finger into her wetness, she moaned softly, preparing to bring herself to a climax. Privately, she wished that her husband would feel some way about this, but she knew he would pretend to know nothing of her self-satisfying activities. And he would not awaken to participate, though she hoped he would.

Suddenly, her husband sat upright, wide-eyed as he roughly reached for the digital clock on the nightstand. "Why didn't you wake me?" he asked in a groggy, waking voice, oblivious to her interrupted pleasure.

I tried she said to herself. "Wait, come here," she said, reaching for him as he swung his legs off the bed. He looked back at her with a frown

"It's too early for that," he complained, seeing the smoke in her hooded eyes.

"Come on," she urged, grasping the back of his pajama top. "I'll do all the work." He turned to her with a softened expression.

"Sherrelle, I've really got to get to the office. We can't do this now. Tonight. I promise I'll try to get home early and make it up to you."

Sherrelle released his shirt and sat up in bed as he rose to his feet. "You make it seem like such a hard thing to do."

Percy turned to her with a crooked smile on his face. "You want me to stumble into the office late? You know that right now is a busy time for me."

"I understand that, but I need some time too," she complained.

"You need sex, that's all," he countered before turning to the bathroom with a low chuckle.

"From my husband!" Sherrelle called after him.

He held up one finger, his back to her.

"I can't believe you sometimes," she hissed, tossing the comforter aside and stomping onto the hardwood floor.

Percy turned suddenly, anger in his small, hazel eyes. "What can't you believe, Sherrelle?" he wanted to know.

"Nothing. Whatever," she sighed, waving him off as she turned away from him.

"Oh, excuse me if you feel neglected. Remember, I'm the one paying the bills around here. I'm the one making it possible for you to leisurely do what you do through the day. If I had it like you, I'd be chipper too." Percy flailed his arms in the air in punctuation.

Her eyes narrowed, her hands snapped to her hips. "What do you mean 'do what you do'? What the hell is that supposed to mean?"

He rolled his eyes to the ceiling and threw his arms up. "Whatever you think it means, Sherrelle."

She looked at him incredulously. All she wanted was to make love. A lone tear dropped from her eye.

"Look," Percy began, taking a step in her direction. "I'm sorry. You see how late I got in last night. Right now is just a really busy time. It kills me not to be able to give you the time you deserve. How could I resist you?" he asked, caressing her arms with the same crooked grin as he looked over her shapely figure. This softened her up. "I promise to make it up to you."

"Promise?" she asked looking up at him, thinking that in the time it took for them to fight she could have gotten what she wanted in the first place.

"I promise," Percy answered, kissing her on the forehead and turning abruptly away.

This is getting old, she thought to herself as she watched the door close behind him. She slipped on a nightie and turned into the hallway, her bare feet falling softly on the thick white carpet. Adorning the walls were expensive oil-on-canvas paintings by Gordon, Matisse, and Renoir. In the living room she was reminded of the comfort of how she lived and the success of her husband. Intricately designed wooden tables, Tiffany lamps, Waterford crystal vases, and Chanel curtains spoke of the luxury she'd married into.

As she dropped a half pack of bacon slices into a pan she reasoned with herself that their relationship would get better once his audit was over at work. The bacon began to sizzle as she walked out to the back porch to dump the empty package in the trash. Seeing it full, anger washed over her yet again. *Sorry nigga* she thought to herself as she banged the back door open. *Nigga can't even empty the trash like a real man.* She ran barefoot across the grass and threw the full plastic bag angrily into the bin. On her way back to the door she heard a woman scream out in pain. *Was that her neighbor?* she wondered as she looked toward the window that had to be her bedroom. *Was she being beaten?* She ducked low as she crept along the side of her house, against the fence that separated their property. She couldn't imagine her neighbor's husband—a handsome, buff guy—putting his hands on the frail woman she'd met a week ago.

The curtain was parted to reveal their bedroom. Sherrelle's heart sped up when—her feet moving away from the intrusion but her heart willing them to stay—she saw them naked in bed. Her neighbor had her eyes closed and she was gripping her husband's chest while she rode him. Sherrelle watched her small breasts bounce with her motion. She looked at the man who had his eyes closed too, seemingly straining at a thought. *What was he thinking about and why doesn't he look at his wife?* Sherrelle asked herself. The scene made her hot. Ouch! she almost said out loud when the thin woman reared back, making her husband wince as his dick stretched at a downward angle. "Damn," Sherrelle huffed. She felt for him, remembering that he had a knee injury. "At least his dick worked," she whispered as she tore herself away from her voyeurism, remembering that she had bacon on the stove and at the same time wishing it was her who was having a stiff dick plunged into her.

Sherrelle was surprised to find Percy out of the shower and dressed so quickly when she stepped back into the house. He was at the kitchen door, looking at her disapprovingly. "I had to empty the trash," she explained, trying not to make it sound like a complaint. He simply nodded, looking to her dew-wettened feet, blades of grass stuck to her ankles. Sherrelle saw a wild look cross his eyes and became aware of the short, transparent, cream-colored nightgown she was wearing, and the fact that she had on no panties. She could smell the smoke of burning bacon.

"You should really put some clothes on," he said before turning away from her.

Sherrelle watched in silence as he grabbed his leather Coach satchel from the living room couch and headed toward the door. When it closed behind him, she angrily grabbed up the sizzling pan of bacon and threw it into the sink. As she stomped her way back into the bedroom, snatches of her neighbor's lovemaking danced across her mind. She could feel the moistness between her legs returning from her interrupted morning interlude.

Her body was moving of its own volition, plopping its bare ass down on the edge of the bed and reaching under it for the black leather doctor's bag. She reached inside for the thick dildo. She breathed out hard at the sight of the deep black, thickly veined phallus. "This is what I do," she mumbled to herself in mockery of her husband's earlier comment as she touched the dildo's bulbous tip to her throbbing pussy lips. She pressed the head in, closing her eyes and recalling the flexing muscles of the dark man next door. She pushed any thoughts of this being adultery from her mind, eager to feel a semblance of the pleasure her neighbor had enjoyed.

Leaning back on the bed, spreading her legs wide, she used one hand to push the dildo in and out while the other stimulated the sensitive knob between her wet pussy lips. Her breathing grew heavy as soft moans escaped her lips. The dildo was flexible, bending with her movement. She withdrew it to place it in her mouth, sucking her juices from the warmed rubber. She slurped the juices from it with enthusiasm, tasting her own flavor with sensuous abandon. Working her fingers rapidly over her now swollen clitoris, she inserted the dildo into her throbbing pussy again, sliding it deep inside. She rotated her hips against the meaty rubber as she felt her passionate heat concentrate itself at the center of her body.

"Ahhhhh...!" Sherrelle screamed out in ecstasy as her juices flowed from her. Her body shuddered and her legs collapsed to the bed as she pulsed around the dildo, which she squeezed as if milking it dry.

★ ★ ★

Sherrelle walked naked through the house after taking a shower and curling her hair; Mary J. Blige sang her rich sermon about staying strong through tough times. Sherrelle had made up her mind to go shopping. *If he wasn't good to fuck, at least his money was good to spend* she thought to herself and not for the first time. The phone rang as she sat down to the computer in the den.

"Hello," she answered lazily.

"Wassup, Homeslice. Whatchu doin'?"

"Hey, Peaches. Just got out the shower," Sherrelle replied, surfing MySpace.com profiles.

"Mmmmm, sounds good," Peaches taunted. "I can hear it in your voice."

"Girl, I wish. If you count my trusty handheld then you're right on point," she commented, clicking on the HoodSweet site, quickly reading about an opportunity to sell HoodSweet apparel for women.

"Girl, you need to come down to my job and find you a part-time lover."

Sherrelle chuckled. "And then I'll have to beat off them sorry niggas who think I'm there to dance. Thanks, but no thanks."

"It ain't like that," Peaches assured her. "Okay, let me not be the one to try to sabotage your marriage, but you can at least come and see me dance."

Sherrelle frowned. "What I want to see you dance around a pole naked for? You're my best friend, but I ain't into that."

"See, now you trippin'." Peaches sulked on her end of the phone.

"I'm just kidding. But for real though, girl, I ain't trying to be around a bunch of horny niggas."

"They pussy cats. Look, whatchu 'bout to do?" Peaches wanted to know.

"Finna spend some money in a minute, but right now I'm sitting here naked in front of my computer," Sherrelle answered as she typed an e-mail inquiring about how she could sell HoodSweet clothes. *Maybe this was something I could do* she thought to herself.

"Well, girl, get dressed. I'll meet you at the Cheesecake Factory on the patio," Peaches suggested excitedly.

"Okay. I'll be there in thirty minutes," Sherrelle

answered before hanging up.

After waiting several minutes for a reply from her e-mail, Sherrelle got up to peek out the front window. Her neighbor's Lexus coupe was still in the driveway, so she knew she hadn't gone to work yet. Sherrelle wanted to see what good sex looked like in her eyes.

After putting on a sexy peach dress that stopped just below her ass, she waited by the door for her neighbor to emerge. She checked herself in the mirror—bronze coloring for her full heart-shaped lips, hair whipped and cascading to her shoulders, her dark legs shining and toes pretty. When her neighbor stepped out into the driveway, Sherrelle stepped innocently from her front door. She waved to her neighbor, noticing that her husband was following behind on his cane. *Poor thing* she thought to herself as he looked up at her. There was a gleam in his eyes that she knew she'd caused. This made her feel good. A simple validation that she sorely needed. She waved, smiling big and bright as she stepped off the porch holding her Fendi bag.

She held on to her private knowledge like something sweet and delicious. *He didn't even have the decency to put on a shirt* she thought to herself, struggling to avert her gaze so as not to cause any undue suspicion. She looked away from his chiseled shoulders, stomach, and chest. Her eyes blinked against his powerful thighs peeking from under shorts that stopped just above his knees. It pained her to see him hobbling on the cobblestones, like a powerful horse with a thorn in its hoof. And she pretended not to notice the way his eyes brushed over her breasts, aware of the way her hips swayed. She saw herself in his eyes and realized she was absolutely gorgeous. This look had been absent from her husband's eyes for some time, and she missed it.

Chapter Two

Marlin

Waking up in this new house was still taking some getting accustomed to, with its unfamiliar smells and the odd angles the sun streamed across the high walls and onto the wooden floors. Even the new bed his wife had insisted on buying felt awkward and hard; its extra fluffy comforter damn near smothering him in its wrap.

With the new scent of strawberry body wash coming from the bathroom (the baby blue tiles too cold to walk on barefoot), he peeled the comforter away from his neck and chest, letting it rest at his hips. He placed his hands behind his head and looked up at the ceiling, not excited the way he used to be with the knowledge that she would soon appear in the doorway. Her long, slender neck would be shiny brass above the soft V shape of the heavy cotton robe. Soft wisps of bronze-colored hair would be stuck to the skin just under her perfectly shaped ears. She would be smiling broadly, expecting his admiring eyes to compliment her.

He chased these thoughts away to make room for the more pleasing ones that danced across his mind as he stared toward the ceiling. He reached down to release the hold the comforter had around his erect joint. It was extra hard and he knew that it was not in anticipation of his wife emerging damp from the steamy shower. He'd reluctantly followed her across the country when she was offered a new position. She had the ups on him since he wasn't playing ball, and the new position meant enough money to pay for his rehab and bills. This was taking some getting used to. He was just about to get some playing time and was hoping to get a new contract—he'd blown his signing bonus—when his knee twisted in a way that dashed his hopes. When his contract wasn't renewed and Stacy got the new job offer, she didn't have to argue with him for long to make him leave Seattle for Indianapolis.

Thoughts of the beautiful woman who lived next door invaded his mind. He knew this wasn't healthy, but old habits were hard to break. He'd thought nothing of her in the beginning, but then there was something in her smile that opened him up like a spring flower. She made him feel the way his wife did when their love was fresh. She was not as pretty as Stacy, but there was something hood about her that he found irresistible. Dark chocolate skin, thick hair that hung to her soft shoulders, and long legs that stopped near her elbows to support a wide, sculpted ass. She reminded him of the girls from back home in Arkansas where he played college ball; thick like molasses and just as sweet. There weren't many ball players with dark-skinned sisters, and he was one of them.

"Is that for me?" Stacy asked with wide, sensuous eyes as she appeared in the doorway. Her gaze followed his hand as he slowly, gently stroked his meat. Marlin looked up at her, trying to orient himself to the figure before him. She'd interrupted his thoughts.

"How did you know?" he answered, forcing a smile. What went unspoken between them was their impending divorce before his injury. Neither had put words to the feeling, but when it became clear that Marlin would need her now, what was left unsaid was covered over with a mutual need—hers being that she could now earn his love and respect. Marlin detested her new position over him and her smugness at the knowledge that he needed her.

"He's saluting me," she observed, letting her robe fall from her slim frame. She strolled leisurely to the bed and fell to her knees. Marlin felt his hardness waning and quickly recaptured the image of the woman who'd served as his fantasy for the last week while his wife went on and on about how great her new position was and how life was going to be so good in this dry-ass town.

Marlin's imagination had leapt over the fact that he'd never seen her naked. All his mind had to work on were the long, dark legs that escaped from the skirt she wore the last time he caught a glimpse of her as she disappeared inside her front door. He was sure she saw him pull into the driveway, and maybe she smiled a little. Maybe she didn't linger at the doorway the way she did the day he saw her at the mailbox because her husband had pulled into the driveway beside him. Marlin had taken him in with one glance, barely hearing him ask how he was enjoying the city in his perfect white man's English. Briefcase, suit and tie, Marlin noted, thinking he was some sort of executive.

Stacy had replaced his grip on his penis with hers, stroking him tenderly as she ended a story about a jealous rival who was upset with the size of her office. "But the hell with her," she said, as if speaking to the swollen head between her fingers. She then covered the swollen, ribbed helmet with thin lips. She sucked off of him making a popping sound. "I know he loves me," she sang before wrapping her lips around the head again and closing her eyes in concentration as she sucked hard.

Marlin closed his eyes, remembering the bronze-colored lips that smiled through the screen door a week ago. They'd barely moved in and she was over to introduce herself. Stacy had answered the door. When Marlin hobbled up behind her on his cane, he thought there was a small glimmer in the woman's almond shaped eyes. The sun had shown her thickness beneath the flower-printed sundress she wore. Her hips and thighs spoke a secret language that only corn bread and grits could pronounce. Her breasts strained against and bubbled over the thin material of her dress. Marlin had briefly wondered if her husband—was he at work? —paid her the amount of attention he knew a body like that needed.

"Mmmmm...," Stacy moaned over the rim of his stiff joint, breaking him from his thoughts. "You're going to make me late," she complained happily as she climbed onto the bed. She straddled him with thin, long legs and narrow hips, inserting him gently inside of her wet pussy. Marlin let his hands lay over her thighs and closed his eyes again, listening to her slow moan as she worked herself over him.

Then there was the time Marlin saw her dash out of her back door to empty garbage in the early morning. He'd been on the back porch doing laundry when he heard her door slam. She had on a silk nightgown that barely reached the bottom of her round ass. On tiptoe she'd raced to the back fence where the garbage cans were. At the time he'd thought it a shame that her husband hadn't taken care of that for her.

Her dark hair hung long and thick to her shoulders, bouncing with each soft trot. He thought she'd looked his way and was frozen in place—caught like a thief stealing a wicked glance behind the screen door, not sure if she could see him standing there. Still, he watched until she disappeared from sight, shaking his head and gritting his teeth at the vision of her full breasts threatening to escape the thin fabric as she focused on the ground in front of her, hands out to the side for balance, daintily taking the stairs in cotton slippers. Out of view, the door slammed behind her, signaling that she'd returned indoors.

"That feel good to you, baby?" Stacy asked, her fingers gripping his muscular chest. This forced his eyes open. Marlin nodded subtly, the image of his neighbor's sexy form running from his mind. Stacy rode him with urgency, chasing an elusive high. "You love this pussy, baby?" she wanted to know, leaning over so that she was whispering in his ear. He squeezed her ass cheeks hard in answer, making her squirm from his grip and yelp out in pain. She reared back on him, making his dick strain downward with her awkward motion, her hands now braced on his massive thighs.

Only two days ago, Marlin had seen her again. He wanted to say hello, but before he could get up from the couch and to the door, she had already retrieved her mail from the curbside box and scampered back up the walkway. She left him with the image of her ass bulging and straining in a pair of cut-off jeans that barely concealed her flesh. He imagined that her large, two-basketballs-sized ass was on top of him now. He dared not open his eyes and prayed his senses would not betray his fantasy. She was riding him with passion, her firm ass able to absorb his squeezing. She pounded down onto him, throwing her thick, curly mane into the air every time she arched her neck back in pleasure. Her large breasts swung over him invitingly. He leaned up to take a nipple between his lips. She enjoyed this—he knew—because she ground down onto him hard, her sweet voice whispering in his ear.

"Ohhh...baby...that's right. That feels so good when you suck my nipple like that," Stacy moaned, pulling him from his imaginings, making him realize it was Stacy's small, familiar nipple between his lips. He struggled against the reality, gripping Stacy hard as the sexy neighbor urged him on with smoky glances. Marlin pumped into his wife with urgency before she could say another word and chase the dream from his mind completely. He exploded into her with such ferocity that she bucked on top of him before allowing him to ease his thick meat to her bottom for the final milking of his juices.

"Ohhh...mmyyyy...," Stacy gasped, chasing her own orgasm as Marlin pulsed inside of her. She shuddered and moaned on top of him, her breathing soft and hot against his neck. "What got into you?" she asked, gently pulling her burning, adhesive flesh from his so she could look into his eyes.

Marlin blinked before answering, "It had to be the way you looked when you got out the shower."

She rubbed her fingers through her damp hair. "You always did like it when I was wet."

Marlin slapped her on the ass. "Come on before you late for work."

★ ★ ★

Marlin was at the computer in the living room when Stacy stepped from the bedroom dressed for work. She was beautiful in a two-piece, cream-colored Chanel pantsuit that hugged her model-thin frame with grace.

"You look nice," he said, turning from the computer screen.

"Thank you, baby," she answered in that cold way Marlin had come to resent. Stacy could switch her emotions on and off like a faucet. He hadn't noticed this before because he was too busy being a professional athlete, but now that it was apparent that she was in charge, she could be a real bitch at times. Maybe this was her way of reminding him that she knew he was going to leave her before his injury. And it was not the first time Marlin had entertained the thought. "Are you walking me out?" she asked by way of apology for her funky attitude. *The finest women seemed to be the most unbalanced,* he thought to himself as she stopped by the front door in a pose to await his answer.

"Yeah, I'll walk you out. Looks nice out there," he answered grabbing up his cane.

The bright, early morning sun met Marlin warmly as he stepped onto the porch. He breathed in the fresh air, feeling it coarse through his lungs as the sun warmed his broad muscular chest. He was glad he hadn't put on a shirt. Stacy was already at the car by the time he got to the last step on the stairs. Just as he turned toward the driveway, maneuvering the cane so that it wouldn't slide on the cobbled walkway, the neighbor's door opened. He was thinking that he would kiss Stacy and tell her to have a good day when a flowery vision of swirling cotton and dark curls and swaying hips and smiling pearl-white teeth seemed to erase all of his thoughts. She moved in slow motion down the steps, lustrous hair framing large, dark eyes with dangling curls. She was waving.

"Good morning, Sherrelle," he heard Stacy sing over the top of the car.

Her body swayed and knocked under a peach-colored cotton dress.

"Isn't it a beautiful day?" she asked, looking from Stacy

to Marlin with a wide grin. A diamond necklace raced into
the cleavage of her full breasts, resting happily above the
swells. She threw her Fendi purse into the open door of her
convertible Jaguar.

"Isn't it though?" Stacy answered. "Too bad I have to
be stuck in an office all day," she added with complaint,
though smiling.

Sherrelle waved her off. "Girl, twelve o'clock be here in
no time. Take a long lunch and the day is over after that."
She let her hair swivel with that as she turned to open the
car door. "Are you going to make it, homeboy?" she asked
Marlin, watching with furrowed brow as he navigated the
walkway with his cane. There was a sweet timber in her
voice that caught at Marlin's stomach. He'd noticed quickly that Stacy was stuck between making a joke of it and taking his plight as seriously as Sherrelle had.

Marlin looked at her with a crooked smile, holding her
eyes for one moment longer than was comfortable for
Stacy.

"You're killing that dress, girl," Stacy chimed in to
break the connection.

Sherrelle moved behind her opened door. Marlin imagined how her hips must have shifted. "I need to lose some
weight!" she complained before laughing out loud. Just like
a hood chick, Marlin thought to himself. She made it sound
like an invitation to see what she was really talking about.
He wanted to say that she didn't need to lose a pound, but
instead he sidled up next to Stacy and smiled graciously,
now in view of her long legs. Her toenails were painted
pink, a silver ring around the second toe on her left foot
gave her added sex appeal. She looked at him now with
smoky eyes. "So how long are you going to be hobbling
around on that cane?"

Stacy answered before he could get any words out. "Forever if he doesn't go to therapy." Sherrelle shifted her eyes to Stacy slowly, coming into some realization of her own. Marlin knew that Stacy was playing herself so he just stood there, letting his eyes soften on Sherrelle"s image. She looked back to him with raised eyebrows.

"Oh, you're in therapy? Are you a football player?" she asked directly, as if daring Stacy to answer for him.

"Yeah. I used to play for the Seahawks."

"Oh, really?" Sherrelle was impressed.

"Until he blew out his knee," Stacy added somberly.

"Yeah," Marlin agreed as he noticed the sparkle in Sherrelle's eyes. "But I'll be back," he assured her with a smile.

"I'm sure you will," Sherrelle answered before letting her dark eyes slide over to Stacy. "We'll have to get together some time. I'll show you guys all the hot spots."

Stacy smiled generously. "Sounds like a plan," she replied as Sherrelle slid into the soft leather of the Jaguar.

Marlin tried to occupy his attention with Stacy as the beautiful, ebony-skinned woman situated herself and lowered the convertible top on the luxury sports car. "I'ma leave in a minute for rehab," he said to answer Stacy's question. She'd asked it when she looked up at him after getting comfortable in the Lexus. Marlin was aware of her eye contact; she was trying to catch him paying special attention to their neighbor. He was glad he was looking at her instead at that instant.

"Good," she responded, which could have been for either of the two answers she was seeking. Sherrelle was backing out of her driveway, giving Marlin an excuse to look up. She waved at him with twirling fingers and a mischievous smile. He nodded shortly before returning his attention to Stacy, who'd never taken her eyes off his face.

"Have a good day at work, baby," he said, letting a smile spread his lips while leaning in to kiss her on the lips. He steadied his cane and stepped away from the car. He waited until she'd turned down the block before turning to walk carefully back up the cobbled driveway to t he house, Sherrelle's bold eyes still creeping into his soul with a private knowledge.

Chapter Three

Sherrelle

Sherrelle could not wipe the wicked grin from her lips, nor could she shake the feeling that warmed her insides, making her giddy with her private knowledge. She'd appraised Stacy in one glance, noticing how she became protective and insecure when she stepped off the porch. *Poor thing* she thought to herself. *It must be hard not knowing if you can hold onto your man.* This gave her a jolt of laughter. She was sure people thought she must have been crazy for the way she laughed out loud and smiled, being the only one in the car. She was used to this though—women suspecting that she wanted their man. She didn't though. "I can't help it if I'm stacked like a bookshelf," she commented to herself, drawing the stares of a trio of white children in a Volvo wagon's back seat that had stopped at a light beside her. Sherrelle waved at the blue-eyed, cherub-faced kids and smiled broadly. They were surprised at this, waving sheepishly in return—one of them a girl with a toothless grin.

Sitting high on a hill overlooking downtown Indianapolis, the patio of The Cheesecake Factory was sparsely occupied. The odd couple of the older white man with the young black woman spoke of the discretion of the hour. Sherrelle wished it had been noon so her entrance could have had a more dramatic effect.

Her Jimmy Choo heels clacked on the hardwood floor as she made her way to the last row of tables in a secluded section. Peaches was looking in her direction through a pair of Chanel shades (making her regret not wearing hers) and from under a pretty straw hat, which she made a mental note to ask Peaches about. She was smiling with Peaches at the three sophisticated white women seated in the next aisle who tried not to appear impressed with her fabulous approach—diamond rings, tennis bracelets and the Rolex necklace gracing her dark skin. "Y'all know you love me, so don't hate," she sang to herself as she passed the table, swaying her hips for the two who would no doubt watch as she took her seat.

"I love that hat," Sherrelle said as she sat down across from her friend.

"I know," Peaches smiled. Where Sherrelle was dark as midnight with a cocoa-brown underglow, Peaches was high-yellow with a mocha pearl. She'd inherited the dark red hair and sparkling grey eyes of her Irish mother, and the full, rich features of her Nigerian father. Her firm breasts hung deliciously inside of her spaghetti-strapped, mustard, linen dress. "I ordered us some drinks," she said with a mischievous grin. "Don't worry, it ain't but two percent alcohol," she added, smoothing the frown that crept between Sherrelle's eyes. Just then the waiter placed a blue-tinted drink in front of her with a soft-blue paper umbrella resting on its rim.

"What is this?" Sherrelle wanted to know as she brought the drink to her lips.

"Noon orgasm," Peaches hissed before letting out a tight giggle. "So what's new?" she asked, setting her own glass down after taking a long sip.

"This is good," Sherrelle commented, looking across the table as Peaches removed her sunglasses, her eyes reflecting the sunlight like diamonds.

"You can thank me by coming to see me dance. I've just been made the feature performer," Peaches said with obvious pride.

"So what does that mean? You get to be the one to shake your ass more than everyone else?"

"Don't even try it. When you start seeing my name in the papers, on coupons for tourists, and hearing it on the radio, you know you gon' look for somebody to tell that you know me." She sat back with this observation to take another sip of her drink.

"Who do I know to tell?" Sherrelle was smiling now. Her friend was truly touched in the head.

Peaches looked at her devilishly. "You could tell your neighbor."

Sherrelle laughed out loud now, her head thrown back. "You are so crazy. What am I supposed to do? Walk up to the man and say, 'Ey yo, my friend is an exotic dancer, she's famous'? You really need to get a hold of yourself."

Peaches let this go. She was more interested in getting Sherrelle to come to the club. "So you not gon' come see me?" she pouted.

"Don't even try it, Peaches. You know that ain't me."

"Remember that time you got that job at Applebee's? You know how much money I spent in there just so you would have somebody to serve?" Peaches asked, leaning over the table.

"And here it was I thought you just liked the apple pie,

cuz that's all you ordered!" They both laughed at this. "I tell you what...I'll think about it. I might come in disguise or something. Maybe wear a fat suit and paint pimples on my face." This caused more laughter as the waiter sidled up to the table and patiently stood by as the giggling subsided.

"Okay, girlfriend, I'll make a deal with you. Come in during a slow day, a weekday."

"And what's your end of the deal?" Sherrelle asked suspiciously.

"Well, seeing as how you hate for me to date so many men, I'll start concentrating on somebody to marry."

"That doesn't sound like a deal to me. You're probably already engaged." They became aware of the waiter at the same time. He was listening intently to their conversation. Peaches was the first to speak up, as if to dismiss him.

"I'll have a chicken salad," she said, then looked to Sherrelle. "You want to share a rack of oysters?"

"You trying to get my sex drive up when you know it ain't got nowhere to go?" she replied around more laughter.

"That handheld is going to be happy!" Peaches exclaimed, clapping her hands together.

Sherrelle was almost embarrassed, noticing the red circles on the young cheeks of the waiter. "I'll also have a chicken salad, and bring us a dozen shelled oysters." The waiter grinned at this, looking at them both with a nod of appreciation for the education.

"He's hot!" Peaches noted after the waiter left.

Sherrelle had an idea. "I tell you what. If I come to see you perform, will you help me sell t-shirts?"

"What! Are you serious?" Peaches asked in surprise. "Sell t-shirts?"

"Yeah. I saw it on Myspace. HoodSweet apparel for

women. I figure I can run Indiana and make a fortune."
Peaches was looking at her dumbstruck. "I need something
to do," Sherrelle added somberly.

"Well, that's how FUBU started," Peaches said in support.

"The tagline is: If you're not HoodSweet, then you're
just a dyme. We can have all the girls at Applebottoms wear
them. I'll give you a few shirts and a pair of boyshorts to
wear on stage!" Sherrelle said excitedly.

"Pump your brakes, girlfriend. Have you even seen the
clothes yet?" Peaches asked.

"No, but they're really cute. Trust me." Peaches looked
doubtful. "I still want you to settle down though,"
Sherrelle added.

"See, now you're asking for too much. I love all my
honeys. That's why you're so frustrated. You don' locked
yourself onto one man and he can't satisfy all your needs."

"Oh, really?" Sherrelle said, knowing where this was
going.

"See, you have to know their roles."

"Like Tequan?" Sherrelle asked smartly. This was the
man Peaches thought she was in love with until she found
out he was a bank robber.

Peaches swooned. "Ohhh, girl! I thought he was the
one! How was I supposed to know he wasn't really a bank
manager that had to travel?"

"That tattoo across his neck didn't give him away?"

"You couldn't see it when he wore his button-ups,"
Peaches said in wide-eyed defense.

"So what happened to him?"

Peaches began pressing a finger against her other hand
like a piano. "One, he lied—which I could have lived with;
two, those phone bills had started to kick my ass; and three,

all of a sudden I was like his errand girl—go pick up this and go drop off that. I ain't into that shit," she finished with finality. Sherrelle was smiling at her across the table.

"So you were telling me the benefit of having more than one man."

"Okay. See you got your square dude who's going to go to work and bring home the bacon for momma to fry in the pan." Sherrelle resisted the urge to tell her about the pan of bacon she threw into the sink. Peaches continued, "And then you got your thug who might or might not have a job, but he's going to give you the loving you need because your workaholic square is too tired to bang that pussy."

The waiter caught the last of what Peaches said, his cheeks red again as he set the salads and rack of oysters on the table. Sherrelle was amused at his embarrassment. She shook her head and was thankful for the interruption, her mind going back to what she had seen through her neighbor's window.

"You need to find a friend on the side," Peaches advised.

"Percy has just been really busy lately."

"And you have to suffer." Peaches tasted her food. "Mmmm," she moaned. "This salad is gooood!" She shook her head slowly with her eyes closed.

Sherrelle looked at her friend and wondered how she could be so happy with her life. She couldn't imagine being with so many different men and playing them out like Peaches did.

"This is good," Peaches said, going in for another forkful with chunks of chicken and green salad with ranch dressing. "It wouldn't even be cheating either," she said with a mouthful of salad, returning to their prior conversation. "See, if your heart isn't in it and you know what it's all about, then it's not cheating."

"That sounds crazy. I can't believe you're trying to justify infidelity."

Peaches looked up at her with wide eyes. "Men have been doing it for ages. Girl, you better get a grip and I'm not talking about gripping that dildo either. You are too fine to be having to stick a piece of rubber up your pussy. I'm serious!" she pronounced, trying not to laugh, but Sherrelle was making it difficult because she was grinning so hard, holding her jeweled hand over her mouth.

"I know one thing—you are going to give our waiter a heart attack," Sherrelle said, catching the slim, dark-haired man looking back at them before he stepped into the main restaurant area.

"That's the only way he'll catch the feeling," Peaches joked in response, raising her hand for a high five across the table. "So I think Thursday is a good day to come to the club. Will you have the clothes by then?" Peaches asked, reaching for a shelled oyster.

"I'ma have to check my e-mail when I get home."

Peaches was looking at her intently, eyes narrowed with suspicion.

"What?" Sherrelle asked before sucking down a raw oyster.

"There's something you're not telling me. And for you to think I can't tell is, like, so disrespectful."

Sherrelle began chuckling, holding her palms up in a plea of innocence. "Ummm...No, I can't think of anything," she said, rolling her eyes in mock thought, though she was itching to tell her juicy secret.

Peaches grabbed one of the glasses of iced tea the waiter had brought them. "Girl, I'ma dash this tea over you!" she threatened.

Sherrelle looked at her in thought, deciding whether or not to tell her. She knew what reaction she would get. "I saw my neighbor having sex," she whispered.

"SHUT UP!!!" Peaches shouted. It was exactly the response Sherrelle wanted to avoid. "Are you serious? How? Where? The one with the bourgeois wife? Oh my God! What happened?" She was looking across the table at Sherrelle with both elbows on the table.

"Would you calm down?!"

Peaches shook her hands in the air in anticipation. "Tell me, tell me. You saw it going in and out?"

Sherrelle was shaking her head slowly, her long, dark curls bobbing in slow motion. "You are so nasty," she sang in a sweet whisper.

"You the one playing peeping Tonya," Peaches responded accusingly, her bright, grey eyes sparkling with their own passion. There was a new trio of young, chic, white women who'd taken a table behind Sherrelle. They were trying to act like they heard nothing of the sexual intrigue just a short distance away.

Sherrelle looked both ways before leaning forward over the table and cupping her mouth with one hand. "I was taking out the trash," she whispered. Peaches rolled her eyes, popping her fingers forward to urge the story along. "And she kinda screamed out." Sherrelle shrugged her shoulders, accepting that this was a legitimate reason to see what was going on. She skipped the part about seeing her neighbor straddle her husband naked. She skipped the part about how his eyes were closed and how she had wondered what he was thinking about. Instead she said, "They were just doing it plain missionary, under the covers!" opening her eyes wide for emphasis and alarm.

Peaches had been grinning wide until now. Her eyes

narrowed and she pressed her lips together tightly. This transformation of face accompanied a slow easing of her body back into her chair. Now she was nodding, and she flicked her fingers forward one last time, as if ridding her hands of excess dishwashing suds. She interlocked her fingers and rested them delicately under her chin, observing Sherrelle. "YOU ARE GOING TO FUCK HIM." She mouthed the words slowly.

"NO, I AM NOT," Sherrelle mouthed more slowly, her dark skin shining and her eyes wide. "So what size are you?" she asked Peaches, her mouth spreading into a smile. She'd kept some for herself and all her friend could come up with was something she could handle. Lame. Peaches was sipping her blue drink now, her eyes looking curiously into Sherrelle's.

"You must be a size ten," Sherrelle teased. Peaches laughed and held one hand high in the air, diamonds and gold sparkling and tumbling light.

"Girl, you crazy," Peaches said. "You know we the same size."

"No, honey. I'm a little thicker than you. I'm what is called a full grown woman." She said this proudly, her cinnamon breasts bubbling over the top of her peach-colored, cotton dress.

"I know that's what you said, but that truly is a delusion of yours," Peaches said smartly.

Sherrelle narrowed her eyes in sympathy, leaning toward Peaches. "And you see this delusion so well, don't you?" she asked, as if to a child.

Peaches caught her meaning. "Me? I'm not delusional. I know exactly what's what and what ain't. I just get straight to the point. And it all boils down to sex and money. And bitches like us need both. We just got our own way of going about it. But see, I know you play that you can't get down like that. You ain't changed that much just because you went to college and I didn't. You still that little chickenhead girl running around Baltimore right with me." Peaches reached her hands across the table. Sherrelle placed her hands lightly in her palms, feeling Peaches squeeze her gently. "It's about the sex and the money," she said low and sincerely, brow furrowed gently to convey her meaning. And you should get everything you want. That's all I'm saying."

Sherrelle directed her eyes to the diamond ring on her left hand. Peaches followed her gaze. The sparkling rock sat atop a platinum band. It sparkled and pulsed like it had a heartbeat.

"That's sexy," Peaches sang, entranced by the rock. Her eyes followed it reluctantly as Sherrelle slowly pulled her hands from her grip.

"I have some shopping to do, girlfriend. Feels just like sex," she assured her friend.

"I know that's right," Peaches replied with a snap of her fingers.

When Sherrelle rose to leave, she politely smiled at the chic, white women at the next table. Their faces revealed wonder at the sight of her. They, too, had looked at her ring finger. And each, in turn, would express her approval and envy with a furrowed brow, pressed lips, and an open mouth that formed an O.

★★★

Shopping did feel like sex. Shoes especially. Three pairs were like an orgasm. And, of course, a few dresses quickly doubled the price of that orgasm. So she was feeling satisfied when, at around dusk, she pulled onto her tree-lined street. Toward the middle of the block she could see Stacy's car in its driveway. Coming in the opposite direction was Marlin. *He is so hood,* Sherrelle said to herself. Twenty-eight-inch chrome rims, low profile tires, wood grain and candy spread on it like butter.

He drove slow; the beat of whatever it was in the CD player moved through her. The words became more clear as they neared each other. Sherrelle reached her driveway first, steadily looking in Marlin's direction, hoping he'd be the first to wave. Then he did. With a small grin. She waved in return with what she hoped was a conservative grin before turning into her driveway. She took her time, gathering shiny, decorated shopping bags from the passenger's seat. A short jolt of anticipation and mystery shot through her. She instinctively flipped down the visor mirror to kiss herself once and blink her eyes twice, as if shaking up a dark blessing to awaken its life force. Too Short had just sneered the word BITCH! from Marlin's Escalade when she opened her door. He'd pulled to the curb and sat there fingering his Blackberry, paying her no attention.

Chapter Four

Marlin

Seeing her up close like that had lit a fire inside of him. Marlin felt like they were having their own private communication. He'd simply nodded in agreement when Stacy said that her dress was cute, looking into his eyes for something more than what his simple gesture spoke. The feeling fought inside of him, trying to leap from him. She had done serious damage to his brain just by the way she'd waved to him when she backed out of the driveway. Marlin replayed this over and over in his mind—the way her ass shifted under the thin dress; how her breasts were alive with natural firmness and bounce; the way her large, smoky eyes looked out from perfect, dark, smooth skin that spoke of the deep well of sweet juice it must have sprung from. *The sweeter the berry,* he thought to himself now, feeling with pleasure the way his erect joint swayed under the bubbling, hot water.

"What it do, Pimpin'?" A familiar, high-pitched voice asked. Marlin had his head against the edge of the Jacuzzi—still feeling the effects of the deep tissue massage he'd received thirty minutes earlier—arms spread out along the rim. He lifted his head slowly, opening his eyes to see a thin, dust-colored man before him, purple towel around his neck. A pair of Hawaiian shorts hid the middle of his thin frame while a purple, silk scarf concealed his long, permed hair tied up underneath.

"Wassup, Da," Marlin answered, watching as the thin, chiseled man across from him eased himself into the hot water.

"I kinda figured you'd be here today," he said before exhaling his pleasure, submerged to his stomach in the bubbling foam. "I was saying to myself, 'Dahji McBeth, you gon' run into the Marlin today. And look who I find,'" he smiled grandly, pearl-white teeth trimmed in gold.

He'd approached Marlin his first day at the Sports Medicine Clinic, promising to guide him in his search for the 'right' physical therapist. This required a brief history of Marlin's condition. Dahji had simply nodded—as if he already knew—when Marlin disclosed that he was a professional football player.

"You just gettin' here?" Marlin asked a smiling Dahji. "Go ahead, spit it out," Marlin said, smiling at what the man might say.

"I was saying to myself how I was going to see you here, and here you are!" he exclaimed.

"Here I am," Marlin echoed with a sigh.

"Don't you see?" Dahji thrust his hands into the air. "It's got to mean something. You and me are going to make something happen." He was nodding his head, smiling.

Marlin had found the small, wiry man too animated to take in large doses at first. He had taken Dahji's description of what he did for a living (manager, agent, promoter, congratulator, and disabled FedEx employee) with a chuckle, unable to see the whole of him in one glance. But soon the precocious man grew on him. This was their third meeting and Marlin still had no clue as to how Dahji could afford the expensive clothes, jewelry, and the maroon-colored Range Rover on a disabled FedEx employee salary. When he asked Dahji bluntly if he sold drugs ('I ain't trying to get caught up with no d-boy,' Marlin had said), Dahji threw his hands out in front of him in protest. "Naw, man! I break out in hives any time there's any dope around me!" he'd assured Marlin, shaking his head violently.

"The only thing big that can happen for me right now is for my next x-ray to show that I can play ball again," Marlin said low, closing his eyes and leaning his head back onto the rim of the Jacuzzi.

"Maybe that ain't what God got planned for you, Pimpin'. I'm a strong believer in letting go—and letting God," Dahji pronounced with satisfaction.

Something had to be working for the man with all the riches. "How you hurt yourself?" Marlin asked, looking down his face at Dahji.

"Slip and fall. Just like always," he answered with a direct stare. "See, everybody is meant for different things. Everybody meant for a specific purpose. Ain't no coincidences in life," he added. Marlin couldn't be sure whether the specific thing Dahji was talking about was his supposed slip and fall or his meeting him at the clinic.

"You slip and fall for a reason?" Marlin asked, his head still leaned back with his eyes closed. Without looking, he could see Dahji making an annoyed expression.

"Naw man, you got it all wrong. I have been sent to you for a specific purpose," he responded, pointing his index finger with the large, gold, lion's head ring on it, a red ruby stuck in its mouth. Marlin leaned his head down to look at him then. No less than three gold ropes dangled from his thin neck. The cross, omega, and gold 'black power' fist medallions jockeyed for prominent position against his narrow chest. The water bubbled over them as if threatening a baptism.

"What specific purpose?" Marlin wanted to know.

Dahji jabbed the lion's head at him. "Now see, that's what I ain't figured out yet, Marly Marl!" He exclaimed.

Marlin smiled at this. *What could he possibly help me with*, he thought to himself. Then another thought occurred to him. "You married?" he asked. Instantly, Dahji closed his eyes and shook his head from side to side, as if warding off an evil spirit.

"You see, Marly Marl," he began, grinning with what he intended to say, "Man is not designed to be with one woman."

Marlin nodded. He leaned his head back onto the rim of the Jacuzzi and dropped an arm into the water to massage his knee. The masseuse had spent nearly an hour flexing, bending, and tweaking the rebuilding muscle.

"It's true, Marly Marl," Dahji said excitedly. "Look back through history and you'll see that man ain't never had to deal with only one woman. It ain't right and it ain't natural."

"So, what—you got a gang of women I suppose?" Marlin whispered over the hum of the boiling water.

"More than you'll find at a Oprah show," he answered. Marlin smiled at this. "Think about it, Marl. No other animal in the kingdom stays with one woman. When a boy cow sex a girl cow, he never go back to her. Never."

Marlin waited for him to continue.

"Why? I'll tell you why. Here it is he might run into a cow that don't like to suck dick but she got the bomb snatch. He can't be tied down with the bomb snatch when he like to get his dick sucked. I tell you who can suck some dick. White girls. They come up sucking dick. It's nothing to them. They do that before they have sex. Black women, it's the other way around. If the sistahs could suck dick like white girls, the world would be a happier place. Say I ain't right, Marly Marl! You played ball! Tell me a white girl ain't the best at sucking dick!"

Marlin was grinning at Dahji's animated explanation though his eyes were still closed. He could imagine the splayed fingers and widened brown eyes. "Superhead," Marlin answered simply.

"A rare exception!" Dahji shouted. "She specialize in head, that's why she so good at it. She look at it like an art, which it is. If more sistahs looked at sucking dick like an art, the world would be a better place."

Thoughts of Sherrelle danced across Marlin's mind. He wondered if she thought sucking dick was an art.

"But you're a happily married man, Marly Marl," Dahji piped up. "Everybody ain't so lucky." It must have been the way Marlin raised up to look at him that made Dahji say what he said next. "You need to hang out with me some-time. Let me show you around town," he said. Then he snapped his fingers as if something had just occurred to him. "You know what I'ma do for you, Marly Marl? I'ma show you one of my most favorite spots."

"Let me guess—a strip club."

Dahji frowned. "How'd you know?" Then opened his face. "This ain't no regular booty joint. Nowhere else in the world will you see women like these women. They come from all over the world just to dance here. You know since the Colts won the Superbowl they all trying to be as close to it as they can. And they'll love you," he winked.

"I got two words for you—Magic City," Marlin said, waiting for Dahji's reaction.

"Aww, man!!! I seent Magic City, and I'm here to tell you that Magic City got nothing on Applebottoms. Applebottoms is so fly it's a franchise." He pressed his fingers together one after the other. "They got one in L.A. and they got one in Chicago. Franchise," he added with finality. "I been to all of 'em."

"There's one in Seattle, too."

Dahji threw his arms into the air. "I stand corrected, Marly Marl. Pussy all over the world. So you know what I'm talking about then." Marlin nodded his head.

"You get around good on a delivery man's salary," Marlin noted.

"Don't let the square package fool you, Marly Marl. I got more turns than a Rubik's Cube and I'm tighter than a sailor's knot." Marlin was grinning again.

"I might slide with you," he said.

"Yeah. We gon' have a good time. Get you out the house," Dahji responded before settling into the water to his shoulders, the bubbly water covering his jewelry in a complete baptism.

★ ★ ★

Too Short was knocking through the speakers yelling 'Bitch!' with promise and conceit as Marlin turned onto his block. The beat had him leaned back in the seat. He resisted the urge to sit up when he saw the familiar Jaguar coming in the opposite direction. He cruised slowly, wanting her to pull into her driveway first. He would have to time this perfectly because Stacy was home and, no doubt, would be at the front door as soon as he pulled to the curb. He pulled his Blackberry from his duffel bag and pretended to be engaged in a conversation. He grinned after quickly looking up and finding Sherrelle checking herself in her visor mirror.

Marlin gathered up his duffel bag slowly as Sherrelle pulled her designer shopping bags from the car. Seeing her bend into the door sent a shiver through him. She was so sexy, tossing her hair away when she stood to place the retrieved bags onto the hood of the Jaguar. She looked his way and flashed him a generous smile. Now he could walk up the driveway instead of cutting across the lawn like he'd intended to do.

"You look relaxed," Sherrelle noted with a quick appraisal. Approval. His muscled body was sheathed in a white nylon Jordan warm-up suit, and his deep chocolate face was clean shaven. His cane poked out at her from the canvas duffel bag.

"Yeah. Looks like you had a good day yourself," he said, looking away from her soft face to her purchases.

"Better than sex," she responded and quickly regretted it. Marlin was smiling, looking into her eyes as they tried to take back what she said. There was a moment when they saw each other more clearly.

"You might need to hire an assistant to help with all that," Marlin joked, easing the unspoken tension. He loved her smile.

"I don't shop like this all the time. I got carried away," she assured him. "So how are you liking Indy so far?"

He relaxed. "It's cool. Haven't been out much. But from what I can tell, it's got a cool vibe." He looked more intently at her then. "You originally from here?"

"No, I'm from Baltimore."

"B-Town," he smiled. "You didn't seem like you were from here."

Sherrelle looked at him with questioning eyes. "Oh,

really? What made you assume that?"

He wanted to say it was the way she moved, the way she made him feel. There was something urban about her. Something that house and that car and her husband couldn't hold. She was from somewhere else for sure. Instead, he said, "I've moved around a lot, and I can tell who the natives are." Now she was smiling.

"That's cute," she said. "So where are you from?"

"I was born in Mississippi and played college ball for Alabama."

Sherrelle became animated, her mouth opening with surprise. "I hate you!" she said, laughing. "I went to U of Arkansas. You are my natural rival," she teased, her breasts bouncing softly together. Marlin knew there was something familiar about her. He was ready to ask her what year she graduated when something in her expression changed. Her eyes glanced up to his porch. Marlin knew before he turned that Stacy was standing in the doorway, holding the screen open. She waved, smiling at Sherrelle. Then her eyes rested on Marlin with an unspoken communication.

"Well, it was nice talking to you," Sherrelle said, her eyes darker than he remembered. Though her smile wasn't as wide as when he'd walked up, it said more. There was something hidden in the dimples of her smooth cheeks.

"What did you get for your husband?" he asked, looking quickly to the stiff, creased bags still on the hood of the Jag.

She looked away from Stacy with a mischievous grin. "He got what he deserves," she answered cryptically. She turned halfway to the door, signaling her next move.

"Don't hurt yourself carrying all that stuff."

She looked at him with a quick smile. "It's all in the wrist."

Marlin nodded at this, though he had no clue as to what she was talking about.

Stacy hadn't appreciated the extra conversation that had taken place after she made her appearance in the doorway. She was looking at Marlin with an icy stare as he walked up the steps.

"So you don't need your cane anymore?" she asked before taking a hard step into the house. Dressed in a fluffy cotton robe, her hair tied in a towel, she'd just gotten out of the shower. Marlin could smell the fruity scent of her shower gel. She was walking away from him with hard steps, her bare feet twisting on the hardwood floor with each angry stomp.

She was in the bathroom by the time he finally caught up to her. "What got you stone-faced?" he asked, watching her through the mirror as she unwrapped the towel from her head. She had the blow dryer in her hand when she turned to him.

"Did she have a good day?" Stacy wanted to know.

Marlin smiled. "Are you serious? Tell me you're not serious. That woman is our married, next-door neighbor," he said, as if this made her off limits. This was the part he didn't like. Stacy's insecurity. Ever since she found out he'd been with a few groupies during his away games with the Seahawks, she would relive her anger at the slightest provocation. Marlin still regretted that marital therapy session and wished he could choke the counselor for making him believe that 'full disclosure' would heal their relationship. This was all before he'd made up his mind to divorce her, before the next contract he knew would be huge, and before the injury that dashed those hopes.

He stepped into the bathroom, reaching for her waist. She watched him with steady eyes in the mirror as he stepped up behind her. "Did you have a nice day, baby?" he wanted to know, hugging her around the waist. His fingers gripped the loose knot of the cotton belt.

"Yes," she answered reluctantly, feeling him pull the knot apart. He spread the robe, revealing her tan sculpted body underneath.

"Did you think about me?" he asked running his thumbs along her ribs.

She bucked in his embrace, not ready to give up so easily. "Did you think about me?" she asked in return. They were staring into each other's eyes in the mirror over the marble counter.

"You can't tell?" he responded, easing his palms over the light hair between her legs. Stacy's eyes fluttered and her head leaned back onto his shoulder. "You smell nice," he whispered into her ear as his finger creased her moistening pussy lips. Her breathing became shallow as she reached around to grab his hardening dick through the nylon of his pants. She stroked him through the slick material as he dipped his finger into her wetness.

"You must have had a good day," she gasped, pulling his stiff joint over his waistband, freeing him.

Marlin turned his wife and lifted her onto the sink. She spread her legs and wrapped them around his waist as he stepped in to her. He kissed her hungrily as he slid his dick into her wet pussy. She winced with his entry, gripping his neck tight and burying her head into his chest. Marlin closed his eyes. Through the darkness appeared the smile of Sherrelle. Seeing her caused his rhythm to halt, but he quickly resumed stroking. He was oblivious to Stacy's tight grip around his neck, her fingernails digging into his skin as he roughly went in and out of her, keeping her from scooting back on the sink. She was trapped in his embrace, impaled on his steel pole.

Sherrelle's ass was before him, leaning into her car. It was perfectly round and formed. Not just wide or big, but sculpted, as if two separate organisms were on each side. And he was going deep into his wife. He vaguely heard the whimper from her lips. Sherrelle's smile beckoned to him. Her words were a song for his soul. Like cornbread and grits, she was familiar, like home. And he stroked deep inside of his wife. He moved her to the marble counter and gripped her small ass, pushing even deeper into her as her legs opened wider to receive him.

She'd said that it was all in the wrist, a mystery that worked at his mind. And he could not feel the hot tears on his wife's cheek, could not hear her words as they escaped in a muffled plea from her lips into his neck, "Please, you're hurting me." Deeper, he stroked. Powerfully, he pushed inside of her, Sherrelle's dimples motivating him. His face was closed tight as he lifted and drove his wife down onto him, over and over again, grunting and huffing with the effort. Stacy screamed out in pain, holding on tightly.

"Come on," she pleaded, begging for it to be over.

This woke Marlin from his trance, allowing him to feel his wife's pain. Slowly, he stroked inside of her now, aware of the tears and the hot breath. He felt her grip around his neck loosen, her nails sliding from the dents in his flesh. He breathed out heavily as he came inside of her, holding onto her as he struggled to maintain his balance.

Stacy wanted to look into his eyes. What she saw was a mystery. It was the same look he had when he used to come off the field after a big game, only this one was more clouded and unfocused.

"I've never felt that from you before," she said, looking over his entire face for clues to the riddle.

"Damn," he huffed, managing to set her back on the marble counter.

"You want something to drink?" Stacy asked, not sure what else to do or say.

Marlin had stumbled back and sat down on the edge of the toilet seat. He nodded to her question, glad that he would be alone. The feeling that ran through him was something he had not wanted to unleash on his wife. He reached to his neck, his fingers running across the deep scratches she'd made as if he was reading Braille. The story spoke of pain. He hadn't meant to hurt her.

Chapter Five

Sherrelle

Sherrelle dropped the last of the designer bags onto the silk-braided couch and stood with her back to the front door—hand over her bosom—to collect herself. She hadn't expected for him to cause such a reaction in her. *It's all in the wrist? What was I thinking?* she admonished herself with soft laughter. She was especially glad that Percy wasn't home. "Damn," she said aloud as she fanned her face with her hand. *Girl, you need to stop acting like a teenager. You are a grown woman and, might I mention, married* she said to herself as she dropped her keys on the glass end table.

Before stepping into the shower, she pressed play on an Isley Brothers CD. She let the water cascade over her figure. She tried not to think about him, tried not to think of the way one of his dimples was deeper than the other, didn't want to see the cleft in his chin again. And his Caesar cut was tight. "Damn," she hissed, turning more of the hot water off to cool herself with the cold. This felt good. She felt like she needed to be punished for her thoughts. And he was from the south, she remembered. She shook her head from side to side, eyes closed tightly, trying to toss the image of him from her mind.

"I am married," she said aloud, climbing from the shower and walking over to the mirror. She stood in front of it naked and examined her tight body: full breasts, round hips, firm thighs, small waist, shaved pussy. She looked back up to her face. There was not a pimple, scar, or blemish on her body. *I am married* she thought to herself. "Happily," aloud this time, forcing herself to believe it. And Peaches' words came tumbling back to her: Women like us need all of our needs met to be truly happy, she'd said. *And she was right*, she thought to herself as she ran her fingers down her flat stomach and around her soft hips. Sherrelle was determined to squeeze whatever she needed in a man out of her husband. It was all a matter of pushing the right buttons, she reasoned, folding her arms under her breasts so that they rose and swelled to attention.

A slow smile crept along her wide mouth as she lotioned herself with strawberry-scented body cream. Her smooth skin responded attentively to her sensuous caress. She spread her legs, feeling the fluffy comforter rise to fill the gaps her ass made. She rubbed the thick cream between her legs slowly as she planned how she would receive her husband when he walked through the door. Along the crease of her pussy she rubbed, tempted to please herself on the spot. Instead, she rose from the bed abruptly, grabbed the phone and called Percy.

"Anderson Accounting," a sweet, young voice answered. It was well past six. Sherrelle wondered what time the receptionist would leave the building.

"Hi, Mandy, this is Sherrelle. Is Percy available?"

"Hi, Mrs. Santiago," Mandy replied brightly. "Sure, I'll transfer you."

Light jazz played through the phone as Sherrelle walked to the full-length mirror behind the door. She did a little dance, making her ass jump as her elbows rose to her shoulders. She was laughing at her antics when Percy's voice came over the line.

"Percy Santiago," he answered.

Sherrelle wondered if Mandy told him who was calling. The idea of him saying his full name when he knew it was her sent a cold chill through her. She resisted the urge to dash his surprise.

"Hi, honey," she said in her sexiest voice. Ronald Isley sang in the background, giving her the motivation she needed. He sang of spending a night with a mystery girl, playing hide and seek between the sheets. He wanted to see their bodies moving to the groove.

"Good evening." He sounded so proper. Sherrelle would not be denied.

"Did I disturb you?" she asked, hoping she didn't sound too harsh.

"No, not at all. What's up?" he softened up a bit.

"Well, I was just thinking about you and wanted you home so baaad!" she cooed. She could feel him smiling over the phone line.

"Oh, really?" She'd gotten to him.

"Yes, honey. And I was wondering when you were coming home to me. I have a special surprise for you." She watched herself in the mirror as she spoke.

"What kind of surprise?" he wanted to know. His tone wavered between expectation—of a surprise he wanted, and reluctance—of a surprise he could do without. There was something in his voice that said he needed a reason to leave his office.

"Well, you'll have to come home and find out," she

answered bravely, done with admiring herself in the mirror. There were three beats of silence. She was about to say "Hello?" when he said, "Let me tidy up here and I'm on my way."

"I'll be waiting," she responded with a sugared tongue.

Sherrelle had just slipped on a thong and a silk, pink nightie that stopped just below her ass when the phone rang.

"Hey, girl," Sherrelle answered, sitting down to the computer to check her e-mails.

"What's up, homegirl? Your man at home?" Peaches wanted to know.

"No."

"Good, so you can talk."

"What you know good?" Sherrelle asked, quickly scanning an e-mail from HoodSweet.com. They were responding to her query about selling their apparel. Attached to the e-mail were photos of models wearing various pieces from the line. It also included wholesale prices for those interested in becoming retailers. This piqued her interest. Exactly what she was looking for.

"Nothing, except that I have a hot date tonight," Peaches said, excitement sparking her words.

"Really?" Sherrelle was digging her credit card from her Fendi bag on the couch.

"Yes. And he is in the ten club." She waited for Sherrelle's reaction. Instead she heard the sound of her fingers tapping on a keyboard. "What are you doing?"

"Oh. Just answering my e-mails."

"What? You got a online boyfriend you ain't told me about? Speaking of which..."

"No!" Sherrelle said, interrupting her. "And no, I haven't seen my neighbor and am not going to fuck my neighbor. As a matter of fact, my husband will be home in a minute so I'ma have to go."

"Ohh! Did I touch a nerve?" Peaches asked, smiling.

"That's expensive," Sherrelle said absently, ignoring her question.

"What's expensive?"

"Priority shipping."

Peaches giggled. "What are you ordering? A dildo?"

"I have enough of those," Sherrelle answered around a small laugh. "The clothes should be here day after tomorrow."

"I hope this stuff ain't cheap and make me break out or nothing."

"Girl, if you don't stop. It ain't like you gotta pay for it," Sherrelle assured her. "You are going to be my first model. If everybody at Applebottoms don't buy something, me and you gon' fight!"

"Once they see me wearing it, they all gon' want some," Peaches replied proudly.

"So who's the hot date?"

"Oh, girl. He claim he don't like nothing black but a Cadillac..."

"One of them," Sherrelle said, curling her lips in disgust.

"I know, but he's cool. He just say that because the only ones he can get are white girls," Peaches laughed.

"So how you end up with him?"

"I just had to get me some of that. My friend Kitty said he had the biggest dick ever. She swears it's ten inches!"

"Ten inches? What does that look like?" Sherrelle asked, scanning more pictures of Hood Sweet models on their own personal websites, thinking that she had to get one too.

"Like a fucking porn star!" Peaches exclaimed. "And you couldn't tell by looking at him. He's shorter than me and skinny as hell, but he is all head, feet and hands. Go figure."

"I guess..." Sherrelle sighed, wondering how it would feel to have ten inches of dick inside of her. Hell, eight inches would do. She laughed.

"What's so funny?" Peaches wanted to know.

"Oh, nothing, girl. You be careful, okay?"

"Girl, please. The man work for Federal Express. Now, I might be a little scared if he worked for the post office," she said. Sherrelle laughed at this.

"Okay, girlfriend. Let me get ready. My husband should be home in a minute."

"What you getting ready for?" Peaches sang seductively.

"My wifely duty."

"Well, you be careful," Peaches joked, knowing there was nothing to fear from Percy Santiago.

★ ★ ★

By the time Percy walked through the door—two hours after they'd gotten off the phone—Sherrelle had stored away her earlier purchases, leaving in the middle of the living room what she'd gotten for him—a fire-red Halliburton Monkey Case that cost a thousand dollars. Inside of it she'd placed a Mont Blanc pen that cost fifteen hundred dollars and a pair of gold, Donald Trump cufflinks that equaled the price of the previous gifts combined. He would not buy these things for himself, so it was up to her to use his money to get them for him.

She'd lit the fireplace and drank three glasses of red wine while waiting for him to walk through the door. She was sitting in the chair she'd positioned in the middle of the

room, which she intended for him to sit in, and her mind
wandered. She guessed at what her neighbor might be
doing at seven o'clock at night. *Maybe they were watching television together,* she thought to herself, privately jealous at
seeing both of their cars in front of their house. Maybe
homeboy was watching sports while she cooked dinner.
Maybe they were having sex. A thrill ran through her at the
thought of the secret she could discover if she walked outside and peered through their bedroom window. *Are they
happy?* she asked herself. *Am I happy?* This thought lessened
her excitement and she remembered that she had never
been in love with Percy in the first place. Admittedly, she
had married him for security. Peaches was right. A woman
needed more than security. What was money without sex?
She wished she was the type who could care less about
money. *I used to be like that,* she said to herself, the wine
moving through her. What changed? Life changed.

She'd loved without money before and when the love
faded, there was nothing left but hurt. She'd promised herself then that money was worth more than love. "Now here
I sit, waiting for money to walk in the door so I can show
him some love," she whispered hotly.

I wonder what type of relationship they have, she asked herself, thinking of the thin, insecure, bourgeois woman next
door. What did he see in her? Did he love her? She looked
like the type who hunted down professional athletes. She
looked like all the other women who stood next to pro ball
players. Were they so different than me? But he deserves
more than that, she thought of Marlin.

Sherrelle saw the headlights of Percy's car swing into
the driveway, bringing her back from her journey of self-
pity and questions. She hadn't realized that Ronald Isley
had stopped singing and that the house was absolutely

quiet. She quickly pressed play again and looked around to make sure everything was in its place. The fire was low. She dropped another log into the brick cavern and rushed to the kitchen to rinse her hands and wash out her mouth. She quickly checked herself in the mirror over the kitchen sink.

Now the door was opening.

Sherrelle swayed her hips in his direction, drawing his eyes from the perusal of their living room.

"What's going on?" he asked, standing in the foyer with his black leather briefcase in one hand and his ring of keys in the other.

"You're what's going on," Sherrelle responded, taking his briefcase from him and throwing it onto the couch. Then the keys. She kissed him lightly on the mouth, letting her tongue run across his lips.

"Have you been drinking?" he asked against her open mouth.

"A little," she answered, loosening his tie, her eyes never leaving his in the crackling flicker of the firelight. She could feel the heat from the flames caress her ass through the silk teddy.

She'd managed to unbutton his starched shirt before leading him to the chair she'd put in the middle of the room, facing the fireplace. He was getting the general idea, looking down at the Halliburton case with interest, and Sherrelle stepped in front of the fire. It glowed behind her, framing her body with electric colors.

Percy relaxed, spreading his legs and placing his hands on his thighs. A small grin played on his lips as she moved to a slow rhythm, her arms lifting to the ceiling and her hips swaying from side to side. A tent slowly rose in his slacks. The fire behind her was playing tricks with his eyes. She looked as if she were moving like an old picture show, a series of movements thrown tightly together to make them appear seamless.

Sherrelle liked the reaction she was getting. She liked the way the heat of the fire felt against her skin. She was in her own world, liking the way her body moved and the growing sensuous sensation seemingly seeping from every pore of her body. She danced languidly before him, vaguely aware that he'd lifted his penis out of his pants and was stroking himself. She didn't mind. She moved toward him in slow steps, stopping to run her hands across her body and sway her hips before moving closer.

When Sherrelle reached him, she placed her hand on top of his, cupping the head of his dick. He was hot beneath her palm. She turned from him and placed his dick in the crease of her ass, the thong the only barrier. She was hot over him as she massaged his dick with a smooth grind. He gasped behind her. She turned her head to kiss him, to give his mouth something to do. She felt him growing hot between her ass cheeks. He panted into her mouth.

"Let me inside," he gasped.

Sherrelle turned to face him, moving the thong aside. He slid into her with ease. She spread open to receive him more deeply, but there was no more to go inside of her. She wanted to get off of him so that he could calm down. At this rate he would shoot his load and leave her unsatisfied. Just then, he began jerking into her with uncontrolled spasms. She couldn't believe it.

"Did you cum already?" she asked, leaning back to look into his hooded eyes. He was shaking his head from side to side as if in apology.

"I couldn't help it," he wheezed out, his dick shriveling up inside of her. She squeezed him out and stood from the chair.

"That's for you," she said dryly, pointing to the Halliburton Monkey Case.

"Sherrelle," he called after her, but she had already disappeared into the hallway.

She grabbed her black doctor's bag from under the bed on her way to the bathroom. She locked the door behind her and shut off the light. She sat on the edge of the toilet, placed the bag on her lap, reached inside for the vibrating dildo, then threw the bag to the floor. The soft hum echoed against the glass shower door and ceramic tiles. Her pussy was wet and waiting as the buzz touched her. Her mouth opened with pleasure as she embedded the flexible rubber into her pussy. With short strokes she worked it in and out, leaning back on the toilet with her legs spread open. Her breasts heaved with her growing passion, her eyes closed tight in concentration.

Then there was a knock on the door. He'd tried to turn the handle but found it was locked.

"Sherrelle. You don't have to do that," Percy complained.

"You can't do it!" Sherrelle shot back.

"Let me in."

She could not finish her business with him standing at the door. Reluctantly, she opened it and brushed by him angrily. "Why?" she asked, turning to him.

"Why, what?"

"Why don't I have to do that?" she asked, not regretting the hurt look that came over his face.

He clasped his hands together, having made a decision. "Because, baby, I can do it for you," he said hopefully. He walked over to her as she sat down on the edge of the bed. She was looking at the floor with a sad face, thinking of how hurt he must have been knowing he couldn't satisfy her. He knelt between her legs, scooting his shoulders between her thighs. She was looking down at him now, her eyes glistening with a mixture of sorrow and anticipation. He gently placed his palm against her stomach and leaned her back onto the bed.

Percy parted her fat pussy lips with two fingers and dipped his tongue into her womb. He circled the edges of her pussy, feeling her tense under his touch. He slipped one lip between his and sucked on it before moving to the other side. Sherrelle's legs quivered against his shoulders. He parted the spot that would reveal the man in the boat. The fleshy, pearl-colored bulb winked at him. Percy slid his tongue across her clit like he would a scoop of ice cream. Sherrelle gasped, her legs jerking. The little man was up now. He stood, fat and glossy.

Percy hitched Sherrelle's legs over his shoulders and buried his face in her pussy, taking the pearl between his lips and gently sucking on it. Sherrelle tensed up and squeezed his head with her thighs. Percy endured this pressure, ignoring her hands as they grabbed at his ears. She was at once trying to push him away and pull him into her. He gently massaged her clitoris with his lips while running his tongue over its tip, then letting air hit the sensitive bulb.

Sherrelle breathed hard under him, mouth agape and legs vibrating wildly over his shoulders. He held them in place, fighting her hands as they tried to push him away, diving in to suck on her sensitive clit.

She cummed a thick river of pleasure over his clean-shaven mouth. He lapped at the juices and continued to suck on her pussy, causing her to shiver and convulse on the bed. She was spent, her legs collapsed onto his shoulders. He then turned her over and spread her ass cheeks. He ran his tongue up the center before darting it into the cum-soaked asshole, pressing against the tender flesh.

"Ahhhhh, shiiitt!" Sherrelle gasped, cumming anew.

Percy was on her back now, guiding his newly erect penis into her ass. Sherrelle opened for him, feeling that he deserved it. He slid into her tightly. Sherrelle squeezed him as he stroked lightly into her butt. He breathed heavily against her ear, his breath smelling like her sex.

His grunting was familiar as he jerked inside of her. She tightened on him like a vice grip, milking him dry. *Now that's what I'm talking about,* she thought to herself as he fell onto the mattress beside her, exhausted.

Chapter Six

Marlin

He remembered Stacy rolling from the bed, though not when exactly. He was caught in the space between wakefulness and sleep, a space that allowed for vivid dreams while also absorbing wakeful elements that crept in through the haze, influencing the dream state. There was running water and the scent of cucumber melon. It was a familiar smell, but it had no association with the barren, early morning beach he was on. He knew that he was in his bed but, at the same time, he walked this beach, his feet sinking into the wet sand, looking out into the misty ocean for some sign of life. He could not see very far in front of him because of the intense fog that dropped like thick, misty rain. It coated him in the sweet scene that he knew had to be coming from the shower. This dream would change when Stacy shut off the water and the sound, he knew.

Marlin was happy where he was though. He could feel himself smiling and, for some reason, his limbs felt light and relaxed under the fluffy comforter. There was a breeze coming through the thick, sweet smelling fog, oddly caressing and tingling one of his legs, wrapping itself around his erect joint.

How did I get here? he asked himself as he trudged forward on the sand, his feet turning it from dark to light with each step. The ocean roared to his right, cresting and breaking, sending a creeping shelf of foamy water toward him. A shapely figure was forming in the sweet mist before him, hair fanned out and blowing with the wind. Sherrelle? She smiled, standing nearly naked before him. The mist was obscuring her body in such a way that only the curves presented themselves seductively.

She joined him on the sand, reaching out for his hand. This is where he wanted to be. He resisted the waking part of his mind so he could stay in this dream. Her hand was soft in his as they strolled along the wet beach.

Then she was lying on the sand in front of him. She beckoned to him with her arms outstretched, her legs spread apart. Marlin felt his heart quicken, the mist tightening around his dick, massaging him with gentle shifts. He knelt on the sand between her legs. She wrapped her arms around him as he sank deeply into her. He was pushing, moved by the wind, seemingly floating above the sand.

Then the sound of rushing water ceased. "Are you serious?"

Marlin's eyes fluttered open, breaking apart the vision in his dream. He recognized Stacy's voice and knew immediately that he had his dick in his hand, but when he opened his eyes to look at her he saw Sherrelle. Marlin blinked again to completely come out of his dream. *Or was I dreaming?* he asked himself, opening his eyes wider and looking to the place where he'd seen her face. There was a soft breeze coming in through the open window, the curtains parted.

Now Stacy was in front of him, looking down at him with a concerned expression. "Are you jacking off?" she asked.

"I was sleep," he answered.

"What were you dreaming about?" she wanted to know.

Marlin closed his eyes again and tossed the comforter over his bare leg. He realized that must have been the reason he could feel air on his dick while he slept. His heart was beating fast and he exhaled heavily.

"I just got out the shower," Stacy complained as a way of informing him that sex would make her late for work. He could feel her next to the bed, the cucumber melon scent stronger now. He peeked up at her, his arm crossed over his forehead. "You want me to make that go down?" she asked, looking to the tent over his dick.

No, I want you to leave me alone, he thought to himself, thinking that if he went right back to sleep, he could catch up to his dream. Catch up to Sherrelle. But it was no use now. Stacy was looking at him for an answer. He peeled the comforter away, revealing his stiff joint underneath. Before he could close his eyes, Stacy had knelt on the side of the bed and taken him into her mouth.

★ ★ ★

Marlin awoke with his palm over his dick. The head that Stacy had given him was tortuous but necessary. She had to apologize twice for scraping her teeth across the ribbed head of his joint, and she jacked him off more than she sucked. He was glad when it was over. He'd looked to the window, wondering if he did in fact see Sherrelle there. *Or was that just me dreaming?* he wondered.

While raking leaves in the back yard, he thought he'd glimpsed her at her back door. He knew she was home because her car was in the driveway. Sure, someone could have picked her up, but he could feel it in his bones that she was home. Home and strangely invisible. He'd hoped she would come out to chat.

Not even the roar of the lawn mower could make her appear and complain about the noise. He took his time mowing the slice of grass that separated their property. On the other side of the fence by his window were footprints in the dirt. She had rose bushes running along the fence.

By the time he got to the front lawn with the edger he was sure that she had been looking through his window. But she still had not made an appearance. The mailman had dropped some pieces into her box, which he thought would surely make her come outside. He briefly thought of knocking on her door, but dashed that thought as corny.

It was just past high noon when he'd pulled his Escalade into the driveway to wash it down. Soap and water were everywhere, tied-up bags of grass were at the curb, and gardening tools were strewn about the lawn when the candy-red Chrysler 300C on chrome twenty-four-inch rims wheeled to the curb in front of Sherrelle's house.

He wasn't surprised to see the beautiful, cream-colored woman emerging from a car that surely belonged to a man. Her breasts bubbled over a satin and lace bustier that looked out of place on the street. Large, gold earrings dangled from her lobes, contrasting sharply with the deep burgundy of her feathered hair, loose curls swishing and swirling as she closed the door and turned in his direction. Her small, silver Baby Phat purse hung daintily from her wrist, which was also adorned with glittering diamonds and gold, matching the sparkle wrapped around her fingers. She was like a walking, shiny piece of Jolly Rancher candy stick, though filled out in the most womanly places.

Marlin turned away from her as she rounded the front of the car and stepped onto the sidewalk. He was rinsing the back of the Escalade, pretending not to notice her looking his way. When he'd expected that she would have already passed him by, and was about to turn to look at her ass, he realized she'd stopped behind him. He turned reluctantly to see what had caused the rift in timing. She was smiling at him. A wide, bright, pretty smile. Her gold rimmed, copper-colored Gucci shades hid her eyes, muting the electric grey. She was more beautiful up close but lacked something he'd noticed in Sherrelle.

"Are you the neighbor?" she asked. Marlin realized then that he'd been the topic of conversation.

He grinned. "I guess I am," he answered.

"Yeah, I guess you are," she replied, bringing a manicured nail to her lips. She was watching him, his muscles shaping the Seahawks t-shirt, the powerful legs under the warm-up shorts, his feet in sandals. She brought her eyes back to his before letting them linger at his waist. "So how you like it out here?" she asked, resting her weight on one leg, shoving a rounded hip out.

"It's alright..."

"Alright!" she responded urgently. "You better get you a tour guide."

Marlin smiled at this. "Maybe I better." The water ran from the hose, making a puddle at the edge of the driveway.

"I'll show you around," Peaches said boldly, bringing his eyes back from the swirling water at the edge of his driveway.

"I don't know if my wife would like the idea of you showing me around."

She shifted her weight. "Oh yeah, I forgot," she said. "Wifey got you hemmed up." She was smiling. "Well, my name is Peaches. It was nice meeting you."

"You too. My name is..."

"I already know your name," she said quickly. "So, are you going to play football again?" she asked, looking into his eyes.

"Maybe," he replied, moving the water to the grass.

"Well, keep the faith. I'll be rooting for you," Peaches said, smiling brightly and bouncing as she stepped with a small wave of her dainty, creamy, jeweled fingers.

Marlin watched her walk away, ass knocking in Cavalli jeans. The front door opened when she stepped onto the porch. *I knew she was home,* he said to himself as Peaches disappeared inside.

Chapter Seven

Sherrelle

Sherrelle was up early, waking her husband with a blowjob before getting into the shower. She really appreciated the way he'd loved her down the night before. She couldn't remember the last time he'd made her cream the way she did. *If you can't poke it, lick it,* she said to herself as she hopped into the shower. *Maybe things would be better from now on,* she thought happily as she lathered herself with shower gel. She was sure that their relationship was on its way to getting better. "If he keeps licking me like that, then I have no complaints," she mumbled under the spray of water. She wished he would get up and join her in the shower, and when he appeared outside the steamy door, she thought he was going to do just that. Then the electric toothbrush hummed to life.

"Come get in the shower with me," she urged him, opening the glass door to give him a glimpse of her shiny, curvaceous body. He looked through the smoky mirror at her, smiling over the humming toothbrush in his mouth.

"I'd love to, honey, but I've got a ton of stuff to do at

the office."

"Suit yourself," she replied, closing the door and rinsing herself one last time.

Stepping out of the shower naked, she made no romantic moves toward Percy as he stood in front of the mirror trimming his nose hairs. She'd done enough for one day and privately felt rebuffed at his refusal to join her in the shower. It was not the answer she'd wanted to hear.

"Want some breakfast?" she asked, stopping at the door long enough for his reply.

"Heat me a couple apple Danishes, will you?" he answered.

Sherrelle wanted to comment on the expanding tube around his waist, but instead said, "Would you like some diabetes with that?" She turned to him just in time to see him smile in the mirror, his eyes shifting her way.

"You got jokes, hunh?"

"I'm just playing. You look fine, honey," she said, catching the insecurity in his eyes before turning into the bedroom. She slipped on a pair of boy shorts and a wifebeater before heading to the kitchen, catching him flexing his thin arms in the mirror as she turned from the closet.

The Danish pastry sounded good, but to Sherrelle's dismay, there were only two left in the box. She hid one in the back of the refrigerator and lathered the other one with butter (go ahead and get fat) before setting it in the microwave. A fluttering feeling shot through her when she decided that she didn't want the empty box in the house because it might attract ants. Her heart quickened as she stepped through the back door. The sun was making its early morning arc in the sky, promising a hot day.

Off the porch, she made a quick left around the side of

her house. Slowly she crept along the fence, her bare feet sinking into the dirt around the rose bushes. She held the empty box away from her body so as not to make noise. Eyes wide and heart beating wildly, she slowly eased within sight of her neighbor's bedroom. The curtain was parted slightly, a soothing breeze rubbing against it through the open window.

"Damn!" she hissed, her hand immediately rising to cover her mouth. She narrowed her eyes to make sure she was seeing right. It was almost more than she could stand, seeing the way his muscular leg hung off the edge of the bed like a fallen log. But there he was, stroking himself slowly. Her eyes quickly moved from his big hand— wrapped around a thick dick— to his eyes. They were closed. It was as if he was dreaming. Her heart felt like it was going to leap right out of her chest. *His dick is humongous!* she thought to herself, her mouth becoming dry at the sight of the large head and the way the shiny, black skin pushed up against it every time he stroked.

"Are you serious?" she heard Stacy say.

Sherrelle was stuck in place as Marlin opened his eyes and turned toward the window. She bolted from the window and rounded the corner. She took the steps with one leap and slammed the door behind her. Percy was in the kitchen biting into his Danish. He looked up at her with a concerned expression.

"What's wrong?" he asked. Sherrelle tried to control her breathing. She held her hand over her breasts as she took deep breaths, the image of the massive dick swimming through her mind.

"What happened?" he said, moving closer to her with worry. He was looking behind her, toward the door she'd slammed.

"I...I...I went out to..." she stammered, trying to get a clear lie in her head. "Went to put the box...," she said, raising the empty Danish box, "and there was a snake..." she trailed off. *And it was the truth*, she said to herself, looking into her husband's wide eyes now.

"A snake? Where?"

You don't want to know, she thought of saying, but instead said, "By the trash."

"By the trash? It's probably gone by now," he said, looking toward the door as if he could see the snake writhing away through the back gate.

"Probably," she echoed in a whisper as he stepped away from her.

"Where's my other Danish?" he wanted to know now that he wasn't going to chase the snake.

"That was the last one," she lied, looking at him from where she leaned against the sink. She couldn't believe him sometimes.

He turned the Danish in his hand, looking from it to her. "Want half?" he asked, extending the twice-bitten pastry in her direction.

She waved him off, resisting the urge to laugh. Not at him, but at her own freaky adventures. *I hope he didn't see me* she was thinking to herself when Percy walked from the kitchen. "Shit, I looked right into his eyes. How could he not see me?"

"What's that?" Percy called out.

"Oh, nothing, honey. I was saying that I couldn't see that there was only one pastry left in the box," she responded, tapping herself on the forehead for talking out loud.

"Pick me up a case of Heineken when you go shopping today?" He was near the bedroom from the sound of his voice so she didn't bother screaming out her reply.

She leaned against the sink thinking about what she'd seen in the neighbor's window. *Girl, you done did it this time,* she thought to herself. But damn his dick was huge. She promised herself that she would never look in his window again, but knew that was a weak pledge.

"You okay?" Percy asked, appearing in the doorway. He was looking at her strangely, making her aware of the way her nipples stood fat and erect against the thin, ribbed cotton. She folded her arms over her chest self-consciously.

"That snake," she said, acting as if she was still shaken up from seeing the bogus reptile.

"Give pest control a call and have 'em come out and look."

This was so absurd to Sherrelle. She wanted to cry laughing, but held her composure and looked at her husband with a pensive expression. "Like you said, it's probably gone by now."

He grinned nervously, not sure if she was insulting him or not. He'd never seen her this way. "I didn't know you were scared of snakes," he said, his eyes moving over her in a calculating gaze.

"Since I was a girl." Her response was even, her eyes never leaving his. She dared him to trivialize the way she felt or try to call her a liar. It was an age-old trick women used, and she would be damned if she let her husband see further than she wanted him to see.

"Didn't know that," he nearly whispered. "Good thing it didn't bite you." He made a motion to turn from the door, but something in Sherrelle's eyes made him take another look. There was a glimmer there that he'd never seen before; some sort of mischief. And oddly, that's what he loved about her— the mystery. Like an untamed cat, she was predictable only when she wanted to be.

"You know, I was thinking," Sherrelle began, able to take her arms away from her breasts now. She clasped her hands at her lap, covering the spot his eyes had traveled to, where her legs came together. "I'm thinking about starting my own business."

"What kind of business?"

"Selling clothes," she answered. Percy nearly chuckled.

"Selling clothes?"

"I do have a degree in business," she reminded him.

He smiled broadly now, though his eyes were serious. "Selling clothes," he repeated, his head rocking on his neck with his eyes catching the ceiling. He was nodding his head when he looked back in her direction. "Have at it," he announced, before making a sudden jump to look at his bare wrist, as if checking for the time. "Oh boy, I'm going to be late." With this, he dashed off.

He did not see the pain his words had caused, the pain from his lack of belief in her. He'd moved off before the tear rolled down her cheek. She wiped at it roughly, only to have another one trail closely behind it.

Sherrelle was still standing at the kitchen counter when Percy ducked his head in to remind her to pick up that case of Heineken. She wanted to tell him that she wasn't going to the store and that he should pick it up on his way home, but instead she said, "Okay." She watched him glide across the dining room and through the den. He did look sharp in his Zegna suit and tassled loafers. She knew that he would carry the Halliburton briefcase into the office with pride, eager to show his coworkers the sleek attaché. She smiled at this and was still smiling when the front door closed behind him. Not really so much because of him, but mostly because of the absurdity of the morning.

★ ★ ★

Sherrelle had gone from room to room with disinfectant and a bucket of soapy water. Cleaning the house felt like she was cleansing herself of the impure thoughts that coursed through her mind. She turned the music up loud when she vacuumed the carpeting that ran through the house, Mary J. Blige giving her strength and hope, though she hardly had a rough life to complain about. She laughed out loud when she realized that what she had was something more like *Desperate Housewives*. *I'd call my show Desperate Neighbors* she said to herself. Or maybe *A Neighborly Affair*—but without the affair, she reasoned.

At first she didn't know what the sound was. She turned off the vacuum and cut off the music. A lawnmower. He was outside! Her heart quickened because she had forgotten about him. Not really forgotten— she could never do that— but her embarrassment wasn't at the forefront of her mind.

She crept through the kitchen, ducking down when she crossed the window over the sink, to peek out of the back porch door. There he was. *Damn!* she thought to herself. Now she knew what was under those shorts. She would look at him differently from now on. She watched him from the corner of her back door window. Briefly— very briefly— she thought about walking casually out to her back yard to strike up a conversation, but the thought didn't produce enough steam to get her feet moving. She could not stand to look him in the eyes. He peered up in her direction occasionally, but she was sure he could not see her. He must have seen me at his window, she reasoned, suddenly embarrassed all over again. She didn't want him to think she was some type of pervert.

There was nothing else she could do while he was out there. He commanded her attention even though she did not, could not, be seen. She followed him as he mowed down the side of the house, stopping at the spot where she stood to watch him. *What is he doing?* she asked herself, crouching low in the kitchen, the sound of the lawn mower her only guide to his movements.

Then he was moving to the front yard. She followed him, watching through the bottom of the lace curtains at the side window. It was as if he was looking for her; the way he kept peering at her front door. This made her even more nervous—as if he were waiting to confront her, to make her reveal how perverted she really was.

Sherrelle was shaken from her thoughts when her phone rang. She jumped quickly to answer it—as if the ringing would disturb some private communication she was having with her neighbor.

"What's up, homegirl? What's really real?" Peaches asked in an animated voice.

"Nothing. Just cleaning up," Sherrelle answered, creeping back to the side window. He'd left her line of sight.

"Why are you whispering?" Peaches wanted to know.

"Oh, ummm..."

"Who you got over there? What are you doing?" she asked like a detective, quickly and to the point.

"Nothing. Nobody. Just cleaning up. Why?" Sherrelle said this in a more controlled voice as she moved to the couch. Marlin was raking up the leaves and stuffing them into trash bags. "He is so sexy." She thought she'd only thought the words.

"Who's sexy?" Peaches asked.

"Nobody girl."

"Look. I'm coming over there. You wouldn't believe the night I had with my friend with the ten-inch dick!" Peaches exclaimed.

Sherrelle was smiling privately, thinking that she'd seen what ten inches must look like. And it was a damn fine sight. "Alright, girl. Where you at?"

"Fifteen minutes away. You had lunch yet? I'm starving. Can you believe he wouldn't even make me breakfast? And had the nerve to be upset when I said I couldn't cook."

"Why y'all didn't go out to breakfast?" Sherrelle wanted to know.

"He's cool and everything, but I can buy my own breakfast."

Sherrelle smiled at this, wondering where Marlin had disappeared to. "Let me finish cleaning up. See you in a minute. You feel like IHOP's?"

"Sounds good, honey," Peaches sang.

Sherrelle thought about asking her to pick up a case of Heineken, but remembered that she really did have to go shopping. "Okay. Let me go," she said, watching as Marlin climbed into his Escalade and pulled it into the driveway. *I wish I had a camcorder,* she thought to herself, sure that he would get wet washing his car. *I could put it on YouTube!* she thought before realizing how foolish she sounded. Disgusted at the way she was acting, she jumped from the couch and turned the vacuum cleaner back on and the music back up.

She was singing along with Mary J. Blige, making her final sweep with the vacuum cleaner and thinking that she had to make an appointment to get her hair done, when she glanced out the window. At that moment, she had felt good about not peeking to see if Marlin was still out there, but when she saw Peaches gaily chatting with him, it stirred her insides once more. She stood at the edge of the window observing her friend's light flirtations, wondering what they were talking about.

Then she was waving and walking toward the porch. Sherrelle timed the opening of the front door just as she stepped to it.

"Hey, girl," Peaches sang, breezing into the house with a secret on her lips. Sherrelle resisted the urge to ask her what she was talking about with her neighbor for fear of sounding jealous. Peaches plopped down on the couch as if she were suddenly exhausted, removing her glasses and wiping her forehead with the back of her hand. "Whoo!" she exclaimed. "It's nice outside." She looked at Sherrelle, who had taken a seat next to her, with a plain face meant to hold secrets. "Why you looking at me like that?" she asked, her mouth quivering and her eyes flashing.

"No reason," Sherrelle answered innocently.

Then Peaches burst into laughter, falling onto Sherrelle on the couch.

"You gon' make me hurt you, girl," Sherrelle threatened, pushing her back up. "What the hell were you two talking about?" she wanted to know.

"Whooo!" Peaches exhaled, gathering herself. "I knew you was watching," she nodded her head with the knowledge.

"He's fine, ain't he?" Sherrelle said with wide eyes.

"Fine ain't the word, girl," Peaches responded. "And I can tell he got a nice package," she added. Then she looked at Sherrelle more closely, noticing her hard nipples and the boy shorts. "He see you like that?" she asked with a frown.

"And what if he did?" Sherrelle shot back.

Peaches frowned. "You nasty."

"I was cleaning up, girl. Now tell me what y'all was talking about."

"Nothing. For real. He said he was married." Peaches rolled her eyes at this.

Sherrelle realized that Peaches must have said something flirtatious and he shut her down. For some reason she felt good about this and thought it safe to share her latest news. "Guess what?" she asked in a conspiratorial whisper.

Peaches looked at her lazily. "What?"

"I saw him."

"Who?"

Sherrelle slapped her on the knee. "Him," she said, pointing toward the window.

"Saw him how?" Now Peaches was interested.

"I was going to empty the trash and..."

"And you looked in his window again! You are so freaky!" Peaches said with a smile. "So what happened?"

"Girl...," she began, shaking her bowed head.

"Come on! What did you see?"

"I don't know if he was sleep, dreaming or what, but he was jacking off!" she hissed secretly.

"You saw IT?" Peaches wanted to know, her eyes searching for more than what words could express.

Sherrelle nodded.

Peaches stared into her eyes, in deep thought. "What it look like?" she asked in an excited whisper.

Sherrelle fanned away her question and jumped from the couch. "I only saw it for a second!" she answered, quickly snatching the cord from the wall and wrapping it around the vacuum cleaner.

"It was fat, wasn't it?" Peaches asked, standing up and walking over to where Sherrelle stood.

"FAT!" Sherrelle replied as if describing a particular size fruit to make sure it was retrieved from the fruit bin.

"I knew it! Most ball players got big dicks." Peaches was saying this matter-of-factly as she strolled to the kitchen. "That's how they get their power. Through their dicks.

Bigger the dick the more the power." Her voice had an echo to it now.

"Where did you hear that from?" Sherrelle asked, coming into the kitchen. Peaches was standing in front of the refrigerator, holding the stashed Danish in her hand.

"I'm starving," she said, biting into the cold pastry. "Everybody knows that," she said, referring to big-dicked ball players. "You didn't know that?" she asked between small bites. "This is so good. Why was it in the back and unwrapped?"

"I was hiding it from Percy," Sherrelle answered evenly.

Peaches understood her perfectly. "Seriously? Want the rest?" she asked, pushing it toward her.

"I'll let you buy me breakfast."

"Ooohhh, girl! Let me tell you about my friend with the ten-inch dick!" Peaches swooned, forgetting about the Danish.

Sherrelle was walking out of the kitchen. "Tell me while I get dressed."

"Remember when I told you he said he don't like nothing black but a Cadillac?" she asked, following her into the room and sitting on the bed.

"Yeah."

"Well, me being the inquisitive woman that I am asked him why."

"And what did he say?" Sherrelle asked, about to pull on a pair of jeans.

"It's going to be hot outside, girl," Peaches said, looking at the jeans. "So he tells me it's because white girls suck dick better. Isn't that crazy?"

Sherrelle was smiling as she pulled a white linen dress from the closet.

"That'll work," Peaches assured her. "But isn't that the

most absurd thing you ever heard?"

"How do you find out if it's true?" Sherrelle was in panties.

"I gave him the best blowjob he ever had in his life!" Peaches announced.

"How do you know?"

Peaches turned to her quickly with a frown. "Can you suck dick?" she asked.

Sherrelle grinned nervously.

"I didn't think you could."

"I can..." Sherrelle said in what she thought was a convincing voice. "Percy doesn't complain."

"That's because he hasn't had phenomenal brain. You probably got bomb pussy though," Peaches said, nodding her head. "But if you had bomb throat and pussy, then you could take that bitch's man next door!" She clapped her hands with this.

Sherrelle was looking for a pair of earrings at her dresser when she saw Peaches reach under her bed through the mirror. "What are you looking for?"

"You are so predictable," Peaches answered, producing the black doctor's bag. She unzipped it and pulled out a dull, matted, black and thickly veined dildo. "And you wouldn't need this either," Peaches said, shaking her head. "Percy ain't jealous of this thing?" she asked, waving it in the air.

"What are you doing?" Sherrelle laughed nervously, watching as her friend pulled a smaller dildo from the case.

"You got all kinds of men up in here," she observed, placing the brown dildo next to the larger black one. "Different races and occupations." She was shaking her head. "Come over here, girlfriend. Let me teach you how to suck dick."

"Girl, please. I am starving and..."

Peaches patted the mattress beside her. "Come on. I'ma do you this one solid. Help you turn your man out."

"He's already turned out," Sherrelle countered as she sat next to Peaches on the bed.

"Well, we gon' make sure he kill himself when you bounce on his ass."

Sherrelle laughed at this as Peaches placed the brown dildo in her hand. "I can't believe you got me doing this," shaking her head.

"It's all about the sex and the money. Remember that. Now, put it in your mouth, let me see," Peaches instructed.

Sherrelle slid the dildo between her lips and pushed it in and out slowly.

Peaches was shaking her head. "No. No. No. Are you really serious?" she asked, looking at Sherrelle with a small furrow between her brow.

"What?!"

"That's not how you suck dick!" Peaches announced. "First off, start by wrapping your lips around the tip. Suck on that like there's a prize you want. Go ahead," she urged.

Sherrelle wrapped her lips around the end of the dildo and sucked on it.

"Harder."

She sucked it harder, sounds escaping every time her lips lost contact with the rubber.

"That's right," Peaches said, looking on seriously.

"That makes my jaws hurt!" Sherrelle complained.

"You gotta practice, get your jaws strong. Next thing is the tongue. What is your tongue doing while you're sucking?"

Sherrelle thought about this, realizing that she didn't

know what her tongue was doing.

"That's the secret," Peaches said with excitement. "Now," she pushed her tongue out. "Rub your tongue in circles under his dick as you suck the head."

Sherrelle did as she was told. Peaches was watching the bottom of her throat.

"Move it in circles."

Sherrelle popped the dildo out of her mouth. "I can't."

"It takes practice. Do it again."

Sherrelle did as she was told. It came a little easier this time.

"Good. Now go further down and concentrate on what your tongue is doing. Making sure it's moving...and keep your jaws tight."

Sherrelle eased the dildo into her mouth, making sure to keep her tongue moving and her jaws tight.

"That's good."

Sherrelle popped it out again after a few strokes. She flexed her mouth, opening it wide and rubbing her cheeks. "Damn," she exhaled. "That got my jaws hurting."

"That's why you can't suck dick. And that's why I had that nigga screaming like a bitch last night," she said seriously. "One last thing. You swallow?"

Sherrelle shook her head. "Hell naw!"

"You gotta swallow, girl, and make sure he sees you do it. Men love that shit."

"That's nasty!"

"You don't say it's nasty when he sucking your pussy, do you?"

This was true.

"Swallow. Don't worry, it tastes just like chicken once you get used to it." Then she jumped from the bed. "Oh, that's my song!" She sang along with Mary J. Blige: *I got this baggage with me / don't want to make you pay for what somebody else has done to me / I don't know what to do / I don't mean to hurt you.'* She stood, waving her arms in the air. *Don't be confused, boy, because you know I really do love you / want you to stay with me I never meant to hurt you baby / ... all of this baggage with me / every time I hurt your feelings it's what someone's done to me.'*

She turned to Sherrelle, who'd packed up the black bag and tossed it back under the bed. "Let's go, girl. I'm starving!"

"Okay," she answered, coming from the bathroom. "I gotta make an appointment to get my hair done."

"We can do whatever after we eat."

Sherrelle thought of her neighbor once again, wondering if his wife knew how to suck dick. She was glad to see that he was in his back yard. He was starting a fire on his grill. Sherrelle's stomach growled with her renewed hunger. He was about to grill ribs. She hoped that, one day, she would have the courage to join him for bar-b-que.

Peaches was at the door when she stepped into the living room. "Where did our friend go?" she asked, looking over to the neighbor's yard.

"He's probably in his house playing video games," Sherrelle answered, closing the door behind her, happy that she didn't have to face him yet.

Chapter Eight

Marlin

This felt good. It had been some time since he'd been able to run like this. His lungs expanded with the triumph. His thighs burned with the exertion. His arms swung in sync with his shoulders, feet pounding on the rubber mat of the treadmill. Yeah, this felt good.

And his wind was up. A full hour of swimming laps and another half hour of therapeutic water aerobics. Yeah, he was almost back. He could feel it in the way his muscles responded to the workout. Sweat drenched his Seahawks warm-up sweatshirt. He felt like he could go on like this for at least another hour. His mind raced along with him. His power was returning. He smiled with the thought, watching the noon news on the overhead monitor.

And that business yesterday. He couldn't understand it. *What was she so scared of?* he thought to himself. *Why she have to sneak off like that?* he wondered. *Maybe I wasn't tripping as hard as I thought. Maybe that WAS her at my window. What would she be doing at my window early in the morning?*

This wasn't the first time he'd thought these things.

Ever since seeing her sneak off after he fired up the grill, he knew she had been purposely avoiding him. He wondered if she thought of him the way he thought of her. What was truly up with her relationship? He was seriously thinking of catching her in the back yard when Dahji got on the empty treadmill beside him. He thought briefly that the little man was going to run, but when he made no motion to enter a running pattern into the electronic console, he knew differently. But why was he smiling?

"I was just asking myself, Dahji McBeth, what can you truly do for a man who needs to be playing football? This is what I asked myself." Dahji said this with a smile on his face. He wasn't dressed for a workout. Clad in a money green, velour, Sean John tracksuit, he looked like a television character. Thick gold ropes hung from his neck, the diamonds on his large medallions glistened under the gym lights.

"Is that right?" Marlin asked, looking back up to the news monitor. The camera panned recent carnage in Baghdad.

"This is what I bin axing myself, Marly Marl! See, I knowed all along that there was some reason I was sent to you." Now he was frowning seriously. "Let me ax you a question, Marly Marl," he said, jabbing his jeweled hand in his direction. "Do you have an agent? Of course you don't or you wouldn't be here talking to me. There's a reason for all of this, Marly Marl. And I got some good news for you. Yes, I sure do. But there's one catch." He waited for Marlin to look in his direction, his eyes glued to the side of his head until he finally turned to him in the silence. "You gotta make me your manager slash agent slash P dot R man." He said all this while slicing his hands through the air like he was doing karate. Marlin was grinning.

"You want to represent me in my professional football career?" Marlin asked, trying to keep his smile from turning into condescension.

Dahji held his hands at his waist, palms up. "That's exactly what I'm saying, Marly Marl. I know everything moving and everybody that is somebody!" Now he was sliding his arm across his body slowly. "Don't nothing and nobody move without me. I know all the player haters and the salt shakers. And I know who is watching them too. I'm cut from a special cloth, Marly Marl. It don't wrinkle or ruffle. Cleans with a shake and a shuffle."

Now Marlin was laughing.

"Laugh, Marly Marl. You get on the bus with Dahji McBeth and we both gone laugh all the way to the bank. I already got you an in-ter-view with the In-di-an-po-lis Colts." Now he had Marlin's attention. He'd stopped laughing. Dahji nodded his head up and down, his eyes closed. "Yes, indeed," he began, looking Marlin in the eyes. "Strength and conditioning coach. Wants to get a look at the guy I'm representing."

Marlin slid back to the carpet, his chest heaving as he wiped his sweaty face with a towel. He was looking at Dahji seriously. What was once comical was becoming something of a plan. He could see the light in the little man's eyes, see how his mind worked. Everything about him was real. Marlin had thought Dahji had an act, and he supposed that others thought the same— at first. But this is how Dahji would win— through being underestimated. He was smiling at Marlin now.

"You serious?" Marlin asked.

"Sho nuff is, Marly Marl. One thang about Dahji McBeth is he don't lie and he don't tell jokes meant to hurt people's feelings."

"That's two things," Marlin said, holding up two fingers.

Dahji's face broke into a large grin, gold sparkling around his teeth. "I stand corrected! Two is better than one any day, especially when counting money!"

"So when is this meeting scheduled for?" Marlin wanted to know. A meeting with anybody related to football was a welcome opportunity. Marlin never blew an interview.

Dahji shook his head slowly from side to side. His long hair lay over his shoulders in large waves. There was a part beginning at the top of his forehead, giving him the look of a ghetto Jesus.

"What? You got some kind of contract I need to sign or something?" Marlin asked, nothing surprising him about Dahji McBeth.

"Nothing like that, Marly Marl. I'm from the old school. Way back in the eighteen hundreds. A handshake is better than paper in my world. And my world is the only world that counts."

Marlin held out his hand and covered Dahji's palm with a firm pump shake.

"He's downstairs waiting on us," Dahji announced.

"Downstairs?"

"Dahji McBeth got the success bus gassed up and ready to fly to prosperity and touchdowns!" He was smiling, enjoying the look on Marlin's face.

"Well, let's roll!"

Dahji pressed a button on the treadmill console and it slid him to the carpet. "On to success! On to prosperity! On to touchdowns!" he yelled, pumping his fist in the air as he led the way to the stairs. "Marly Marl," he whispered as a shapely, muscular woman passed them going up the stairs. "Remember when I told you that white girls such dick better than sistahs?"

"Vaguely."

"Well, I'ma have to stand corrected on that. She a sistah still if her mom white and her father black, right?"

"Last I checked. All it take is a drop," Marlin answered.

"I gotta hold to one of them. She suck a golf ball through a water hose."

"She got you open, hunh?"

"Like a whore's pussy," Dahji said emphatically as they stepped onto the landing. The Sports Medicine Clinic juice bar was next to the apparel shop. Further down the thickly carpeted foyer was the entrance to the women's sauna and steam room; the men's were in the other direction, by the vitamin and supplements store.

Marlin saw the familiar face of Mark Richards sitting alone at a table in the juice bar. He was sipping on a white colored drink that looked expensive. His shoulders were broad under the official Colts nylon warm-up jacket. His hair represented his years in the league; salt and pepper marching back in waves from a mocha-colored forehead.

"You don't sleep, hunh?" Marlin said to Dahji.

"Never. Just rest a little, that's all."

Mark Richards looked up at Marlin when he walked in the door. He had a generous smile on his face as he stood with his hand out. "Marlin Cassidy," he said, gripping the ball player's hand firmly.

"Mark Richards. Nice to meet you," Marlin answered.

Dahji was the last to sit down, enjoying what he had brought together.

"How are you feeling?" Mark asked, getting to the point.

Marlin smiled, aware of the way Dahji leaned back in his chair, the way he folded his large hands over his lap. He realized now how big Dahji's hands were. Sort of out of place for his slight build, but maybe a compensation for his big personality. "I'm feeling good," he answered, believing it and feeling it.

"I've seen you at work," Mark said, nodding his head with assuredness. Mark Richards gave off the fatherly demeanor of a black man who was not only physically fit but smart. His skin looked clean, though he was as dark as charred oak. His dark eyebrows sloped like molasses over deep, oil-black eyes. There was Alabama in those eyes. Arkansas. Mississippi. Georgia. In those eyes. From back in the day. Marlin felt the strong bond of brotherhood that set shit off back in the day. Now it was time to set shit off again. Only this time it was about money and winning championships on a professional football field. Not even O.J. Simpson could fuck that up.

"Let me get to the point. Dahji here says that you got what it takes. You don't get to this level without having what it takes. You're anonymous if you don't measure up. So what I want to do is see you back on the field. I wanna do what I can to help your career."

Dahji had barely moved and was somehow able to communicate with the pretty blonde behind the fruit juice counter. Suddenly on the table were three large, frothy, cream-colored drinks, strawberry and banana chips spotting the thick malts.

Marlin had not realized how thirsty he was. He knew he looked crusty. Something in his life was changing. He could feel it. Like the time he'd just walked out of a liquor store and two men brushed past him going in. They'd gone in shooting. And he always remembered the pregnant lady; she was the woman who lived in the next apartment. She'd smiled at him, she was the prettiest woman in the building.

And when people started saying that he was lucky how he got out, he would remember her. He would always remember the pretty, pregnant lady who died that day. And he lived.

"Whatever it takes, coach," Marlin responded, bringing the cold glass of creamy fruit to his lips. He licked them good, his large tongue rolling over thick lips. He was ready.

"I'll be in touch with Dahji," Mark said, pointing a thick thumb toward the silent man. "From my understanding, you are not under contract nor have you been approached by anyone else?"

"That's right," Marlin responded, liking the taste in his mouth.

"First we need to get you medically cleared. We want to get you into our training center, have you work out with the practice squad. Our goal is to get you on the team. We think you'll work out at second string running back."

"I'll share the load."

Mark turned to Dahji. "Come with him to the training center."

"We ready," Dahji spoke for the first time. It was his same beveled voice, but there was power in it, confidence.

★ ★ ★

Sherrelle stayed in bed on purpose. She heard Percy roll from the mattress, groaning because he'd come home late and had had too many dry martinis. He drank a Heineken to relax.

She heard him step clumsily into the shower, screaming when the hot water stung him. She lay under the covers naked. She could smell herself. Feminine. Sex. Sexy. Her long hair fanned out across the pillow. She'd given it to him and he'd loved it, but there was still a fire in her that he couldn't put out. He might get out the edges and maybe even douse the flames, but there was this middle that he just couldn't reach. And so she'd slept with her palms between her legs. Occasionally, when conscious enough throughout the night, she'd rub herself with the side of her palms.

He'd called her from the bedroom to where he was in the den. There were late night golf reports on ESPN. He waved her over with a wicked grin when she appeared at the door in her red teddy, breasts succulent and swollen. She knelt down in front of him, looking into his eyes the whole time. She would give it to him. She unzipped his pants and pulled his bone hard dick from its trap. She wanted to see if it worked. She wrapped her lips around the head and rolled her tongue under it. She felt his thighs tighten. Again. Now his knees jerked. Then she tightened her jaws and sucked on the head, hard. He tried to turn sideways, his only reflex. He shoved her from him and spun her around roughly. She eased down onto him, feeling him crease her pussy. She gripped his knees and rotated her hips into him as he slid inside. He jerked quickly, not reaching bottom, and then his legs started jumping under her. It was over.

"Where did you learn that?" she heard him whisper before she left the room, leaving him to his golf reports.

Even now she grinned with satisfaction. He'd stepped from the shower and she could feel his eyes on her. Then she opened hers. He didn't know what to say, so he bravely said, "I'm proud of you." She smiled at him.

She slept late on purpose. She wanted to hear him close the front door, wanted him to give that some thought. That shit he talk, that shit he do, that shit he don't do well. That shit he need to think about. 'Cause I'm about to start my own business. It's about to be some changes.

After he was gone she lay in bed, warm and tender, the

sides of her palms rubbing against her pussy. Because she was thinking about some shit too.

She was getting out of the shower when the doorbell rang. She appeared at the door damp and wearing a thick terrycloth robe. She saw the UPS truck first. Then there was a tall black guy pushing a loaded dolly of brown boxes up her walkway. "Mrs. Sherrelle Santiago?" the pudgy Latin man asked. He looked like beer was his water. Everything was fat on him, yet proportioned.

"Yes," she answered, opening the screen to provide enough space for him to slide the paperwork to her, attached to a digital clipboard.

"We have a shipment for you. Please sign at the bottom of the screen."

Now here she was in the middle of her living room surrounded by ten newly opened boxes of HoodSweet apparel. She called Peaches to tell her to come by, and to bring some Rocky Road ice cream because she had a strong taste for some.

"I know what you got a strong taste for," Peaches had said, already on her way. She just had to hit another corner of the Palladium ice cream store.

Sherrelle had received most everything in three colors: pink, red, and white. She had boy shorts, strap Ts, wifebeaters, hoodies. She thought those were real cute. She put one on, feeling sexy and brave. HoodSweet was scrawled across the front in raised letters. There were sweatpants, hats, headbands, scarves, and sports bras.

Now Peaches was at the door. She didn't even notice the clothes strewn on the couch and table. She walked in carrying a plastic bag, handing it off to Sherrelle. "I ran into my high school principal in the ice cream store," she exhaled as if this was the worst thing that could happen to her.

"For real?" Sherrelle answered absently, already leading the way to the kitchen for spoons.

"The ho was shook. The last time she saw me she was kicking me out of her office," Peaches said, laughing.

"Why?"

"The bitch had the nerve to say I wasn't really black so I should be doing better in school."

"WHAT?!" Sherrelle said, turning in shock, extending a silver spoon to her.

"Yeah! Bitch sitting in her office with them big ass titties sittin' on the desk. She got Malcolm X, Martin Luther King, Harriet Tubman—you know, the big shots," Peaches said, flinging one thin arm at her, the gold bangles on her wrist knocking together.

"Right," Sherrelle said, digging into the rich chocolate ice cream, careful to get a marshmallow and walnut chunk on the spoon.

"So I say, 'Here it is, Miss Robichalk'—I mispronounce her name," Peaches said, grinning.

Sherrelle was smiling, moving the ice cream around her mouth with her tongue.

"She corrected me. 'It's Robicheau,' she said. 'Okay, cool. But I say you all up in here with all this black art and pictures and sayings, but here it is you done dyed your hair blonde and you wear blue contact lenses."

Sherrelle's breasts jumped to the zipper and quivered inside the HoodSweet hoodie. She laughed softly.

"Crazy bitch!" Peaches said, licking more ice cream onto her tongue, the spoon upside down.

"What did she say to that?" Sherrelle asked, wide-eyed and smiling.

"She told me to get the hell out of her office." Peaches

went in for more ice cream.

"Did she recognize you?"

"Hell yeah," she smiled. "She gon' remember that shit the rest of her life. She didn't have the blue contacts in, but her hair still blond though."

"She couldn't let that go!" Sherrelle laughed.

It wasn't until the laughter subsided and they were preparing to move back into the living room that Peaches noticed what Sherrelle's hoodie read. Her eyes opened wide. She quickly looked into the living room and threw one fist in the air. "Power to the people!" she screamed, turning to Sherrelle and hugging her. "Congratulations, girl!"

"It's nice, too," Sherrelle said, following Peaches into the living room, running down her own descriptions and likes about everything, and talking about what would look good on each of them. Peaches held up a pair of white boy shorts and suggested that Sherrelle take out the trash in them. She had no idea that Sherrelle went outside with less than that on her body.

"I'm wearing this tonight," Peaches said, holding up a red wifebeater with matching boy shorts. "They gon' like this, Sherrelle."

"I hope so," she replied, confident that the women would all want something.

"Just bring a couple sizes of everything. Especially these," she said, holding up the top and shorts she was wearing that night at Applebottoms. "So what time you gon' get there? You should come early so you can meet the girls before it gets busy."

"What time does it get busy?" Sherrelle wanted to know.

"When it gets dark."

"Well, it'll probably be after six, depending on what Percy is doing at the office or if he makes it home early."

"Just call that nigga and tell him you goin' to the club to sell your stuff and start an empire for women who get good lovin'."

Sherrelle was laughing. "You are so wrong."

"I'm serious though."

"I'll be there early. Don't worry," Sherrelle assured her.

Chapter Nine

Stacy

Stacy was coming into the house as Marlin was sitting down at the dining room table. He had a plate piled high with bar-b-que chicken and ribs that he'd just gotten out of the microwave. There was a new bounce in his step. Never in his wildest imagination would he have believed that Dahji would be the one to get him back on the field. He had to give the little man his props. He'd proved, once again, that you can't judge a book by its cover.

She appraised him as she dropped her purse and brief-case on the couch, her eyes taking in the change in his posture and the way he looked up at her. There was something new in his eyes.

"What's going on?" she asked, reaching to take one high-heeled designer shoe off after the other, then hobbled his way.

Just then, Marlin remembered he'd forgotten to get something to drink. "Hey, babe," he replied cheerfully. "You mind grabbing me that Pepsi out the fridge?"

She stopped in mid stride, the hallway that led to the

bathroom to her right, and a closer look at what was in Marlin's eyes a few steps further. She was undecided as to which direction to take, her curiosity pulling her away from the feeling in her bladder—never mind that he should have gotten his own drink before he sat down. "I've got to pee!" she decided, making the right and darting knock-kneed into the hallway.

Marlin grinned and hopped up from the table with energy.

Stacy wanted to say something about him drinking from the two-liter bottle when she stepped back into the dining room. Marlin had his head bowed over his plate, ripping through a chicken breast. There was definitely something going on. She felt her power ebbing. "What's going on?" she asked, pulling out a chair and sitting next to him, her elbow resting on the table, her palm under her chin. She knew it was something good and was looking into his sparkling eyes for the prize. He was licking his lips like a lion after a bloody kill, dark red bar-b-que sauce dotting his chin and the right side of his cheek.

"I met with the Colts today!" he said, looking at her quickly— just long enough to see the confusion—and biting into the rib between his fingers.

"The Colts?" she asked, remembering the celebration after they'd won the Super Bowl, and how Marlin had said then that all he needed was some playing time and that would be them celebrating.

"Yep," he answered shortly before taking another bite of chicken.

"That's great!" It didn"t come out like she'd intended it to, and Marlin caught the undercurrent of fear in her voice. His eyes cut to her after the words tumbled from her lips. "Aren't you happy?" she asked, hoping to mask her insecurity by getting him to forgive her.

"Ain't no promises right now. They wanna see me run and cut." He shrugged his shoulders. "After I get cleared, then it's just on to the practice squad." He was deliberately downplaying his excitement. Forgiving her. Now she had cause to really be happy. She wrapped her arms around his neck and kissed him sloppily, loving the taste of bar-b-que sauce on his cheek and chin.

"I'm so happy for you!" she exclaimed, relaxing into her seat with one final tap on his knee, observing the way he gripped the soda bottle with fat fingers and turned it up. His neck muscles pulsed as he gulped down the fizz then came up with a large burp. He was back.

"So, how was your day?" he asked, looking at her from a fresh rib held loosely between his fingers.

"It was nice. I'm really enjoying the people I work with. Everyone is so supportive," she responded, her mind retreating from the feeling she'd fought before he was injured. She'd always felt that he was halfway somewhere else and that she was holding her breath for the eventual day when he announced he wanted a divorce. But then he got hurt and everything changed. It was her chance to convince him that she was the right one for him.

"So, how did you meet with them? I mean..."

"Guy at the clinic," Marlin answered around a mouthful of sweet beef. "He got me a meeting."

"Is he some kind of agent or something?" She was digging through the possibility of him returning to the field, upset at herself for thinking that it may not be official.

"You could say that. I gotta meet with him tonight."

"Tonight?" Stacy asked, her face registering a mix of animated joy and confusion.

"At Applebottoms," Marlin added, though he didn't

have to. He was enjoying her lightweight doubt in him.

"Applebottoms," she said in low voice. "What is that?"

"Strip club."

"Oh." Her eyebrows raised and her mouth formed an O. Marlin had returned his eyes to his plate. He was feeling extra good now. He dared her to discount his newfound lease on life. And he didn't even want to share who Dahji was and how he could possibly arrange such a meeting, this man who held meetings at strip clubs. She wouldn't get it at all.

Fed and burped, Marlin killed time playing Madden football on his X-box in the den. Stacy came in to ask him some odd question (Did you let your mother know about the good news?) or make a statement (You should look through this Caribbean vacation catalog. It's absolutely beautiful.) or make a request (I need you to rub my back. I think I twisted something.) This was the last of her intrusions into the den, at which he said he'd be there in a minute. The game was almost over.

Stacy was fresh from the shower, lotioning her legs with thick cream. It took a long time for her to get it to disappear, Marlin noticed as he watched from the door. She was enjoying performing for him, naked on the edge of the bed with her leg high in the air. She'd turned on a jazz station, the piano stroking at him under the soft pull of trumpets singing. Marlin's dick stirred. She was grinning mischievously at him.

"Are you going to massage my back?" she asked, looking up into his face as he stood between her legs. He held her lotioned ankle in his palm at his shoulder. Her pussy winked up at him as she lay back on both elbows.

"Is that what you want?"

She didn't answer, just looked at him with a serious

expression. There was the feeling of a last dance between them. She wanted to mark this point in their relationship. Her eyes barely shifted as Marlin pulled his running shorts over his growing dick and let them drop down his legs to the floor.

Without a word he leaned over and grabbed her knee, pushing her legs wider. He continued to hold her ankle in his other hand, lowering his dick, a missile now, to her waiting pussy. He entered her with a nudge, catching at the entrance and then easing in with slow, warm strokes. With his feet firmly planted on the hardwood floor, he drove down into her, opening her up with her legs spread apart. She was all pussy and legs.

"Ahhhhh," Stacy moaned when she'd wettened enough for him to slide deep inside her. She tried to tighten up so that he couldn't get too deep, but his leverage while standing allowed him to push his dick past her barriers. Her pussy swelled and pulsed before him.

Marlin grabbed her other ankle and held both up by his ears. He slid into her deeply, she having relaxed and having decided to take the dick. She cried out with each stroke, creating a rhythm that allowed Marlin to hit his groove. He knew he was doing damage, the energy of her sex feeling like a breakup.

Stacy abruptly slid back onto the bed, causing him to slide out of her. She turned over on the bed and raised to her knees. Marlin grabbed her hips, guided the missile into her wet flesh and sunk deep inside of her. She rotated her hips in a way that offset the force of his strokes; she didn't want to take the dick straight on. Marlin held her in place as he chased her motions.

She grabbed a pillow and shoved her face into it. Her muffled cries turned into shrieks every time he pounded into her, forcing her to bounce up from the pillow, letting some of her cries escape. She had no choice but to allow him deep inside because her pussy muscles just couldn't handle the pressure. She bore the pain, feeling him grow hot and swollen inside of her.

Marlin was blind with passion as he pounded into her, gripping her hips so hard his fingers dug into her skin. She was locked in his grip as he filled her with his thick, long, shiny meat. He could not hear her cries as he jerked powerfully into her, pulling her shoulders and breasts off the bed as he emptied himself.

★ ★ ★

That's all she wanted, Marlin thought to himself as he stepped off the porch. Stacy had watched him dress— Rocawear turtleneck sweater with matching brown corduroys, diamonds hanging from both ears and a Rolex watch on his wrist. A Kangol apple cap sat rakishly on his head. She lay across the bed, observing his every move. He kissed her before walking from the room. *Yep, that's all she wanted. For me to beat that pussy up.*

He was nearly off the porch when he heard a man's voice yell, "Why the hell didn't you discuss this with me first!" Marlin knew right away that it was Sherrelle's husband.

"I did!" she responded. Marlin was at Stacy's car, looking back toward Sherrelle's picture window. She and her husband were in the living room, their silhouettes opposite one another. It looked like he was holding something in his hand. He was waving it over his head now. "So this is your idea of a business?" he yelled.

"What are you so scared of?" Sherrelle asked.

"Me?! Scared?! All of a sudden you want to open up your own business! And what is this shit you're selling?! It's for prostitutes!' Percy laughed loudly, throwing his head back as he tossed whatever he was holding to Sherrelle. Marlin watched as she caught it quickly. He'd made up his mind to knock on the door if he heard a crash or heard her scream, but Percy stormed off toward the back of the house. 'That shit ain't gon' work!" he'd yelled back to her.

Marlin watched as she stood in the living room, her head bowed in her hands. He knew she was crying and wished he could comfort her in some way. Then she started moving again, with purpose. Marlin knew then that she would be fine. She was bending low and pulling what looked like clothes from the floor, folding them slowly before stacking them on what must have been the couch under the window. He turned toward his Escalade parked at the curb. There was a meeting he had to attend. Now he wasn't so bored with the idea of going to a strip club.

★ ★ ★

Applebottoms Gentlemen's Lounge was situated in a commercial parking lot next to a huge OfficeMax megastore, which had already closed for the night. Marlin could see the lights of the mini commercial zone ahead of him in the distance as he traveled a long, dark road. Past the city, Applebottoms lay nestled on the outskirts of the suburbs. If a woman screamed out there at the top of her lungs, no one would hear her who didn't already know why she was screaming.

For a Thursday night it was unusually crowded. The front parking lot was full with parked cars and two-way traffic. At the canopied door, a midnight-colored bear of a man met stopping cars to open their doors. A similar dark-suited man was at the door with his arms folded across his massive chest. He was opening the door for sharply dressed men, ladies, and laughing groups to enter, and letting the red light from within seep out.

Marlin spotted the familiar burgundy Range Rover parked at the third spot away from the door. *Dahji had juice*, Marlin thought to himself as he pulled around to the back of the large building. He found a space under a lamp in the corner of the lot, near the rear. A group of men were emerging from a big-bodied Benz as he stepped from his Escalade.

"What it do, Bru?" a dark-skinned, wiry-limbed man said, his diamond-bezeled grill sparkling under the light. The three men following him were similarly dressed in designer jeans, reptile boots and thick sweaters. All were weighed down with thick gold ropes with large, round, diamond-studded discs hanging from them, including a star and crescent that were surrounded by the words "Live rich, die ready." The men moved with confidence and leisure.

"What's up?" Marlin answered, looking over his shoulder at the mysterious men. He relaxed once they started joking amongst themselves, forgetting that he even existed. The dark-skinned man who'd spoken to him started to remind the peanut butter-colored man next to him—large diamond earrings weighing his earlobes down—about those broads from Kansas, and asked jokingly if one of them ever gave him that money she'd promised.

"Bru," he answered with a grin, revealing more diamonds, "she asked me to loan her ten racks so she could make it an even hundred."

"What you tell her?"

Everyone waited for his response. "I told her punk ass to get back on the track and get the rest of my money!" This was followed by laughter as they strolled nearly next to Marlin.

They were Marlin's type of folks, he knew, and he was

glad they were beside him when he got to the front door. They'd surrounded him as if he was with them. The wide man at the red leather, padded door nodded big when he met the eyes of the slim, Hershey-colored man with the diamonds in his mouth.

"Jon Ansar!" the doorman exclaimed, extending his big paw.

"What it do, Bru?" Jon Ansar answered.

Big man shrugged, "It's all good." Marlin had heard the man's name before. He was famous among the circles of those who didn't file taxes and had no social security numbers, and he lived like royalty. Nothing to do with guns or drugs—Marlin would know—but they moved in the same circles as bankers, lawyers and city officials. White-collar crime and favors kept them above the law. Big man opened the door with a smile, nodding at Marlin as he passed by, Jon Ansar behind him.

"Yo, Bru," Jon Ansar said, sliding up next to Marlin. "Don't I know you?" His eyes were like two deep wells of black ink.

Marlin was hesitant, caught up in his gaze. "I used to play for the Seahawks," he replied.

Jon Ansar snapped his fingers. "That's it! But naw, that ain't all of it. You ever stomp through Arkansas?"

"I played my college ball there," Marlin answered. "I'm Marlin Cassidy."

Jon Ansar smiled big, spreading his arms out and looking around at his crew. "This him right here. This Cassidy. Remember, Talib?" he asked, looking at the mocha-colored man beside him. "We ate big off this cat right here." Talib was nodding in agreement.

Jon Ansar turned back to Marlin. "In the championship game against Ohio State, y'all didn't win but you rushed for over two-hundred yards that day and covered the spread with that last touchdown from twenty yards out." Marlin was smiling now. He remembered that day. It was a good one for him. It was the play that got him into the NFL. "We ate big off you. Look, tonight I got you covered," Jon Ansar said, giving Marlin dap as he nodded his head. "So what you doing now?"

"Interviewing with the Colts right now," Marlin answered.

"That's good business. We eats big off them every year," he assured Marlin with an exaggerated expression. "Good luck, Bru. I'ma be lookin' out for you." He pushed off, leading a procession through a beaded curtain and into the dimly lit room beyond.

They'd entered a sort of foyer where a man stood ready to scan them for weapons. It was then that Marlin noticed—his arms up as the wand moved down his body— that no one in Jon Ansar's crew got scanned. He briefly thought he should have rolled with them when they pushed off.

The large room was dominated by a round, wooden platform where a shapely, cream-colored blonde woman moved to a hypnotic beat. A runway from the platform extended to the back where it was met by a hanging red velvet curtain. There were four more platforms at each corner of the room where a woman, each representing a different nationality, danced. These smaller stages were surrounded by leather-upholstered booths that were partly hidden in darkness. To the right was a long bar that ran the length of the wall; a giant, bearded white man moved behind it under dim light. To the left was a raised platform sealed off by a velvet rope. This is where Jon Ansar had gone. Marlin could see him and his crew settling into one of the U-

shaped tables at the middle of the row. Then he saw Dahji.
And Peaches. He knew her? They were laughing together,
seated closely in one of the booths. Marlin headed toward
the velvet rope.

Marlin was stopped by a muscular black man in a suit.
He held firm at the spot where the rope clipped to the silver pole. This was his duty and he took pride in reserving
this space for privileged individuals.

"Marly Marl!!" Dahji sang from his seat, catching the
gatekeeper's attention. Dahji waved him up, making it
alright for the velvet rope to come loose. Peaches was
watching him with curiosity as he strolled down the aisle to
their table.

"You know him?" Peaches asked Dahji after he'd given
Marlin dap over the table.

"Have a seat, Marly Marl." Dahji beamed, looking at
Peaches. "This here is my folks in a real way," he replied.
He turned back to Marlin, noticing how Peaches was react-
ing to him. "You know Marly Marl?" he asked, not sure if
he wanted to know the answer.

"He stay next door to my friend, that's all," she assured
him.

Dahji relaxed. "Like I always say—it's a small, small
world after all."

"I didn't get your name," Marlin said to Peaches,
extending his hand across the table. Her tight body with all
the right curves was sheathed in a bright blue, Chanel,
velour tracksuit; her dark red hair contrasted with the pale
of her skin. Her palm felt light and delicate in his.

"Peaches," she said sweetly. Marlin knew right away
that she was the one who had given Dahji the blowjob that
changed his opinion about white women being the best at
it. He'd had no idea she was a stripper, but wasn't at all sur-

prised. Though he did wonder how Sherrelle factored into her life.

An Asian lady dressed in a long, maroon, silk kimono stepped to the table. She held in her hands two, large, silver buckets with a bottle of Dom Perignon peeking over the top of each. She cast her eyes to the table down the row. Jon Ansar was smiling their way.

"Marly Marl," Dahji said happily after the bottles had been set down and the waitress stepped away. "That's Jon Ansar right there. You in the big leagues already and don't even know it."

Marlin nodded, trying not to notice the silver sparks coming from Peaches' eyes. Seeing her made him think of Sherrelle and the fight she was having with her husband. Marlin reached for a bottle.

"I'd love to stay, but I have to get ready for my show," Peaches said.

"You ain't seent your friend slide through?" Dahji asked.

"No. She shoulda bin here by now," Peaches responded, looking out over the railing for the friend Dahji mentioned. "Well, I'll see her when she comes in." Then she looked at Marlin. "Sherrelle is coming," she said with a grin. Marlin's heart leaped as he filled the three glasses on the table with bubbly.

He didn't trust what would have come from his lips, especially the way Peaches was smiling mischievously at him, so he just pressed his lips together and nodded nonchalantly.

"So help me keep a look out," Peaches said then, hopping up from her seat, and swiveling down the aisle and through the velvet rope. Now Marlin could see for the first time how Applebottoms was alive with lust and money.

Three 6 Mafia thumped with heavy bass through hidden speakers, giving the room its rhythm and bounce.

"Here's to a small world and touchdowns!" Dahji said, holding up his glass for a toast.

When the glass came away from Marlin's lips he saw the familiar brown skin and long, thick hair. She looked his way but couldn't see into the raised, dimly lit cavern. Marlin caught the passing Asian waitress and pointed Sherrelle out to her. "Would you mind showing that lady to this table please?" he asked.

"Sure." She took tiny steps. Marlin watched her the entire way. He heard Dahji ask who she was and he absently answered that she was his neighbor. He watched the waitress approach her, say something with a smile, then lead her in his direction. Marlin stood and stepped into the aisle so as not to appear flossy. She smiled when she saw him.

"I didn't expect to see you here," she said, almost nervously, because she'd been avoiding him ever since she saw him through his window.

"I could say the same about you," he answered.

"Dahji, a good friend of mine," Marlin said, stepping aside so she could shake Dahji's hand as he stood up from the table.

"Is he a good neighbor?" Dahji asked, smiling at her, almost eye level if it weren't for her heels.

Sherrelle looked quickly at Marlin, noticing the slight grin on his face. "I couldn't ask for a better one," she answered gladly, feeling Marlin's eyes on her.

There was a break in the music. The silence filled with anticipation until the microphone crackled to life. A sexy whisper said, "Please welcome to center stage, our featured dancer, Peaches."

"Oh my God!" Sherrelle said in a low voice, barely

audible under the deep bass that pounded through the speakers at that very instant. Dahji was looking toward the stage.

"Excuse me for a minute," he said, before sauntering down the aisle.

"This your first time seeing her dance?" Marlin asked after she'd slid into the semi-circular booth beside him. It felt good to be next to her.

"Yes," she replied, looking across the room at her friend twirling around the silver pole dressed in a HoodSweet wifebeater and pink boy shorts.

Marlin was watching Dahji stop to speak to a sharply dressed, olive-skinned white man halfway to the stage. The man leaned in close to say something in Dahji's ear. When he backed away, Dahji nodded and shook his hand. "What's in that bag? You dancing, too?" Marlin asked, gesturing with his chin at the large Louis Vuitton duffel she'd dropped onto the seat next to her.

She smiled. Her hair was pulled into a tight ponytail and her gold hoop earrings dangled against her soft cheeks. "Oh, no...no. These are my clothes. I'm starting a clothing business!" she said, growing excited as she unzipped the large leather bag. "Peaches is wearing this on stage." She lay a pair of boy shorts on the table. "You like them?"

Now Marlin understood what the fight was about. "They cool for inside the house."

Sherrelle leaned back in her seat, looking at him with twisted lips that threatened to smile. "Inside the house? Oh, so you the type that won't let your woman wear this outside?" Her voice had a sweet melody to it, Southern.

Marlin was shaking his head. "Not any wife of mine. Not even my girlfriend for that matter." He liked the way her cardigan sweater shaped itself around her body. And the black jeans she wore did justice to her thick shape.

"So what would you do if your wife wanted to wear this to go get the mail?"

Marlin grinned, relaxing next to her. He looked out to the center stage quickly. Peaches was bending over, and as she touched her toes, she pulled the boy shorts down to reveal her pretty, creamy ass creased by a thong. Dahji was throwing a wad of money onto the stage. "She wouldn't do that," Marlin replied, turning back to Sherrelle. "Now let me ask you a question."

"What kind of question?"

"A general question. Nothing to ruffle your feathers," he assured her with a shrug.

"You have to pour me a drink first," she said, looking for an empty glass on the table. Upon seeing none, she looked at Marlin's. "Can I drink from your glass?"

Marlin pushed it to her without hesitation and then proceeded to pour her a drink. "Now. My question. Do you always look into your neighbor's window?"

Sherrelle nearly choked, bringing her hand to her mouth to control her coughing. Marlin was smiling at her. "I'm sorry. I am so sorry," she said with doe eyes.

"Did you like what you saw?"

She took a minute to study him. "Why would you ask me something like that?"

"It's a simple question. I would tell you if I liked what I saw if I was peeking in your window."

"Touché," she said, jabbing the air with her finger. "Okay. Yes. I liked what I saw." There was a falling, crumbling wall disintegrating between them. Her chin was up in defiance.

"I ain't even gon' ask you what you saw. How many times?" he asked, looking up at her with a frown.

"Do we really need to go there?"

Marlin eased back into the seat, looking out to the stage again. Peaches was on all fours, making her ass bounce in the air. She was surrounded by money. Men shouted and hooted around the center stage, vying for her attention. Dahji was surrounded by a group of women, each leaning in to whisper into his ear in turn.

"How long have you two been friends?" Marlin wanted to know, looking back at Sherrelle.

"Since we were little. Who is that guy you introduced me to?"

"That's Dahji. He got me an interview with the Colts."

"Really?" Sherrelle said, genuinely happy. "So homeboy about to get back on the field?! That's great!"

"And you're about to be a real deal business woman," Marlin nodded.

Sherrelle lifted up her glass. "Oops, I can't toast you. But here's to us," she said before taking a sip of champagne. "So let me ask you—how would you answer your own question to me?"

"Which one?"

"About liking what you see in the window?"

Marlin looked at her carefully, wondering if she was happy in her marriage. "I ain't seen you. But you are a beautiful woman, so I don't see me having any complaints," he assured her.

"Can I ask you a personal question?"

"Am I going to need a drink?" Marlin asked, laughing nervously.

"No," she assured him. "But you can have your glass back just in case."

He held up a palm. "Naw, I'm cool. What's up?"

"Are you satisfied? I mean it's just a simple question.

Me and Peaches talk about it all the time—about how people get together for certain reasons and they're not really satisfied."

Marlin knew then that she wasn't satisfied and had probably married her husband for financial reasons. "Do you love your husband?" he asked her.

"Answer my question first."

"Your question is a little deep. Maybe we can get to it later."

She smiled. "Okay. We'll get to it later. Yes. I love my husband."

"Are you in love with him?" Marlin asked.

"No." Her answer was quick. It was as if she'd already given this some thought and had no problem voicing it. "And don't think I go around telling this to people."

"I'll take that as a compliment."

"You should," she said. "And what about you? Love or in love?"

"Same as you," he answered, meeting her eyes.

"That's lonely, isn't it?" she asked after a few beats. It was as if Snoop Dogg wasn't rapping through the speakers and cheers weren't erupting around the stage, as if they were alone.

Marlin shrugged, "Love and starvation can't eat out the same bowl."

"Wouldn't it be nice if they could though?"

He nodded, giving this some thought.

"And wouldn't it be better to be in love with someone who satisfied all that you needed?"

"Sounds like a dream," Marlin whispered, her smoky eyes still on him. Somehow she'd gotten closer to him.

"Do you dream?" Sherrelle wanted to know.

"All the time."

"About what?"

"A woman," he answered.

"Not your wife?" She was interested in the juicy details and leaned both her elbows on the table. She was close enough now that she had to turn to him. She rested her chin in her palm. Marlin shook his head. "Who do you dream about?" Her eyes were wide.

"That's something else we might talk about at another time."

"Well, is she beautiful? Do you know her? Do you have sex with her in your dreams?" she asked with childish glee. "Is she good in bed?" She laughed low now, looking at him in anticipation of his answer. Her knee rubbed against his under the table. It was like a bolt of electricity going through him. Her eyes sparkled with the contact.

Marlin nodded one time. "Yes to all of the above."

"She must be hot," Sherrelle teased, privately hoping that it was her whom he dreamed about.

Dahji sauntered up to the table and slid into the seat beside Marlin. "I don't know, Marly Marl," he said, shaking his head before taking a long swallow of champagne.

"What's that?" Marlin asked.

"She got a hold of me something fierce. I don't know..." Dahji trailed off. Neither man saw the smile on Sherrelle's lips. She realized that this was the man Peaches said had a ten-inch dick, the man she'd given the best head of his life. Better than a white girl. It was all falling into place.

"Hey, homegirl!" Peaches screamed at the edge of the table. She'd changed into her velour tracksuit, though it could not hide the energy underneath. She was absolutely on fire with sex appeal. Marlin could see how Dahji was hypnotized. Peaches was looking from Dahji to Marlin then to Sherrelle. "It's a small world, ain't it?" she asked with her nose wrinkled up.

"I was just thinking that," Sherrelle said, grinning with wonder.

Peaches waved her up from her seat. "Come on, girl. Everybody wants to see your stuff. Grab your bag and let's go," she said before turning to Dahji. "I'll see you later?" she wanted to know.

"Sho nuff," Dahji answered.

Sherrelle looked at Marlin with a knowing gaze. There was a question on her lips.

"See you around, neighbor," Marlin said, giving her a smile. He felt like he was on cloud nine. Sherrelle made him feel alive all over again. He looked forward to seeing her out front at her mailbox, knowing that she would wait for him to come outside and chat.

"We got an early morning, Marly Marl!" Dahji said, slapping Marlin on the shoulders. "On to prosperity! On to touchdowns!" he whispered, raising his glass for a toast.

When Marlin raised his glass, he realized that Sherrelle had left her bronze lipstick print on the rim. He placed his lips over hers and took a sip of champagne. She was as sweet as he'd dreamed she would be.

Part Two

Chapter Ten

Dahji

Dahji exhaled softly as his soft-bottom Gators sank into the thick carpeting. He removed the dead reptiles from his feet, walked over to the entertainment system and nudged the glass pane. It popped open to allow him to press play on the CD console. Soft jazz swept through the luxuriously appointed open space (camel skin couches, a suede covered wall under stairs that led to the loft where the fluffy red comforter hung over his king-size bed along the brass railing, stainless steel appliances in a black ceramic kitchen) that he was always happy to get back to. He pressed the oval button on the answering machine as he shed his clothes, dropping first his shirt across the headrest of the couch on his way to the kitchen.

"Hello, Dahji," a woman's syrupy voice sang, the 'l's and 'j' pronounced with meaning. "Well, you have absolutely got to call on me." In the background were the wailings of an opera singer. Dahji could see Mirabelle as she called him, no doubt lying naked in bed with her thin, pale fingers rubbing across her pussy. "It is a shame that I must go to sleep in this state," she complained helplessly. "Not one to grovel. Please don't make me grovel." Her voice was husky now as he slipped on a pair of Romeo house slippers, their hard soles tapping on the tiled floor of the kitchen. She moaned, "This is absolute torture, and Lord knows that I do not deserve this treatment. Perhaps I have been very naughty."

Dahji made a mental note to call her in the morning as another message came to life, squeezing between the burping of a trumpet through hidden speakers.

"Mr. Dahji McBeth. Of course you are not home. Pleased to know that all went well with your new client. My husband seems hopeful. I think we should meet for lunch to discuss your end of the arrangement. Love you, sweetheart."

Dahji still did not know what Gloria Richards would ask of him in return for her speaking with her husband about giving Marlin a shot at training camp. He lifted the thick gold ropes from his neck one by one and laid them on the marble countertop, their heavy, diamond-encrusted medallions dropping with expensive thuds. He rubbed his hands across his small chest before opening the refrigerator for the jug of cranberry juice. Whatever it was, he was prepared to keep his end. If Marlin was offered a contract to join the team, this could mean a whole new life for him. He would call Gloria in the morning.

It was nearly two o'clock, he realized as he unhooked his Rolex, wondering where Peaches was. He checked himself for the feeling that crept through him at the thought of her. Still, he couldn't resist going against his rule of not having women come over to his house after midnight when she asked if they'd see each other later. He absolutely had to see her after her performance on stage.

There was something special about her. She was something more than a beautiful woman who danced exotically.

"Roger," his mother sang through the answering machine. Dahji cringed every time he heard his government name. He was glad no one was there to hear it. "Are you there, dear? Well, we were just thinking about you and praying for you." There was rustling in the background. Dahji could see his father trying to tell her to hang up the phone before she said something stupid.

"Well, okay," she was back. "Be good, and if you get a chance, come on by and say hello." That's what his father didn't want her to say. The good reverend didn't like the way his son's life had turned out—meaning that he wasn't a preacher and would not be taking over the church he'd pastored for thirty years. He complained about everything concerning Dahji, beginning from the day he announced that his name was Dahji McBeth. His father nearly fell where he stood, instead stepping backwards to be caught by the plastic-covered couch.

Then there was the jewelry and the rumors. Yeah, the rumors. Women in the church were quick to speak about how he earned his money. They would speak about it with wonder, with a mixture of shock and longing. Reverend Reed did not like the things women said about his son. And then there was the long hair that hung past his shoulders. No, he would not be a preacher's son, but his mother loved him still. And to spite his father and return his mother's love, he would show up with groceries tomorrow.

He downed the dark red juice and refilled the glass. He carried it with him to the living room and sat down on the couch before a stack of mail he'd dropped onto his coffee table earlier in the day after retrieving it from his post office box. He grabbed the silver letter opener from a large

seashell atop the glass table and zipped through one envelope after another, most of them stamped with addresses of
correctional facilities. Inside each of these envelopes was a
check and a list of semi-nude photos requested by inmates.
Most of the checks were in the amount of fifty dollars but
there were plenty in the amount of a hundred dollars—no
doubt because an extra ten photos came with a one-hundred-dollar order.

When the night desk guard called to tell him that
Peaches was downstairs, Dahji had the checks and orders
stacked in separate piles. A box of photos was on the table
alongside a stack of envelopes and stamps. This was the part
he hated—addressing, stamping and stuffing the envelopes
with photos. It was too much like work.

"Let her up," he answered, deciding that he would leave
the stuff out. Maybe he would get Peaches to finish
addressing, stamping and stuffing the envelopes. Maybe
not.

By the time she rang the door chime, Dahji was coming
down the stairs having just changed into a pair of white silk
pajama bottoms. He wished he'd had enough time to take
a quick shower, but decided to wait until he could take one
with Peaches.

She beamed with big silver eyes when he opened the
door. "I could get used to this," she said, smiling. She stood
still with her giant Coach bag propped against her leaning
hip, allowing Dahji's eyes to roam quickly over her lithe
body sheathed in a velour Baby Phat tracksuit.

I could, too, Dahji thought to say but instead said, "What
all you got holed up in that?" He jabbed his finger toward
the stuffed brown leather satchel. She walked past him
through the space he made in the door and he inhaled her
jasmine scent, his dick stirring beneath the soft silk of his

pajamas.

She turned to him once she'd reached the space that gave her an opportunity to decide where next she would go. Kitchen. Living room. Upstairs. Or maybe the bathroom next to the bottom of the wooden stairs. Electricity shot from her eyes as her lips twisted sexily in preparation of her answer. "It's my lady stuff," she said, then looked around her as if suddenly noticing the low-playing jazz and the photographs and mail stacked neatly on the coffee table, given more attention from the focused recessed lighting overhead.

"What's all this?" she asked, dropping her sack on the floor and swaying over to the edge of the couch for further inspection. She stopped before reaching the table to look back at him. "Is it private?" she wanted to know out of courtesy.

Dahji had been watching the way her hips moved. Her ass was perfectly shaped, and she had hips that rounded just enough before coming back to her thighs for the long journey that was her legs. "Lightweight materials," he answered, walking to where she stood, thereby giving permission for her to sit with him as he finished what he was doing.

"I had no idea," she said, watching as he sorted through the photos of beautiful women in thongs and lingerie. "You take all these pictures yourself?" she wanted to know, her eyes scanning the neat stack of checks at his elbow.

"Most of 'em."

"So how much do the girls get paid?" Her mind was all business.

"It depends," he answered evasively.

"How much would you pay me?"

He looked to her then. "What are you worth?"

She wasn't expecting this question, and as she was thinking of a good number, she noticed how there were gold flecks in his brown eyes. She saw those same flecks in his long hair that bounced on top of his shoulder when he turned to her. She shrugged her shoulders and looked back to the table. She picked up a picture of a coffee-colored woman with a huge ass creased by too-small panties. She was smiling back at the camera. Peaches looked at the picture closely and then up at the heavy red drapes parted around the tall windows. "You took this here?" she turned to Dahji now. He nodded, looking down at the photo. "How much did you pay her?"

"That's confidential."

Peaches looked at the picture again, as if to figure the woman's worth. "So all you do is take the picture and what? She get a cut every time someone buys one?" She knew this wasn't the way it worked but it was the way she would want it to work. When Dahji smiled, she knew she was right. She made a sound with her mouth to indicate that this was not something she wanted to do.

"Could be a way to get your girl's clothes out there," he suggested, already able to see the clothes on the websites of the women he photographed. "You gotta get your own website first though."

"That's what Sherrelle was talking about," she said. Now she was seeing the possibility in her mind. She picked up another picture and looked closely. This one was light-skinned with blonde hair. From what she saw, none of the women in the photos could hold a candle to her or Sherrelle. She sat back on the couch, satisfied with her realization. "I'll talk to her about it," she whispered, feeling the tiredness from her day fall on her as Dahji went back to addressing envelopes and stuffing them with photos he was lifting from numbered slots inside a shoebox.

She doubted that selling pictures could pay for this high-rise apartment, the clothes, the jewelry, or the Range Rover he drove. But she knew enough to know that he wasn't selling drugs or robbing people, something that would put him in jail like her absent boyfriend Tequan.

"Sherrelle says you're Marlin's agent," she stated it as a question, looking at him from the side. Though she couldn't fully see his face, she could see the dimple from his smile.

"Something like that," he answered. *Agent*, he repeated to himself. Something real. Something he could tell any and everybody he was. This is what had made him smile. Even his father couldn't be shamed by that, especially if he could eat off of it. But first Marlin had to do well in training camp.

"That's cool. Sherrelle likes him," Peaches commented in a low voice. She was watching Dahji's profile the whole time, studying him.

"I kinda figured that." He turned to her now. "Ain't they both married? And next door neighbors?"

Peaches nodded with a grin to match his.

"It must be hard," he said, shaking his head, knowing that there was bound to be some creeping going on. He saw the sparks between them when she'd joined them at the table earlier at Applebottoms.

"Do you have to finish that right now?" Peaches wanted to know. She was ready to take a shower and go to bed.

Dahji let the envelope he was holding fall to the glass table and stood up. He stretched his arms out as if directing traffic toward the stairs. He bent to grab up Peaches' Coach bag as she led the way, the heavy blow of trumpets following them, seemingly buoyed by a cloud of snare drum.

Through the floor-to-ceiling window that was framed by red velvet curtains, the city winked with the early-morning lights of downtown.

"Did you enjoy yourself tonight?" Peaches asked as she reached into the glass-paneled shower. There was room enough for at lest ten shapely women holding a dozen roses in front of them. She'd shed her clothes on the way upstairs and now stood naked as she looked at Dahji through the oval mirror over the black porcelain sink.

Dahji was tying up his hair so the water would do minimal damage, tucking it safely under a flower-printed shower cap. He was reminded that Peaches had white blood in her when she stepped into the water without covering her hair. He liked this about white women; the way their hair wouldn't nap up under water. He'd forgotten just that quick that she wasn't all sistah.

"Yeah, I had a good time," he said, shedding his pajama bottoms and mesh boxers. His joint swung to his thigh as he sauntered to the shower and stepped under the spray of water. Peaches looked at his thick dick, admiring the way it hung over his long balls.

"Do you like ending your day with me?" she asked, squirting the shower gel she'd left there the last time into her palms. The water sprayed between them as she reached forward to rub her hands over his chest, bringing the liquid to a soapy lather.

"You cool," he answered sleepily, the effects of the hot water, the long day, and Peaches' gentle fingers rubbing on his body taking their collective effect.

"I'm cool, hunh?" she questioned, sliding her hands down to his hanging dick and using it to pull him closer. The water sprayed across his chest as she stroked him softly. He grew inside of her palm under the slick, soapy water.

"What you doin' here anyway?" he asked smartly, looking down at her smoke gray eyes. Her burgundy hair turned dark under the water as it trailed away from her shiny pale forehead.

"I'm here because you want me to be here," she said bravely, pulling on him hard as he reached his full length. She looked down at him now. "Damn! You should be a porn star. You ever thought of being a porn star?" she asked, turning her burning eyes up to his. She held him tenderly in her palm, feeling the weight of him across her fingers, making him bounce solidly in her palm. She was holding a weighty prize that she didn't have to rush to. She was enjoying the look in his eyes.

Dahji grinned. "How you know I ain't got some plan for you?" he asked huskily.

Peaches frowned. "Like what? Taking pictures?"

Dahji's smile grew wider.

"'Cause if that's all you want," she continued, "you can have your funky pictures." She squeezed his dick with this remark, the feeling of him in her palm something she could not enjoy any more if she'd wanted to.

"What do you think about when you're on stage?" Dahji asked, brushing the meaty head of his dick against her navel.

"Ummm...," she considered this.

"Naw, don't think about it. Come out with it."

"Nothing," she answered.

"Nothing?"

"That's right. Nothing." She turned her chin up to him as she pushed his dick down so that it grazed the soft mound of her pussy. "Are you going to answer my question?"

"What question?"

She was moist, guiding him to the spot that would send a jolt through her. She was amazed that he was long enough for her to navigate the way she was doing. "Why aren't you a porn star?"

"My father's a reverend," he answered hoarsely as she rubbed his swollen head through the warm crease of her pussy. His dick was at such an angle that the top of his ribbed head caught at her entrance. She moved on the tip, not letting him escape her gentle ride.

"Really..." she breathed out with her eyes closed. "That...must...have...been..." Her voice trailed off as she turned away from him, still holding on to his hard joint. She rose on tiptoes in invitation.

"Besides, I can't act," Dahji said as he bent his knees and slid up inside of her. Her narrow back swooned with his entry and she gave out a slow yelp against the tiled wall. He filled her slowly and fully, finding an easy rhythm inside of her. Gripping her breasts, he held her up, impaling her on his rod as she moved up and down on him.

"Yes," Peaches panted, throwing her head to the side. "Let me see. Let me turn around so I can see," she commanded.

Dahji eased her up off of him in a smooth, long glide. After she turned to face him, she wrapped her arms around his neck and folded her legs around his waist. He lifted her on top of him and slid into her once more. He let her lean back in his embrace so that she could watch as he slid in and out of her. His thick meat was surrounded tightly by her pink folds. Her center grew hot as she watched and felt him go inside of her, thankful that he was gentle and tender.

Dahji felt himself grow hot under the spray of water. She was squeezing herself around him as he slid in and out of her. Every time he hit bottom, a jolt of ecstasy shot through him. She rose up on him and grabbed him tightly, burying her face in his neck.

His knees buckled as he shot into her tight pussy. She let her legs unwrap from around his waist and slid him out of her as she stepped back down onto the floor of the shower. She knelt before him—water cascading over her head—and took him into her mouth to drink the rest of him up. She gripped his narrow ass tightly as she sucked hard on the swollen head, making him jerk with each pulsing release. He was so drained he had to lean on one of the glass shower panes for support, lest he crumble to the tiled shower bottom.

Chapter Eleven

Peaches

She watched him sleep on his back, his large hands folded over his chest; studied the way his fine eyebrows thinned out at the edges. She examined the way his thin mustache grew a grade thicker at the corners of his thin lips. His skin reminded her of clay, a brown that looked like it would dent and take its time to recover if she touched her finger to it. His eyelashes were long, forming an umbrella over the closed orbs that seemed to see all when open. She lay next to him and snuggled in closely, feeling the warmth emanate from his body, draping one arm across his stomach.

Peaches had to smile to herself. Sometimes it stretched out into a full laugh, drawing stares from the occasional driver who happened to notice her. Snatches of her night and morning with him raced across her mind. Why did she dance? This was a fair question since she kept pestering him about being in the porn industry. He'd asked it while they were lying in bed after early-morning sex. She loved the way he could make her smile and think at the same time. And the dick was the bomb. Just thinking of the way he fucked her from the back sent a jolt through her sore pussy. It was a kind of sore that felt really good. Like after a good workout. She knew that she would feel this way all day and looked forward to it—her pussy steadily reminding her of how she'd turned him over and straddled him. All day she would be reminded of how his eyes rolled to the back of his head as she only allowed the head of his fat dick inside of her, controlling her motion on top of him.

She wasn't even mad that he didn't get up to make breakfast. She'd had all the breakfast she needed. She smiled even now when he'd suggested that she was trying to drain him so he wouldn't look at another bitch. She'd only grinned mischievously at him in answer. Clever that he could know such a thing.

Still, she'd toasted bread, afraid that she would fall out in the elevator if she didn't get something into her body. She loved the look on his face when she brought him two slices slathered with strawberry jam. Breakfast in bed. She suspected that this wasn't something he usually had done for him, even if it wasn't a full meal of eggs and bacon or whatever. The look on his face was enough, even though he let the toast lay on the fluffy comforter as if he wouldn't eat it. That was okay with her. A kiss on his forehead and she was out the door with no mention of when they would or should get together again. She'd made up her mind to wait for him to call her.

Peaches turned onto her block and didn't want to be there. It was all too clear to her how the landscape slowly deteriorated as she drove from the plush neighborhood where Dahji lived to her own decrepit hood. Liquor stores replaced the markets and fresh fruit stands. Thugs hanging out on the corners in jeans and tracksuits (this early in the morning) replaced the old white men who stood at the edges of the park in wooly sweaters and slacks (this early in the morning), two blocks from Dahji's high-rise apartment.

Even the apartments were different. They went from shiny and well-tended to what she found here, standing as if they were barely constructed. Traffic had worn these too-close-together, brightly painted buildings (as if to promote charm) down to what they were—faux projects with a patch of grass out front to soften the ugliness of the black iron gate that rarely worked and the intercom system that never did. Thankfully the underground parking gate lifted when she pushed on the white button of the door opener attached to her visor.

Her Toyota Camry, which had too many miles on it to be reliable, was parked at the back space of her stall. *Why did I dance?* she asked herself, thinking of Dahji's question to her. She'd seen a show on television that talked about how strippers were privately seeking the attention of their absent fathers. 'Bullshit,' she hissed in defiance as she swerved the front end of the candy-red Chrysler 300C behind her bucket. She was gathering up her large Coach bag and her smaller Gucci purse when she noticed her next-door neighbor coming from the elevator at the end of the dim parking garage. She took a deep breath in preparation for the encounter.

Shonte had a way of trying to insult her in a friendly way, though they both knew that their situations did not compare. Especially since Shonte had two children—whom she toted with her now as if they were inconvenient luggage—and a husband who got locked up for trying to break in to a key shop. That was funny in itself, but Peaches would never make her feel bad about it. She often wondered, though, what was to be gained from a key shop. Did they keep that much money in the safe? And since they specialized in locks and keys, could he really have hoped to break in to the safe?

"Hey, girl. Where you coming from?" Shonte asked, her peanut butter-colored face frowning up. She'd rounded the back of the 300C laden with a large, fake Louis Vuitton purse and holding her daughter's (the youngest's) hand for fear she would fall behind and further stall her morning.

"Hello, Darius," Peaches called from her seat in the car to Shonte's ten-year-old son. He was growing into a broad-shouldered teenager, his black eyes large and observant. Shonte looked down at him to see what expression he wore in response to Peaches' sweet greeting, forgiving her for ignoring her question, which was meant as an insult anyway.

"Wassup," Darius answered, far older than his years. Shonte looked back at Peaches with an expression that said she was proud of her manly little boy and his well-versed ghetto vernacular.

"Yeah, girl," Peaches began, looking at Shonte with a smile as she stood with her designer bags hanging on her shoulders. The chirp of the alarm on the 300C was its own indicator of ghetto privilege. "So how is Darnell?" she asked, tossing the hot ball back into her corner. She knew Shonte's husband couldn't be but one of two things—good or on lock-down.

"He's okay," she answered in a newly tired voice as she snatched her key from the door of her raggedy Dodge Stratus. Her daughter climbed into the front seat, but only after Shonte gave a stern warning look to Darius when he looked like he was going to push her out of the way.

Peaches could have had sympathy for Shonte, but

instead felt that she deserved her lot in life because of her funky attitude. The way her Wal-Mart uniform hung off her slim body made her seem impoverished. "That's good," Peaches said to this, smiling at Darius as he looked at her admiringly through the back window.

"So you got Tequan's car again, hunh?" Shonte asked, her eyes wide after running them the length of the bright paint and chrome rims. She was looking at Peaches for the info.

"Just for a minute. He'll be home soon," she lied.

Shonte's mouth formed an O and her painted eyebrows arched over beady eyes, though no words escaped. She nodded subtly, wanting to speak more on how this meshed with her coming home so early in the morning, but she would have to hold this bit of conversation for a later date.

"Girl, you gon' be late for work so let me let you go," Peaches said before looking at Shonte's daughter. "Bye, precious little angel," she sang, smiling and waving at the bright-eyed girl who waved back eagerly.

Peaches heard the Dodge coming to life in fits and starts as she waited for the elevator door to open. She knew Shonte was embarrassed. The engine rattled as the Dodge warmed up but seemed to settle down a bit by the time the elevator opened its staid doors. When she looked out, Shonte was putting the car in reverse, one of the lights showing white where the red plastic had been busted out. *That's a nice-sized ticket*, Peaches thought to herself as the doors rumbled together, sealing her off from the noise of the clattering, screeching engine.

Peaches dropped her designer bags onto the overstuffed black, leather sofa by the door. Her apartment was appointed with the kind of high-end electronics (plasma screen in every room, Bose surround sound system) that were more suited to a five-digit-square-foot home than a two-bedroom apartment. Platinum-framed photographs of her and Tequan (in Vegas, Disneyworld, Atlanta in front of Magic City, Universal Studios) lined the far ledge over the nonburning fireplace. They were reminders of not only the life they had shared but, sadly, his absence.

She listened to her answering machine as she walked through the apartment, getting undressed for a much-needed soak in the tub.

"Hello, Peaches," Arthur's familiar voice sang out at one in the morning. She remembered the look on his face when she told him she couldn't give him a private dance last night at Applebottoms. He had to make do with what everyone else got—a sexy, feature-length dance on stage. "I really enjoyed seeing you last night," he continued in his whiny voice. "I'd love to see you for lunch if you're not busy," he added.

Peaches was at the tub, running her hand through the running water to find the right temperature. *Lunch. That'll work*, she said to herself, knowing that he would have a fresh thousand dollars for her time.

"Peach," blew the stilted voice of her Korean friend. "I see you last night and bery nice. We see each other after close, yes?" he said. Peaches smiled when she heard his voice. She rather enjoyed dressing up and going to the doctor's office. She would make that appointment, she decided, as she sat on the edge of the tub with the water rushing behind her. The voices felt far away while she listened from the bathroom.

Then the phone was ringing anew. She knew who it was before she heard Sherrelle's voice call out to her through the answering machine. She was up from the tub and picking up the phone before Sherrelle could call her name again and accuse her of being a tramp because she hadn't made it home.

"Hey, homegirl," Peaches breathed into the phone and started walking back to the bathroom. The water had reached halfway up the white ceramic tub.

"What's up, girl? You just getting in or something?" Sherrelle asked as Peaches dropped scented oil beads into the water.

"Unh unh...I was here," she answered evasively.

"Liar. Where were you? I called you earlier but I didn't leave a message."

"Dahji," Peaches answered simply, her voice betraying her usual detachment when speaking of any man except for Tequan.

"Ooohhh!" Sherrelle hooted. "You sure have been spending a lot of time with him. You must like getting slapped with that monster dick!" This was followed by laughter. "I don"t blame you."

"Percy home?" Peaches wanted to know, sensing freedom in her friend's voice.

"Girl, he just left. I am too through," Sherrelle breathed out in exasperation. "So tell me about your night."

"Same ol' dick, girl. Long and thick. My pussy sore!" Peaches complained. "I wish I could let you feel it," she joked.

"I wish I were so lucky."

"You would know how it felt if you weren't so trying to be faithful to your husband. Ain't nothin' wrong with a little bump and grind." Peaches was easing herself into the water, sighing at the feel of the warm, slick water washing against the tender folds between her legs. "Your neighbor is some type of hunk though. I think he likes you, too," Peaches said, laying her head back on the cushioned bathtub edge.

"You think so?" Sherrelle knew the answer to this already.

Peaches sucked her teeth. "Bitch, you know he do," she answered.

"You want to go to lunch?" Sherrelle asked, wanting to get off the subject. She knew that Peaches would eventually tell her the virtues of getting some dick on the side while being married.

"I have an appointment. But I'll be over there before the sun goes down. I got something to talk to you about."

"What is it?"

"You are going to have to wait," Peaches teased.

"Heffa," Sherrelle said around a smile.

"Backatcha. Love you," Peaches responded before ending the call.

She closed her eyes to enjoy the feeling of the warm water coursing between her legs and soothing her tender pussy. The jasmine scented water eased her mind, letting it travel to a world where she lived in a big house with a husband who could protect and provide for her. There were happy sounds of children laughing. Her children. Their children. *Did Dahji have any kids?* she asked herself. She made a mental note to ask him the next time they spoke. The phone hung loosely in her grip over the edge of the tub. She was almost tempted to call him to tell him that she enjoyed her night, but that was the man's job. Damn, she wanted to hear his voice!

She tried to concentrate and return to the house where there were children laughing and she had a husband who lived an honest life, and the threat of him being arrested or leaving her unexpectedly was non-existent. This was a good feeling. There were trees in the front yard; from one of them hung a swing her husband had built with his own hands. She was at the sink washing dishes with a flower-printed apron on. She would tidy up and call the kids from their rooms so they could go shopping with her. A feeling of peace surrounded her as she looked out into the front yard from her kitchen window.

She knew not how long she'd been in this fantasy world when the ringing phone broke her from her reverie. She opened her lids slowly, the cold water making itself known to her limbs with a gentle shock. The phone was ringing still. This is what woke her, she realized, feeling her sense of peace and security slowly evaporate like steam into the air. She looked at the caller I.D. and knew right away that it was Tequan. His call could not be identified. She thought this was funny for the first time. He was so invisible that the phone company couldn't even say who he was until she came on the line and was forced to make a decision about whether to say yes or no to a call that would cost her nearly ten times what a normal phone call cost. Yes, she would accept his collect call. His name was Tequan in case anybody cared. I do, baby. I do.

"Hey, honey," she answered in a cheery voice, though she felt unhappy for some reason. She struggled to place the reason as Tequan started talking.

"What it do, boo? How my girl doin'?" he said over the beep, beep of the prison phone that recorded their call.

"Nothing. Waiting on you to call."

"That's right, baby." She could see him smiling on the other end. He was calling so she knew it had to be after nine. That meant she'd been in the tub for at least forty minutes. Damn, no wonder the water was cold. She made a move to get out, the water sloshing over her legs.

"Where you at?" he asked urgently. She knew where

his mind was headed.

"Getting out the tub."

"Serious?" he said. "What you fitna do? Go lotion up?"

"Yeah," she answered. She noticed his tone change. His voice grew deeper, as if he was preparing for a romantic meeting.

"Check it out," he began. "I already hollered at Bo. He gon' have that ready for you when you slide through. What day you coming?"

"Probably Sunday," she answered, looking at her shiny body in the full-length mirror behind the bathroom door. Her thighs were toned and shaped from dancing, hips tightly rounded and ass firm to the touch. She cupped her hands under her breasts to test their bounce.

"Sunday." He said this with disappointment. Peaches knew he would rather that she come Saturday. "What you doing on Saturday?"

"Working."

"That's what I'm talking about!" he pleaded. "If you come both days this weekend, I'ma make it so you don't have to work." This is what Peaches was afraid of. She wasn't trying to be a major drug smuggler, surely not the kind that would give up her job to do it. She was already trying to decide if she should get used to the idea of driving her own car. Meanwhile, she was estimating in her head how much time was left on the call. He was only allowed fifteen minutes and she'd already decided that she wouldn't answer if he called back.

"I can't miss work, Tequan," she said as she walked through the house and into her room. The bed dominated the small space. The plasma screen was attached to the wall. It was positioned between two large paintings of children boxing in a small ring. Tequan said they'd cost nearly a thousand dollars each. He'd been doing good back then. A heavy wooden dresser stood against the far wall, its oval mirror reflecting her image. She was surprised at the bored expression on her face.

"Okay. Sunday. That's cool. But be sure you stop by Bo spot."

"What spot is this?" she asked, frowning at herself in the mirror as she dribbled body cream into her palm.

"The one on thirty-ninth. You remember, I took you over there when the fight was on," he explained.

The operator came on to remind her that the call was from an inmate and that it was being recorded.

"So where you at now?" Tequan asked, the interruption reminding him of his earlier pursuit.

"Laying on my bed, getting ready to lotion myself up." She knew what he wanted to hear.

"Is that right?" His voice grew husky. "Damn, you got my dick hard, baby!"

"Stroke it for me," she whispered, letting lotion dribble down her leg.

"I am, baby," he breathed out. "That pussy wet, baby?"

"Yeah," she answered, rubbing her leg.

"That pussy ready for me to slide inside?"

"Yeah."

"Spread them legs for me." She let lotion dribble down her other leg. "I want to hold them legs apart and slide into that hot pussy. Is that what you want, baby?"

"Yeah," she answered, rubbing the lotion in. "Put that dick inside this hot pussy, baby. Ooohhhh! I'm so tight and you feel so good!" she hissed. She could tell he was positioning himself better to jack off.

"Yeah, that's right, baby. Let daddy slide between them thighs." His breathing was heavy now. Peaches was up, looking at herself in the mirror and rubbing lotion over her stomach.

"Come on, baby. Slide that dick inside of me. Oooooh, you feel so good. I'm about to...ahhh...ahhh...give it to me, give it to me," she urged him as she searched for a pair of panties in her drawer. She found a pair just as Tequan let out a muffled gasp and breathed heavily into the phone.

"Damn, baby! Damn..." he wheezed, recovering as the operator came on the line to let them know they had one hundred and twenty seconds left to their call.

"I love you, baby," Peaches said after the interruption.

"That's real," he responded. "What you about to do?"

"I gotta go to the doctor for a pap smear." She was smiling, knowing that the visual would quickly ease his erotic nature.

"That's cool. You gon' be home later?"

"Sherrelle is expecting me to come by later. She's starting a clothing line. I was thinking..."

The phone clicked off. Peaches decided that she had just enough time for a much-needed nap before she would meet Arthur for lunch.

Chapter Twelve

Dahji

Dahji watched Peaches leave the loft. He lay naked under the covers, his dick laying heavy between his legs, its head pulsing with its own beat from the attention she'd paid to it. He waited until the door closed behind her before he took a bite of the sweet-with-strawberry-jam toast. He nodded his head in approval; that was exactly what he liked to see in a woman. Serve your man in bed. He was confident that she would start cooking, even though she claimed she didn't know how.

Long after she left, with the wall-mounted plasma screen on at the foot of the bed (showing an early-morning sports show), Dahji lounged with one knee up as he took an occasional bite of toast. He held the stiff bread between the fingers of his hand, arm slung over his raised knee. Thoughts of Peaches floated through his mind, creating new space where multiple women resided. It was almost two hours 'til noon by the time Gloria called. He'd meant to call her but had been so comfortable in bed that time slipped by unnoticed. With alarm he realized that Peaches was beginning to move inside of him in a way that hadn't been done since his ex-wife was killed in a car accident. This was at a time when he followed all the rules, before he changed his name and earned the disapproval of his father, before he learned that his dick was a commodity. Now here was Peaches to awaken those long-ago feelings for a woman who commanded attention.

"Top of the morning," he said into the phone as he climbed from the bed on his way downstairs.

"Good morning, Mr. McBeth," she smiled from her end. He could imagine her in her giant sunroom drinking tea. Maybe her husband had just left, and yes, Marlin should be at training camp. This thought gave him a light feeling. It was like remembering that something good had happened but forgetting what it was exactly. He stood over the toilet and let his dick hang low as the piss parted the blue water.

"Are you urinating?" she asked in alarm.

"Naw. Rinsing out the bowl," he answered, entranced by the way the thick stream made the blue water bubble up and separate. Feet spread and with one hand on his waist, he stood ready for what the day would bring.

"I don't think so," she mumbled. There was a secret between them. She'd called on him at a time when things were uncertain in her marriage. Back when he was delivering packages for Federal Express and just after the death of his wife. He'd often dropped packages off to her house that were for her husband or were the purchases of a bored housewife who couldn't shop leisurely in public for fear of being harassed. The Colts weren't winning at the time and everyone was catching shit from the fans. She'd cried on his shoulder and got a touch of his swelling dick. They were both sad and had helped each other in a time of need. It was only one time, but that one time solidified their friendship and introduced Dahji to the power of his dick.

"Are you just rising?" she wanted to know.

"Not all of us are roosters," he responded coolly, reaching down to squeeze the length of his manhood for those last drops.

She laughed in the comfortable way women of privilege laughed, more like a smile with sound. "Maybe not a rooster, but cock for sure." She enjoyed her own humor. "Where shall we meet for lunch?" she asked in a clear and proper voice.

"Are you going to be wearing a bra?" Dahji asked, walking into the kitchen. She liked to be talked to that way. It was their foreplay and sex since they both knew that real sex was not going to happen. Too much was at stake for her and for him. He knew he couldn't go back to her once he'd performed that first favor for her. Though it had earned him five thousand dollars, the thought of him sexing another woman for the benefit of money changed their relationship.

"I feel like sushi," he answered, thinking that all of his mojo had been drained.

"Sushi?" she asked. He could see her professionally trimmed eyebrows raised above eyes rimmed thickly in black.

"Sushi."

"Well, okay," she sighed. "And I suppose you'd like the back table at Hirohito's?" she asked, knowing his preferences well enough.

"High noon, pardner," Dahji said with mock menace. This made her laugh like a song that crashed to the floor like metal pans, forceful enough to startle children if they'd not heard it before.

"It's your world, young man. I'll meet you there."

Dahji grabbed a one-ounce bottle of ginseng from a box of thirty he kept in the kitchen drawer and drank it with his morning orange juice. He made another call on his way back upstairs.

"I hear you got a problem with your plumbing," he said when the proper voice of Mirabelle came on the line.

He could see the straight smile on her narrow, pale face, which was highlighted with the sky blue of her large, round eyes. They were the biggest things on her besides her long pussy that went with her long limbs.

"Oh, yes!" she shrieked, her voice echoing through the large room he knew she was in no matter where she was in the big house.

"It's terrible! I am in quick need of a skilled technician," she moaned seductively. Dahji had grown to love these games as much as she did. He discovered her one day while delivering packages. She'd answered the door on a day not long after her rich husband died. He consoled her and her hand had brushed across the large mound in his snug pants. When she looked up at him with those eyes, he knew that something had changed, and not just the bright blue that grew smoky.

"Well, I can send somebody by there to check on that clog at about dinner time."

"Well, that will be perfect. Please be sure that he comes with the right tools because I do believe this is a serious matter!"

Dahji was smiling. He liked the white lady who appeared older than her forty years, though she worked hard to look thirty. "I'll be sure of it."

"Thank you. I'll leave the door open, and I believe you have the passcode for the gate?"

"Yes. We do have this information on file. Be prepared when he arrives."

"Oh, I will!" she assured him, the words erupting from her like a pistol shot. Sometimes he felt it was a shame that she took her husband's death so hard, given the fact that he left her his millions. But true love had no value, he reasoned, glad that she parted with some of that money so easily when it came to him.

Dahji replaced the phone in its cradle before stepping into the shower. Gloria would like to see him in a suit, he reasoned, almost sure that whoever she needed him to service would also appreciate his conservative dress. The day he would have passed before him. It would be sex and business. *Not a bad day*, he thought to himself as he rinsed and stepped from the shower.

When the phone rang he was dressed in the bottom half of a dark blue, Hugo Boss, two-piece suit with square-toed Cole Haan hard-bottoms. He buttoned a soft white, cotton Hugo Boss shirt as he strolled to the phone. Scanning the downstairs from the loft, he realized that he'd not finished filling the orders for the photos. The envelopes, stamps, and photos lay in neat stacks on his glass coffee able.

"Hello," he said into the phone, thinking that he had time to finish them and drop the photo-filled envelopes into the mailbox on the way out. And then take the checks to the bank.

"Good morning, Mr. McBeth. This is Gerald at the lobby desk. There is a woman..."

"Ebony," she sang from where she was standing on the other side of the waist-high, black marble partition.

"Ms. Ebony," Gerald repeated.

"Damn!" Dahji whispered next to the phone. He'd completely forgotten that she was coming over. "Send her up," he said, now knowing that he would be pressed for time.

Dahji opened the front door with a smile on his face. Ebony stood before him in a stretch cotton dress that hugged her shape dexterously. Her milk chocolate breasts bulged over the ridged cotton while her hips stretched out above her thighs. Gold bracelets jangled on her slim wrists as she waved at him with both hands in front of her breasts, temporarily obscuring the view of her thick nipples through the stretchy, white material.

"Hi," she said, smiling with surprise when she saw that he was dressed up. She looked around him with wide, brown eyes. "Did I interrupt something?"

"Naw, baby girl," Dahji answered, stepping to the side. "I damn near forgot you was sliding through."

She was behind him now as he closed the door. "I woulda called but my cell battery died," she explained, rubbing along her neck where her tapered, old-school Halle Berry cut ended.

"It's cool. Don't trip. What's bin up with you?" he asked, walking toward the kitchen. "Want something to drink?"

"Thank you. Ev'ry thangs cool. I'm still trying to get in *Smooth* magazine or something." She was looking around her, noticing the box of photos and envelopes on the table. "So how am I doing?"

"Everybody love you," he answered, referring to how popular she was in jail. Most of his orders were for her.

"They like my ass, hunh?" she asked, taking the glass of grape juice from him.

Dahji smiled, "You have a cute face." She liked this. "And pretty skin," he added, liking the wide, full-lipped smile she was giving him. Her slanted eyes, which were set under thick, black lashes, gave her an exotic look. She had a nose that turned up at the end, though this only added to her mystery.

"That's good to know, but I need to make a change. I might have to move out to L.A. or something," she complained, dropping the woven, brightly colored cotton purse from her shoulder onto the couch. Now she was unburdened and free to swivel her hips to the window. She was looking out over the city with her hands on her hips. "I could be a star," she was saying. "I just need for people to see me." She turned to Dahji now who stood with the camera raised to his shoulder. "Know what I mean?" He liked the look on her face when she asked this question. Innocent. Vulnerable.

"Wassup with your website?" Dahji wanted to know.

She was walking toward him, her eyes on the photos stacked on the table. "I'm working on it, but I didn't realize how expensive it was," she pouted. Dahji was looking at her feet inside her leather sandals, the straps wrapping up around her ankles. She had some pretty toes. There was a gold band on her left big toe.

"You ever thought about dancing?" he asked.

She looked up at him now with a frown, forgetting about what was on the table. "And have all those men grabbing all over me? Unh unh. I can't deal with that. Grinding on dicks all night. That ain't me." She made it sound dirty. Dahji didn't like her in that instant. He wondered how Peaches would respond to that.

"Buffie used to strip," he said simply.

"Damn. I know," she huffed. He knew then that she would do it; she was just trying to be uppity.

"Some of my best friends are strippers."

"Really?" Now she opened up like a flower.

"Yeah," he answered, lifting the camera to his eye. "Think like a stripper," he suggested, taking a picture of her. She was smiling. "Imagine yourself on stage." Click. "Everybody throwing money at you. Strut to the window." Click. Click. "Now look over your shoulder at me." Click. Click. Click. She was feeling it now, smiling back at him.

"You think I would make a good stripper?" she asked, peeling from her dress.

"Yeah," he assured her. Click. The dress peeled over her hips like a banana being exposed. Click. Her eyes were cast down, the city behind her. Her fingers worked inside the dress to get it over her round hips. This was going to be a good picture. Click.

"Turn around. Hands on the glass." Click. Her beautiful ass was creased by a black thong. Dahji shook his head. She saw him and was pleased. "That's nice. Move like that again." Click. She swayed her hips and then touched her toes. Black ass and the city skyline. Click. Click. Click. Bestseller, he knew. She was eighteen and ripe like a plum. Tender to the touch.

"Like that?" she asked, raising up from touching her toes.

"That was good. Now cover your titties and face me. You've never done this before. Remember when you were a little girl? You're kinda shy," Dahji informed her. She transformed instantly, and it was then that Dahji knew she was special. She looked like she was sixteen and a virgin, even though she was nearly naked except for the thong, gold, and strappy leather sandals.

She was smiling and he knew why. His dick was marching down the leg of his slacks. He'd tried to stop it, but she'd turned away from him again and placed one hand on the windowpane, looking back over her shoulder with an innocent expression. It was a model's pose.

"That's right, baby. Do it the other way." Click. Click. "Left hand on the windowpane. Look like you got caught at something." She wasn't smiling anymore. Click.

She turned to the city. She could have forgotten that she was being photographed judging by the way she stood. Something had crept into her mind and held her captive. Her feet were together; one heel was up, her knee pressed to the glass. She was nearly in profile, her gold hoop earring swaying in the early morning light. Click. Click. That was the one.

After a few beats of silence, she reeled her mind back in. When she looked back at Dahji, who stood watching her, she appeared as if she'd been lost. A slow smile teased the corners of her mouth. "Was that okay?" she asked shyly. He'd pulled something from her she didn't know was inside of her.

"That was the bidness," he assured her, aware that she was trying to avoid looking directly at the rod stretching along his thigh.

"You got hard." She looked embarrassed. Dahji shrugged, making no effort to move.

"You liked that, hunh?" she asked, bringing a French-tipped nail to her bronze-glossed lips.

Dahji shrugged. "You awright."

"So what you gon' do now?" she was looking directly at his hard-on now.

He looked down at himself and then back up at her. She looked at him hungrily. "Nothin'. I gotta be out."

"Let me see it," she said urgently, her words stopping him as he turned to lay the camera on the table.

"You don't wanna see it," he answered, figuring that he would give her three hundred dollars—a hundred more than last time—and send her on her way.

"Yes I do." She was closer to him now, her brown eyes taking on her innocent persona. "I do. Let me see it. It's big, hunh?" She was nearly naked before him, her breasts high and swollen. Dahji straightened up and faced her. She ran her tongue across her bottom lip as she reached for his zipper. When he didn't protest, she became more deliberate.

She knelt in front of him as she unzipped his pants. After realizing she couldn't lift him from where he lay trapped in his slacks, she breathed heavily with anticipation and unbuckled his belt. She slid his slacks down to his ankles, moving her chin out of the way as he sprang up before her. Her eyes grew wide as she looked up at Dahji's face.

"It's the biggest," she whispered, looking along its length as she reached up to touch it. She grasped the swollen head in her fingers and then rubbed him to the base. Slowly, she parted her lips and touched them to the head. Her tongue licked across the helmet as if expecting for it to dissolve in her mouth. She breathed in deep and opened her mouth wide, taking him inside with a long gulp. She choked.

"I'm sorry," she apologized after regaining her composure, looking up into his eyes. "I can't put it all in my mouth," she said in amazement.

They'd come all this way and now she was playing. She wasn't a pro, Dahji realized. "Suck the tip," he advised her.

She wrapped her lips around the head and sucked on it like she was sucking marrow out of a bone. Gradually, she was able to slide more of him into her mouth and really began to enjoy what she was doing. She cupped his balls in her hand and massaged them gently while rotating her head for a circular suction.

Dahji was not impressed. She didn't know how to suck dick. He closed his eyes in concentration and was surprised that Peaches came to his thoughts. He could feel her tongue roughly rubbing along the base of his dick and the way her lips wrapped tightly around the thick meat. He tensed up and grabbed Ebony by the ears. She gagged when he shoved the whole of him down her throat and squirted his load. She choked and tried to grab at his hands but it was of no use. He had her locked onto his dick until he reached the last of his violent spasms.

Ebony fell back onto the carpet, wiping the back of her hand across her mouth. She looked at him lustfully with wide eyes, her legs spread. "Come on," she huffed, reaching to pull away her thong. "Come on," she repeated, her breasts heaving with passion.

Dahji was already stuffing his dick back into his pants. "I ain't got time right now." He reached into his pocket and pulled out a folded wad of money. He flipped three one-hundred-dollar bills from the stack. "I'ma see about getting you a website," he said, handing the money to her. He ignored her hurt expression as she got to her feet. Now she was covering her nakedness, caught between embarrass-ment and shame, though aware enough to take the money from his hands.

"Serious?" she asked, dropping the money to her side. "You gon' help me?" She looked like a small child now, the way her eyes pleaded.

"Yeah. Check with me next week," Dahji assured her before sitting down on the couch to occupy himself with the photos. He was already planning to take another show-er and change into a tan linen suit. It looked hot outside. He tried to concentrate as Ebony got dressed and gathered up her purse. She stopped at the edge of the couch when she was ready to go.

"Thank you," she said, looking over at him.

"Ain't nothing. We gon' get rich together." He smiled now, glad that she'd recovered. And she smiled back. He got up from the couch and walked her to the door.

"Monday. Check with me Monday or Tuesday."

"Okay. I'll call first." And she was out the door.

Chapter Thirteen

Peaches

Peaches spent more time at Arthur's office than she'd intended. It must have been due to her pinstriped, navy blue, two-piece skirt suit. A pink, silk scarf, flung carelessly around her neck, was tucked into the cleavage that her white cotton blouse left exposed. She'd rolled her long hair into a loose bun and let it hang at the nape of her neck. The gold-rimmed Carolina Herrera glasses set off the outfit while her legs stood from Jimmy Choo pumps, giving the whole office body aches when she showed up.

Consequently, Arthur took his time walking her through the front lobby area where his underlings toiled in small cubicles. She didn't mind it at all, the way he stopped here and there to give an order or check on some seemingly important matter, all the while giving his colleagues a look at the beautiful woman next to him. They craned their necks into the aisle to get a look at her ass as she walked away. She knew she'd done her job when they were finally in Arthur's office and he smiled broadly with his accomplishment. She stood at the closed door for his further inspection, smiling wickedly. He was on the clock and if he wanted to use his time using her as a prop, that was fine with her.

She didn't even mind that he wanted to spend time telling her about the vacation he had planned for the upcoming three-day holiday. Sure, she loved the sun. And yes, the sand was okay, too, except when it got between her butt cheeks. He'd liked this. He laughed so much that his face turned red. And from it being as fat as it was, she thought it would surely rupture. His bulging blue eyes disappeared behind the folds of his face, and reappeared when he'd settled back down. And when he suggested that she join him for his vacation, she assured him that she would give it some thought.

In her mind she was calculating how much she would charge him for this. It would have to be something that could get her halfway to a down payment on a house. She knew women who were kept by men like him. The men had bought them houses and had a key so they could drop in whenever they wanted. Peaches didn't want this for herself. A simple fee for services would be just fine. She couldn't stand the thought of being kept like a bird in a cage by a fat white man who could make demands on her.

By the time he rose from his desk, an hour had already passed. His phone never rang, which made her curious. He must have given the secretary a signal that he was not to be disturbed. She wondered if everyone in the office knew the real reason for her visit and not the one he gave them—that she was looking to invest in pharmaceutical stock. She doubted they believed this, but anything was possible.

He stepped around the desk with a crooked smile creasing his pasty cheek. He reached out for her hand and situated her on the desk. He reached behind her and shoved the photos of his wrinkled wife and two children (wearing college graduation gowns) to the middle. They tumbled and folded down to the black mat on the desk. With his movement he breathed hot cigar breath on her.

He sat in the chair he'd pulled her from, his breathing labored, and licked his fat, purple lips. He parted her legs, pleased to find that she was wearing no panties. She opened them wide for him. This is all he wanted. To suck her pussy. She creamed onto his tongue over and over again. He lapped at her pussy like a dog, covering his clean-shaven face with her sweet nectar. Just when she thought she would fall off the desk in exhaustion, he raised up. Forty more minutes had passed.

Thankfully, he had a private bathroom where she could freshen up. She washed his saliva from her pussy and emerged from the bathroom as if she'd purchased major stock in a pharmaceutical company, just the way he lied about it to his coworkers. And when he handed her the thick stack of hundred dollar bills, she briefly considered stock investing, but decided to add this to her savings instead. Getting out of the ghetto project apartment building was her first goal. She dreamed of a house with two trees in the front yard.

After spending a nice chunk of change on a new Versace dress that she planned to wear when she convinced Dahji to take her out on an official date—this was another goal—she pulled to the curb in front of Sherrelle's house just as the sun began to make its arc from the sky. It was sliding behind the high roof of the house across the street. The hard-top Benz Sherrelle's neighbor drove pulled into the driveway shortly after she drove up. Peaches had never seen Marlin's wife. She waited, acting as if she was looking for something, so she could see what the woman looked like. When she saw that she was pretty in a model kind of way, she got out of the car. The thin, toffee-colored woman was pulling a bag of groceries from the trunk.

"Good evening," Stacy said, giving Peaches a quick glance and a cheerleader smile.

"I like your shoes," Peaches answered, not really liking them at all. They were the style that cost less than the style a woman bought if she were truly being stylish and didn't have to count pennies.

"Thank you. But I'd much rather have yours," Stacy replied, exchanging a knowing look with Peaches. They'd sized each other up just that quick, each calculating their separate benefits to outweigh the hidden insults. "Are you Sherrelle's friend?"

"She's my sister," Peaches responded, feeling like it was the truth. Besides, it was none of the woman's business. She wished that it was Marlin who had pulled up in the driveway so she could tease him about Sherrelle and ask him if he enjoyed seeing her dance. She wondered if his wife knew that he was at the strip club the night before.

"Hey, homegirl," Sherrelle yelled from the porch. "Hi, Stacy," she waved across the lawn.

"Hello, Sherrelle," the smiling woman answered as she moved up the walkway. "It was nice speaking with you," she called back to Peaches.

"You too." Peaches licked her tongue out to Stacy's back and exchanged a frowned face with Sherrelle as she walked past her husband's red Corvette and then her Jaguar.

"You look nice, girl. Where you coming from?" Sherrelle asked after they hugged on the porch.

"Having a meeting with a stock broker," she answered. "I was thinking about investing," she added with a wink and a smirk.

"I hope the dividends are good," Sherrelle said, coming into the house behind her.

"Believe me. They are." Peaches scanned the living room. "When are you supposed to get some more clothes?" she asked. "Girl, everybody is asking for the boy shorts and wifebeaters."

"I e-mailed them today but I didn't get a response yet."

Peaches was stretching her neck to see where Percy might be. She looked back at her friend for the answer.

"Bathroom," Sherrelle mouthed silently.

"You're going to be a millionaire, girl," Peaches said loudly, knowing how much Percy would hate not only her loud voice and her being here, but also the fact that she was giving Sherrelle confidence—the confidence she would need to divorce his sorry, little-dick ass. She laughed into her hand as she dropped down on the couch. "Whew!!" she exhaled loudly.

"You are crazy," Sherrelle whispered, walking past her toward the kitchen. "Want something to drink?"

"Beer."

Sherrelle looked back at her then. Peaches urged her—eyes wide and fingers pushing her toward the kitchen—to grab one of her husband's beers and bring it to her.

If Percy felt any kind of way about seeing Peaches in his living room drinking his beer, he made no comment. He just walked past the living room into the kitchen, attempting to suck in his stomach and look nonchalant.

Peaches exchanged a surprised look with Sherrelle who was seated on the opposite couch folding clothes she'd recently washed. Peaches tried to stifle a laugh as she jumped up to go sit next to Sherrelle. She turned around on the couch to peek through the curtain for a sign that Marlin had come home.

"He mad at me right now," Sherrelle whispered, bringing Peaches back from her observations.

"Why?" she asked, looking up quickly at Percy passing by the door of the kitchen. He was grabbing a butter knife from the drawer by the sink.

"He wanted dinner ready when he got home. He really mad that I went to Applebottoms last night to sell my clothes." She leaned close to Peaches to say this in a cool whisper.

"Fuck him," Peaches hissed.

"Then he say I look like a stripper in these shorts."

Peaches had privately thought that herself when she first walked into the house. She said instead that Sherrelle could make money just walking around the club. She wouldn't even have to dance, just conversate with the horny men. "For real?" Sherrelle had asked, eyes wide in mock disbelief.

"You seen your neighbor?" Peaches changed the subject to one that erased the cloud from her friend's face.

"Girl," Sherrelle began, tapping Peaches on the arm, "he left for football practice this morning. Oh my God!" she swooned with her hand over her full breasts, which were pressing against the inside of her pink HoodSweet t-shirt.

"That man is so fine," they said in unison. Their laughter was interrupted when Percy stuck his head out the kitchen door.

"There isn't any mustard," he complained, looking at them with a mixture of jealousy and nosiness.

Sherrelle cocked her head to the side as if looking at a retarded dog, a dog that, when hungry, would nose his bowl over and spill the food on the ground. "Really?" she said, making her face look dumb. "Well, I guess I'll have to pick some up next time from the store." She tried to hold her expression when he rolled his eyes and turned back into the kitchen muttering that he would have to use mayonnaise.

Peaches and Sherrelle leaned into each other with muffled giggles after he moved from the doorway. "He need to do some sit-ups," Sherrelle whispered, laughing louder this time in complete rebellion, shooting the disrespect through the house like missiles seeking a target of insecurity.

"That reminds me," Peaches began, lowering her voice to a whisper, "Dahji said that you should find out more about how the clothes are being sold. I had never heard of them before, had you?"

Sherrelle shook her head no and looked at Peaches with interest as she held a pair of cotton boxers in her hand.

"See, that's what I mean. Dahji...he's so...smart. Anyway, he says that you should get your own website and model the clothes yourself. He has all," she waved her jeweled hand in the air in a wide circle, "of these girls that he takes pictures of."

"What for?" Sherrelle asked.

"Apparently he sells them to people in jail. I saw it for myself. You wouldn't believe how much money he makes doing that."

"How much?" Sherrelle was excited, seeing it all in her mind: the website, modeling, getting other women to model, getting paid. And far away, in the midst of this accomplishment, was a certain freedom that beckoned her. It drew her toward a future that didn't include her husband. Her heart felt hollow with the thought, light with the vision.

"I counted at least five thousand dollars in checks from

jail. And that was just what he picked up in the mail that day."

"You spent the night with him?" Sherrelle wanted to know, almost jealous. Not because she had been with Dahji, but because it was obvious that she'd had a great night with a man she really liked.

Peaches smiled and folded her palms together over her lap like a schoolgirl. "Do you want to know about my night or about getting this business started?" she finally said.

"All of it," she responded in a voice laced with laughter and a bit too loudly, causing Percy to peek around the corner to see what the excitement was about. Sherrelle ignored him. "Come on. Tell me. Tell me." Her large, dark eyes were wide with expectation. She was being transported from a place that was steadily closing in on her. And it felt good.

★ ★ ★

Peaches had hoped to run into Marlin as she left Sherrelle's house. She wanted to look him in the eyes and in some way let him know that he needed to drop his wife and convince Sherrelle to divorce her husband and marry him. She shook her head at this absurd scheme, but what were friends for if not to plan absurd schemes for their friends? It was crazy, she knew, and she would never voice such things, but she did hope that he could have read it in some way in her eyes. Maybe she would joke about it if she saw him.

And she felt good too. More and more she was seeing how having a website with a clothing business could change her life. Change Dahji's life too, that is, if he needed it changed. Maybe they could change together. But she knew that, for both of them, the money would have to be right. In her mind, she saw herself coming to work at a store called HoodSweet and seeing Sherrelle everyday. They would be working side by side. And they could even have modeling shows and contests, and have celebrities wear their clothes. She could see it all. Now it was up to Sherrelle to contact whoever it was she needed to talk to and find out what the deal was with these hot clothes.

Jamie Foxx was singing about leaving the club early and having great sex as she pulled in to the nearly empty parking lot of the mini-mall. Dr. Kim's small family practice was sandwiched between a Baskin-Robbins and a Rexall Pharmacy. *This was cute*, she thought to herself as she parked next to the BMW 745iL she knew belonged to the big-headed Korean doctor. If people came from the doctor with good news, they could get ice cream, and if not, they could go to the pharmacy.

Dr. Kim was at the front desk handing a file to his secretary when the door jingled with her entry. He looked up and upon seeing her over the rim of his glasses, pressed his pink lips together and nodded, though there was a noticeable jerk in his body. Happiness. Peaches smiled at this as she strolled to the front desk, holding his eyes along the way. The perky white girl sitting at the desk looked from the doctor to Peaches with a question in her small, blue eyes.

"Hello. This way, please," Dr. Kim said, a bit too officially. Peaches smiled at the receptionist before turning to walk through the knee-high wooden partition. The receptionist turned to her computer monitor with a flurry to either check for the appointment or the name of the woman who had walked into an empty reception area and gotten invited immediately to an examination room, as if she had been expected.

"How are you?" Dr. Kim asked as he led the way down a carpeted hallway to the last door on the left. On the walls

were landscape prints with positive messages scrawled
across the bottom. Peaches had grown to like the short doctor with narrow shoulders. His white coat stopped just
below his knees. She liked the way he combed his hair—
back away from his forehead so it looked like a black, shiny
helmet. But what she liked most about him was that he paid
her very well for her time. Plus, he had a little dick.

"I'm fine, Kim. And how have you been?" Peaches
responded as he gestured for her to enter the sterile examination room ahead of him.

"I have been well, thank you." He smiled with a perfect
set of white teeth, his skin stretching to the corners of his
kind eyes. The door closed behind him as Peaches sat on
the reclining paper-covered table. It rustled and wrinkled
beneath her as she crossed her legs at the ankles.

"It is so good to see you," he was saying as he moved to
a cabinet over the stainless steel sink. He pulled a yellow
envelope that bulged with the shape of money from a shelf
and handed it to Peaches, slowly, smiling all the way.

"Thank you," she said, sliding it into the Coach purse
beside her. Dr. Kim was moving back to the cabinet. "Did
you have a good day?" she asked as he took a bottle of
Hennessy from the shelf and poured a drink.

He was nodding, paying attention to the drink he was
pouring. "Yes, very good. And you?"

"This is the best part," she answered with a smile.

Dr. Kim toasted her before taking a sip. "That is good,"
he said, smacking his lips. Peaches couldn't be sure if he was
responding to what she had said or the drink. She smiled
anyway.

"So, tell me. How are you feeling?" he asked. She
would have thought this was the beginning of an examination, except that the doctor removed his coat and was

unknotting his brightly striped tie. Peaches knew he was nearly ready to get down to business.

"I'm feeling fine, thank you. I just left my friend's house..." He looked at her sharply. Peaches thought it might have been a look of jealousy. "And she..." now he relaxed, "wants to start her own clothing company."

"Really?" Dr. Kim liked talk of business. His forehead creased as he sipped on the cognac, loosening the first few buttons on his blue shirt.

"Yes. How would that work exactly?"

Dr. Kim was happy to educate the beautiful woman in his office. "Well, the first thing, of course," he began as he carried his drink to a leather stool and rolled himself over to face Peaches. He looked up at her. "Does she have the design of the garments?" he asked, his brow furrowed.

"Pretty much. She knows how she wants everything to look."

Dr. Kim grinned before taking another sip of cognac. "It's simple really. The biggest thing is the manufacturing. You see...if you're successful you will need superior manufacturing to meet the demand." He said this while his body adjusted to the sting of the liquor. His mouth worked against itself to cool his tongue. Peaches simply nodded. "But quality is very important," he added.

"Manufacturing, hunh?" Peaches said in a low voice, practically thinking to herself.

"Yes. Manufacturing." Dr. Kim saw the far-away look in her eyes. "When your friend is ready, I will help," he said, pleased that this had brought her silver eyes back to him. "Sure. This is not a problem. She only needs the cash. Not much, but some. I can get her a good deal."

Peaches wanted to jump from the table and tackle him, but instead she said, "I'll let her know." She didn't want to talk about what it would cost. She would ask Dahji first. She knew she could always get a discount when it came down to it, but she needed to know what was fair first.

Dr. Kim was satisfied and feeling a pleasant buzz. He'd rolled to the wooden counter and slid his empty glass across the countertop to the wall where it bounced back and threatened to tip over. He looked at Peaches sheepishly, a wide smile making his skin wrinkle around his eyes. "You look nice," he said.

"Thank you. I was hoping you'd like it."

"Very nice," he repeated, his eyes roaming over her body. He was ready. Peaches reached into her purse and pulled a small condom from the side pocket. She held it quietly in her hand while he let his trousers drop to his ankles. He stepped out of them, his shirt hanging past his waist like a child. There was no indication that he was aroused as he stepped between her legs.

"That's nice," Peaches said, reaching through the opening in his boxers and pulling the stub through. He smiled graciously, appreciating the compliment. She wrapped him in her palm and stroked him softly as she looked into his eyes. His breathing became heavy as he grew to his full length. He was no longer than her middle finger and not as thick.

"I really miss you from last time," he said, not able to hide his lack of discipline with his broken tongue now that he was aroused.

"I've been thinking about you all day. I couldn't wait for it to be the end of the day," she replied, expertly slipping the condom over his penis. "How do you feel?" she asked, smiling as she stroked him.

"Fine," he stuttered.

She stroked him lightly as she unbuttoned her blouse

and pulled the scarf from her neck. Her breasts bubbled between the buttons of her shirt, catching his attention like a light would catch a moth. When he looked back into her eyes, she stepped from the medical bed and knelt in front of him. She took his condom-sheathed penis between her lips and pressed them lightly around his small tip. Her hand rested under his shirt; her fingers ran through the soft hair on his stomach. He strained under her attention. With her other hand she cupped his balls. They felt like doughy marbles between her fingers.

"Ahhhh..." he moaned over her, struggling to keep his balance, his hands pressing down on her shoulders.

He's almost ready, she thought to herself as she gave him one good suction through the condom, feeling him tense under her touch. It was like holding a baby carrot between her lips.

She stood and retrieved her KY Jelly from her purse. Without much delay, she squeezed some onto her finger and pushed her skirt down to her ankles. She bathed his dick with jelly and turned from him, bending over the medical table. This was his invitation. She didn't bother to remove her pink thong, instead she just spread her ass cheeks for him, the string moving under her thumb. He put his dick against her asshole and pushed softly. She barely felt him, even though she made it tight. As he pushed for a second time, she opened a little for him. He slid into her, the jelly making his entry smooth. She reached back for him and gripped his hips. He moved inside of her reluctantly, not wanting it to be over.

"Come on, baby. Give it to me, daddy. I want it so bad!" she moaned, urging him on.

He grunted, holding on to her tightly as he pumped urgently, chasing a feeling yet running from the conclusion.

Peaches squeezed her ass cheeks around him as he barely made an impression in her asshole. When he'd first suggested that she let him fuck her in the ass, she knew that it
would be nothing, but still made it hard for him. He appreciated grandly that she let him do this. Peaches helped him
to realize all of his fantasies. Things his wife would never
do, she did.

"Ahhhhh...," he groaned behind her. He jerked and
twisted as he shot into the condom. Peaches felt all of his
energy leave his body. He shriveled out of her instantly and
fell back on his heels with clouded, satisfied eyes.

When she looked back at him there was no indication
that he had been erect at all. His penis had ducked behind
his shirt as if running from the sun. The end of the condom
peeked through an opening in his shirt, like a turtle's head
poking hesitantly from its shell.

Chapter Fourteen

Dahji

After leaving his lunch meeting with Gloria at Hirohito's sushi bar, Dahji left Peaches a simple little message saying that he enjoyed their evening and the toast, too. Player shit. He smiled to himself, knowing that she would not expect this. Warren G. thumped through his speakers as he slid smoothly onto the interstate. He was following the directions Gloria gave him. Over brightly colored raw fish, she harmlessly flirted with him, batting her dark eyes and biting into the sushi with unintended meaning. She'd dutifully complimented him on his satin-lined, tan, linen suit. It fit him with a tailor's precision. Mr. and Mrs. Warrington would like that. It was the first time she'd mentioned their names. They were a married couple and very, very rich, she'd assured him. His discreteness would be valued most of all. No problem.

He'd tied his hair into a ponytail. It hung down past the collar of his linen coat. She'd also complimented him on the fact that he was conservatively jeweled in a thin, Movado gold watch and simple, half-carat earrings, though

she would have liked to see him with bare earlobes. But this
was asking too much. The diamond pinkie ring gave him
added personality. It ain't my jewelry they want, he said
with a wink. Gloria smiled wide at this.

There were more trees; taller trees and less property the
closer he got to his destination. From the freeway he could
see the peaks of columned homes in the distance. They rose
above the tree tops, dotting the landscape like beacons in a
sea of green. Fuck the wife. He could do that. Let the husband watch. Sure, no problem. As long as...no, no, no,
Gloria assured him with a wicked laugh. He just wants to
watch, she said, laughing some more at the expression on
Dahji's face. He exited the freeway and followed the quiet
street to where the large elm tree nearly hid the signpost
that led to the half-mile private lane enclosed by overgrown
trees, which led to a small booth. A guard post. Beyond the
gate he could see a fork in the road, a private community of
mansions. *Freaky white people*, he thought to himself as he
pulled his Range Rover to the yellow metal bar that
extended from the booth. There was a young black man
inside. He smiled when he saw Dahji, his blue security uniform fitting his beefy frame snugly.

"How may I help you?" the large man said, half leaning
from the open space in the booth. His words betrayed his
looks: black, greasy, everything shaved, yellow eyes around
deep black orbs.

"I'm here to see Mr. Warrington," Dahji answered,
ignoring the skeptical look on the man's face. Dahji felt
sorry for him. He'd be stuck guarding white folks until he
died. He was probably the kind of dude that took it person-
ally when the house burned down.

"What's your name?" he asked, squinting at a clipboard.

"Mr. X," Dahji answered, knowing that this wasn't on

the board. Brotha trying to be cute, he reasoned. His name tag said his name was Frank. It was written across the pocket of his uniform like he was a mechanic.

Frank nodded his head as if he'd just located Mr. X. "Go 'head," he said, reaching down in the booth. The yellow bar rose with a smooth grinding motion. "Turn left, go straight, house at the end," he added in a clipped slur.

Dahji followed his instructions. Through high iron gates and shrubbery he could make out glimpses of the mansions on the other side. He couldn't tell where one ended and the other began, or if on either side of him there was just one property. The trees blocked the sun so he drove in the quiet shade. He didn't bother turning up the music. There was something about this rich landscape that needed to hear itself. This was how people got rich—quiet, so they could hear themselves think.

At the end of the quiet lane, a wrought iron gate was opening between two brick pillars topped with gold lions heads. Passing through, a large courtyard fronting a columned white porch was revealed. A black limousine was parked to the side of a water fountain, the water squirting from the mouth of a flying white dolphin. A black Lexus sedan was parked near the porch. A broad-shouldered white man with gray lacquered hair was standing on the porch, dwarfed by the high ceilings and general expanse. He was smiling down at Dahji, waving for him to park behind the Lexus.

"That's Edith's car," he yelled out in a happy voice. Everything was great in his world. "I always tell her to park it to the side but she never listens. How are you, Mr. X?" he asked as Dahji climbed the wide steps. He held his large hand out so that Dahji had to look at it for the last three steps before he could finally grasp it.

"I'm fine. Mr. Warrington, right?" There was a giant gold ring on the white man's fat middle finger. It sparkled money green light as he released Dahji's hand.

"Sure, that's me alright. All my life," he answered gladly. "Glad you could make it. Come on inside," he said grandly, waving a big arm for Dahji to follow.

The inside of the house was like something out of architectural digest. No expense had been spared. In the small foyer there were expensive-looking rugs on the marble floor. The two chairs that stood beside the shiny wooden desk were padded with a muted paisley print on the seat and back. Beyond the foyer was a long hallway, at its end a swinging white door. To the right was a closed mahogany door that Dahji suspected was a study or library, like rich people often had.

"Come on in here. Make yourself comfortable," Mr. Warrington said, gesturing toward the airy room to the left. It was fitted with white furniture, either wicker or cotton. Along the front, lace-curtained window was a deep sitting chair. Around a low wicker table stood a white couch and two facing chairs. Dahji sat in one of the chairs. He looked back to Mr. Warrington who trailed him with a grin.

"Comfortable?" he wanted to know.

"Sure."

"Good. By the way, call me Tom. My wife, of course, is Edith. We'll be joining her in a minute. First, let's get you a drink. What's your style?" he asked with his thumbs hanging from the pockets of his slacks.

"Cranberry juice," Dahji answered.

"Great choice!" Tom said, as if he were proud of it. He spun on his heels and left Dahji alone.

There was no sound. Through the window he could see the front gate that led to the lane he'd just come down. He looked around carefully, wondering what kind of business this man was in that could get him into a crib like this. In this room there were no indications of what he was like or if he had other family. It was a room for strangers. The only thing it said was that they paid attention to detail, comfort, and privacy.

"Here we go," Tom announced, bounding into the room. In one hand he had a glass of cranberry juice and in the other he carried a larger glass of what Dahji knew had to be vodka. That accounted for Tom's bloated, but otherwise smooth, tanned face and swollen hands. He handed the juice off to Dahji and continued walking to the other side of the room. It was the first time Dahji noticed that there was a door in the wall. It was painted with a fresco of angels flying above the clouds. Tom stepped through it quickly and closed the door behind him. Through the slice of space the opened door created, he could see that the room was bathed in hot pink and bright purple. He caught the edge of a poster bed. He tried to guess how many rooms the house had as he sipped on the cranberry juice. He looked at his Movado more out of habit than to see what time it was. Nearly three. Mirabelle would be expecting him in a few hours. Sitting here now, he looked forward to seeing her.

"She's all set!" Tom announced, stepping back through the door he'd gone into. He'd changed clothes. Now he was dressed in a pair of leather cowboy chaps, his groin covered with a black, mesh jockey strap. The black leather straps of his vest stretched around his ribs and pulled at the leather across his stomach. His feet were wedged into a pair of shiny leather house slippers. Dahji tried not to smile.

"Go ahead and laugh. I know I look ridiculous but Edith likes it, so…" he said, looking down at himself before shrugging his shoulders.

Dahji decided suddenly that he liked Tom as he rose from his seat.

"There's a bathroom in here," Tom said, pointing Dahji to another room. "Take a shower. The soap is some good stuff. Knock on the door when you're ready." Tom stepped to the side as if showing Dahji his newly purchased property. Tom closed the door behind him.

This is a woman's room, Dahji thought to himself. Lace and ruffles were everywhere. Even the bathroom was done up in a woman's hand. Everything seemed new and unused; shiny chrome and polished marble. The soap bar was wrapped in thick cellophane and stamped with a white English lady in profile. There was a set of fluffy white towels on the huge marble sink, their tags still on. The bathroom was big enough to park four Range Rovers in it. Hanging on the back of the door was a brand new, blue, terry cloth robe, its Polo tag hanging from the sleeve. There was even a shower cap available for his hair. *What white person wore a shower cap?* he asked himself before realizing that Gloria must have had a hand in making sure he was well taken care of.

Lathered and rinsed, Dahji stepped from the bathroom followed by steam. He was naked under the thick robe, a row of Magnum condoms in his pocket. There was another door that doubled as a floor-to-ceiling mirror on the wall across from the tall window, a bed between them. Behind the door must have been where Edith and Tom had escaped to.

Dahji was not prepared for the woman he saw step through the door. Her pink, silk nightgown slid down her long body like a caress. She was the palest woman he'd ever seen. Her blonde hair trailed down her back in a shiny river.

She had legs to her shoulders and lips that pouted pink and sumptuous. She was beautiful; like a model but more. Like she didn't belong on earth at all. She smiled and her blue eyes sparkled like the sky under a hot sun. She gave him a short wave, her fingers tapered and gentle.

"Hot damn!" Dahji muttered to himself, bringing his fist to his lips and narrowing his eyes to see her better. The padded chair he sat in held him like a prince.

She smiled appreciatively and cast a sexy glance at him as she turned to sit on the bed. She had ass like a petite sistah and breasts that swelled the silk of her negligee.

"Good afternoon, Mr. X," she said, her voice like a musical note. There was a combination of mischief and humor in her eyes. She was aware of the effect she had on him, yet shy about it nonetheless. She crossed her long spider legs at the knees. The light streamed in from the window, sparkling her large, powder blue eyes like diamonds.

"Ms. Edith, right?" Dahji asked.

She raised her palms slightly, as if framing a prize. "The one and only," she assured him. "You approve?"

Dahji nodded. "No doubt," he responded. This tickled her. He liked the way her breasts moved under the silk. Her cleavage was a creamy, mild valley that breathed and shifted with her.

Then Tom stepped through the mirrored door with a big smile on his face. He was proud of himself and enjoying the satisfied look on Dahji's face. "You've met my wife," he stated, rocking on his heels as if buoyed by joy.

Edith smiled. She had a beautiful smile and Dahji was glad of it. The pearl necklace she wore turned in the hollow of her neck just between her collarbones.

"Yes, we've met," Dahji replied, holding the sparkling blue in her large eyes. She should have been a model, he thought. Probably is already. Dahji made a mental note to keep an eye out for her in fashion magazines. He had to buy some fashion magazines. She rose from the bed on small pale feet, holding his eyes all the while, as her husband stood by the door.

"I'm glad that you could come," she whispered as she knelt to the floor in front of Dahji. She slowly reached for the lining of his robe—holding him in her gaze—and pulled it apart. Now she looked to the lounging joint between his legs. Her lips parted and her small tongue touched the back of her bottom teeth. There was a small intake of air as her eyes shifted quickly. Tom saw her sudden jolt.

"What is it, Edith?" he asked, his eyes growing wide for her answer. He was careful to stay near the door.

"It's beautiful!" she breathed out in a hot whisper. She was like a child who'd opened a mysterious present. She reached for him with both hands, as if going to retrieve a rare artifact that had only been speculated about, but never beheld. She lifted him and he grew in her palms, stretching forth across her hands, unfurling like a beast. Tinted browns and burned beiges turned onto one another, running veins carried the fluid that inflated his pulsing organ. He came alive before her eyes, his bulbous head leading the way across her palms and stretching over the edge of her hand. Just under the ridged head he turned a darker brown, while a soft tan rose to a cliff that descended smoothly to a rounded tip. Like a missile, like a sports car, this organ was built for stealth and power.

Tom didn't move. Edith's breasts swelled with her breathing and she held the stiff meat in her hands gently. The weight of him floated and jumped over her palms.

"Beautiful," she whispered, leaning toward him and

pressing her smooth cheek to the side of his swollen head. With closed eyes she rubbed her face along the length of him, communing with the organ. She turned and kissed the small arm with its throbbing veins that forked and traversed the brown-black, pearly, stretched skin. Her soft lips were a whisper as they touched him like a feather. She looked into Dahji's eyes.

Now Tom moved. "Sumvabitch!" he whispered, surprised that he'd spoken out loud. Edith grinned without showing her teeth. She stood from the floor and let her silk gown fall from her lithe body. She was perfect and pink. Her breasts were loosed from the lace bra, standing high and firm, the nipples perfect little pink knobs. Then she pushed her pink panties from her slim hips and over her knees. She stepped from them slowly, all the while watching Dahji's dick jump and rise and fall with her movements. She had a soft down of blonde hair— like someone had swept up the floor of a barbershop and stuck it to her pussy— that formed a heart between her legs.

"Do you like me?" Edith asked, her arms out to her sides. She had no idea how beautiful she was. Dahji nodded quietly, his dick making a jump across his lap, from one thigh to the other. He reached into his pocket for the gold-wrapped Magnum condom.

"Oh no, not yet!" she said quickly with a step in his direction.

She knelt between his legs, a hand on each thigh. His dick swiveled up toward her chin. "Please. Not yet. Don't cover this up just yet," she said before kissing the tip. She grabbed the swollen meat with both hands like she would a bat and spread her lips for a kiss. It was a loving kiss, like she was adoring a small child. He was hot in her palms as she sucked on the head like candy. Her breathing was light and her breasts moved over her chest.

He was an object, not much to speak about. She was the fair princess who, by special request and a promise of discreetness, was able to taste her fantasy. And the prize was the biggest dick she'd ever seen. It was a sight to behold. Something she would privately know. Perhaps she would not tell this to her friends when they spoke of or speculated on the size of passing men as they sipped wine on a veranda. No more than a swinging dick. Dahji was detached as the fairy princess, Cinderella, Snow White, the beautiful model, took part in his blessing.

She'd tasted the whole of him, held him like a cob of corn and raced down the length of him hungrily so that her soft cheek met the curly pubic hairs on his stomach. She savored every inch of him, as if discovering a new taste and texture at every stop. Her lips were raised, bruised and worn from her attentions. She grinned naughtily when she had satisfied herself orally.

"Now I'm ready," she said breathlessly and Dahji knew what she meant. "But let me do it," she added. He handed her the condom. She peeled away the gold and pulled the large, rubber, folded circle from its holding cell. With the tips of her fingers she placed it on the head of Dahji's swollen dick and gently rolled it snugly down to the base of him. Tom had moved to the bed and sat with his knees apart. Dahji could not see him. Edith turned around and gripped his knees, lowering herself onto him slowly. Her back swelled with anticipation.

She stopped when the head of his dick met her pussy lips. She was soft and hot, her small hands with long fingers holding on to his knees as she sampled him, pushing down so that he entered her slowly. She was wet and firm, a snug fit. Her body shuddered and she breathed out heavily. Her hands gripped him tighter as the head creased her moist walls. She gasped with his entry, her pussy breathing and relaxing over him.

Tom strolled to the window and stood behind Dahji. He watched as Edith lowered herself onto the thick meat. "Lovely," he whispered hoarsely.

Edith moaned, her back arching as she moved him further inside. She grew wetter and he slid a couple more inches. Dahji watched as more of him disappeared inside of her, the pink folds of her pussy peeling away tightly. She was going slow, trying to keep her breathing normal and accept him.

"You can do it," Tom urged her on, watching from over Dahji's shoulder. He licked his lips and rubbed his palms together.

"Ahhhh...," Edith moaned as she bucked down onto the hot shaft. Her elbows shook and wobbled. She held fast to Dahji's knees like a pilot holding a plane in flight during turbulence. She breathed out hard and relaxed her pussy muscles, letting even more of him inside. She was hot like an oven. Now she was getting comfortable. Slowly she rose up and left her shining wetness gleaming on Dahji's pulsing dick. Tom breathed hard behind Dahji.

Edith was ready to slide down onto him again. She gripped his knees tightly and ground him inside of her with a smooth rhythm.

"Oh, yessss!" she gasped, dropping onto him, her face closing up in a frown with the good pain.

This is what it was all about. Through the centuries. The black dick. It was freedom and a trap. She devoured him. They devoured him. An object of derision and fascination. He disappeared inside of her as much as she could stand. Her moans, groans, and little shouts of pleasurable pain were centuries old. Beads of sweat broke out on her pale back, running alongside her spine with its knots pressing through her skin. Hung. From trees. Hunted. Castrated. Hung. This is what they wanted. This is what she wanted. Big black dick. She opened like a flower and filled her pussy with the artifact of centuries-old conflict. Her hair tossed and swung with her abandon.

Dahji was detached from the feeling. He saw well enough the way his dick slid in and out of her, felt how this was a real treat for Tom. He was witnessing the big black dick in action. More than theater, he was sharing in the experience. This thing was alive. It throbbed with life, with history, with power, with stealth. Black power.

"Ooooh, my God!" Edith moaned loudly, shivering and shuddering over him as thick, milky cum squirted from her pussy, drenching his meat and coating it with cream. She smelled sweet, like cinnamon. Yet strangely tart, like a lemon. These aromas mixed themselves around his dick as she widened and sank deeper to his lap.

Suddenly, she jumped off of him and ran to the bed. She fell to her back and raised her legs high in the air, leaving Dahji with his dick bobbing in the air. Her cream cold and warm over his skin.

"Go get her!" Tom instructed with glee in his eyes. "Gotdammit, pound the life out of her!" he hissed, looking from the dripping, drying joint to his wife.

Dahji's dick bounced heavily in front of him as he took the few steps to the bed and guided his missile inside of her glistening, waiting pussy. She was red and swollen, her gold hairs matted with thick, clear-white cream. He grabbed her ankles and held them wide at his shoulders, going into her in one smooth motion. She turned her head to the side and shut her eyes tight.

Tom was at the foot of the bed, looking eagerly from his wife to the long, thick dick sliding into her. The show. Just like when little white kids would come to watch the hung black man. Cutting off his joint was a special thing to see. Some folks talked about how these dicks were pickled and kept as souvenirs. What a fascination. What a curse. What a blessing.

Edith threw her head from side to side with her mouth screaming silent words. Her golden hair stuck to her forehead and perspiration slid from her temples.

Dahji pounded into her. She quivered under him, gritting her teeth and then bellowing loudly, "Awww, shiiiiit!!" The word sounded strange coming from her magenta lips. Then she was limp and unmoving. Tom raced to her and held her face in his hands.

"Edith," he called, "Edith." Still, there was no sound, only a murmur of incoherence, her eyes rolling to the back of her head before their lids shut her off from the world.

Dahji slid out of her carefully. She folded her legs together and rolled to her side with her hands clasped between her knees. She rocked in a fetal position and moaned very low. Her body shined with sweat. Light seemed to emanate from her pale skin.

"Incredible," Tom muttered, shaking his head. He looked up at Dahji with raised eyebrows and shrugged his broad shoulders. "That'll do it. She's done for. Thank you, Mr. X." He spoke as if she were not in the room.

Dahji had never seen this before. Sure, he'd made women convulse and cry, but never fold up and leave the room while their body remained.

★ ★ ★

Tom carried Edith from the room like a small child. She didn't seem to notice that she was being lifted. She whimpered softly in his arms and rubbed her knees together as if cooling herself.

Tom returned with a proud smile, holding a white envelope. Dahji knew what it was before he handed the heavy package to him. That was something to see, Tom had said before inviting him to shower and show himself out.

Dahji sped along the interstate, fresh from the strange foreign soap. His balls were beginning to ache. He'd never released himself and decided against jacking off in the shower. Instead he called Mirabelle to say that he was on his way. She was happy to hear it and he was happy that she was ready for him.

His dick jumped in his trousers as he pulled to her gate at the center of a secluded, tree-lined street that spanned her property. He pressed the numbered code box and the wrought-iron gate swung open.

Up the graveled driveway he came to a clearing where two Bentleys were parked. One a GT, the other a touring sedan. She was at the door, smiling, her blue eyes sparkling. Her black hair cascaded to her shoulders. Her thin, graceful frame with delicate curves peeked through the sheer black silk of her three-piece negligee.

The sun made its final descent from the sky as he stepped onto the porch.

"Hello, Mr. McBeth," she said, stepping aside to allow him into the mansion. She was frying chicken in anticipation of his hunger.

Dahji turned to her on the marble floor and grabbed her roughly by the waist. She was in the process of asking if he had checked his account lately. He could wait for this. He was sure that she'd made her regular wire transfer, which afforded him his lifestyle. Right now he had to unload his nut sacks. She looked at him with wide eyes, not expecting this.

"All day you bin on my mind," Dahji said as he turned her away from him and slid the silk gown from her shoulders. She'd turned her head slightly to watch him, allowing him his way with her. She placed her hands on a waist-high podium where a wooden statue of Buddha looked on in a cross-legged pose.

"You smell nice," he whispered against her neck as he shoved off his linen coat with one hand and slipped his other up the front of her, grasping a silicone breast. She gasped, throwing her head back and pushing her ass out to him.

"You're so soft," he muttered, moving a hand down across her taut stomach and running his fingers through her pubic hair. He felt her wetness and dipped his finger inside. He brought the shining digit to her tongue. She wrapped her injected lips around his finger and tasted herself. She moaned as he popped his finger from her mouth.

"I've missed you," he whispered against her ear. She gasped, growing hot under his spontaneous touch. He managed to loosen his pants. They slid to his ankles and he stepped from them. His dick sprang forward with a recent memory, the tip hot and pulsing.

"Ohhh, goodness," Mirabelle hissed, working to free herself of her garments.

He lifted her up at the waist and lowered her onto his dick. She reached her toes toward the floor. Only when she had half of him inside of her did she feel the marble under her feet. She moaned with passion as he squeezed into her. The cross-legged Buddha was knocked to the floor as she bent over to receive the impaling better. Her black hair hung wildly and shook violently with each of his thrusts. With every forward motion, a small cry escaped her lips.

Dahji slammed into her with urgency, long-stroking her and bending his dick inside of her so that she reached for him to control his pounding. He would hear nothing of it, and realizing this, she braced herself against the wall and took all of him.

He grew hot. His throbbing meat expanded beyond limits with passion and anger and history. Mirabelle yelped out in pain as he slammed into her with a powerful force, gripping her hips tightly and shooting a much-needed release into her, grunting and grinding and twisting into her wet pussy.

He groaned loudly as he shuddered and jerked inside of her, feeling the pain and tightness in his balls ease. She was wet and dripping over him.

Mirabelle rose up, squeezing his limp but solid dick inside of her, to look at his face. She searched for the reason behind his assault, the source of the energy that passed through him into her. She wanted to know what story was written across his heart. All she saw were his hooded eyes that sparked with fire. The fire of being hung.

Chapter Fifteen

Peaches

Friday nights have always been the busiest. She'd danced no less than three feature-length performances that spanned three songs each. Then there was the floor work with the smiling conversations that all centered around how the men could get her into bed. Most tiring were the lap dances, and then there were the private shows at the back of the club. It might not have been so bad except that she'd started her day early and, by the end of the night, she was emotionally drained.

The sun had already arced its rays across her bedroom window signaling her usual time to get up, but she was tired and went back to sleep. She remembered the phone ringing several times, but whoever it was hung up before the answering machine picked up. When she heard Dahji's voice, she was barely awake, living somewhere between a dream of a house with two trees in the front yard and swimming with dolphins. She heard his smooth voice say good morning. She remembered that she'd smiled, and she hoped that he didn't think she was out somewhere or over another man's house.

Peaches stretched under the covers, ignoring the car alarm outside her window, the girl asking her mother why they had to go to Grandma's house, the dog barking in the courtyard of the apartment next door. These disturbances were no match for the rest she needed.

She didn't know how long she'd been sleeping when the incessant ringing of the telephone woke her and held her awake. The answering machine wasn't allowed to pick up. Instead, the ringing propped her up in bed, her eyes staring the phone into a submission that would not be had.

"Hello!" she answered harshly, groggy from sleep, reaching across the bed and holding the phone tightly to her ear.

Her eyes rolled hard when the recording came to life announcing that the call was from a correctional facility. Reluctantly she pressed the number five as instructed to accept the charges.

"Where you bin at?" Tequan asked when they were connected.

"Sleep."

"It's damn near ten o'clock. I bin callin' you since nine." There was hurt in his voice. A sort of powerlessness that came with being locked up. "And all last night!" he added before falling silent.

"What's up?" she asked, ignoring his complaints.

"You what's up. You out there in traffic and a nigga can't even get in touch with you. Why you didn't transfer the house to your cell phone?"

"I forgot." She rolled to her side and laid the phone on her cheek, closing her eyes.

"Tell me you love me," he said, his voice losing some of its anger. She hadn't tossed any fuel into the fire so he sounded stupid trying to argue.

"Love you."

"Damn. Nigga barely heard you. Who you got over there?"

"Please. Don't start," she warned.

He was smiling nervously, squeezing too hard on something that he didn't want to squirt away. "What you wearing?" he wanted to know.

She had on a HoodSweet t-shirt and no panties. "Pajamas," she answered.

"Serious?" He was disappointed.

"It rained last night," she lied.

"Serious?" There was disbelief in his voice. "When you gon' stop by Bo house to pick that up?" he asked, going to something he could get a better answer to. This is what it was all about anyway.

"I'ma go by there," she assured him.

"Make sure you check the oil before you drive up here tomorrow." He was seeking confirmation of her visit without questioning her about it directly. He listened for her reply. There was silence.

His voice seemed far off. She heard the part about oil and driving, but through a dim haze of sleep, she envisioned a tractor moving over corn fields.

"Peaches!" Tequan shouted.

"What?" she answered, called from her semi-dream state.

"Damn, P. You pregnant or something? You got a nigga over there or something? I'm talking to your ass and you act like you sleep and shit. What's really going on?" Now he was angry.

"I'ma go by Bo house and I'ma see you tomorrow. Call me later," she said.

"Yeah," Tequan agreed with menace. "I'll see you tomorrow."

"Bye. Love you," Peaches responded in barely a whisper before ending the call and throwing the phone across the bed. She covered her head with her thick comforter and fell back to sleep.

There were the two trees. Lemon, so when she walked out onto the porch, she could smell citrus in the air. The streets were made of corn stalks, and the roaring slow idle of a tractor moved down the empty street, cutting through the stalks and laying them flat on the ground. The sun shined brightly overhead. Peaches looked up into the glare with her hand over her eyes. A bluebird flew across the sky, its chirping like musical notes. She followed it with her eyes to where its small, forked feet landed on a high telephone wire. Another bird, this one red, soon joined it. They surveyed all that was around and beneath them as they sat on the high wire. Peaches wrapped her hands in the dish towel she carried. There were no other houses on the street, just her and the two lemon trees in the front yard. This was all she needed. It was peaceful.

★ ★ ★

Peaches woke up around noontime. The sun was at its zenith, straight up in the sky, blazing down on the hot concrete and steel of the city. She stretched under the covers, feeling as if a blanket of calm had been placed over her. Something had occurred to her during her sleep. She was closer than she realized to what she really wanted in life. Yet there was a tide moving her in the other direction. Two kinds of love lived in her heart. There was the dedication to and the love she had for Tequan. This love represented their past and the bond they'd forged through hood struggle— drugs, jail, collect calls, strife. It was a dark love. Passion. Its

basic tenants predictable by history and closed in by
options. Then there was a brighter love. This she thought
of with a smile. It made her feel good. Anything was possible; the future held all of her dreams. No drugs, no strife,
no collect calls, no jail. This new kind of dedication
involved only that she shed her darker love. This occurred
to her during sleep. She woke up thinking about Dahji.

The shower was running, the steam fogging up the
bathroom mirror as she dialed Dahji's number. The phone
was to her ear as she stood naked, watching her figure in the
mirror be obscured by the steam.

"Yada, yada, yada," Dahji answered, Snoop Dogg rapping in his lazy drawl in the background.

"Yada yourself. Hi," Peaches answered, smiling to herself, feeling light and airy.

"Wassup, Sunshine? You at the crib?"

Peaches smiled at his new nickname for her. She felt like
sunshine. And it was a validation that he at least had been
giving her some thought. "Yeah. You wouldn't believe that
I just got out of bed."

"Felt good, hunh?" he asked.

"Ooh," she cooed. "I feel like a brand new baby. Friday
nights are the worst at the club."

"I can imagine. Stay at work, earn the perks."

"That's cute," Peaches smiled in answer. It was a relief
that he didn't question why she was just getting out of bed
or try to make her feel bad for it. "So how was your yesterday?" she wanted to know, wondering what he did with
himself during the days.

"Gathering the dough to put it in the oven," he replied.

"Is it rising?"

"Like an accordion. But as a matter of course, I really
don't check often."

"Checking ain't cheating," Peaches said to this. She enjoyed their light banter. Privately, she missed not waking up next to him, and wondered if he felt the same way. Her phone line clicked. "Would you mind holding on for a second?"

"Check your trap," he answered as if he had all the time in the world.

"Hello?" Peaches was not in the mood to hear a correctional facility recording.

"What's up, homegirl?" Sherrelle asked.

"Hey, girl. I got Dahji on the other line."

"Ooohhhh!" Sherrelle moaned. "It must be nice."

"It is."

"Well, I won't hold you then. But guess what? The guy who owns the HoodSweet name is in jail."

"Serious? That's why it take so long for him to get back to you," Peaches added.

"Yeah, but get this—he's looking for somebody to run it like it's theirs. He just wants his cut."

"That's you, girl."

"He asked me to write him a letter with my own business plan. This might be it, girl!" Sherrelle said excitedly.

"The clothes and the name are hot. Well, let me get back to my..."

"Your man? It's like that?" Sherrelle screamed.

"I didn't mean it like that, but let me get back to him." Peaches was smiling broadly.

"Okay, girl. We'll talk later," Sherrelle smiled with her as she cleared her line.

"Dahji? Sorry about that. That was Sherrelle. She says the dude with the HoodSweet clothes is in jail. He's giving her the green light to run it like it's hers."

"Sounds like a plan," he answered.

"So what are you doing today?" Peaches asked, steam continuing to fog her mirror.

"Gotta go see my momma."

"That's cute. But you don't sound like…"

"Naw, it's cool. My pops is a reverend and he ain't really feeling my get down."

Peaches could understand him perfectly. "So what is your get down?"

"I can't really speak on it like that," he answered cryptically.

"Well, are you free after you visit your dear mother?"

"Like a date?" he asked, thinking how long it had been since he'd been on an actual date that didn't involve business.

Peaches was smiling, dipping her hand under the spray of shower water. "Yeah. A date."

"I'm down. Get with me around three or four."

"It's a date then." Peaches was smiling so wide her eyes were nearly closed. She ended the call and hopped into the shower like a little jig of a dance. "I'm going out on a date," she sang as she bobbed her head under the water.

Her joy had ebbed by the time she got out of the shower. There was the business—the grimy business—of going to Tequan's homeboy's house to pick up the drugs she'd agreed to bring to him. She was returned to the land of the gritty. The pleasant skies with birds chirping on telephone wires and lemon trees with citrus aromas planted in the front yard—all of this was in the future. Right now she was still in the world where she danced half-naked on a stage nearly every night, and had sex with men for money. She loved a man in prison, and she was going to bring drugs to him. She didn't buy into his promises of making her financially stable, she knew this was his cap and she pretended to believe it. What he didn't know was that she would do it simply because she loved him. But that love was being challenged by dreams that were slowly showing themselves as a possible reality.

★ ★ ★

This neighborhood was deceptive. Though it was well-placed with clean homes and freshly tended lawns, there was an underside, sinister and evil in its application. This illusion of calm is what made the occasional shooting and yellow tape so alarming. The sons and daughters of middle class parents had inherited this neighborhood and turned its insides into something their parents had never intended. The epitome of laziness, these offspring had failed to build upon the success of the previous generation. The few who did promptly found shelter outside of this neighborhood, leaving it glittering with new cars and the flashy clothes of those who never worked a day in their lives.

Peaches turned onto the now familiar street and knew which house Bo lived in even before she got to the middle of the block. It was the house where most of the new cars congregated. There was an obscenely fat man leaning against a Viper Dodge truck. His fatness bulged against the soft material of his blue Nike tracksuit. In his embrace was a thin, brown woman with long, weaved braids who played like she didn't want to be pawed. She giggled and laughed in her attempt to keep his hands off of her high, round ass. They both swiveled their necks when Peaches pulled to the open space behind the Viper truck on chrome twenty-six-inch rims. The fat man was smiling at Peaches while the paper bag-colored girl looked at her as if the sun had been blotted out and moved on.

Peaches stepped from Tequan's Chrysler 300C in a pair of hip-hugging Cavalli jeans and BAPE sneakers. She'd left the top button undone on her LRG, white, button-up with stitched red roses trailing from the collar down one arm.

"Whaddup, Peaches?" fat man said.

"Hi, Bay Bay," she responded, now glad that she'd wrapped her hair in a red, polka-dot, Lucille Ball headscarf because the chickenhead woman in Bay Bay's arms looked hostile.

"You and Tequan still doing it, hunh?" Bay Bay asked with a wry grin.

"Something like that," she answered, stepping to the curb. "Is Bo inside?" she wanted to know, seeking his permission to walk past the two dudes lounging on the porch who looked from the steps eagerly.

"Yeah, he in there."

"Thank you," Peaches said, ignoring the beady eyes of his hood-rat plaything. She knew the men on the porch, their oversized t-shirts hiding the pistols in the waists of their jeans. "Hi, Drew. Hi, Bam."

"Damn, girl!" Bam hissed, looking up at her as she stepped up the stairs between them.

"We need somebody for my bachelor party. I'm getting married!" Drew said behind her, craning his neck up the stairs.

"I don't do bachelor parties." Peaches turned to him on the porch. He had a wicked grin on his face. "Who you getting married to anyway?" she asked, aware of Bam ogling her ass.

"You wouldn't know her. But for real though, what it take for a nigga like me to get a woman like you to do his bachelor party?" He pulled a wad of oddly stacked money from his pocket and held it close to his stomach for her to see.

"Ten thousand dollars," she answered in a plain voice.

"Gotdamn, Peaches!" Bam shouted. "What a nigga gon' get—a coupon for five more bachelor parties and a free pass to Disneyland?" His laughter crackled as he dapped Drew.

Peaches smiled with him. "Naw, boy. I can hook you up with somebody though. Who are you marrying? I might know her."

"That nigga ain't getting married," Bam said with a smile. "That nigga just trying to see you, that's all."

"I don't like strip clubs," Drew offered, stuffing his money back into his pockets.

"Why?" Peaches asked, willing to entertain him in her duty to keep the lion calm.

"What I'ma pay for something for and leave with my dick all hard, and the bitch go home paid and ain't spread her legs?"

"Then you should get married," she answered smartly, pointing a manicured finger at him playfully.

"That's what I'm trying to do." Drew looked out to the street where a blue Chevy Caprice was passing by. "You know them?" he asked Bam, turning toward him with a serious expression.

Bam was looking after the car and rose from the porch with his hand under his shirt when Peaches knocked softly on the screen door.

"Go on in. Bo in the back," Drew said without looking up at her.

Black leather couches formed a U shape in the living room. In the center was a low table with various video consoles and their paddles strewn about. Empty Kentucky Fried Chicken boxes were on the leather sofas, left there after a recent foraging. Against the empty fireplace was a big screen television. A porno movie was playing mutely.

The shapely white woman mouthed her agony wordlessly as the buff black man pounded into her from the back. Sweat glistened on his muscles and his face contorted in concentration.

"Come on back here," Bo said from the hallway, waving his beefy arm from a door. Just as quickly, he'd disappeared from the doorway.

His back was to her. He was seated at a desk in a room at the end of the hallway. His shirt was off, showing the large cross tattooed on his broad back. His shaved black head shined with a recent application of grease. His thick thighs spread from the small stool upon which he sat and his feet gripped the rubber straps of his slippers. She could smell sex the closer she got to the room.

"Tequan just called," Bo said, not looking back at her. He was concentrating on something on the desk before him. The room was bathed in light whereas the hallway was dark. The doors to the other bedrooms along the hall were all closed.

Peaches wasn't surprised that Tequan called. He was probably checking to see if she'd arrived yet. "Is that right?" she asked rhetorically as she stepped through the door. A light-skinned woman smiled up at her from the bed against the window where the light was coming from. She made no motion to hide her huge breasts. They spilled across her chest as she lay propped up on a pillow with a smoking joint between her fingers. She was naturally pretty and thick, just the way the hood liked her. Her long, brown hair lay in plaits over her shoulders and were wrapped at the ends with blue rubber bands.

"Your name Peaches," the thick woman said, exhaling a plume of sweet-smelling smoke through her small button of a nose.

"That's Marvelous," Bo said, his head turning for a brief second from his work.

"You work at Applebottoms?" Marvelous wanted to know.

"She wanna strip," Bo said before Peaches could answer. Marvelous rolled her eyes to the ceiling.

"How long have you been dancing?" she wanted to know.

"Not that long," Peaches answered, wondering what it was Bo was doing at the desk. It was a small room. Along the wall at the foot of the bed were football trophies lining several shelves of a bookcase. Pictures of Bo in various baseball and football uniforms were attached to the walls. Then there were the high school graduation pictures and the Grambling University team football pictures. He'd returned to this room and this life after a brief flirtation with the outside world.

"She ain't finta be dancing," Bo announced. "She just thinks it's hot. She got it in her head that she gon' make a million dollars and then end up in all the magazines." He turned from the desk now and handed her four, finger-length, stuffed balloons. "There you go. Make sure you tie a string to the end so you can pull 'em out."

"Right," Peaches answered, something catching in her chest. The vision of her sitting in the visiting room pulling the drugs from her pussy made her pause. She could feel Marvelous looking at her in appraisal.

"Tell Tequan I said hi," Marvelous said, breaking Peaches from her stutter of motion.

She made a small smile. "Okay," she replied, feeling the denseness of the balloons in her palm. They were shaped like fat fingers.

"Remember, just decline a search if they ask to search

you. All they gon' do is not let you visit," Bo instructed, his large hands down between his legs. Peaches could imagine him sneaking under the covers to fuck Marvelous whenever he felt like it. She was there for whatever he needed. Like a can of beer, he could open her up when the thirst hit him.

"Okay. No problem," Peaches responded bravely, her courage chasing away the doubt. Bo raised his beefy frame from the stool. Muscles and mass flexing to his full height.

She turned with his signal to follow him out. "It was nice meeting you," Marvelous sang behind her.

"You too," Peaches replied, striding back through the dark hallway and the smell of chicken, beer, and sex.

Drew and Bam were out in the middle of the street. They were at the windows of a Maxima, smiling and playing with two women inside. Bay Bay was in the truck. Peaches thought it strange that he sat straight up and looked over at her while seemingly frowned up in agony.

"Be careful," Bo said beside her, standing with his hands on his hips, surveying the scene before him and looking both ways down the sunny street. This was his domain and these were his soldiers.

"Awright, then. See you later," Peaches said before stepping off the porch. The women in the Maxima craned their necks to see her as she stepped around the front of the 300C, alerting Bam and Drew to her departure. The paper bag-colored woman who'd been in Bay Bay's grasp earlier, raised up in the passenger seat of the Viper truck. She wiped at her lips, shaking off her embarrassment at the look Peaches gave her for sucking dick in public.

"Tell that nigga don't drop the soap!" Drew shouted, raising up over the hood, a big smile on his face.

"Yeah! Give homey our love. Tell 'im to sleep on his back!" More laughter as Peaches waved at them and got into Tequan's car.

She watched the scene grow small in her rearview mirror. This was going to be their day. Perhaps they would all go to the pet store for dog food, or make a similar short excursion away from the house. She knew this because this was her. Marvelous was her. Bo was Tequan. And here she was digging back into this life with hesitant hands. Suddenly this just didn't feel right. She felt bigger than this. The drugs, sex, pistols, gangsters, lewd conduct, and the trappings of the ghetto used to have a powerful allure, but now it seemed so destined to end one way—jail or death. She would speak to Tequan about this. She wanted to know what his plans were after his release. She looked at her watch and thought it wasn't quite time to give Dahji a call. She called Sherrelle, wanting to hear more about the dude in jail who owned HoodSweet. *That was some boss shit*, she thought to herself as Sherrelle answered the phone.

Chapter Sixteen

Dahji

Dahji ended his call with Peaches with a curious smile on his face and returned his focus to matching new orders for photographs and stuffing envelopes with sexy poses. The stack of checks he picked up from the mailbox was even higher than the day before. That *King* magazine advertisement was paying off. There was something mysterious about her that he liked. She was the type of woman who knew how to give a man space. He liked that she didn't question him more about how he stacked his money. For his part he could care less why she slept late or how she earned her bread besides working at the club. He suspected that she might have a few select clients. He briefly entertained the thought of how their lives could mesh if they became more than fucking friends. What was obvious was the fact that she had a mind for business. And if she was right about HoodSweet apparel, then it was something he would definitely be involved with. His mind worked at how to market the product using his connections and make it a global phenomenon. He envisioned women everywhere replacing their 'dyme' status with HoodSweet. If you're not HoodSweet then you're just a dyme. He smiled to himself at the smooth slogan, realizing he was onto something special.

Then the phone rang. It was a busy morning. Gloria had called earlier to ask about his meeting with Tom and Edith. She wanted to know if they'd given him a tip. A little something, he answered, deciding not to share with her exactly how much. She might have been jealous.

"What it do?" he said into the phone, stuffing a large envelope with twenty pictures of a J. Lo look-a-like who was on her way over with a friend. She was popular among the Mexican prisoners across the nation. He had a woman for every taste.

"Mr. McBeth, you have guests. A Ms. Maria and a Ms. Rosie."

"Send 'em up," he answered into the phone and looked at his watch. They were right on time—one o'clock. He gathered up the shoebox full of photos, envelopes, stamps, and prison checks and headed upstairs to stow them away, Snoop Dogg's smooth delivery following him up the stairs about being a pimp and sending a ho so he wouldn't have to be broke no mo.

The doorbell was ringing as Dahji started back down the stairs dressed in a pair of Phat Farm denim jeans and a blue rugby shirt. His hair hung to his shoulders in loose waves. His bare feet sank into the thick carpeting as he stepped to the door with his camera in hand.

"Hola, Papi." Rosie grinned. She looked edible in a sheer, flower-print, spaghetti-strapped dress that stopped at the top of her thighs. She was a blonde, blue-eyed, Spanish hottie that could pass for J. Lo with her ass, waist, and face, only with enhanced breasts that stood pert and plump.

"Hola, Mami," Dahji answered, looking at her friend

who he'd never met before.

"This is Maria." Rosie introduced the statuesque brunette with legs as long as Texas and breasts that rose like twin peaks, making the strands of her silk dress suspend tightly in the air to her shoulders.

"Rosie says so many nice things about you," Maria sang, her hazel eyes sparkling as she pressed her soft palm into his. They were moving inside the apartment.

Dahji closed the door behind them. "That's because I pay her," he joked, enjoying the smiles on their faces and the way their bodies danced with movement even though they were standing still.

"You have a very nice place," Maria said in her sweet Latin accent.

"I told you, didn't I?" Rosie asked in a low voice as Dahji moved toward the kitchen.

"Told her what? What y'all drinking?"

"No soda or liquor," Rosie answered for them. "We made a bet that you would answer the door with your camera," she added with a smile, making herself comfortable on the couch and dropping her deep brown leather purse at her feet.

"I didn't believe her," Maria said, sitting in the wicker king chair by the window overlooking the city. She looked like an ancient Aztec princess. Her eyes sparkled under the light.

Dahji handed Rosie a glass of cranberry juice. "I hope you won something nice," he said.

"You are the one who won," Maria said as he turned in her direction.

"Me? What I win?"

"We can't tell you yet," Rosie giggled, exchanging a knowing glance with Maria, her breasts bubbling inside the thin material of her dress. Without a bra they stood firm against the thin, cotton, flower print, her fat nipples pressing against the flowers dancing across her chest.

"Sounds like a good bet," he said, walking to the sound system against the wall and changing the CD to The Pussycat Dolls. They sang about wanting a man to loosen up their buttons and do something nasty to them. Maria and Rosie immediately started moving their bodies in their seats, asses massaging the cushions to the beat.

"I love Pussycat," Maria giggled out.

"Pussy is the best," Rosie added from the couch with a wicked grin.

Dahji knew a good call when he made one. They were the same coin but different sides. One tall and shapely like a model and the other petite and curvaceous like a hood chick.

"So when are you going to make a video?" Rosie wanted to know, reminding Dahji of their last conversation. She wanted to be the first to introduce his line of porn videos.

"Right now," he responded with a wicked grin, looking from her to Maria. It was obvious to him that they'd given this some thought.

"Will you be joining us?" Maria asked, sipping her cranberry juice and looking at him seductively over the rim of her glass. Dahji smiled.

His dick stirred in his jeans at the thought of stuffing their hot pussies, but today wasn't the day. "We gon' have to do that off-camera," he replied. Maria made a playfully sad face.

"You promise? Rosie says you have a nice package," Maria said, opening her face up again.

Rosie produced a midnight black dildo from her leather satchel. It was attached to a leather jock strap. A strap-on dildo. He wondered why they chose the blackest dick they could find, then realized it was more about the color than the size. "It's big like this, girlfriend," Rosie said simply, holding the thick appendage in the air. They both looked to him for confirmation and estimation.

Dahji raised a finger in the air. "Hold up. Let me go get the camcorder."

When he came back downstairs, Rosie was over by the window with Maria. They were kissing tenderly, the sun a halo behind them through the window. Dahji began filming, The Pussycat Dolls providing the soundtrack.

Hands rushed through hair as they kissed each other lightly on the lips, fabric moved up over hips. Legs long in stiletto heels, feet spread apart, Rosie reaching under Maria's dress to fondle her. Maria's head thrown back in pleasure. Rosie's breast in Maria's palm, then her nipple between Maria's heart-shaped lips. The passion was rising as Rosie returned the favor, peeling the strap from Maria's shoulder and exposing her to her touch. She caressed Maria's bare breasts as Maria raised them for the camera. As Rosie kissed and sucked one breast and then the other, Maria slipped the straps of her dress from her shoulders. The women stood facing each other, their breasts marching forward to meet like magnets. They rubbed their nipples together, kissing them like Eskimo noses.

Dahji filmed. He directed them to the low, sloping-backed couch on the other side of the window. The sun bathed its paisley print cushions in light.

Maria lay down, reaching for Rosie as Rosie's lips sought her breasts. She kissed her slowly and tenderly down the center of her body, peeling away her dress as she got lower. With the silk dress free of its host and laid carefully on the floor, Rosie lifted the string of Maria's thong and kissed her along her softly rounded hip. This made Maria's body wave up while her lips parted in a soft moan. Maria lay seductively, looking down the length of her body as Rosie slid the thong down her long legs and let it drop to the carpet. She kissed Maria along the long leg hanging from the couch, on up to her firm thigh. She rubbed her hand across Maria's smooth stomach and kissed the soft mound of her shaved pussy. Maria's breathing became heavy with anticipation. Rosie dipped her tongue into Maria's pussy, her ass in the air.

This was a nice shot. Dahji had them in full view. Maria watched as Rosie nibbled on her swollen clit, her moans like music. Then Rosie moved up her body and kissed her breasts tenderly, letting her tongue soothe the burning nipples with loving, sensual care. Their mouths met and this was a beautiful sight. There was passion in their kiss, and it shot through the camera lens as Dahji moved around them for the best angles.

They switched positions, all the while never losing touch; hands caressing breasts, lips kissing softly and hungrily. Now Rosie lay on the couch naked as Maria kissed her from the hollow of her neck down through the center of her breasts. She stopped there to squeeze the fat nipples between her lips. Rosie gasped under her, her body coursing and squirming with energy.

Dahji worked to control himself as he filmed, moving to the head of the couch for a better view.

Maria eased the thickly veined dildo into Rosie's wet pussy. Rosie's lips parted and her neck arched back as she gasped in ecstasy. Their hands were intertwined over Rosie's head as Maria kissed her, sliding into her with smooth strokes. The leather straps of the dildo were tight around Maria's ass, tightening and flexing with her thrusts.

Rosie raised her legs over Maria's shoulders as Maria plunged into her.

"Come on, Mami!" Rosie hissed. "Come on, Mami!"

Maria's black hair shifted and fell with her thrusting. Her breasts bounced against Rosie's mounds as they met with each slow grind.

"Ahhh, Mami! It's there, Mami! Come on, Mami!" Rosie thrashed under Maria, her legs spread in the air like rabbit ears.

Maria let the dildo slide all the way out of her pussy, leaving only the bulbous head at Rosie's rim before sliding it back inside of her hot pussy. Beads of sweat trickled down her spine as it curved and bent with her grinding motion.

"Ahummm! Oooweeee! Unnnnnhhh! Ahhhhh!" Rosie panted and screamed as she creamed onto the dildo. She shuddered under Maria as their lips met for a wet kiss.

Maria raised up and unstrapped the dildo. She handed it to Rosie who promptly placed it around her hips. Her lips were pouty and her hair frizzy. It was as if they'd forgotten Dahji was in the room.

Maria stood and leaned over the couch, spreading her legs wide. Rosie slid the black dick into her waiting pussy. Maria swung her long, black hair from one shoulder to the other. Rosie gripped her hips softly and began to slowly stroke in and out of her.

Dahji moved to the side to watch Maria's expression as the dildo, which was attached to Rosie's curvaceous hips and ass, slid in and out of her pussy.

Maria began to breathe heavily as Rosie found an easy stroke. The dildo was shimmering with cream. It glistened with shiny passion. Rosie used it as if it were her own dick. She twisted and turned with it, bucking against Maria's ass so her flesh vibrated.

"Yes, Mami, Yesss!" Maria moaned, moving against the dildo as Rosie pounded it into her.

"You like that, Mami?" Rosie asked, her face flushed with passion.

"Yesss, Mami! Give it to me! Come on, Mami! I'm cumming, Mami!" she screamed, her face tight.

Rosie let the big, black, dick slide in and out of her at a downward angle. This seemed to cause a volcanic eruption in Maria. She shuddered and shook, falling to the couch and gasping.

Dahji couldn't control himself. His dick pressed against his jeans ferociously. Rosie was the first to notice as she looked up after exchanging a passionate kiss with Maria. She grabbed Maria by the hand and lifted her from the couch. Without a word, they walked over to where Dahji stood with the camcorder in his hand, and knelt before him. They both worked at his zipper and freed his stiff meat from its bondage. He raised the camcorder and filmed their attack on him, thinking that he could always cut this part out.

Their lips met on either side of his dick. Rosie's small hands moved up and down the length of him, knowing exactly what to do. His dick was hot to the touch from the arousal their lips created. They kissed over the head and sucked on him from both sides. It was a challenge to keep his balance as they rubbed their lips down the length of him like a Big Stick icee.

Maria wrapped her lips around his swollen head and rolled her tongue across it as Rosie nibbled at the shaft and massaged his balls with her soft fingers. As Rosie kissed her way up to the head, Maria moved along the other side. They were playing a game to see who would be the one to catch the prize. He swelled and pulsed between their lips.

Both of them grabbed hold of his dick and pulled on it softly while they kissed the tip, their lips meeting and smacking, their tongues rolling and darting over the sensitive
skin. They kept massaging him, his skin hot under their
touch. When he climaxed, they were both at the tip of his
dick, both having won the game and sharing the reward.

★ ★ ★

Dahji didn't want to see his father. It was going to be more
of the same thing—the good reverend giving him the cool,
silent treatment at first, then pouncing on something he
didn't agree with as he listened to his conversation with his
mother. Dahji suspected that his mother was trying to
bring him and his father together, but the gears just didn't
click right. His Pops wouldn't be satisfied until he cut his
hair off and started referring to himself by his given birth
name. And let's not forget coming to church so the reverend could proudly announce him as his born-again son.
But his mother had called again, checking on his arrival
time after Rosie and Maria left with a thousand dollars each
in their designer purses.

That was some good business, Dahji thought to himself
about stepping up his mail-order game to include porn
videos. He already had the stable of women. That bogus fall
on the loading dock at Federal Express was the best thing
that happened to him, he reminded himself as he turned
onto his parents' quiet suburban street. A certain sense of
joy spread through him when he saw the house he was
raised in standing from the recessed, landscaped lawn, its
trimmed, green bushes guarding the entrance and its rose
bushes lining the front of the two-story house. His mother
kept his attic bedroom intact with all of his childhood
mementos and bowling trophies. His father's Cadillac was
in the driveway. *Every reverend had to have a long Caddy*, he

thought to himself as he pulled in behind his mother's Volvo sedan.

He could smell the pork chops before he reached the front screen. The door was open behind it. It was about three hours past lunch; his mother didn't need a special time to cook. All the curtains were open, giving the antique furniture and interior a clean and airy look. The shiny, black, baby grand piano stood under a high window, giving him remembrances of his youth—Christmas carols around the burning fireplace, piano lessons that he hated, his father practicing an upcoming Sunday sermon perched against the piano with Dahji as his audience.

He opened the screen door and stepped into the warm living room. He looked to the left, almost expecting that his father would be in the den watching college basketball. But he wasn't. With his absence, Dahji lost the rhythm of the house. He scanned the room for any differences since his last visit. Photographs chronicling his boyhood and adolescence were spread across the ledge of the fireplace. A giant oil on canvas of his mother and father at the renewal of their vows ceremony. They had been celebrating thirty years of marriage. The furniture was still wrapped in thick plastic and, further into the house, the dining room table sat heavily on wooden paws. So many dinners at this table.

"There's my baby," his mother sang from the kitchen doorway, a World's Best Mom apron wrapped tightly around her slim figure. Her skin shined caramel; her long hair wrapped tight, making her smooth forehead shine. Her face was open and bright. The privilege of being a reverend's wife and living a healthy lifestyle—if you don't count the pork in everything from collard greens to pinto beans—was in her smile.

"Hey, Momma," Dahji responded, smiling and taking

long strides to her open arms. She held the greasy fork out
to her side to receive him.

"Mmmm," she moaned, swaying with him in her arms.
She smelled of good cooking. She stepped back to appraise
her son. "Have you been eating?" she wanted to know, a
look of concern wrinkling the brow of her brown eyes.
She'd scanned him from feet to head.

"Nothing as good as what you got here," he answered,
moving to the pots.

"You haven't been gone so long that you forgot to stay
away from my stove," she warned, catching him by the arm
and pulling him to her. They were nose to nose, unmoving.
"You be nice to your father when he comes in here, okay?"
she instructed with a straight face. Then she released him
and moved to the stove with the long fork extended.

"Where is he?" Dahji asked, watching as she poked and
flipped the pork chops frying in the grease.

"Where who at?" came the high-pitched voice of the
reverend. He stepped into the kitchen from the service
porch, holding on to an old book that Dahji reasoned he
must have searched out in the library he kept in the garage.
He looked at Dahji with penetrating dark eyes. He looked
the same as when Dahji had seen him last, almost two
months ago. They held each other's gaze for a minute
before the reverend broke contact.

"See you still got that girly hair," the reverend said,
leaning against the cabinet by the sink. The window behind
him let in the sunlight. It brushed over his thinning, gray
hair, which he combed away from his forehead. The
straight strands spoke of his Creole heritage. They marched
together and divided in salt and pepper strands away from
his smooth face, a youthful face only betrayed by the salt
and pepper stubble he kept cut low. Every now and then

he'd shave it, but this only gave him the appearance of a turtle outside of its shell. The lower half of his jaws wrinkled into a permanent row of baby sausages. Dahji liked to think that this was God's way of punishing him for his hypocrisy.

"Leave him be, Cleotis," his mother said, busying herself with the mashed potatoes, their brown skins mixing with the yellowed meat as she pressed the metal utensil into the bowl.

"The boy's fine," his father said, folding his arms across his narrow chest, making the strap of his overalls jump into the air. "I just want to know if he's ever going to go back to work and earn a decent, honest living?" This was said more to his mother, but the words hit Dahji like a dart.

His mother looked to him for the answer to the question his father had thrown into the air. Her expression pleaded with him to give him a good answer. "You are going back to work, right?" she asked softly.

Dahji parted his lips, hoping that what he was about to say sounded as real as it was. "I gotta man playing for the Colts." He said this to his mother but could see the baby sausages on his father's face wiggle and jiggle with the next question on his father's lips.

"What do you mean you got a man? What kind of man are you talking about?" his father challenged.

"I represent a player in training camp. You know, the football team?" he replied sarcastically. His mother shot him a warning look.

His father looked confused, his brow furrowed like he couldn't understand English. "Mabel, what is this boy talking about? Does he mean to say that he's some type of sports agent?" These words came from the side of his mouth with his head turned to his wife and his eyes shifting back and forth with confusion. He could pretend to be a baffled fool when it suited him best. Like the time his church was being investigated for embezzlement. It was around the same time his father bought a boat to park at the new vacation house on the lake. The role he'd assumed as the unwitting fool followed him home. The head deacon of the church ended up going to federal prison.

"Yeah, Dad. Like an agent," Dahji answered straight away, looking into his father's face and capturing his eyes so they would stop jumping to his mother for confirmation.

"That's great, Roger!" his mother said, looking at him with a wide smile. She wanted to hear more. He had his father's silent attention, too.

"Well, I got a meeting for a guy that used to play for the Seahawks and..."

"Who?" his father asked quickly.

"Marlin Cassidy," Dahji answered, watching as his father placed the second-string running back. He nodded when he'd successfully done so.

"I got him a meeting with the coaches. And now he's in training camp. So..." Dahji shrugged his shoulders.

"So he's not officially on the team yet?" his father asked, doubtful.

"Naw. Not yet, Pop."

His father smiled then. "He will be though," he said. "I've seen him run in Seattle. Colts would be a fool to pass on him. Did he clear his medicals?"

"Yep," Dahji answered proudly. It made him feel good that his father approved.

"You coming to church tomorrow?" his mother asked. Dahji felt the weight of his father's stare.

"Yeah. We got a special guest tomorrow. Gonna be a good day the Lord will make," his father added.

"Coretta's coming," his mother said with a smile, cutting the fire off on the last of the pork chops.

"Coming where?" Dahji asked, his face screwing up with renewed anger. Coretta lived down the street. They were high school sweethearts. She went to college and found a new love and got married. She came back home and they'd sexed on a couple of occasions. When she became pregnant, she insisted that the little girl was not his. Then her husband was sent to prison for life. This is when she started demanding that Dahji take a DNA test because she now believed that the girl was his.

"And she's bringing your daughter, Aryn," his mother added.

"She got yours and your mother's eyes. My hair," his father noted, looking at Dahji with a sparkle in his eyes. They wouldn't let him deny the little girl, no matter Coretta's trifling ways. They wouldn't allow his anger to deprive them of a grandchild.

"Bringing her where?" Dahji asked. He still hadn't provided a DNA sample. His mother's word had proven to be enough for Coretta.

"Here," his father said plainly, unfolding his arms and picking up the dusty book from the formica countertop. "Little girl can eat, too," he added, walking past Dahji and patting him on the shoulder.

Dahji waited until his father turned into the den at the front of the house. "Momma, why you didn't tell me she was coming over?"

His mother looked at him sternly. "Because it's about time you do the right thing and acknowledge that she's your daughter. You can't go around pretending that she's not just because of the way her mother acted," she instructed in a low whisper, her small brown eyes narrowing in on him.

Dahji wanted to leave immediately. He didn't want to see Coretta. She'd played him, he felt. "Why she just didn't say I was the father in the first place?" he asked, a measure toward pouting and anger.

Mabel busied herself with the cream corn that simmered low in a small pot on the stove. "Maybe because she was married and didn't want to hurt anybody," she answered, never looking at her son.

"Not until her man go to the bing."

"Whatever happened to her husband is of no consequence." She turned to him now, the plastic stirring spoon pointing in the air. "God make everything come to the light. And you need to start being a man and not a little hurt boy about the situation. Now she's coming over to dinner and you best make yourself the man I know you to be." Along with her words were the face of her intentions (eyes, nose, mouth, ears) all making themselves clear in her determination that he do as she said. She shook him without laying a hand on him.

Dahji nodded and let out a deep breath as if a pin had been stuck into him. "She shoulda said something before," he complained for the last time. Then a feeling of relief came over him. He had a daughter. Denying her had closed something in him, but now he was free to be a daddy, something he'd always wanted to be. *Funny how God gives us what we want*, he thought to himself as the doorbell rang. He knew, without his father calling through the house, that Coretta was at the front door.

"You be nice," his mother warned him one last time with big eyes and a pointing of the plastic spoon.

His father had Aryn in his arms, making her smile with his slow questions about what she'd learned in first grade.

Coretta looked at Dahji as he stepped from the kitchen. Light from the open door framed her shapely body in an angelic glow. Hershey chocolate-colored with long black hair, her facial features were even and plain. She smiled with perfectly set teeth in a small mouth. She still had a cheerleader's body, her thick thighs beginning at the end of the brown skirt that hung from her ass like a tent. She watched him until she was within speaking distance.

"Hi," she said simply. Aryn looked from Dahji's father's arms with a mixture of deciphering grown folk talk and fierce recognition. The smile was replaced by a quizzical gaze. She was let to the floor slowly. There was a moment where everyone watched father and daughter examine each other. Then Aryn looked up at her mother for an answer.

"That's your father," Coretta said with an instruction mixed in.

"How are you, Aryn?" Dahji asked, bending to his knee and holding out his arms for her. The last time he'd seen her she was two years old and still another man's daughter. She dutifully walked into his arms and let him hug her to his body. Dahji could feel his mother's eyes on him from where she stood in the kitchen doorway.

"Hi, Mrs. Reed," Coretta said, waving to his mother across the room.

"Hi, Coretta. Bring that girl in here so she can learn some cooking," she instructed. Aryn knew they were talking about her. She broke away eagerly.

"Hi, Grandma!" she called out excitedly, scampering over the carpet and throwing herself into her arms.

His father eased into the den like a ghost, leaving Dahji face to face with Coretta. There was the excited chatter of their daughter in the kitchen like glue bringing them together.

"Hi," Coretta began. "How have you been?"

"I'm cool," Dahji answered.

"We need to talk," she responded in her grown-up, motherly way.

Dahji led the way up the stairs next to the den. His room looked the same as when Coretta used to come over after school. Baseball mitts, basketball, football, baseball, and bowling ball all in a net sack by the door. He sat down at the wooden desk by the window that overlooked the street. She sat down on the twin-sized bed, facing the poster of Jay-Z and Mac Dre on the opposite wall.

"Talk to your husband lately?" Dahji wanted to know first of all.

"No. We got divorced."

"Why?"

"Mainly because Aryn's not his daughter," she answered defiantly.

"How did you come to—all of a sudden—change the daddy?" This was the first time they'd had a real conversation since the arguments surrounding her birth six years ago.

"I always knew she was yours, but I was married. I know what I did was messed up. And I don't blame you for being mad at me."

Dahji got the feeling that this moment had to come. She'd given it some thought too. "Why else you divorce him?" he asked.

"It was over before he went to jail. He got laid off and just lost his mind," she said, opening her eyes and spreading her arms wide in frustration. There was a smile teasing her lips. Dahji grinned, feeling how easy it was to spend time with her, how good this felt.

"So what you doing with yourself nowadays?" he asked,

leaning back in the chair and folding his hands behind his head.

"I'm in school. And I work for a lawyer as a paralegal."

"That's cool. You wanna be a lawyer?"

"Yep. You think I would make a good lawyer?"

"I don't see why not. Maybe you could get ol' boy out of jail," Dahji said, smiling. But she wasn't smiling.

"Can we please not talk about him?" she asked, her face serious. Dahji made a movement with his lips to say okay. "Your daughter is so smart," she began, "she has your sense of humor." She was looking at him for a response.

"She's cute. She get her looks from me."

Coretta laughed at this. "I ain't mad at that," she responded easily, crossing her legs at the knees, one leg swinging over the other. Her smooth, chocolate-brown thigh hinted at a good memory.

Dahji's phone was ringing inside the pocket of his jeans.

"Hello," he said into the small device, watching Coretta as she looked around the room.

"Hey, yourself," Peaches said cheerily on the other end. Dahji checked his watch. Nearly four o'clock.

"Hey, Peaches. I'm running a little late. We still gon' do that though."

"Are you busy?"

Coretta pretended she was absorbed in his yearbook pictures. She'd picked up the book from his nightstand and flipped through the pages.

"I'm at my mom house right now. I should be outta here in the next hour. She cooked so you know how that go," he explained, already feeling like it was going to be too late to go out on the date.

"Well, call me when you're about to leave. I'm at Sherrelle's house," she said. There was no anger in her voice.

"That's cool. I gotta check on Marlin, so I'll be through there in a minute."

"Okay, but maybe we should do the date thing another time. I have to be at work in a few hours."

"Damn. Okay. I'ma make it up to you though." He could feel her relaxing into a smile on the other end of the phone. Now Coretta was looking at him with wonder.

"I'm counting on it. Are you going to stop by the club?"

"I should be able to see you before then." He checked his watch again.

"Well, I'ma leave here in a minute. Her husband gets mad when he comes home and I'm here."

"It ain't my fault!" Sherrelle yelled in the background.

"Well, I'll call you when I'm about to roll. We'll hook up before you go to work," he suggested, stopping Coretta from leaving with a hand in the air.

"Sounds good. Bye."

"Later," Dahji responded, ending the call. Coretta was standing at the door.

"Sounds special," she said.

"Friend of mine," Dahji answered, slipping the phone back into his pocket.

The sound of his mother's voice traveled through the house and up the stairs, just like it had when they were up here all those years ago together. They both smiled at the memory as Dahji rose from his seat. His stomach moaned in anticipation of the hot food that would be set out on the table. He knew without seeing that his mother would sit him next to his daughter, which was fine by him.

Chapter Seventeen

Peaches

She wasn't upset at all. Not like she thought she should have been. After all, they weren't boyfriend and girlfriend. But she had to admit to herself that she was feeling Dahji in a real way. She'd hoped that she would have still been at Sherrelle's house when he stopped by to see Marlin. Then again, maybe it was best that he hadn't. Marlin's wife and Sherrelle's husband may have thought it strange the way the four of them would have been hanging by the curb, laughing, talking, Sherrelle and Marlin trying not to appear interested in each other. Yeah, maybe it was good that she missed Dahji.

And she couldn't explain her joy when he called her. He had asked her to come over before she went to work; said he had something special for her. Really? She'd asked. But he wouldn't say anything more. Only that he'd been thinking about her during the day and was sorry that he couldn't get free in time to make their date. This meant a lot to her—that he would think of her and that he would apologize for standing her up. He usually kept his appointments, he'd assured her. No problem, she thought then. I'll stop by there and see what Mr. Man has for me as his apology.

He'd dimmed the lights and lit candles, complimented her on her Fifth Mart jeans and the way she wore her hair (feathered to frame her shining face), and led her to the glass dining table. There was a dinner of pork chops, cream corn, mashed potatoes, and garlic bread. It was very thoughtful of him to think of her while at his mother's house. And even more cute that he admitted to not cooking the food himself. She wasn't mad at him for reheating it. What he did was a nice gesture. Luther Vandross play low throughout the plush pad as they conversed lightly about their day. It was a real date after all, Peaches thought to herself then.

And the pork chops were good. Secretly, she made a plan to meet his mother. Of course, that would mean that by that time they would, in fact, be girlfriend and boyfriend. She'd smiled over her plate then. He'd asked what for and she replied that she was just happy. Truly, she was. Like a little girl with her very first crush. Happy that he'd given as much thought to Sherrelle and her HoodSweet apparel as she had, happy that he respected her business sense and didn't question who the Korean man was who promised to give her a good deal on manufacturing, happy that Dahji thought enough of her to include her in the bottom line of the operation. He'd planned to set up the website and make her the spokesmodel. You and Sherrelle together will carve the heart out of the rest of these fake bitches, he'd assured her. Yeah, she was happy about this.

Then there was the bubble bath. It was scented with oils. He'd scrubbed her down with an oatmeal sponge. He spoke about his father and how their relationship was frac-

tured because of his lifestyle. Peaches thought better than to
question him about the particulars because she was, after
all, an exotic dancer, and hadn't spoken to her own parents
since leaving Baltimore after high school. And Dahji never
seemed to mind this. Though she did sense that he was
slowly positioning her so that she wouldn't have to strip any
longer. She recognized the man-in-control in him. It came
naturally to him and she felt protected in his company.
He'd rubbed her along her long legs with the sponge and
made no sexual innuendos. This was all about her and not
about sex. She didn't know how to feel about this. She was
horny at his touch, yet she appreciated the gesture of him
simply serving her for the night.

By the time he'd taken her out of the tub and laid her
on the bed to rub her down with massage oil, she was thor-
oughly relaxed and wanted very badly to feel him inside of
her. But she was patient, allowing him to first massage her
back. He made small talk about seeing a video on pandas in
the wild. He could come up with the most obscure observations about nature and apply them to life. A baby panda
was sometimes discarded by the mother if there was something odd about it. Peaches had looked over her shoulder to
ask what sort of oddness he was talking about. Retardation?
Down syndrome? She didn't believe that pandas could be
retarded. They laughed at this. He rubbed the oil along the
back of her legs, massaging the soft muscle at the back of
her knees and making her laugh. He told her a joke about a
man who used to come home from work and sex his wife
without showering or foreplay. Dahji was at her ankles
then, rubbing her small heels between his fingers and
pulling on her toes. The man's wife complained and asked
that he be more smooth, show some finesse.

Dahji rubbed back up her legs and made circles on her

ass, parting the firm mounds of muscle with his thumbs. He blew along the crease of her ass. Peaches closed her eyes and moaned into the satin covered pillow. So the next day the man came home and showered and put some good-smelling cologne on. He asked his wife if he was doing a good job, if he was showing some finesse and being tactful. She said yes to all of this. Peaches was smiling as his hands rubbed along the sides of her body, his fingers brushing against the softness of her breasts. Then the man asked his wife if she would please pass the pussy.

Peaches was still laughing, asking where he'd heard that joke when he raised one of her legs, bending it at the knee so that her calf was perpendicular to her body. The smooth silk of his pajama bottoms rubbed against her as he positioned himself over her back. This was what she had been waiting for. Her pussy had been throbbing from the outset; his dick occasionally brushing up against her during the massage. "I forgot where I heard it," he whispered as the head of his dick slowly eased through the lips of her waiting pussy. At this angle, her ass was turned up slightly and she could feel him rub against her g-spot. He grabbed her bent knee and opened her up a little more. He eased in a bit more and stopped with his head poking just inside of her, feeling her warmth.

"You mind if I just stay like this?" Dahji asked, feeling her pussy pulse around his still joint.

"Unnhh unhh," she moaned, her cheek lying on the pillow. She had mixed emotions. He was in her but was not moving. There were slight adjustments and the hot pulsing that sent waves of heat through her, but there was not the stroking and grinding she'd expected. This was something new and different. And it felt good. Like lovemaking.

"What are you looking for?" he asked, making the head

of his dick pulse against her walls.

Peaches wanted him to at least stroke her one good time. "In what?"

"In a man."

He was what she was looking for. "Somebody that treats me nice," she answered, moving her hips so that he inched a little further inside of her.

Dahji resisted, backing up just a little, filling her with the short, hot, knob of meat. "That's what everybody wants," he said, feeling her pussy breathe and grip him. He inhaled deeply to control himself.

"Ummm," Peaches mumbled and then wished that she had not. She raised her hips so that his dick edged into her. She smiled when he tried to stop the movement. Then they rested. The weight of him lay inside of her temptingly. "Respect," she answered, feeling her center grow hot and concentrate to a fine point.

"Who's car is that you drive?" he wanted to know.

Peaches didn't hesitate. "He's sort of like my boyfriend in jail," she replied.

Dahji slowly slid inside of her, feeling her body shift under him. Her ass pushed against his stomach to help guide him. Left and then right he scraped against her walls and then settled halfway out of her, his head throbbing in place. "Sorta?" he whispered against her ear.

"It's complicated," she moaned, her pussy dripping with cream, making her even slicker.

Dahji filled her again and then slid out of her until only his head remained. Slowly he shoved his dick inside her again, arching his back so that he went up at an angle. She groaned under him as he stopped with his nut sacks nearly reaching her pussy. "You like complicated?" he asked, slowly easing out of her so that she had to wait to answer.

"Nooo," she sighed finally.

"I can't tell," he said, filling her up again with a slow stroke. She was hot and wet. He fit snugly as he slid out of her in a smooth grinding motion and then changed his angle slightly to fill her up again. She moaned under him, gripping the edges of the pillow. Her face was screwed up tight as she took his thick dick bravely.

"Please," she moaned, raising her hips to influence his stroke.

He turned her over and raised her leg to the air and held it across his shoulder as he rose to his knees. He watched as his meaty dick went into her sideways. Her mouth fell open with silent moans. Now he was putting his back into it, dropping into her with measured force. Her pussy was tight around him, glistening with her juices. Her breasts jumped and shifted with each downward thrust. Her body shook as his swinging nuts slammed into her, making a wet, clapping sound.

Then she was on her stomach again, shoulders on the bed and ass in the air. She buried her face in the pillow as he piloted his dick inside of her pussy. He long-stroked her, smacking into her pussy so her ass cheeks turned red. He gripped her firm hips like handle bars and slid in and out of her, her muffled moans and groans in the pillow encouraging him. She raised up from the pillow letting an exhausted gasp escape.

Peaches wanted to switch positions but was determined not to give in to his pounding. He wouldn't have that to say about her—that she couldn't handle the dick. She fell into a rhythm with his strokes, tightening her pussy as he pulled out. She could feel the effect this was having on him. His hands gripped her tighter every time she gripped him with the walls of her pussy. Now she was enjoying the tension it created. She felt him swell and shudder, his grip tightening and then loosening before he collapsed beside her on the bed.

Peaches rubbed his bare back, shiny and warm from sex. She was proud of herself. She had taken the dick and made him collapse. He breathed heavily beside her. She still had not answered his question about whether complicated was what she was looking for. She admitted to herself that it was not what she wanted. She made up her mind to tell this to Tequan. She would drop his car off at his mother's house. She would call off her complicated relationship. Not that Dahji had made any promises, but she knew she needed to close one door so another one could open. There was a stab of pain at the thought that she would wake up in the morning and smuggle drugs to him. This would be the last time, she was thinking to herself as Dahji rose from the bed. His heavy dick swung outside of his silk pajama bottoms like a meaty pendulum. She wanted to taste it but he reminded her that she would be late for work.

★ ★ ★

Peaches woke up the next morning still sore from Dahji's lovemaking. She had been late for work. She couldn't resist him. She squirmed under the covers remembering how she'd tasted on his dick. She'd caught him about to take a piss and hurriedly stopped him in the bathroom and knelt before him. She'd taken him into her mouth, tasting with relish the mixture of their bodies on his meat like a specially seasoned dish.

She dressed in a pair of jeans, then remembered she couldn't wear jeans into the prison. She decided on a pink, Nike, nylon jogging suit. Though it was baggy it did nothing to conceal her curves. Then she remembered that she had to pull drugs from her pussy. She stood in front of the mirror for a long time, thinking about if she should do what she said she would do. She didn't need Tequan's money. She didn't need him to make her financially stable. But she reasoned that maybe he would not be upset with what she had to tell him if he had something in his hands as a parting gift. But she didn't want to wear a skirt. *I'll just put it in my socks*, she thought to herself, thinking that she would deny a search if they asked to do one. They might not let her come back to the prison, but she had no intentions of coming back anyway.

The drive to the prison was two hours, down long stretches of highway, past cows and old barns. She played two new CDs (Mary J. Blige and India Arie) that marked the time. The prison loomed in the distance with its barbed wire and tall gates and gun towers. The women waiting in line all looked the same—fatigued from the long drive and bored with the process.

Peaches was reading a newspaper—the headlines spoke about prison overcrowding—when a female officer approached her. She was seated on a bench inside of a small room. She'd already gone through processing and had her hand stamped with an invisible sign to claim her arrival. She was waiting on the shuttle bus that would take her—along with twenty other visitors, mostly women and small children—up the long hill to the main visiting room.

"Excuse me. Ms. Helen Adebenro?" the blonde lady in the starched prison guard uniform asked.

Peaches looked up, her heart leaping inside of her tracksuit. "Yes?" she answered like a question.

"Would you please come with me," the hard-eyed lady said. Her smile was meant to say please. Peaches was trying to figure out how a lady with blonde hair and blue eyes got a name like Rodriquez as she rose from her seat, her eyes on the black name tag attached to the guard's flat chest. It was surrounded by little gold handcuffs and a gold American flag. Her badge glistened gold and shiny, making her look bigger than she actually was.

Peaches was aware of the stares of the other visitors as they passed through the small room and out into the sun.

"Is there a problem?" Peaches asked, looking to the guard with what she hoped was an innocent expression, though her heart was pounding in her chest.

"No, not at all. Please step this way," officer Rodriguez instructed, moving in the direction of a door Peaches hadn't noticed until that very moment. She followed her.

There was nothing in the tan-walled room. She faced a giant mirror along the far wall, her reflection staring back at her. A table was in the middle of the floor.

"We've selected you for a random search," the officer said. The door closed with a hiss, blocking out the sun. There was a green, metal door on the other side of the room. Peaches suspected that it led to some offices.

"I decline a search," she answered, casting her magic key into the dark lake. But nothing happened. The officer just smiled. They stood in front of the table. Somewhere there was a fan humming. Peaches was afraid to look up, her mouth was suddenly dry.

"Not a search, a simple pat-down. We're allowed to pat down visitors without notice. It's on the notice board at the front of the prison." She said this with the ease and elegance of a predator cornering its prey.

Peaches could feel the air leaving her body. Her face was cold from the blood leaving. She was thankful that the guard didn't remark on her suddenly changed appearance. She simply motioned for Peaches to lay her Fendi purse on the table and spread her arms. *Not a search?* Peaches asked herself, the woman's talloned hands roughly sliding across her arms and down her body. She dug her fingers along the ridge of her bra. At this, Peaches realized that a proper search would allow the guard to reach under her bra and into her panties and down along her hips. She was feeling for something hidden beneath the clothing. Peaches wanted to run but there was nowhere to go. She'd followed this woman into this bare room, and now the woman was running her hands down her legs and stopping at the bulge in her sock. A weird relief washed over Peaches. When the guard stood—drugs in hand and a clipped smile on her chalky face—Peaches was thinking of who she would call to bail her out of jail.

Part Three

Chapter Eighteen

Dahji

Dahji lay in bed, the morning sun stretching warmly across his chest. It streamed in through sheer, dull red curtains that hung over a high window. The silk sheets were soft under and over him, still holding Peaches' aroma in their soft folds, along with the scent of the massage oil and sex. His dick hung heavy between his legs, getting much-needed rest. His mind worked over Peaches' situation. She was the type of woman he could spend quality time with, but her boyfriend in jail gave him pause. She was loyal, no doubt about that. It also said something about her that she had decided to end it. He wanted to say that she should give it some thought, but he had to admit—while he hated to deprive a brother of his broad—that he wanted her for himself. *Charge it to the pimp game*, he thought to himself.

And then there was the matter of his daughter. He'd always known Aryn was his. It angered him even now, even though his mom told him to forgive, that Coretta would deny him the privilege of a daughter, just to keep her bogus marriage intact. True, he had been married and so had she, but that shit shouldn't have gone down like that. Dahji was game to the fact that she may have felt slighted because she was his No. 2 female. Still, a child changed everything.

Shit was about to get real beautiful. He could feel it. If Marlin made the Colts football team, then it was over for this hard grind. Dahji grunted with this thought. He could taste success and would do anything to make it happen. He couldn't believe his luck meeting Marlin at the Sports Medicine Clinic. He said it then and would continue to say it: There's a reason they met each other. And it was showing itself now.

And the clothing business with Sherrelle was just icing on the cake. This was going to take his side hustle to a new level. He swung his legs over the side of the bed triumphantly, ready to see what the day would bring, how the pimp god was going to bless him for keeping it way too real. Before he could get to the bathroom, the phone rang. He picked it up on the way.

"What it do?" he answered as he pulled his dick through the opening of his silk pajama bottoms.

Gloria chuckled wickedly. "So you're fucking women unconscious now?" she asked with shock. Dahji knew she was going to make this a running joke between them. "Are you peeing?" she wanted to know, recognizing the sound of his piss hitting the water.

Dahji squeezed down the length of his dick, squirting quick bursts into the toilet.

"That is so rude," Gloria complained.

"You scared of rude," Dahji commented, flushing the toilet.

"No. Just careful, that's all. I'm happily married. Once was enough for me." She spoke of their one-time sexual meeting. He'd sweated out her perm in his effort to give her what her middle-aged coach of a husband couldn't or was too busy to give her. "Well, I must compliment you. Tom and Edith were very satisfied," she said.

"Yeah. That was kind of weird." He was in the kitchen, pouring two vials of ginseng into a glass of cranberry juice. He ripped open a vitamin pack that held no less than ten pills, bright gels and dull solids.

"Well, whatever you did to make an impression on them, it worked. Edith wants to see you again."

"I don't think so," Dahji responded.

Gloria lowered her voice as if they were in a crowded room. "She wants to see you alone. Away from her husband and the house. She's prepared to compensate you very well," she assured him.

"That's bad business. What are you, a pimp now?" Dahji asked, forcing the tart vitamins down his throat.

"Well, excuse me for trying to help."

"You can help me by convincing your husband to get my man on the team." That was better. He felt his energy rising already as he refilled his glass with cranberry juice.

"About that," she began. "Your man, as you say, he's on the practice squad."

"The practice squad?" Dahji shouted, nearly choking, his face frowning up in confusion. He wasn't about to tell Marlin that he'd made the practice squad. "He's a running back. Your husband knows this. You trying to hustle me, Gloria?"

"No, sweetheart," she answered calmly. "You want him on the team yesterday. I'm not the coach. I can't make the decisions. But I can motivate my husband in some ways," she said sweetly, as if Dahji could envision how this motivation might occur. "Now, we have discussed an early addition to the special teams."

"What?"

"Hold on, now. This would get him past the first cut. I can give you what you want. You want Marlin Cassidy to play behind the starting running back, sharing the load, right?"

"Right."

"Well that's what I want. And I want it for you," she assured him. Dahji had not moved from the kitchen counter. He looked across the living room and out to the city outside his floor-to-ceiling window. He felt it coming. She wouldn't make it as simple as fucking a white broad unconscious to get his man on the team. She was hustling him and he couldn't be mad at her.

"So what is it going to take to get him to where you and I want him to be?" he asked, feeling her smile through the phone.

"Well, there's one more favor I need from you," she announced. He knew that it wasn't going to be simple. He was silent, having already made up his mind that he would do whatever it took to be a real live sports agent.

"What is it? And don't think you won't owe me for this," he said.

"She's a friend of mine. She's married."

"What she need me for?" he asked, already knowing the answer, yet hoping it wasn't anything too weird. He still shuddered when he thought of the white woman who'd wanted him to shit on her stomach.

"She's just...well...her husband doesn't...he can't satisfy her."

"Come on, Gloria. Keep it real."

"She's a little overweight," she confessed.

"Is she white?" he asked. The only thing worse than a fat black woman was a fat white woman.

"She's my friend and she's African."

"What, you mean, like, from Africa?" he asked.

"Yes. She's from Ghana. Her husband owns an import-export company. Will you meet with her?" She sounded like he really had a choice.

"My man is sharing the load for the starting position, right?"

"Sharing the load," Gloria repeated.

"Set it up for tomorrow night."

"That's perfect. Thank you, Dahji! You don't know how much this means to me."

"Marlin Cassidy. Running back. That's how much this means to you."

"Don't worry, sweetheart. He's on the team," Gloria assured him.

"In that case, your friend is as good as served. Hit me back later on."

"Will do, sweetie. I love you so much." This was said with sincere appreciation. Her friend must have been complaining about her lack of sexual healing.

A little overweight, Dahji thought to himself with a chuckle, envisioning a jet-black woman with a flat nose and a wide ass while he dropped two strawberry Pop-Tarts into the toaster. He'd spun around to grab the butter from the refrigerator when the phone rang again. Briefly, he thought it might be his mother calling to make sure he was coming to church.

"Mr. Dahji McBeth," the gruff voice of the lobby desk guard began. "You have a visitor by the name of Coretta Haltom."

Dahji was shaking his head with the realization that his mother must have given her his address. She must have taken his excitement at spending time with his daughter and eating dinner with them as a sign that it meant more than it did.

"Send her up," he said, a small thrill going through him with the memory of yesterday's dinner at his parents' house. They'd shared easy laughter. It was so easy to communicate with and be around her. Yet so much had changed and come between them. Dahji stood with his hands on the kitchen counter, waiting to see which bell would sound first—the door or the toaster—all the while aware of the morning hour and wondering what Coretta was doing coming by his place. He had given her no indication—at least he didn't think he had—that they would get together in a real way. He was amped about being in his daughter's life but hadn't entertained the thought of rekindling any type of relationship with her.

The toaster bell rang first. The Pop-Tarts lay hot on a napkin in front of him when the doorbell rang. She was dressed in a short, flower-print, sheer, cotton skirt and strappy leather sandals. Her cocoa-brown skin glittered with diamond appointments gracefully ringing her limbs and earlobes. Small, bronze lips smiled her surprise; long, black hair feathered to her shoulders. Her breasts strained against the sheer cotton of her matching, flower-print tube top.

"Hey, you," she greeted him casually, standing in the doorway with a surprised gleam in her eyes. "Your mom was nice enough to give me your address. Hope you don't get mad at her," she said, cocking her head slightly to observe his expression.

"You didn't bring Aryn?" Dahji asked, moving so she could pass by him into the foyer.

Coretta sauntered into the luxury apartment, dropping her soft leather purse onto the suede sofa. She nodded her head in approval and turned to watch him cross to the kitchen where he concentrated on slathering jelly onto his Pop-Tarts.

"This is nice. You're really doing good for yourself," she said, following him. She climbed onto a high bar stool, watching him.

Not until Dahji had taken a bite of the crisp pastry did he look up at her. He chewed and observed her in his environment. She wanted to be fucked, he realized. It was in her every move—the way her gold, hoop earrings danced against her brown cheeks; the way her French-tipped nails tapped against the black marble of his countertop. He took two more small bites, maintaining eye contact with her soft browns that smiled back mischievously. He held the half eaten Pop-Tart out to her silently.

"No, thank you. We had breakfast already."

Dahji shrugged before taking another bite, nearly finishing the pastry.

"Where's Aryn?"

"She's with your parents. I'm here to take you to church. Your mother sent me." The last part was an explanation, so as to defer the blame for her showing up unexpectedly. Dahji was sure she had agreed with passive enthusiasm when his mother suggested it.

"What time service start anyway?" he asked, biting lazily into the second Pop-Tart. Out of view, his dick stirred against the smooth silk of his pajamas. Her diamond, heart pendant lay cradled at an odd angle between her sugary breasts.

"Ten," she replied, turning her wrist so the diamond face of her Lady Rolex showed. "You better get dressed or we'll be late."

Suddenly Dahji was curious. "What your husband go to

jail for?"

A cloud passed over her face. "He was selling drugs," she answered simply, her eyes not moving from his.

"And let me guess—you had no clue," Dahji said suspiciously.

"Not a clue," she replied.

Dahji pointed to her watch and then moved his finger around to point out her gold and diamonds. "And all this you thought what about?"

"That's what was so crazy. He had a good job working for the bank. He didn't have to do what he was doing."

"And all this time you thought he was a square." Dahji was smiling.

"It"s really not funny."

"The hell it ain't funny. You played that nigga all the way to jail. I know you,' he said, pointing his finger at her as he rounded the counter. "You made him think he had to do it to keep you. The same way you told him Aryn was his to keep him." He was standing at the edge of the counter, ignoring the way her ass hung off the stool.

She stared at him for two beats before she blinked. "You right. But he made that choice."

"And he can't be mad at you for shaking him like a raggedy car and—Do he know Aryn not his?" he asked suddenly.

"Yes, I told him."

"You went to see him?"

"No. Over the phone," she answered.

Dahji was shaking his head. "That nigga gon' kill you," he hissed with narrowed eyes.

This is when the ghetto in her surfaced. "Nigga, please. He got a hundred years," she said, waving her pretty hand in the air. "He was out of his league anyway." Now she looked at Dahji with meaning.

"So, what you want now? How you see this playing out?" he asked, knowing that she must have a plan. She raised her eyebrows quickly and let out a slow whistle. She was satisfied with herself. "Well, first, we gotta get to church before your mother has a fit." Then she laughed. It was the soft timber that he'd loved all those years ago. He was smiling before he realized that his face was spread.

"I gotta shower and get dressed," Dahji said, moving toward the stairs.

"Take your time," she called after him.

"Stay outta my cabinets," he responded from the rail of the loft. She waved up to him with a careless grin.

She was crazy, Dahji said to himself as he lathered with scented body wash Peaches left in the shower. She was slowly leaving little items to mark her territory. He'd noticed them here and there: a silk scarf left on the couch, a pair of diamond earrings on the bathroom counter, a pink watch on the nightstand, and then this morning he'd noticed a small bag of toiletries by the closet. She was easing into his space with measured steps. And he wasn't mad. Not mad at all. *She's a boss bitch*, he thought to himself.

When Dahji stepped from the shower and into the loft in his cotton robe, he was both surprised and amused. Coretta was under blue satin sheets. The red silk sheets had been thrown on top of the wicker laundry basket by the closet. She'd changed the linen and had a wicked grin on her lips.

"You had a woman over here last night," she said, her nose wrinkled from the scent of the previous night's sex and massage.

Dahji nodded slowly, his dick already rising with the confirmation that she indeed wanted to be fucked. She was bold and he'd always liked this about her. *This is what had that nigga selling dope*, he thought to himself as he dropped the robe from his shoulders. Coretta smiled wide at the sight of his rising joint. It pointed the way to her pussy.

Dahji pulled the blue satin sheet to the side, revealing her nakedness; thick thighs leading to a hairy pussy. Her small waist was hidden by her thighs as they rose into the air, tiny feet dangling above her head. She was ready for him and knew that he could not deny the invitation.

Dahji knelt onto the bed and scooted up the mattress, his heavy dick bobbing in the air stiffly, leading the way. Coretta held her ankles as he neared, spreading wide for him. The head of his dick sank into her with a sucking sound. Her eyes rolled into the back of her head as she received him. She spread her legs wider, allowing him deeper inside. He braced himself on the mattress, his chin near her mouth, as he eased into her wetness. She was open and wide under him. He bent to kiss her, tasting her tongue and its warmth. She opened further, allowing the bulk of him inside of her as her breathing grew harsh and soft moans escaped her lips. Her ankles rocked beside his head as he slid in and out of her.

"Ohhh, baby," she moaned, her French-tipped nails scratching across his arching back. She reached down and grabbed his ass cheeks, encouraging him further into her.

He grunted as her pussy unfolded itself with a hot breath. He sank into her depths as she moaned into his ear. She was taking the dick with pleasure; it was something she'd been waiting on. She creamed over him silently. He could see the whiteness of it as he looked down the length of himself as he disappeared inside of her.

She was wet like a river, allowing him deeper, her moans growing louder. This encouraged him and his stomach grew tight with the effort. She pulled him into her hot body and held him in place while he ground into her snugly. The tension of hitting her bottom tingled and swelled his head. She rotated her hips under him for added sensation. He pounded into her at varying angles, sinking deep as her hardened nipples smashed against his chest.

"Ohhhhh, baaybeee!" she shrieked, scratching him across his back, her eyes shut tight and her legs rocking beside his head with his pounding. They swayed together in a smooth rhythm as he went in and out faster, chasing an elusive early-morning orgasm.

He rose up and grabbed hold of her ankles, spreading her legs wide. She was all pussy as he dipped into her with precision. She reached back and grabbed the edge of the low bed to brace herself. She pushed back every time he pushed through her wet wall. His thick meat was shiny and pulsing as he stroked. Her stomach was wet with a light sheen. Her breasts bounced hypnotically with each thrust, followed by an open-mouthed moan.

She creamed onto his thick shaft in smooth waves of milky pleasure. His tip grew hot as the center of him jabbed into her. She grabbed hold of him tightly as he released into her. Her mouth searched his hungrily as she rubbed and soothed his smooth back.

"That's right, baby," Coretta whispered into his ear. The ring of the phone made her jump, interrupting their moment of tenderness. Dahji reached across the bed. The caller I.D. read that the caller could not be identified.

"Hello," he answered. He expected a voiced reply but got a mechanical prompt that clued him in that the person calling was in a correctional facility.

"It's Peaches," came the familiar voice. There was shame and panic in it.

The recording asked him to press five to accept the charges. He pressed five, his heart beating hard inside of his chest.

"Peaches?" he said into the phone. "What happened? Where you at?" he asked, rolling from Coretta, his dick meeting the cool air outside of her warm pussy.

"Hi, Dahji. I am so sorry to be calling you like this. There was no one else I could..."

"Don't trip on that. What you need?"

"I need you to bail me out. They arrested me for drug smuggling!" Her voice relayed the shame she felt.

"Don't trip. You'll be out before dinner. Hold tight. Don't worry."

"Okay," she breathed out. "Thank you. My bail is..."

"Just give me your name and I'll find out the rest and be there to get you."

"Helen Adebenro. A-d-e-b-e-n-r-o."

"Got it. Be at you in a minute," he assured her before hanging up.

"Is everything alright?" Coretta asked with worry.

"Yeah." Dahji hopped up from the bed with the phone in his hand. He reached for his phonebook in the dresser. "I gotta handle something right now. I ain't gon' be able to go to church. You can take a shower if you want to." He absently gestured toward the bathroom while he flipped through the small pages of his phonebook.

Chapter Nineteen

Sherrelle

There was a lightness flowing through her body. She could feel her essence like a ripe fruit ready to fall from a high tree—soft yet firm to the touch, sweet and tasty on the tongue. The seed within the thick pulp heavily ridged and weighted with unyielding potential. That's what she felt like—an unyielding seed full with sweet potential. All she needed was the proper rich soil in which to plant her womanhood. And she knew where to find this earth that was so powerful, that so wanted a full seed. She would love to be planted in this soil. There was an open sky before her with this firm earth wrapping her in its warmth and nurturing her glorious growth.

Sherrelle stretched naked under the thin cotton sheet. It was getting hot. She slept naked and this was the excuse she used on her husband. He could not know that throughout the night she had thought of Marlin and rubbed herself. She'd awakened Percy in the middle of the night with her moaning and rubbing of her clit with her hands as they lay wedged between her thighs. She'd been dreaming deeply about a sexual encounter that didn't involve her husband. She wondered briefly if what she was doing was cheating. Briefly. Percy complained and rolled over to return to sleep. This was the excuse she used for her anger, wanting to return to her dream of infidelity. It felt better than real-life sex with her husband.

Yes. Her essence called to her while her husband was in the shower. She considered laying in bed until he left for work, but there was an urge that pulled at her. She smiled to herself and threw the sheet over her head, giggling like a little girl with a private memory. He was everything she could hope for and she was sure he felt the same way about her. He knew that she peeked through his window, knew that she saw him having sex with his wife. Her essence was ripe. The soft undersides of her breasts, round part of her hips, tender inner thighs, backs of her ankles, swollen nipples, soft shoulders, smooth neck, full lips, puffy cheeks—all felt on fire. Her body tingled with the thought of her next door neighbor. Last night, sitting in the booth with him at Applebottoms was like a surprise date. She wanted to see him again. Now.

Sherrelle threw the sheet from her excitedly. It was a nasty little game. She wondered if he was still in bed. Would he wait until she appeared at his window to watch? Slipping on a pair of HoodSweet boy shorts that hugged her tightly, she listened for Percy's progress in the shower. Her breasts stretched the sheer, ribbed cotton of the wifebeater, nipples fat and wanting attention. The shower stopped just as she walked from the room.

At the bottom of the kitchen trash bag there was an empty cup of yogurt. This was enough to take outside and dump in the larger can. A perfect opportunity to satisfy her urges. The brightness of the day at first caused her to

squint. It was going to be a beautiful day. She stepped down
the three stairs in wool slippers and crouched down against
the side of her house. Her heart was beating wildly, just like
it was the first time she ventured this way. She was almost
to his bedroom window. She gripped the excuse of the
trash bag tightly, crouching low in her voyeuristic pursuit.
    There he was. And his wife was between his legs on her
knees. She was naked, wet, fresh from the shower, her cotton robe at her feet. A familiar routine. Sherrelle wondered
if he liked getting head from his wife. His face was screwed
up and he jumped in anticipation of some pain. He braced
himself against the edge of the bed, his legs spread apart.
His wife slid her head sloppily up and down his dick. She
gripped his muscled thighs and made a bold move to twist
her mouth over his dick. Marlin jerked his eyes open and
inhaled sharply, his body tensing. His wife looked up at him
in apology before bending over him again carefully. She
sucked on him slowly, careful not to try any new tricks. He
looked bored.
    Sherrelle smiled and quickly looked out to the street
and behind her, as if she were sure she'd be caught. "She
can't suck dick," she whispered to herself happily. Marlin
pulled her onto the bed and stood up behind her. Sherrelle
unconsciously swallowed dryly and licked her lips at the
sight of his thick dick hanging in front of him as he positioned it to slide into his wife's pussy. His hands were on
her hips, and Sherrelle could feel her own hips burning and
her pussy twitching.
    "Sherrelle," Percy called above from somewhere in the
house. She looked up instinctively, picturing Percy at the
kitchen archway. She quick-stepped along the side of the
house, sure that he was on his way to the back door. She
rounded the corner just as he stepped onto the porch, the

white plastic bag at her side barely weighted with the single empty cup of yogurt. She saw herself in his expression as he stood above her on the porch. She was dressed like a hooker in the early morning, wide-eyed and carrying an excuse for trash.

"What are you doing?" Percy asked, his forehead frowned up in confusion. Sherrelle had already begun thinking of her answer when she stepped away from Marlin's first thrust into his wife. The way her small body vibrated was in her mind. While she thought about what she would say to her husband, she thought about how her body would react to Marlin's lovemaking.

"I was going to get the dead petals off my roses," she answered, looking back at the healthy rosebushes lining the space between the houses.

"Dressed like that?" he asked, pointing at her wildly to bring attention to her warm body. He saw how ripe she was, the way her pussy was creased and bulged in the tight pink boy shorts. Her nipples must have seemed about to explode. Her hair must have been shining under the sun with its long, loose curls caressing her warm shoulders. His small eyes scanned her and he decided in his anger that he would not be taken in by her obvious sex appeal. He turned from her, his fingers gripping the phone he held at his side, a pair of leather gloves peeking from the back pocket of his slacks. He was dressed for golf. She wondered what Marlin would be doing on this Sunday.

Sherrelle followed him into the house, returning the near-empty plastic bag to the bin by the back door. "You want breakfast before you leave?" she asked before he could step away from the kitchen. He turned to her then. There was something new in his small, hazel eyes. They were partly curious but still held something like anger. But this was hard to manage in such a small frame. The way his stomach was now falling over his belt was funny and a shame. No, he could not let anger be his master. It would only cause frustration and whining.

"Who you know in jail?" he wanted to know.

Sherrelle shrugged, not ready to move the image of Marlin's dick from her mind, and already knowing that Percy didn't want breakfast. "My cousin Darryl is locked up, but he calls my mother." She looked out the kitchen window as if in thought, her nail pressed against her bottom lip. She was mentally preserving the size of Marlin's dick, she would need this soon. "He doesn't have this number," she replied, turning back to him.

Percy held up the phone like it was evidence. "Somebody from jail called here."

It was obvious that he hadn't accepted the call. Sherrelle just figured it must have been a wrong number because she knew of no one who would be calling her from jail.

Something else had occurred to Percy. Now that he had denied her sex appeal, he was free to criticize it. "And what did I tell you about going outside dressed like that?" He used the phone to illustrate his point, moving it up and down her body like a metal detector. She resisted the urge to laugh out loud.

"What's wrong with it?" she asked innocently, now looking down over her body and enjoying the sight of her soft brown thighs. The back of her knees tingled.

Percy's whole face showed his anger, twisting and turning until it settled back on her plainly. "You're dressing like a ghetto hoodrat, going out to these strip clubs with that Peaches girl! You call yourself selling clothes. You might have better luck selling it to prostitutes!" He was trying to cut deep into her, attack her dreams of freedom. Freedom from his inadequacy. She held his gaze, not at all thinking about what he was saying. She wasn't going to respond. Instead she would make him feel like he did what he'd intended to do—hurt her.

"So there it is," she whispered, brushing past him and hoping she was successful in looking like she was about to cry. She'd been holding the image of Marlin in her mind and had decided it was time to be alone just when her husband meant to insult her. She felt him turn to her, perhaps wanting to apologize, but she was already slamming the bedroom door. She grabbed her black medical bag from under the bed and stomped into the bathroom with a small grin on her lips. "You don't have a clue," she whispered to herself as she turned the taps on in the bathtub.

Water rushed into the porcelain basin as she reached inside the black bag for the biggest, blackest dildo she had. There was an attachment that went with it, specially designed to work under water. This she stuck to the bottom of the tub. It was a base that held the dildo straight up.

She heard the bedroom door open, then Percy was on the other side of the bathroom door. He called her name once and when she did not answer, (instead she threw another handful of scented oil beads in the water) he halted his attempt at reconciliation.

Sherrelle stood up from the tub and looked at herself in the full-length mirror behind the door. Her fingers pulled at her long, silky hair, making the curls bounce across her shoulders. Her big eyes with their long lashes stared at themselves in thought. *Yes, you are ripe, honey.* Maybe Percy knew this. Maybe they'd run their course together. Maybe they were no longer good for each other. Maybe he felt like he couldn't hold her in her new ripeness. Sure, he'd married her and promised to give her a good life, but that had been when she didn't know what a good life was. It wasn't driving a Jaguar and shopping all the time. It wasn't being quiet and denying her own needs and wants. A good life was being in love. And now that she'd met Marlin, she knew she wasn't in love.

With Percy, she had been in need. Sometimes, when a man comes along who can give you a good lifestyle, you want to make it love. You learn to love him, convince yourself that you're in love with him. But your heart was never in it. It never jumped and skipped at the sight of him.

She pulled the wifebeater over her head and tossed it to the floor. Her breasts stood firm and ripe. She caressed them gently, feeling their need to be tended to, to be pinched properly, nibbled properly, handled with care.

She turned to see what her ass looked like in the boy shorts. She was proud of their snug fit. She was ripe. There was not a bit of flab, fat, or excess skin on her toned waist, ass, and thighs. Her back was smooth and defined. She peeled the shorts from her body, bending over and looking in the mirror at the way her ass stayed closed and how her thighs fit perfectly together. Ripe.

The water was exactly how she wanted it: nearly too hot to get into but just cool enough to make her pause with each new wave of water coursing over her tingling skin. Once she was submerged to her breasts in the water, she leaned back and closed her eyes. She was in her own cherry-scented world, the oils washing over her in slick application. Between her legs, the currents rushed, licking her burning thighs and caressing her rounded hips. She recaptured the image of Marlin's thick joint as it hung suspended in the air before him. She grabbed the dildo from the rim of the tub and placed it between her legs under the water.

His stomach was flat. The muscles in his hips framed his manhood. The head was round and sloping. Sherrelle spread her legs for the dildo, her eyes closed with the image in her mind. He'd pressed into her, her body moving like a wave to absorb him. She pressed the dildo into her tight pussy, and sighed in pleasure, feeling her lips come apart. The way he gripped her hips was not, in any way, meant to be subtle. There was desire in his touch, but not for her it seemed. She pressed the dildo in further, letting it fill her with its thickness. Her knees were over the rim of the tub, she was lost in her fantasy.

She was before him, her ass in the air and her pussy waiting for the thick meat to press into her tight folds. He gripped her thighs firmly, the caress Sherrelle knew was meant for her. He wanted to be inside of her. She was tight for him, gripping him for his effort. The dildo moved inside of her, making small waves in the water. She could feel his hands on her, feel him inside of her. His scent was intoxicating. Her fingers gripped the dildo tightly, shoving it with meaning into her wet pussy.

She wanted to be on top of him. She put the dildo on the base she'd attached to the bottom of the tub. She held on to the rim of the tub as she squatted over it. She pressed down onto it, the water rising with her movement. He was waiting for her to slide over him. His hands were on her waist, guiding her down onto his thick dick. The dildo was waiting. She slid down onto him, feeling him ride straight up inside of her. Water splashed over the rim of the tub, wetting the tiled floor. Her eyes were closed in ecstasy, her lips parted with soft moans as she slid through the water onto the dildo. This is what he wanted—a real woman who could handle it. This is what she wanted—to ride him until she could feel him swell inside of her.

Water splashed violently with her motions. She concentrated hard on her mission. She gripped his thighs firmly and felt him tensing beneath her. She urged him on, splashing water as she pounded down onto him. She felt him release himself and moan hungrily. She cummed over him and tightened around him to squeeze out what was left.

Sherrelle breathed hard as her eyes opened slowly, still clouded with passion. There was very little water in the tub and the floor was soaked. She smiled with satisfaction, wondering if Marlin was thinking about her this morning. As she rose from the shallow basin, the dildo was not deflated. It stood straight up and warm, ready for more of her passionate sex.

Chapter Twenty

Marlin

A gift and a curse. That's what this was. It was a gift to be accepted into training camp and be on a football field again. The smell of the locker room, putting pads on—the real possibility that he would be playing again. Let Dahji tell it, he was already on the team, but no one who mattered had said anything to him.

The curse was two-a-days in the blistering heat under pads. His body ached from the contact. His thighs burned and his hamstrings felt like fire was literally moving through them. There was a constant pain shooting through his shoulder. Yet he welcomed the curse. It was all necessary, and he was relieved that he hadn't had to report to training camp. Coach had given them this Sunday to be with their families and attend church. Marlin was planning for his church to be a therapeutic massage and a soak in a Jacuzzi to ease his hurts.

He stretched under the comforter gently. His muscles stretched and popped with his movements. He was tight all over. He smiled with the memory of his dream. Seeing

Sherrelle the night before at Applebottoms had done something to him. His dream shot images through his mind— her straddling his lap, facing him, her body obscured by a sheer, white, silk negligee. Her breasts were so close to his face that he'd lost focus. The feeling that came with these images was peaceful and satisfying. Then there was the feeling of his hand rubbing along the softness of her thigh. Her toes were pretty, he remembered. There was an image of the sun behind her, her long, black hair fanned out. She looked like an angel coming through some arched doorway. It felt like he was in a church. He struggled to remember how these images went together. He wanted to remember his dream. Maybe since they spent so much time together the night before, there was no need for him to dream so clearly, he thought to himself as his dick twitched under the covers. The unfurling meat knocked against his thigh. There was still this, this commitment to hardness at the thought of her. Would she appear at his window? he asked himself as he reached to stroke the stiffening joint. It was all too much to handle. He groaned with the thought of actually having her in his arms.

His dick finished growing and was lying under his palm, trapped against his thigh. Stacy was singing a Mary J. Blige song in the bathroom. Her voice was clear now that she'd turned off the shower. He knew she would be stepping through the bedroom door soon and would look at him with a mixture of remorse, thinking she was neglecting his needs, and her own hunger if she saw him stroking himself. Never once did she consider that he was thinking of another woman. She'd come up with her own reason for his increased sexual desire: training camp.

Her smile was genuine and sensual. He stroked himself. Her skin was dark like chocolate. He stroked himself. Her eyes were like deep wells of seduction. He stroked himself. Her thighs were thick like molasses. He stroked himself. Her breasts bubbled like boiling brown sugar. He stroked himself. Her smile was like a sweet invitation. He stroked himself. Her lips were shaped like strawberry hearts. He stroked himself. Her hands were soft like cotton. He stroked himself. Her voice was a tender song. He stroked himself.

"Marlin...you are too much," Stacy said with a mixture of excitement and criticism, stopping him in mid-stroke and breaking him from his thoughts. He looked at her with hooded eyes as she walked over to the bed in her robe. She was wet from the shower, wisps of sandy brown hair stuck to her long neck. "Is it really training camp? Are you taking steroids?" she asked, looking from his eyes to the tent his dick made under the comforter.

"Just the regular vitamins," he answered, swinging his legs from under the covers and placing his feet on the carpet. This was their ritual. Though she couldn't suck dick, he allowed her to continue to try and get it right.

Stacy smiled at the thick erection shooting up in the air from his lap. "Shouldn't you be getting ready to go to the sports clinic for your massage?" she asked as she shed her cotton robe and knelt between his legs eagerly. Her copper skin shined with moisture and smelled of lilac. This was enough for Marlin. She was sexiest just from the water. The way her eyes glittered and her skin glowed continued to move him. Though their marriage had changed in its dynamics, there were still glimpses of their former attraction. She continued to give their marriage her best effort even though she had the feeling he was moving away from her in some fundamental way.

She opened her mouth wide over his swollen head, not

wanting to scrape her teeth along his tender skin. Her mouth was warm and she sucked on him slowly, enjoying the feeling of him inside of her mouth, rubbing across her tongue. Marlin watched as she concentrated on what she was doing. She was making a serious effort and getting better at it. He wondered if there was some school she could attend to learn how to suck dick in a professional manner. She was basic with the straight up and down—no suction and no magic tricks with her tongue. Maybe Dahji was right when he said that white girls gave the best head. But he did say that Peaches had changed his mind about that. This made him think of Sherrelle. Maybe Peaches had shared her secrets with her best friend. He closed his eyes thinking of Sherrelle. It was hard to imagine her lips around his dick because he was in constant fear of being scraped by Stacy's teeth. Then, as if on cue, she tried to rotate her head while sucking down and pinched the ridge around his head. He winced, his legs jerking.

"Sorry," Stacy whispered, looking up into his face.

Marlin was ready for her to go shopping and eager to get to his massage. He lifted her from his dick and positioned her on the bed on her hands and knees. Taking up position behind her, he guided his dick into her waiting pussy between narrow hips. He held her in place and sank into her slowly, then he came out of her, scraping her walls. Suddenly he thrust quickly into her, making her body shake. She sucked in air with his assault.

As he was about to glide inside of her again, he heard someone call Sherrelle's name. He looked toward the open window and saw a blur of chocolate, white cotton, and flowing hair dart from his line of sight. He smiled to himself. She'd been watching. This aroused him instantly, making his dick swell inside of his wife. He went at her with a hot passion—in and out, in and out, in left and out right, in right and out left, in down and out up, in up and out down. Her body moved with tight jolts upon his impact. He gripped her hips tightly, pulling her into him with each thrust. His toes dug into the carpet like eagle claws as he pounded into her. Ignoring her loud moans and hoarse grunting, he jammed into her with fierce urgency. He hit her bottom repeatedly, controlling her like a rag doll, lifting her knees from the mattress and shoving his dick into her in mid-air.

"Marlin! You...are...hurtiiiing..." she shrieked, her hands grabbing at the mattress for some leverage.

He ignored this in his blind passion. He smacked into her repeatedly, his thighs shining from her wetness. Her pussy lips would be raw and sore after this pounding. His whole body felt like firecrackers had been lit against his skin and popped over his muscles. His back arched, his arms flexed, and his fingers dug into Stacy's hips as he exploded into her with a final thrust. He held her to him as he jerked inside of her in quick spasms of ecstasy.

"Marlin," Stacy gasped, curling into a fetal position and looking at her husband with wonder and fright. He stood at the edge of the bed with his hands on his waist, breathing hard, dick hanging powerfully between his legs like a weapon equipped to do more damage. There was something in his eyes that she hadn't seen in the bedroom before. It was a look of dominance and passion that he usually reserved for the football field. It scared her. She wondered again if he was taking some type of performance-enhancing drug. She couldn't imagine that her next-door neighbor was responsible for this reaction in him.

"You okay?" Marlin asked, shaking himself from his

trance. He reached for her.

"I'm fine," she answered near anger as she scooted from the bed and disappeared into the bathroom.

Marlin followed, opening the door behind her. "You okay, baby?" he asked again, reaching out to her as she shed tears in front of the mirror.

She looked at him with tear-stained eyes. "You tried to hurt me. What was that about?" she asked, her face quivered with fright and confusion. She searched his face for some indication as to what was going on with him.

"We were making love," he answered plainly.

"No," she said quickly, raising a finger in the air. "That was not making love," she added, pointing past him to the bedroom. "That was something else entirely."

"I'm sorry, baby. What do you want me to do?"

"How about being considerate for once. I know things haven't been easy for you lately, but there's no need for you to take it out on me." She was reaching through the shower door to turn on the water.

"You're right, baby. I should be more considerate. Mind if I join you?" he asked with a smile.

She looked him up and down, stopping at the hanging joint between his legs before looking back to his eyes. "You'll keep that thing to yourself?" she asked, attempting to smile through the pain of disrespect.

"I'ma tie him up with a rope," Marlin responded with a wicked grin, following her into the shower.

He was tender with her this time, his soft touch an apology. Tender, wet kisses were what she wanted to feel, assuring her of his love for her. But Marlin still had his private plans. All he had to hear from the coaches was that he was going to be playing for the team, and he would be free to divorce her as he'd planned to before his injury.

When the phone rang, Marlin had a feeling it was Dahji before he answered.

"Marly Marl!" Dahji sang into the phone. "Man, you wouldn't believe how busy the man got me." Marlin could feel him smiling on the other end. He imagined him lying across the laps of a bed full of women. He doubted that 'the man' had him doing anything he wasn't profiting from.

"I doubt that, brother," Marlin replied, standing near the bed with a towel wrapped around his waist. Stacy looked at him through the bathroom mirror while she pulled on a pair of jeans that did nothing to hide her narrow hips. He mouthed Dahji's name to ease her curiosity.

"Marly Marl..." he sighed as if he'd just now felt his exertion. "If you only knew what I do for you."

Marlin's stomach turned, a flock of birds stabbing at his guts. "So what you saying?"

"What I'm saying, Marly Marl, is that I got an important meeting with some important folks to discuss your future."

Marlin was confused. "On Sunday?"

"Naw, naw, naw. Tomorrow, tomorrow. We getting close though. If I say there's cheese on the moon then you better grab a spoon," Dahji said around a wide smile.

"Awright, man," Marlin answered, remembering that it was he who got him onto the practice field in the first place.

"So how's training camp? I bin hearing good tales about you. Passed your medicals and running circles around the defense. That's good business!" he said excitedly.

Marlin stretched, watching Stacy walk to the closet, her small breasts standing up like figs. She searched through a row of brightly colored silk blouses. "I'm on my way to get a massage. You coming through?"

"Aww, Marly Marl!" he began in agony. "You wouldn't believe where I'm on my way to right now."

"Try me," Marlin said, quickly trying to imagine where the little man could be going at eleven on a Sunday morning.

"I bet you a cheeseburger and a pack of mustard you couldn't guess," Dahji tested. He sounded relaxed.

"Church," Marlin ventured.

Dahji chuckled loudly. He was driving, Marlin knew this for sure. But there were no sounds of traffic around him. Soft music played in the background. "You know, Marly Marl, if this certain situation had not come about, I would owe you a cheeseburger and a pack of mustard— which I would not take out of my commission, mind you— but as it stands, I am on my way to jail."

Marlin was still trying to picture the flamboyant man in church when he said he was on his way to jail. "What?" He shouted when he didn't mean to. For all of his doubt about Dahji, he realized he was truly afraid to lose him. He knew at that moment that he was far better off with him than without him. All of his dreams evaporated in an instant. Dahji was laughing on the other end. Stacy stopped to see what the sudden outburst was about on her way back to the bathroom to check her makeup. Marlin averted her questioning gaze, instead focusing on the shiny hardwood floor. His toenails needed to be clipped.

"Not me, Marly Marl," he said, his laughter turning into a wide smile. He appreciated Marlin's concern. "Our girl, Peaches, done got herself snatched up by the law folks."

"How?" Marlin could see the fine, cream-colored woman sitting in a cell with a mad expression marring her pretty face.

"Can't speak on it now. I'll clue you in at a later date. A player's work is never done, Marly Marl!" he sang like a superhero who loved putting out fires and rescuing women in distress.

"Awright. Give her my best. Holla back." This got Stacy's attention—the mention of a woman. She paused as she passed him to go from the bedroom into the hallway.

"Will do, Marly Marl. Will do," Dahji replied cheerfully, as if Peaches' arrest was only a minor setback, and that he would take care of everything. He spoke as if being associated with him was a privilege, like there was a benefit to being his friend. This occurred to Marlin with clarity. If there was no privilege, then there was no relationship. With this, he thought of Sherrelle. It was a privilege to see her smile.

"Is everything okay?" Stacy asked, coming back into the room with a banana in her hand. Marlin was caught up in a thought. He wondered if Sherrelle knew. Surely she would want to know. Did Peaches call her first or did she just call Dahji instead? He looked up at Stacy.

"Yeah. That was Dahji. He ain't gon' be able to meet me at the sports clinic." There was no need to share what happened to Peaches. In his wife, he saw insecurity. She would only judge Peaches. She would feel that she had it coming because of her obvious hood-chick appeal. Besides, it was none of her business.

"Any word on you making the team?" she asked after he'd stacked a wall between them. This question was meant to remind him of this.

Marlin was shaking his head, walking past her on his way to the closet. "Naw. Not yet. But it look good though." He slid on a pair of Colts football sweats. He didn't have to look at her to know that there was fear in her

eyes. There was a part of her that didn't want him to make
the team. Making the team would mean a return to his role
as provider and a return to his independence from her.
These selfish feelings competed with her love for him and
her wanting him to achieve his goals.

"Is there anything I can get for you while I'm out shopping?" she asked. This was her way of apologizing for her
selfish thoughts.

Marlin stopped at the door of the bathroom, a finger
pointed to the ceiling in thought. "A jock strap and mouth-
piece," he said. He could get these things at the sports clinic and really didn't need either of them, but the look on
Stacy's face said that he'd made the right move. She needed for him to give her something to do.

"Do you need more tape or wraps?" she asked.

"Naw. I'm cool on that," he replied shortly. That was
enough.

Marlin was late for his massage. Inga could be cruel if
she was made to wait for her clients. He changed into a pair
of workout shorts after realizing it was going to be a hot day.
He stepped out onto the porch with a duffel bag on his
shoulder. His heart leaped when he saw Sherrelle at her
mailbox. Her ass bulged inside of the blue shorts she was
wearing that stopped at the top of her firm thighs. She
turned when she heard his door close. There was a communication in her eyes that he was glad to see. He was
happy to see her too. Then she was bashful. Yeah, I know
you saw me this morning, he smiled back at her as he
stepped from the porch. They met in the middle of their
driveways.

"Hey, homeboy," she said, the mail held absently in her
hand. Marlin was struck by how effortlessly she maintained
her beauty. Her breasts made perfect, sensuous impressions

under the short-sleeved HoodSweet t-shirt.

"What's up? No boy shorts and wifebeater?" he asked, letting his eyes move over her body. She didn't need to expose herself to be beautiful.

Sherrelle shifted her weight to one hip and screwed up one side of her face. "I was afraid I wouldn't be respected that way. My husband doesn't like it either." She looked at him for his response, her lips curved like plump, sweet orange slices.

"Respect is different from insecurity," Marlin answered, watching with wonder as her face relaxed into a smile.

"So you're not the insecure type?"

Marlin shook his head before he answered. "By no means."

"That's good to know. Did you enjoy yourself last night with all those beautiful girls walking around showing their asses?" He wanted to reach across the slice of grass that separated them and grab her into his arms.

"It was cool," he replied absently. Such a beautiful day and her husband wasn't home. He thought it a crime that she should be left here and not taken out to enjoy life. He looked up toward her house. "Your husband leave you stranded?" he asked.

"Not hardly. He's playing golf."

"That's a shame."

"Where is your wife?"

"Shopping." They exchanged knowing glances. Both had this absence in common. "So you enjoy the show?" he asked, grinning wide.

Sherrelle laughed out loud. "I know you didn't." Her giggles were musical notes, moving her body to its symphony. "I'ma have to stop that, hunh?"

Marlin shrugged. "It's apparent that you got issues." He stepped back when it looked like she was going to cross their invisible boundary. "It's just a shame that I can't see you do what you do," he said, dimming his smile that prevented speech.

"You wouldn't be impressed," she answered coyly.

"I bet."

"You'd lose all your money, too." She was observing him now. Something had moved forward in their interaction. There was a bet on the table. "So you're on your way to practice?" she asked, backing away from the cliff of their intentions.

Marlin suddenly remembered his appointment. "And I'm late, too. I'm on my way to the sports clinic for a massage and whatnot."

"A massage, hunh?" There was an insinuation in her voice, a flirtation.

"It ain't even like that. Inga is, like, six-two and one-eighty, with fingers like steel."

"Damn. That sounds like it hurts," Sherrelle complained.

"A necessary pain," he replied, hoisting his duffel bag onto his shoulder in preparation to step away.

"Well, let me let you go then," she sighed, making a move toward her house.

Marlin thought to tell her about Peaches but decided to keep this moment to himself. He didn't want to see what she looked like when she was worried. He couldn't have answered any of her questions anyway. Besides, he was sure that Dahji had it taken care of. "So what's on your p-g for the day?" he asked, bringing her back to him.

"Shopping," she answered. This was not the kind of shopping his wife indulged in. This was the kind of shopping that made up for something lacking in her life. Marlin nodded.

"Don't hurt the bank now," he responded with a smile and turned to leave.

"Oh, it's going to hurt," she promised after him, her words sharp with meaning.

Marlin resisted the urge to look back. He felt warm inside when he finally got into his truck and saw that she was waiting at her front door to wave to him as he drove away.

Chapter Twenty-One

Peaches

Cold. Hard. Depressing. Dull. Boring. Time. That's all it was being in a cell. A stainless steel sink stood in the corner of the concrete room like a monument. And the inside of the toilet bowl was so pasted with grit and grime that when it was flushed, the water created its own tributaries. The gray door was solid steel and let light in through a small, wire, mesh window, which was at eye level. In the middle of the door was the tray slot, which opened and closed like a steel mouth at meal time. A lunch was passed through there. She searched it and found an orange. She would need her energy.

She passed the hours by reading the walls—testaments to those who'd passed this same way. Names scrawled in lipstick and what could have been shit testified to a love missed or revenge promised. Then there were the scratches made by sharp objects. Some spoke to a city or gang, some were hate signs, some just lines to mark the time.

Peaches was without her gold and diamonds. Her limbs felt bare, stripped of their ornaments. She was done crying.

The stainless steel excuse of a mirror showed her own misery and red, crying eyes. In an effort to avoid the puffiness that would result, she decided to quit the tears. They would do no good, she'd said to herself. It was time to be tough.

There was relief in this arrest. She moved seamlessly through the process of answering the detective's questions. No, Tequan did not know she was bringing him drugs. It was going to be a surprise. No, she'd never done this before. Sure, search my car. No, it's not in my name. Yes, it belongs to Tequan. Yes, he lets me drive it. No, I am not his wife, just his girlfriend. No, I do not have children. The address she gave was made up. Yes, I've moved. That's why this address was different from the one on her visitation form. Can I get bail and a phone call? she asked when she decided to be fed up and remembered that she had this coming, and that she didn't have to answer any questions. May I please see a lawyer? She was tired of looking across the wooden table under the bright light at the pale white man with the big stomach. So many white people who looked at her like she was a specimen. Judging her and discussing what she had done. They passed the drugs from one to another like a prize. Her request for bail and a lawyer prompted her one phone call. No more questions were asked.

First she called Sherrelle. She knew when Percy answered that there was going to be some drama. He pretended not to know who she was. Hadn't Sherrelle ever called her Helen in front of him before? Obviously not. Then she called Dahji. Her heart raced as the phone rang. She was lucky. The man responsible for allowing phone calls had recognized her. He'd been to Applebottoms. He smiled generously, saying she should try someone else, and then complimented her on her stage performance as she struggled to remember the number.

That was nearly three hours ago. She'd been warned that if she wasn't bailed out by dinnertime, she would be transported to the county jail in the city. The guard who found the drugs had informed her of this before she was put on a van to the municipal jail. She feigned ignorance when Peaches asked what the bail might be.

Twenty-five thousand, five hundred dollars. Damn. How did they come up with that number? she thought to herself when the deputy sheriff handed her the arrest forms. She'd scanned them in her boredom when there was nothing left to read on the wall. And she thought of Tequan. She wanted to kick herself in the ass. How could she be so stupid? She knew she was reaching backwards when she left Bo's house. Her heart hadn't been in it. Her ass hurt. Her head hurt. There were only so many times she could read the small print on the pink paper, only so many times the numbers to her crime in penal code could be read. How could they get three charges out of one single act?

Time seemed to stand still. She paced the small, cold room with her hands stuffed in the pockets of her tracksuit. Even it had lost its shine. She swore not to ever wear it again. It smelled of the dank cell. She would burn it. No, she would just throw it away. Her skin itched. Her scalp tingled. Her only comfort was her Nike running shoes. They absorbed her every step as if comforting her in her time of need. "Sorry, I gotta throw y'all away, too," she said apologetically, speaking out loud to no one but herself. She had to pee but willed herself to stay away from the toilet. She paced some more, wondering what time it was. Outside the eye-level, mesh, wire window was a white wall. She twisted her face against the window, looking for a clock, but there was just more white wall. Now she really had to pee. She squatted over the rim of the toilet bowl and listened to her piss echo loudly through the cement room.

There was activity outside. A woman was asking what time she could get her phone call. The deputy said some time in the next half hour. There was a fleeting movement outside of her door, then the closing of a cell door somewhere along the hallway. She heard the deputy's keys as he walked back in her direction. She wanted to ask him what time it was. It sounded like he was slowing down. Then he peered in at her, his keys slamming roughly into the iron locks. He opened the door.

"Adebenro?" he asked.

Peaches nodded at the back of the cell, looking hopefully at him while trying to keep from rushing forward. It was taking too long for him to say what he was supposed to be saying.

"You made bail," he said simply, and then stepped back to signal that she should walk free.

She stumbled forward, nearly expecting him to say that he was sorry, that there had been some mistake.

"Don't forget your paperwork," he said, pointing over her shoulder to the pink papers that lay in a neat pile on the cement bench. It was the nicest thing she'd heard all day.

Peaches didn't bother putting any of her jewelry on. It all looked like meaningless trinkets inside the plastic bag the deputy handed to her over the cold, wooden counter. She signed where the deputy told her to sign, promising to appear in court two weeks from today, promising not to leave the state. The papers also explained how to get her bail money back at the outcome of the case. She signed a form agreeing to pay court costs should she be found guilty, a release form stating that she had been treated humanely and without malice, another form stating that she had not been violated in any way, harassed, or civilly obstructed in any way. Her ass hurt and her head ached. That was all she could complain about.

Dahji was like an angel dropping into hell to rescue her. He stood as the sliding glass doors opened with a hiss into the clean lobby of the municipal building. Here, there was traffic, people walking to and fro handling important business. Dahji stood out from the crowd of official-looking people in uniforms and disheveled men and women there for tickets and minor offenses. He wore a maroon, silk, short set and gold, soft-bottomed Gators. His hair hung parted at the forehead in loose curls over his shoulders. Gold and diamonds twinkled around his neck, wrists, and fingers. He was a living protest to conformity. He lived on his terms. Peaches flew into his arms. He hugged her firmly, absorbing her tart breath of relief.

"Thank you," she sobbed into his shoulder.

He rubbed her along her spine. "It's alright. You know I wouldn't leave you out here."

How could she think he would? He wasn't that type of man. "Thank you," she repeated more coherently, stepping back so he could see her eyes.

"Let's shake. This spot give me the creeps," he whispered. She smiled, some weight being lifted off her.

He held her to him silently as they walked from the building and across the parking lot to the Range Rover. There were no words for what she felt or anything he could say to make her feel better.

"Take this," Dahji instructed, reaching into the center console and handing her a small vial of dark liquid and two white pills.

"What's this?" she asked, already having decided that she would take whatever it was.

He pointed to the dark liquid. "Korean ginseng and aspirin."

She smiled gratefully, twisted off the vial's small, white cap, and washed the pills down with the herbal remedy. Just as she thought of how thirsty she was—the ginseng merely wetting her throat—Dahji produced a bottle of Mango-Strawberry Snapple from a small, brown, paper bag he'd plucked from the backseat.

"Got some Twinkies, too," he said, offering her the yellow sponge cake.

"You think of everything, don't you?" Peaches asked as the cold drink reached her palm. She was in no mood to eat, but the Snapple felt good going down her throat after the bitter ginseng.

Dahji asked no questions and she was thankful. Adjusting the seat back, she leaned against the headrest and closed her eyes. It was all so surreal. She thought she had it all together, thought she was on her way to a better life. And just that quickly she had tossed herself into a situation that only fools found themselves in. She was a fool. Tequan was a fool. How could he expect to direct her when he couldn't even direct himself? Love could make you very stupid. *Peaches, you are stupid.*

These thoughts tumbled through her mind as the smooth jazz soothed her and the comfortable ride hypnotized her. She was thankful that Dahji was not full of questions, that he didn't judge her or demand to know exactly what happened. It didn't seem important to him. He knew when to give space, she thought to herself as a sweet horn solo moved through her. If not for the nightmare of her arrest, this would have been nice. This was a poor substitute for a real date. It was amazing how they could find time to spend with each other in a moment of crisis.

As the music soothed her, she promised herself a new direction in life. She couldn't care less what happened to Tequan's car, she was through with him. This was the ultimate embarrassment. A renewed sense of gratitude passed through her at the realization of just how crazy she must seem, and Dahji acted as if it was nothing. She felt herself smiling as she leaned back in the seat with her eyes closed. She knew then that she loved him for sure. *And he must feel some way about me*, she reasoned. Who *would spend twenty-five thousand to bail me out?* Nobody. And he had it. This meant something special. Her body tingled at his boss status. No regular nigga could have pulled this off—would have pulled this off. She felt protected. That he was able to protect her sent a hot rush of emotions through her. And the jazz wailed its soothing melody, relaxing her body and calming her mind. She was entering another world, quickly leaving the state of mind that opened her up to these pitfalls. From now on, there would be nothing but reward and a welcome struggle that didn't involve such heavy risks.

Peaches hadn't realized she'd fallen asleep until they slowed down at a freeway off-ramp. Dahji looked over at her and asked for directions to her house. She was thankful for this, too. She wanted to tell him that she was saving up for a house but quickly realized that it wasn't necessary. Darkness covered decay. The haggard men loitering on the corner in front of the liquor store, the rusted black van sitting on milk crates at the corner she told him to turn on, the apartment building that looked like it was struggling to hold itself up—none of these things would he associate with her. He was opening the driver's side door before she could ask if he was coming up. She felt nothing when she bypassed the telephone pad that was supposed to be used to gain entry, or when she simply pulled the creaking, black, iron gate open without using her key. All of the security apparatuses meant to protect the community had given out long ago due to constant assault.

But she was proud that inside of her apartment, there was some sense of who she really was. There was the large, comfortable leather couch and the big-screen television. The place smelled like her and moved around her like a familiar blanket. It was an oasis of green surrounded by ghetto gray.

She was happy to serve him a cold glass of cranberry juice, not bothering to explain—after his curious glance—that she'd bought a big jug after finding out the dark red liquid was his drink of choice. Thoughtful. He filled up the space with his presence, yet moved around it with grace and respect. He was unassuming, waiting for her to relax and come to herself. When his phone rang, it was her opportunity to excuse herself for a much-needed shower.

There were loose ends to tie up that he made no mention of. She was grateful for this. She would gather the money she'd earned over the last four months—leaving ten thousand dollars for herself—and repay him for the bail. She would have a discussion with him to find out how he planned to play his hand. She wanted to tell him how much she liked him. His laughter followed her under the water. He'd found the remote control and turned on the television. Redd Foxx was telling Ester to get out of his house. She liked Dahji's laughter. The water soothed her. It rinsed her clean of the dirt, the shame, the foolishness, the stupid choices, Tequan. She was done with it all. It was time to make room for something—for someone—new.

Dahji found a basket of strawberries in the refrigerator. They lay on the couch next to him and he reached for them like popcorn. Peaches walked into the living room carrying the money he'd paid to get her out of jail. She smiled when she saw his eyes move over her scented body, still warm from the shower under a silk robe. Her soft curves moved with purpose. Her silk negligee was open at the front, revealing the diamond navel ring pushing through her creamy flesh. When he didn't reach for the envelope, she tossed it onto the glass table and moved between his legs. She smiled at him as she knelt before him. Silently, she undid his thin, snakeskin belt and slid his silk shorts down his legs. The theme song to *Laverne and Shirley* was playing on the big screen. She thought it was cute how he loved old-school shows. She wrapped her lips around his dick and sucked on the flaccid meat, feeling him come to life inside of her mouth. She reached down to slip his Gators off his feet. Then she unbuttoned his shirt and moved it over his shoulders, his dick still in her mouth. Slowly and tenderly, she worked her tongue across the base of his fat head. She felt his thighs tighten against her cheeks when she slid down onto him tightly. Her lips massaged the fleshy meat. It pulsed against her tongue.

Now it was her turn to converse with him while controlling their session. She raised up, letting the soft silk fall from her shoulders, and straddled him. Her entire body was on fire. She shivered with a sudden jolt as she pressed his dick past the folds of her pussy. His breath came short as she wrapped her arms around his neck and grinded slowly over him, moving at an angle to make him wince and huff. She moved slowly, her breasts brushing against his chest. With him comfortably filling her up, she allowed him to see the mist in her eyes. She held his gaze and relaxed onto him like sand settling after an ocean wave had washed ashore.

"Hello," she said, smiling as a tear dropped from one eye.

"What it do?" he drawled hoarsely, looking softly into her eyes. There was a current of emotion racing through the silver orbs.

"Are you mad at me?" she wanted to know, squeezing her pussy around his thick meat.

"Naw," he whispered.

"I need to make some changes," she said, a pair of tears racing down her cheeks.

Dahji was silent, his hands resting on her hips. He was at a disadvantage. With her knees up on the couch, there was only so much of him that could go inside of her. She worked this with expert precision, squeezing and releasing him at will. Hot-tipped needles poked at his skin.

"Wanna know what I dream about?" she asked, more tears falling. She made no move to wipe them away. She didn't want to take her arms from around his neck. She didn't want to stop looking into his eyes.

"What's that?"

"I dream of owning a house with two trees in the front yard," she whispered hotly. "I dream of washing dishes in a beautiful kitchen and having two children and a husband that loves me for real." Tears streamed with her emotion, dripping from her chin onto Dahji's stomach. He let them run down into his lap, meeting the place where he entered her.

"That's a good dream to have."

"What do you dream of?" she asked, sliding up on him and watching his eyes grow dull with pleasure, before settling back down on him. Her movement caused a burst of activity: swelling, pulsing, massaging, opening and closing.

"I don't dream. I plan." She grinned at his reply.

"What are your plans?"

"You know my plans," he said vaguely.

"Do your plans include me?" she wanted to know, her heart racing. Maybe it was unfair that she was on top of him.

"I got a meeting with your lawyer tomorrow." He stated this plainly. Peaches smiled nervously, new tears falling from her eyes.

"I can't afford a lawyer," she sobbed happily.

"It's already handled."

"I don't know what to say." She knew no words to explain to him how grateful she was. There were no words that would help ease the swelling of her heart. Her tears felt like warm blood coursing over her hot cheeks. "I must look like a fool," she huffed, attempting to wipe away her emotion.

"Not to me," Dahji assured her.

Peaches exhaled and gathered herself. She looked at the ceiling before casting her gaze back on him. She could feel him inside of her. He fit perfectly and snugly. "That's great, but it doesn't answer my question."

"About you being in my plan?"

She nodded hopefully.

"You make me happy," he answered simply. "You choose me and I'll take care of the rest." This was the pimp in him. "You know what I'm saying?"

Peaches grinned. She knew exactly what he was saying. And she would not try to change him. She would love him. And they would get rich together.

"I choose you," she answered, making her pussy tighten over him as she leaned in to kiss him softly on the lips. She hugged him tightly, her tongue probing his strawberry-sweet tongue as her hips moved into him gently, pressing his thick meat against her walls with smooth strokes. *Yes, I choose you*, she thought to herself, feeling him warm inside of her and grow to meet her demands. Her pussy breathed over him, allowing more of him inside. *Yes, I choose you.* Her lips were hot on his and her breasts tingled against him. His hands gripped her ass as she slid him inside of her and tightened to squeeze his thick head. "Yes, I choose you," she breathed out against his ear as she increased her rhythm and showed him just how much she appreciated him. This was a choice she wanted to make with all her heart, and he felt so good inside of her. Boss.

Chapter Twenty-Two

Sherrelle

She was glad it was going to hurt. When Percy got the bill from her shopping excursion, she knew it would cause him pain. But she didn't even care. Trina thumped through her speakers, rapping about dropping her ass down low and letting it roll. Shopping was better than sex. Her pussy tingled as she thought of her earlier meeting with Marlin. He looked so fine the way his muscles bulged under his clothes. There was a mystery around what they could do.

It had been a long day of shopping. The sun had fallen from the sky by the time she pulled onto her block. Her heart jumped when she saw Marlin stepping off his porch. Her eyes quickly scanned their driveways to gauge how much time she would have to converse with him. His wife was home and her husband wasn't. She could give him the gift she bought for him.

"Wassup, homeboy?" She smiled as she pulled to a stop in her driveway. He was at the edge of his lawn, behind his wife's car. He wasn't dressed to go out so she figured he was just getting something from his Escalade parked at the curb.

"What's up, homegirl?" he answered. She loved his smile. The way the corners of his mouth turned up did something to her insides. His creamy caramel complexion glowed under the night lights.

She opened her door with ceremony, giving him a glimpse of her thick legs under her long, linen dress.

Marlin was shaking his head. "He gon' kill you," he said, smiling at the designer shopping bags piled into her Jaguar.

"Not hardly, honey," she breathed out, standing away from the car. "It just looks like a lot. Just some shoes and a few cute dresses," she explained, not mentioning the small boxes of jewelry that would hurt Percy good.

"He's better than me," Marlin acknowledged.

Sherrelle looked at him sharply. "You don't let your wife buy nice things?"

"Keep it real, Sherrelle. You shop for the same reason a middle-aged man would drive a sports car."

She smiled. "Or a man with a little dick."

"You feel me then."

She turned to a bag she'd dropped on the hood with a quick look to his porch. "I got you something. Is that okay?" she asked with a twist of her lips.

"What is it?" Marlin asked curiously. He felt like they were having a relationship that hadn't been consummated yet. She turned to him with a black box.

"Just a little something I picked up to encourage you," she replied, stepping back to watch him, her fingers burning from his subtle touch as the transfer was made.

Marlin peeled back the top flap on the palm-sized box and pulled up a round, glass ball. Inside was a small running back dressed in a Colts uniform. He held a football in his arm while the other stiff-armed a defender as he maneuvered through other oncoming defenders.

"Shake it," Sherrelle instructed joyfully, her eyes wide with excitement.

Marlin shook it one time. White snow raced around the inside of the glass ball. It was a scene, the glass ball anchored to a wooden, square, black base. He smiled at her thoughtfulness. He shook it again when the white powder settled back onto the playing field. "That's cool," he whispered like a happy child.

"I'm glad you like it."

"This ain't gon' be enough for your peep show entertainment, though," he said, grinning at her mischievously.

"Oh yeah. That." Her pinky fingernail came to her lips. She sucked on it in thought. "We'll consider that a down payment then. Cool?"

Marlin nodded. "A down payment, hunh?"

Her smile promised a good reward. "Yeah. A down payment," she answered. "But can I ask you a question?"

Marlin looked at her doubtfully. "What?"

Sherrelle pinched one side of her face tight. "Why you act like you're in so much pain when your wife sucks your dick?"

Marlin laughed louder than he'd intended to. "Are you serious?" he asked, bouncing back to look at her, wide-eyed.

"You're like this." She closed her eyes and shot her arms out to the sides, tensing her body as if waiting for someone to bite her in a place she didn't expect.

Marlin laughed some more. "That ain't right."

"It is right," she smiled, enjoying the feeling he gave her. "What's up with that?"

Marlin shook his head in dismay.

"It really shouldn't be a horrible experience," she said

sweetly, her voice a seductive whisper.

He looked up at her, thinking about how badly he wanted to grab her up in his arms and kiss her. She was watching the emotions and the hesitation pass over his face. Then she looked up at his porch. His front door was opening. He noticed the change in her expression. Their connection had been broken. She turned away from him to retrieve another bag from her car, but more to prevent his wife from seeing the look in her eyes than from any duty to get into her own house.

"Thanks," Marlin said, shaking the ball one more time before stepping to the curb. He didn't bother to look back at his wife who he knew was trying to figure out what was in his hand.

"Hey, girl," Sherrelle sang as she stepped onto her porch, laden with the spoils of her shopping spree.

"Hi, Sherrelle. You look like you had a good day," Stacy answered politely. Sherrelle could see more written on her face than what was on her lips.

"Just the necessities, that's all." She smiled, thinking that all she wanted to do was get into her house. Her face was on fire and she wondered if Stacy could tell. Women could always tell, and a part of her really didn't care.

She dropped the last of the bags onto the living room floor and peeked out the door before she closed it to get a glimpse of Marlin as he stepped onto his porch. He carried his Blackberry in his hand. He must have left the gift she gave him in the car, she reasoned. She rushed to the bathroom and dropped to the toilet to pee.

Maybe I shouldn't have bought Marlin anything, she thought as she changed out of her high heels and linen dress. *What was his wife going to think?* She slipped on a long, white, HoodSweet t-shirt and slipped off her panties. Her pussy needed to breathe. She stood in front of the mirror on the back of the bedroom door and stuck her finger in her pussy as she thought of Marlin. *He really did like the gift,* she thought to herself. His eyes lit up, bright like stars. This excited her for some reason. That he could appreciate something so small moved her in some way. The ringing phone made her dislodge her finger from her pussy and walk to the bedside table to answer it.

"Bitch, where have you been?!" Sherrelle shouted into the phone, standing beside her bed with her hand on her hip.

"I tried to call you!" Peaches answered, "But your punk of a husband wouldn't accept my collect call."

Sherrelle suddenly remembered Percy questioning her about who she knew in jail early that morning. "Were you in jail?" she asked, worry on her face.

"Yes!" Peaches answe red with indignation. "I was going to see Tequan and, girl, bitch got caught up."

"Are you serious?" she asked, not wanting to question the specifics of her actions. "What they say you did?"

"Some crazy shit. Like I tried to smuggle drugs into the prison. That shit was so fucked up, I can't even believe it was real."

Sherrelle was walking into the living room. "I know you can't," she responded in support. She was shaking her head with the notion to chastise her friend for her stupidity, but instead she said, "So what happened?"

"Dahji bailed me out and came and got me," she swooned with pride.

"I'm sorry I couldn't be there for you," Sherrelle said, a flood of dark emotions running through her. Percy could have accepted the call. He had to know that it was an important call. *But that's all right,* she thought to herself. *It's damn near over for your ass.* She lay across the couch with the phone to her ear.

"Don't trip, girl. I'm cool now. I have to go back to court in two weeks."

"Damn. That's trifling. So how do you feel?"

"I'm good," Peaches answered in a long whisper. "Dahji just left. He got me a lawyer already, girl."

"Now that's what I call good looking out. He must really like you."

"And I like him, too," Peaches assured her. "Girl, we really need to get this HoodSweet thing on deck. You got some more clothes on the way?"

"Yeah. They should be here tomorrow." Sherrelle was looking out the front window. Percy was pulling into the driveway.

"I'm going to see my Korean friend tomorrow. He's going to give us the hook-up for manufacturing. It's on after that, girl."

"That would be big," she responded, watching as Percy tripped while walking up the steps. He looked down dumbly, as if something had purposely gotten in his way then disappeared. He was drunk.

"What you do today?" Peaches wanted to know.

"Shop," she answered, her attention on her husband as he struggled to get his keys out of the door. He stepped into the living room and looked at her, surprised. His eyes scanned her body slowly, brightening when he got to her thighs. Her t-shirt barely covered her ass, and she lay on the couch with one foot on the floor.

"I'm sorry, baby," he said in a voice trying to control itself.

"Sorry about what?" Sherrelle asked, an edge in her delivery.

"Percy home?" Peaches asked.

"What I said this morning." He threw his hand toward the kitchen to indicate the spot where the offense took place. Now he looked at the department store bags strewn on the carpet. His face registered understanding before he looked at her. "Shopping," he whispered absently, moving to the edge of the sofa. Sherrelle moved her leg so he could sit down. He laid his hand on her foot.

"How was golf?" she asked, feeling sorry for him.

"Terrible. My shot was off," he answered, his eyes trying to figure out why she still held the phone to her ear.

"You should practice more," Sherrelle advised him, pulling his eyes to her mouth. She smiled.

His fingers felt across the top of her foot while his eyes concentrated on a spot near her ankle. "Yeah. I need to practice." His eyes traveled up her thigh. "You are so beautiful."

Sherrelle's eyes let down a curtain. She observed him as if from a long distance. It was at times like these that he seemed so vulnerable. This was when he saw her like he did the first time. It was at times like these that he must have realized that he didn't measure up. He had to know he didn't make her happy. At times like these, he must have questioned why she stayed. His eyes said as much while his mind lost itself in her beauty.

"I'ma have to call you back," Sherrelle said into the phone.

"Awright, girl."

Sherrelle dropped the phone beside her. "Are you hungry?" she asked softly, remembering with sadness how they used to be. Their world was new. Everything was possible. Then they'd settled into a predictable routine. He tried to satisfy her sexually and she shopped to make up for the lack of satisfaction.

His eyes were glassy, moving slowly over her body while his hands felt along her thigh. In answer to her question, he bowed his head slowly to her pussy. He pushed up her t-shirt to expose her pussy. He kissed her softly along her thighs, leaving a wet trail.

"Are you hungry?" she asked again, not in the mood for his sloppy pussy sucking. Then he stuck his tongue inside of her and she caught her breath, her body arching involuntarily.

Percy was motivated by this movement. He positioned one of her legs over the back of the couch, letting the other hang toward the floor. He kicked off his golf shoes as if this would help him in his endeavor. He relaxed himself between her thighs and pushed his tongue into her again. He tasted her with relish, moving his tongue around inside of her fervently. She squirmed under him, her legs wide and her pussy accepting his attention.

He hummed with pleasure as his tongue lapped between her thighs. She raised her legs into the air to allow him to lick her from her asshole to her clit. He sucked on the swollen button hungrily, making her squeeze his head between her thighs. Still he sucked, and then dipped his tongue into her pussy again. His lips moved from side to side, taking her pussy lips between them, nibbling softly.

When she creamed onto his face, this encouraged him. He licked it up enthusiastically, moaning with pleasure. He slid his hands beneath her ass to hold her in place like a platter of food. He slurped, sucked, and licked her until her body shook and shuddered.

Percy continued to suck on her pussy and freed one hand to work at his belt buckle. He unzipped his pants and pushed them to his knees. He pulled on himself as his tongue went in and out of her. Sherrelle encouraged him with soft moans, calling his name sweetly. He raised up when he got to his full girth. Positioning himself between her legs, he sunk into her.

"That's it, boo," she cooed, rubbing his back and wrapping her legs around his waist as he pumped inside of her.

His motions were deliberate and quick, chasing an elusive moment and working himself into a frenzy. Liquor sweated out of his pores as he huffed against her ear. She whispered to him, knowing that this would send him over the edge. She barely felt him inside of her and squeezed tightly around him. He tensed and pulsed, finally releasing himself with a shudder and a whimper.

"You hungry, baby?" she asked again, the weight of his frail body collapsing between her legs. He withered inside of her pussy, slipping out of her unnoticed.

Sherrelle smiled proudly, happy that she'd excited Marlin with her gift.

Chapter Twenty-Three

Dahji

That was the business, Dahji thought to himself. Not since his wife had he felt a woman so much. Peaches was way too real, and he had real feelings for her. He'd fooled himself into thinking that he was just being helpful by bailing her out of jail and getting her a lawyer. The truth was, he felt a stabbing pain in his heart when she called and said she was in the bing. He didn't truly realize until that moment that he felt for her the way he did. It was beyond the fact that she could suck a good dick, hush a room just by walking into it, and carry herself with a hood chick mentality and be glamorous at the same time. His feelings for her went beyond this.

She had a way of letting him know, without words, that he was the boss and that she was down for whatever. She was the kind of woman he needed on his team. He didn't realize how lonely he'd been until he met her. He had wondered what it was about her that tugged on his emotions. Now he knew and had poured water over the fire that burned in him. She saw this need in him and chose. She understood him perfectly, this moved him as well. She was no square and was ten-toes-to-the-concrete in the game.

And when she cried over him, they had been tears of joy. He felt this, and it was a burden. He smiled to himself at how well he had maintained his composure. She expected no less of him, he knew. He was proud of himself. Knowing that she'd broken the law for her dude meant more than money to him. Dahji lived by the pimp code of directing a woman to her highest potential. He felt that one of the main problems in the world was dudes misdirecting their women. Peaches had been misdirected, but she proved how loyal she could be. Her actions proved that she was the type to hold her man down and raise him up at the same time. He loved this about her. And the bonus was that she knew the business of choosing. And a chooser's prize would be her eternal love for him. She would be committed to him and he would direct her in a way that would make both of them rich. She had potential, and Dahji was proud to make her his woman.

They made slow, passionate love. She shared more of her dreams with him. He shared some of his dreams with her. She promised she would learn to cook. He promised he would eat her cooking. They laughed together, becoming one in their intimacy. The deal was sealed.

Dahji was tired. She'd milked him dry and sucked him raw. He'd already decided that, in order to do what they needed to do, he would buy a house with two trees in the front yard. But he would keep the high-rise loft for business purposes. He was glad to be home. His answering machine was lit up with messages. Through the picture window, the bright lights of downtown sparkled in the night. Dahji let the messages play.

"Roger. Your father really wished you could have made

it to church today. We hope everything is okay. Coretta said that you had gotten an important call. I love you, sweetheart. And your father loves you, too, even if he can't say it for himself. Bye, baby. Call your mother."

Dahji really wanted to go see his father preach. He pressed for the next message.

"Hello, Dahji. This is Viola. Hope everything went okay with your friend. Call me so we can talk about keeping her out of jail. Toodles."

Dahji smiled at this message. He'd known Viola for quite a few years. They'd gone to high school together, and if she hadn't been his wife's best friend, she could have easily been his number one woman. It would have been a challenge because, even back then, she knew what she wanted to be in life—a lawyer. *Everything happens for a reason*, Dahji thought to himself. She turned out to be a trusted friend.

"Hi. This is Peaches. I really enjoyed the time we spent together. And I want to thank you for everything you've done. I'll see you tomorrow, sweetie."

Her voice was on the edge of sleep. Dahji could picture her being swallowed up by her thick comforter. Luther Vandross sang in the background. Her voice was low and sexy, nearly a whisper. *Yeah, see you tomorrow*, he said to himself.

"Hey, Dahji. This is Ebony calling. Are we still on for Monday? I feel like I've been cheated. You know I want some of that dick. Why you playing with me?" Dahji pressed forward.

"Hola, Papi. You know me or do I really have to say? Did you get all the footage you needed? Call me, Papi. Adios."

Maria was so sweet. His dick jumped at the memory of how it felt to have two women suck his dick at the same time. He dialed Marlin's number.

"Hello. Cassidy residence," Stacy answered.

"Hey, Stace. This is Dahji. How's the weather on your side of town?" he asked, walking into the kitchen. He pulled his box of ginseng from the drawer and ripped open a bag of multivitamins. He stood still, trying to figure out whether he wanted something else.

"Hi, Dahji. We're fine. Hold on, I'll get Marlin for you."

"Cool." Dahji was already fishing two bananas, two eggs, orange juice, half an avocado, and a jar of raw oysters from the refrigerator.

"Waddup?"

"What it do, pimp?" he replied when Marlin's gruff voice came on the line.

"It do what it do. Just lounging. Everything cool with Peaches?" Dahji cracked the eggs into the blender over half the jar of oysters. He began slicing the avocado. "Yeah, that's straight. She just needs good management."

Marlin was smiling. "I feel you on that. She's good people."

"This is true. I'ma go ahead and lock her down and show her the blueprint."

"The famed blueprint?" Marlin joked, his hand over his mouth in his mock excitement.

"Marly Marl, you know what the blueprint feel like. What would you say if I can damn near guarantee you sharing the load at running back?"

"I hear you speaking on it, but like I say, ain't no coach spoke on it. Until that happen, it ain't official."

Dahji sliced the bananas into the blender and poured orange juice over the concoction. "What I tell you, Marly Marl? If I tell you a flea can pull a tractor, then you better find a rope and hitch him up. If I tell you a fat girl float, then you better throw her ass over the boat." Marlin was laughing. Dahji turned the blender on. "If I tell you I got a cure for cancer, then you better get a loan and invest in me. If I tell you the sun is going to burn out tomorrow, then you better go buy some flashlights."

"Awright, awright! Man, I got you!" Marlin said through his laughter. "I believe you man!" More laughter.

"Naw. I don't think you do! If I tell you there's ice in hell, you better get a coat. If I tell you Jesus coming back, then you better go to church!"

Marlin was laughing so hard, he was silent. A hard yelp barked from him when he recovered between fits of mirth. "Stop it," he managed in a hoarse plea. "Stop!" He was still trying to recover. In the background, Stacy was asking him if he was okay.

Dahji filled a glass with the drink that would bring his mojo back. He screwed his face up tight as the rough mixture passed down his throat.

"Awwwwrrghh!" he belched, swallowing hard and refilling his glass. "Remind me to make my special mojo drink for you, Marly Marl. Guaranteed to make your dick grow an extra three inches overnight. You don't believe me?" he asked, preparing to down his second glassful.

"I believe you!" Marlin replied without hesitation.

"Uuuharrrgggghhh!" Dahji roared, having drank the thick sludge. "I'm meeting with a lawyer tomorrow. Figure we might need to have something on paper. I'm meeting with some special folks to holla about your contract tomorrow, too, Marly Marl," Dahji said.

"Yeah."

"You feel good?"

"Yeah."

"You feel like a boss?" Dahji asked excitedly, feeling the potent drink rush through his limbs.

"A true boss."

"'Cause only a boss can write his own ticket. Get at you tomorrow, Marly Marl."

"Tomorrow," Marlin responded before hanging up the phone.

Dahji had some more calls to make. He dialed the first number that would make his situation with Marlin official. He lounged on the sofa with a row of Fig Newtons and a glass of cranberry juice as Gloria's phone rang.

"What's up, Glo Glo?" he said when she answered.

"Hello there, mister agent man. How are you?" she wanted to know, her voice laced with the privileged life of being a professional football team coach's wife.

"You hold the key, Glo Glo." He sipped his drink while chewing on a Fig Newton.

"There's no denying that." A piano played in the background. Dahji could picture Gloria's teenage daughter sitting at the baby grand. "Her name is Sasha Grand. I gave her your number so she would be calling you sometime tomorrow. Are you free tomorrow night?"

"For her I will be," he answered.

Gloria smiled on her end. "That's great. She's looking forward to meeting you. Thank you so much. She really has no idea what to expect."

"I'll be good. Don't worry."

"Oh no. I'm not worried about that. Actually, I believe she expects you to be very bad."

"Bad like how?" Dahji asked, becoming wary. He knew that this was going to be more than simple.

"Ummm...well...I'll let her share her desires with you." She laughed wickedly. "Nothing you can't handle, I'm sure. Well, I must be going. We'll speak soon?" she asked in a way that indicated that they would.

"Yeah," Dahji responded, wanting to press her about what her friend might want from him, but deciding against it. Since she wasn't a gray girl, there was no real fear of her being extra'd out in her sexual deviancy. Then there was the satisfaction in knowing that this would be the beginning of a certain freedom. He popped another Fig Newton into his mouth, thinking about how good it will be to become a real sports agent and have a man playing for the Indianapolis Colts.

His next call was to his lawyer friend.

"Viola Sparks."

"What it do, V?" he asked. She sounded like she was just waking from sleep.

"Who is this?"

"Dahji. You sleep? You still at the office?"

"No. No. I mean, yes. I must have dozed off." The rustle of papers spoke to her all-business life.

"You need a vacation," Dahji admonished her. Ever since he'd known her, she was always studying and working. She never played.

"Right. I'll get right to it after I pay off my student loans, mortgage, credit cars, car note, oh and find a husband to take a vacation with. Enough about me though."

"You need a vacation," Dahji repeated, this time saying it lightly with a grin.

"Thank you, Dahji. You going to take me on a vacation?"

"I ain't got no problem with that. I tell you what. My man playing for the Colts. He's going to need a lawyer to handle his contracts."

"Right. I believe I was the one to suggest this."

"So when my man goes to Hawaii to play in the Pro Bowl, we all get to go. That is, if you're his lawyer. There go your vacation right there."

"You've got a lot on your plate, I see."

"Just trying to tighten up my hand, you know?"

"Well, I applaud that. So how is your friend who was arrested?"

"She's good. They charged her with possession, attempted trafficking, and intent to distribute."

"That's nothing," she said. "I'll take care of it."

"What is this going to cost a friend?" Dahji asked, smiling through the phone.

"Well, come see me tomorrow at noon and we'll discuss it." Her voice had grown soft and inviting.

"You still like those hot dog burritos from that hole-in the-wall on Tenth Avenue?"

Her laughter was pleasing. "I can't believe you remember that. I haven't had one of those in ages."

"Go home and go to sleep. See you tomorrow, V."

She was smiling. "You know I just might do that. My cat is probably worried about me." She let out a hearty chuckle to mask her loneliness.

"Be good to yourself, V."

"I'll try," she said, before ending the call.

Dahji leaned back on the sofa, biting into his Fig Newtons slowly and sipping the cranberry juice. There wasn't enough of him to go around, he thought to himself. So many women needed a good man. *It was going to be a powerful day tomorrow,* he was thinking to himself when the phone rang.

"Hello, darling," Mirabelle sang in her sultry voice. Dahji had expected her to call. After sexing her in the foyer of her mini-mansion in a way that he'd never done, he had expected her to swing back for an explanation after the storm had dispersed.

"I was just thinking about you," Dahji answered. Though his lifestyle was about to change, she was one woman who could always command his attention. She had been responsible for introducing him to the finer things in life. He didn't remember when she first suggested that he needed a sponsor. He'd come to understand that a sponsor was another term for sugar momma.

"Oh, really," she cooed. "That's great to know because you've been on my mind all day. You wouldn't believe how boring it was. Oh, gosh!"

"Yes, I would," Dahji grinned.

"I don't blame you for refusing to accompany me to my art shows. This one was especially drab."

Dahji had gone with her one time. It had been one of their first outings after he'd put his ten-inch dick inside of her. She had wanted to do him a favor now. She'd just bought the high-rise loft for him and wanted him to pick out the signature oil-on-canvas to place over the aquarium she'd planned to buy for him. The painting he chose was of an African at sea. He was stranded on a wooden raft, the sails tattered and fallen along the mast meant to support them. He was surrounded by sharks waiting for him to tread water. For Dahji, the allure of the painting was the calm with which the man floated amidst such apparent danger. It had cost Mirabelle ten thousand dollars. And that was only the beginning of her gifts to him. The Range Rover was next. She'd explained that he needed to ride in class if he was going to visit her regularly. The ghetto-glittered Cadillac he drove just wouldn't do, she'd said before turning into the luxury car lot.

"Dahji," she sang. "I am near your home. Are you

occupied?" she asked.

Dahji could imagine her behind the wheel of her Mercedes, turning a near corner in anticipation of his answer.

"As a matter of fact, I just got in and was about to get in the shower. Do you have your key with you?" he asked. He smiled when he heard her breath catch. He'd always suspected that she had a key though she'd never used it.

"Of course not, Dahji. I would never..." she said before breaking off in silence. "How did you know?" she finally asked, barely whispering. He'd always known.

"I'll be in the water. Where are you?" he asked.

"I'm near and I can't wait to feel you inside of me. Can you imagine what you have done to me?" she hissed erotically.

He knew exactly how he made her feel. "I don't have a clue. Tell me about it when I'm inside of you."

She gave out a low moan. "Please be nice. See you," she said before ending the call.

Dahji pressed the glass pane on the entertainment system and R. Kelly's powerful voice filled the space. After lighting a couple of sticks of African Musk incense and giving a thumbs-up to the man on the raft, he climbed the stairs and stepped into the shower.

Her voice sang out in greeting. "Dahji... It's me, Mirabelle." He'd barely finished washing up with Kors soap and lotioning with Creamy Citrus Pear body cream. It was a combination that she particularly liked. He stepped to the edge of the loft in a red silk robe, his hair hanging loosely to his shoulders.

"You look nice," he said, glaring down at her. She was dressed in the classic fashion: a black, Chanel, two-piece skirt suit that had a tailored fit on her slim frame, accentuating her hips and breasts. A string of pearls graced her long neck and contrasted sharply against her raven black hair. Her ocean blue eyes sparkled up at him. She placed her small, glittering purse on the marble kitchen counter.

"Thank you, but I did not come here for compliments. Come to me now." Her instruction was filled to the brim with need and desire. Her body practically emanated heat. She was undressing as he walked down the spiral staircase, slowly revealing her intentions.

Sheer black stockings. Black garter belts attached to black lace panties. A shiny, black bra that supported her breasts. Black, high-heeled shoes stepping from the discarded Chanel skirt, the blazer already tossed aside. The white, silk blouse and Hermes silk scarf topped the soft heap like a crown of wealth and anticipation. Dahji was glad he'd drank his mojo juice and hoped that it would work right now. R. Kelly was singing through the eaves of a grand cathedral, imploring a woman to marry him. How magnificent this would be.

"You say I've been on your mind, hunh?"

"All day," Mirabelle groaned as Dahji stepped within reach. She pressed her lips to his and explored his mouth with her tongue as her hand found the treasure between his legs and pulled on his thick meat through the silk robe. He came to life in her palm. Her free hand brushed over his hair and rested on the back of his neck as she wilted in his arms.

Dahji lifted her light frame in his arms and carried her up the stairs. She deserved slow romance for his last impaling.

"You smell good," she whispered to him as he reached the foot of the bed.

"Not as good as you," he answered, laying her gently down on the bed. He kissed along her smooth neck as he pulled her bra straps over her shoulders. Her breasts pointed straight up in the air, her nipples straining for attention. He took each one in turn and softly rolled the soft, fleshy knobs between his lips. Mirabelle held his face in her hands as if to transmit emotion through her limbs. He traced his fingertips lightly along her body as he kissed down her stomach to her navel, stopping to twirl his tongue inside of her life port. She rolled her body under his touch. His fingers found the rib of her panties and rolled them past her hips as his tongue traced down the slice of her pussy and rolled across her raised clit. She moved up to meet his lips as he kissed her sensitive spot.

"Ohhhh," she moaned, her ass cheeks rolling across the silk sheets, her heels digging into the mattress.

Dahji slowly kissed down her thighs and stopped to pay attention to the insides of her knees with soft bites. He pressed his thumb against her clit as he kissed the tender skin of her inner thighs, licking a light trail back to her pussy. His tongue replaced his thumb and he inserted it into her pussy. She shuddered involuntarily when he crooked his thumb inside of her sweet sanctum to press against her g-spot. He looked up the length of her curved body. Her head was thrown back, her eyes were shut softly, and her mouth was open. She licked her lips in pleasure.

"Is that what you want?" he asked in a low voice.

"Please," she gasped.

Dahji returned to sucking her swollen clit and pressing against her g-spot. His thumb was slick from her wetness and he slid it in and out of her slowly, rubbing against the roof of her pussy. She bucked under him sensually, her hips rolling from side to side to take some of the pressure of his tongue away.

"Inside, pleeeeese," she moaned, reaching down and

pulling at his shoulders to bring him up and over her body. As he neared her, she reached for his stiff meat and spread her legs wide, guiding him inside of her. She panted with muffled breaths as he pressed into her waiting, hot glove. Her legs were spread in the air, heels pointing to the ceiling. Her mouth found his and she sucked on his lips as he slowly rotated his hips into her.

"That's how you want it?" he asked with his mouth against hers.

"You are the best thing that's ever happened to me," she whispered in ecstasy. She wrapped her long legs around him and forced more of him inside of her. She panted hotly against his lips as her hands framed his face and she kissed him wetly.

She was super wet, her juices dripping and making his entry slick and easy. He long-stroked her in slow motion, filling her and rubbing along her walls with smooth passion.

"Ahhhummmm," she groaned, gently pushing against his chest and rolling him over onto his back. She straddled him and remained on her toes as she lowered herself over him. His long, thick meat slid into her and she gasped and trembled. She braced herself against his chest and teased the head of him with slow motions. Her face screwed up in passion as she moved on top of him in short strokes. Her thighs shook with her effort to control the action.

Mirabelle bit on her bottom lip and closed her eyes as she began to slide down the length of him. She increased her rhythm slowly and opened her eyes to look into Dahji's face. Her blue eyes sparkled as she grew excited and heated. Sparks flew from them as she locked onto Dahji's eyes in a trance. He disappeared inside of her with slick abandon, her pussy opening wide and accepting him warmly.

"Are you going to cum inside of me?" she panted in question. "Please do," she added, finding a higher grip on his shoulders and lowering her chest to his. Her breasts rubbed softly against him as she rolled her hips in a way that made his dick bend inside of her with each motion. She moved down and up on him with quick rolls of her hips. Her pussy swallowed him and released him with a grinding rub along her sweet, hot walls. When she found the angle that allowed him to reach all of her sensitive spots, she controlled and concentrated on her motion. She breathed hotly over him as she spread her legs wide over the bed. Her pussy breathed with its own life as he went into her with hot, pulsing thrusts.

"All day," she gasped before raising up and spinning around on his dick. Her back was to him now and she braced herself on his thighs. Her pale ass slammed down on him as he watched his dick do a repeat disappearing act. Every time she received all of him, she ground down in protest to make his swollen and tender head jam against her deep inside.

Dahji gritted his teeth, determined that she would be the one to cum first. He gripped her waist tightly as she lost herself in her own world of pleasure.

Mirabelle let out a shriek and her body trembled and shook. She shot cum into the air like a magic trick. Dahji was shocked as he watched her ass vibrate and grind on him.

Sated and spent, she rolled off of him and curled up beside him, rubbing his chest and purring like a cat. Her breath was hot and sweet. Her skin was covered with a soft sheen. She shined as if she'd been buffed with a silk scarf and scented oil.

"You didn't cum," she whispered, her hand moving

down to trap the bobbing, unsatisfied head against his stomach. It pulsed under her touch. She raised up and scooted down the bed so that she was eye-to-meaty eye with his dick. She leaned over him and licked her juices from his meat—first the top side and over the head, and then she slid her tongue down the length of him on both sides, and lay her cheek on his stomach. She put his tender head into her mouth and cupped his balls, massaging and prodding them to give up their power as she gently but powerfully sucked on his head, rolling her tongue roughly under its base with care and urging.

Dahji felt as if she was sucking his very essence from him. If there was anything left at the bottom of his well then she was calling it up. She took her time with her mission, rolling his balls between her fingers and sucking the head of his dick, the side of her warm face resting on his tensing stomach and her thick mane of dark hair fanned over his torso like a cape. He grew hot and pulsed in her mouth. This urged her on. Her suction increased and she pulled on his nut sacks. The sensation curled his toes and he gasped as she sucked one—two—three good times, calling up his reserves. Just as his thighs tightened and his stomach muscles flexed, she stroked him quickly, forcing him to swell and pump his fluids onto her tongue. She sucked harder, making him inhale sharply and squirm subconsciously under her assault. A scream escaped his lips, one he had no clue he had uttered until Mirabelle sucked the last drop out of him and his hearing returned. He barely heard her soft voice through the haze of his consciousness.

"There," she whispered, patting his satisfied and spent snake and returning to his side to enjoy their mutual glow of sexual satisfaction.

Chapter Twenty-Four

Marlin

Marlin felt the change in his bones. It was in her eyes, the way she'd looked first at his wife and then at him. She had calculated her hidden desires and her eyes communicated her private wishes to him. It was in her estimation of his wife as she stood across the lawn, bidding her husband farewell. The spouses exchanged smiles. They were plastered across their faces like they had been molded in plastic—fixed and generous. He could feel invisible tentacles reaching across the expanse and attaching themselves to his soul. It was a warm feeling, the soft points of her desire inserting themselves into his skin and taking root.

He wondered if Stacy could feel what was happening. Wondered if Percy could feel what was happening. Were they both blind to the whirlwind of emotions passing across their slice of lawn as they both began their trek to work? Could they sense that a change was coming? Did they notice the possible exchange that could have easily been made, but were just politely being silent? Did they not see that they were mismatched? How simple it would be to switch places and be with the more suitable mate. Surely they must have felt this.

Percy was the first to back out of his driveway, giving rise to an awkward moment when Sherrelle lingered and gave a small wave to Stacy and then a plain-faced look to Marlin before she sauntered back up the walkway and disappeared inside of her house. Marlin kissed Stacy tenderly in a form of apology for his absence of heart while Sherrelle was in his presence. He did not want to hurt her in this way. There was a sense of gratitude that had to be maintained. No good could come from a false note. This is what haunted him. How could he continue in this way with a false note when a more harmonious one lived next door? Where no tuning was needed? It was like stepping into a room and having someone know exactly what he needed to be comfortable, instead of someone stumbling around a guess and falsely assuming his desires. She knew exactly how he felt and he could feel her in his bones.

And there was a change coming. The skies were opening up to reveal a new situation. It was ripe with opportunity. He would be free from the shackles of returning a love that was not full. This half love was slowly being pushed aside. She had to feel this. She'd tried to mask this insecurity with questions about Dahji. Who was he exactly? How could he get him a contract? Is this what he did for a living? Why haven't you heard anything yet? What does he expect from you?

Marlin didn't have the answers she needed. All he knew was that Dahji was responsible for getting him on the field. He couldn't hope to make her understand the way Dahji imparted his brand of confidence to him. It wasn't a confidence that was written on paper, this confidence lived in human interactions and what Marlin came to realize were handshakes and traded favors. He did not care if the man had no credentials, did not care if he'd never been a sports agent before. And Marlin knew what was expected of him. It was the same thing he expected of himself—to play football. They were helping each other out in the most basic of ways: They were offering each other a new life.

This was before the moment when he met Sherrelle in the driveway to see her husband off to work. He didn't understand this at all. Their whole interaction seemed forced. Maybe he could see it so clearly because that was how his own relationship was: forced. This tension only became more apparent when a mirror was placed before him and a riper alternative was shown to him.

How could her husband be so blind? It was obvious to Marlin that Sherrelle was on fire. She emanated a heat that boiled at the surface of her skin like sumptuous balls of nectar. They burst and bubbled along her figure, giving off a soft glow of beaded sweetness. At the proper touch, Marlin was sure that she would open up like a rare flower only found in a secret garden of rich soil; a lush, exotic specimen of botanical desire.

And he could feel her soft, warm embrace around his heart. She squeezed around the muscle tenderly. He smarted at the memory of her thick thighs in the red, cut-off jean shorts that hugged her like a glove. His mind moved over the image of her breasts filling out the HoodSweet t-shirt like melons ready to be sliced and served. How could her husband not know? She was trapped inside of him, making him move with easy strokes for a love unknown. Like a far-off vision of bliss, she appeared on the horizon. Every fiber of his being reached out for her.

Marlin hadn't realized that he'd been standing over the spinning washing machine until the buzzer woke him from his trance. Her smile and the twinkle in her eyes had him captured in their light. He opened the lid to retrieve the damp clothes and drop them in the dryer. Then he saw her. His heart leaped out of his back door and across the small, white fence that separated their houses. He was through the screen door and down the back porch in three strides. She could not hide her sexiness. Not even the heavy gardening gloves and Timberland boots could cool her fire. The pruning shears only added to her allure.

"Wassup, homeboy?" she smiled, watching him stroll up to the fence. She'd stopped to wait for him. It was as if she had been expecting him, as if the fire had not reached its full strength and there was more wood to lay across the flames. There was nothing worse than a fire that had not been allowed to burn freely.

"What it do, homegirl?" Marlin answered, stopping at the fence with his hands over the wooden spikes. He was aware of how the soft part of her throat, just between the collarbones, swelled and dipped with her breathing. The smooth skin along her tender neck moved at the vibrancy of her smile, the veins underneath coursing with the hot blood of a passion untended.

"Don't you have to be about the business of making a football team?" she asked, slapping the shiny metal scissors into her gloved hand. These heavy-duty tools looked out of place in her delicate hands. Her face shined with her hair pulled back into a ponytail.

Marlin looked at his bare wrist. "I've got a few minutes," he replied. "You about to get your Martha Stewart on?"

Her smile was a reward. It formed small crevices that framed her full, heart-shaped lips and made her eyes slant over balled cheeks. "Yeah, right," she sighed, her breasts heaving and settling under the shirt that was cut into a V at her throat, allowing her skin to take in more sunlight. "It helps me think," she added.

"From where I stand, you got everything you need. What you got to think about?" he asked, enjoying the way her eyes cut at him and her lips pressed together at one corner so that only one crevice was formed in her soft cheek. She was calling bullshit on him and he had to smile in return.

"What you think I gotta think about?" she asked sharply.

Marlin shrugged. "I can't speak on that," he answered innocently.

"You the one said I got issues, so you must be able to speak on it." She was confronting him in a playful way though a casual observer might think that they were enemies.

"I feel sorry for your roses," Marlin said, breaking through her mock frown.

"Don't try to get out of it. Tell me what issues I got."

Marlin leaned his head back a little to observe her. She was a little girl and a full-grown woman. Her man couldn't hold her, he realized in that instant. "You ain't getting it right," he ventured.

She shifted her weight to her hip, hand resting on her waist. "Ain't getting what right?"

Marlin smiled. "Dick. That's your issue."

Now she grinned, her eyes revealing the light they were holding back. She looked vulnerable now that he'd spoken her secret aloud. "You didn't make love to your wife this morning. Why not?" she asked, watching the curtain go down over his eyes.

"She kinda mad at me right now."

"So who ain't getting it right?" she shot back. She could have been talking about a number of things, Marlin realized. She could have called him on the way he looked afraid every time Stacy gave him head, but she didn't.

Marlin nodded his head. She was right. "Okay. You got me there." She smiled with satisfaction.

"So how long have you been married?" Sherrelle asked, her eyes soft with understanding. They had admitted their common ground.

"Seven years."

"Really?" she asked, her eyebrows raising in surprise.

"Yep. Right outta college. I'm loyal like that."

"She looks like a ball player's wife—thin and light-skinned."

She was right. Marlin tried not to show that he agreed with her. "How about you? Y'all don't look like a love connection."

"About the same time as you and your soul mate. He was there for me," she replied vaguely.

"So you married him for that? Or is it one of them situations where he had the bread and wasn't too bad in bed?"

"Something like that."

"Why y'all ain't got no kids?" Marlin wanted to know.

"Why don't you have any? Or do you—somewhere in another state where you were playing a rival team?" There was mischief in her eyes.

"Naw. No kids." He shrugged. "I don't know...just hasn't happened."

"You make her take birth control because you plan on leaving her?"

Marlin looked shocked. "Damn, homegirl! You don't pull punches do you?"

"Why should I when it's better to keep it real?"

"You talk to your husband like this?"

Sherrelle was enjoying herself. "Aren't we having a conversation? You came out here."

She reminded him of the girl in elementary who acted mean to disguise her love. "Take some off. You ain't got to be so mean. I know you feeling me. Why else would you be at my window?"

She smiled then. "Alright," she answered, rocking a bit. "So, homeboy, answer me this—are you happy in your marriage?"

"What kind of question is that? You can't go around asking people stuff like that."

"I'm not asking people, I'm asking you. Are you happy in your marriage?" Her eyes were direct, speaking in a language meant for him only.

"She's my wife. If you were my wife and we were not one hundred percent, would you want me admitting it to our neighbor?"

She seemed to give this some thought while she searched his eyes. "If I was your wife, you wouldn't have room to be standing in our back yard having this conversation. You would not even think about being anything less than one hundred percent, as you say."

"If I was your husband," he repeated her words like a question. "You think your husband is one hundred percent satisfied with you?"

"Well, I could answer that question for him, but I won't. The real question is if I'm satisfied," she said, then narrowed her eyes at him. "Do you think I'm satisfied?"

"Why don't you divorce him then?" Marlin wanted to know. The more he talked to her, the more he realized that she was smarter than the average beautiful face. She did not use her beauty to get by. There was a real intelligence in her thought pattern. But there was also a hood mentality. She hadn't forgotten where she came from.

"When you divorce your wife then I'll divorce my husband. Deal?" There. She'd put the hammer on the table. She was as sharp as a shovel and ready to dig a new plot.

Marlin tried not to appear impressed. She was smiling like there was a game being played, yet there was a seriousness to her gaze that stood by her words like a sentry guarding her intentions. "You don't need me to divorce your man. You can do that all by yourself."

"Marlin. Do you really think I would divorce my husband?" she asked, a seriousness returning to her voice that was meant to chastise him for his foolish assumptions. She'd laid a trap and he had blundered into the intricately spun web of deceit and false hopes. She'd used her wile to encircle him in a ring of desire. Now he felt alone and unsure of what he thought of her.

"Naw, shawty. You stay married to your husband. That's the best move you could make." As soon as the words left his lips, he realized how cruel they'd sounded. Her face had taken the insult and bravely gave back a sure smile.

"Well, as long as I choose him, then what you say is right," she responded in what could have easily been a sad voice, except for the grin and the step away that interrupted his reading of her meaning. She looked back at him with a small wave. "Have a good practice," she offered cheerfully. There was nothing else for him to say. She would not give him the opportunity to clean up that last statement. He understood perfectly, resigning himself to finishing his laundry and trying not to think about her. She'd said the more important thing: Have a good practice. This he could focus on. There was something to be done, and this was the first part of completing it. More than ever, he felt the hunger to succeed and get back on the field.

He hadn't realized he'd slammed the back door after climbing the steps until it banged back open and he had to shut it more gently. She was under his skin. He had to get away from here. Away from the windows where she moved outside, seemingly unaware of his existence. The clothes could wait. He grabbed up his duffel bag and walked briskly through the house. He would arrive to practice early. This would be a good thing. Yeah, this would be a good thing. He'd get in some extra workout time. There was this anger to work out, this extra burst of adrenaline that needed to be exercised.

He avoided looking back at her as he got into his Escalade. He turned Jay-Z up and scooted away from the curb. She was under his skin and he would try not to think about her.

★ ★ ★

He had his nerve. It was all his fault. He had no business asking me if I was going to divorce my husband. Didn't he know that I dreamed of doing it? He would have been better off asking me to marry him and telling me that he was going to divorce his wife. Hell, naw, it wasn't the same thing! He doesn't love her. Any fool could see that. And this gave him no right to question me about my marriage. Damn. That man is so fine. Why did he come outside anyway if he was going to be mean? Girl, you know you wanted him to come outside. And you need to quit fronting about how mad you are. You know that if you hadn't pretended like you were mad you would have jumped across that fence and kissed the life from him. And you can't be mad at him for not rolling over when you said to. He ain't a dog. So ain't no reason for you to be mad. But, damn, that man is so fine.

These thoughts ran through Sherrelle's mind like a

track meet as she struggled to concentrate on the roses. She would cut too close to the base, and then too far from the stem. It was no use. She could not concentrate. Then he emerged from the front door. It took everything she had not to make her way to the front of the house so she could say something. Oddly, she was thankful that he didn't look her way when he drove off. She ripped off her gloves and threw them to the ground before stomping back into the house.

The sound of the ringing phone was muted by her mumbling. "Forget him. I was a fool for thinking about him anyway. I am a married woman. Happily. Yep, happily married. Ain't nothing wrong with my marriage. Just because your wife can't suck dick don't give you a right to try to bring me down. Hello!"

"Damn, bitch. What's wrong with you?" Peaches asked.

"Oh. Hi, girl. Nothing. What's up?"

Peaches hesitated, hoping that the sound of her car wasn't resounding over the telephone line. "I'm the one should be mad, but you sound like somebody done took your toys or something. What's wrong?"

"Nothing," Sherrelle answered, falling down heavily on the couch.

"Come on, now. We ain't gon' start holding back now. We bin girls for too long. Spit it out."

"I just had a fight with my next-door neighbor," she admitted.

"Your neighbor? What do you mean you had a fight? What neighbor?"

"Marlin."

Peaches laughed out loud. "Are you serious? What are you fighting with him for?" she asked. There was a pregnant pause. "Oh, snap! Y'all had a fight!" she yelled around her laughter. "Ohhh, shit!"

"Cut it out! It ain't that serious!" Sherrelle protested, ashamed of her own smile. Hearing Peaches' response confirmed what it was: a lovers quarrel.

"Y'all must really be feeling each other. Both of y'all married and fighting like high school sweethearts. That is so sweet," Peaches sang.

"He just gets on my nerves."

"He's supposed to. Percy don't even get your feathers ruffled like that," she giggled.

She was right, Sherrelle realized. Damn. She was right. "What should I do?" she asked helplessly.

"Don't do nothing, girl. We gotta get our shit together before you can even start thinking about what to do about your married neighbor."

"You are so right," Sherrelle agreed. "So what's up with you for the day? What's that sound?"

"That's my raggedy-ass car!"

Only then did Sherrelle remember that Peaches had been arrested and that she refused to pay to get Tequan's car out of impound. "Is it that bad?" she asked, stifling laughter.

"Hell, yeah, girl. I'm about to trade it in though."

"Dahji ain't gon' let you drive around like that for long," Sherrelle said.

"That's my baby," Peaches sang. "He's way too real for me to play like that, though. We go together now," she said like a schoolgirl.

"Listen at you! So y'all moving in together, too? The way you describe him, I can't see how he's going to all of a sudden settle down."

"I know!" she gasped. "I ain't going to try and change

him. That's the quickest way to lose your man. And plus, when Marlin makes the team, everything is going to change."

"What Marlin got to do with him?"

"Girl! You don't know? Dahji is the one who got him the interview with the Colts. And he's going to get him a contract, too. My man is going to be a real live sports agent," Peaches announced triumphantly.

"Well, you go, girl!"

"In the meantime, I gotta go see Dr. Kim about this merchandising business and get back some of my bail money for Dahji. I'ma have to turn a special trick for his ass."

"You be careful."

"I got this. Don't trip. We about to be paid, girl! Did you talk to the HoodSweet dude about contracts and what-not?"

"I should hear something today."

"Awright. I'm at the office now. Let me go do this like Brutus and be out this bitch."

"Awright. Call me later."

Peaches laughed. "Oh yeah. I forgot to tell you. Dahji is going to need us to drop by his crib so he can take pictures of us for the website."

"What's so funny about that?" Sherrelle wanted to know.

"Because I can't wait to see you pretend like you're not sexy in your boy shorts and wifebeater."

"Whatever," Sherrelle moaned. "It's just business."

"That's right, girlfriend. Strictly business. See ya later."

"Call me," Sherrelle sang before ending the call.

Long after Peaches had hung up, Sherrelle still sat on her couch. It was amazing to her that her girlfriend had attached herself to this venture as if it were her own. She wasn't mad at her either. To get a manufacturer to mass produce her designs would mean a lot. And she didn't know much about Dahji, but if he had anything to do with the website and helping the situation, then it was all good. There would be enough money to go around.

She jumped up from the couch with a shriek and pumped her fist. She felt like going shopping but wanted to be home when the HoodSweet shipment arrived. To occupy herself, she got out the wash bucket and slipped on a pair of rubber gloves. She was going to clean the house from front to back. She opened all the curtains and let the sun shine in as Mary J. Blige sang through the house encouragingly.

Chapter Twenty-Five

Peaches

The business park was active with shoppers, the lunchtime crowd leaving the familiar sights to shop and eat elsewhere, and those entering to eat and shop the routinely vacated premises. A parking space opened up two businesses down from Dr. Kim's family practice office. She would have to walk by the 31 Flavors Ice Cream and Rexall Drug store. She coaxed the engine off, hoping that it would not embarrass her in front of the young, copper-colored women crossing in front of her. When they looked toward the hood of the car with horrified expressions, their eyes traveling up the bubbled paint job to her face, she smiled sheepishly as if she was just as shocked as they were. The car shook like a dying animal not ready to go yet. Peaches began to open her door before the shaking ceased and privately hoped the car would not be mad at her for her abandoning it and start again when she returned.

She smiled freely once she put some space between her and the apparatus that spoke of her poverty. No one could know that she was recently arrested and that she lived in an apartment building that failed her at every stop. Just that morning, the cold water in the bathroom would not shut off. She had to call the manager—a fat white man with gray whiskers poking stubbornly from his red, liquor-splotched face—to fix the problem. He'd shown up eagerly, hitching his worn tool belt up to his stomach, which flowed over his waist like molten lava. His white t-shirt told of the pizza he'd had for breakfast and he smelled like the gin he'd drunk to chase it down. He smiled with his pass into her apartment, happy to be of assistance. She'd borne his bland observations about the art of plumbing and accepted his excuse about needing a certain piece to stop the dripping. This would grant him another opportunity to enter her apartment and look around as if cataloging the items that were foreign to this decrepit building.

No. They would not guess that she was in dire straights. But she smiled because she knew that her situation was only temporary. She was on a mission. There would come a time when she drove her own fly ride and there would be a time when she lived in her own house with two trees in the front yard. Yes, this would soon vanish—these meetings with Dr. Kim. She was on her way to the top. She could feel it in her bones.

Her Chanel shades; Fendi purse; silk Versace skirt and blouse, which accentuated her fine curves; dark red hair, which she'd straightened and which lay on her shoulders; Jimmy Choo heels; and diamond appointments, which glittered on her slim arms and neck, separated her from the poverty she was trapped by. Big Blue-Eyes looked up from her desk with the respect Peaches felt she deserved. She stepped purposefully to the young woman's work space and announced herself.

"Oh, he's expecting you," the receptionist replied, gesturing down the hallway and, at the same time, reaching into her bottom desk drawer for her purse. She was about to take her lunch break. As Peaches stepped through the low, wooden partition, she wondered who would answer the phones.

Dr. Kim opened the door just as she neared the end of the hallway. It was as if he'd timed her arrival so that the smile on his face would be newly formed when she looked at him. It was generous and inviting as he moved aside to allow her to pass. He inhaled her soft scent, his body leaning forward like a flower to sunlight. Everything about him was very neat. His dark hair was brushed back from his flat forehead and it shined under the florescent lighting. His white, doctor's coat was open, revealing a shiny, red tie over a brisk, white, button-up shirt. Its collar fit loosely around his neck, giving him a measured, antiseptic appeal. His small, dark eyes twinkled beneath thick lashes.

"Ms. Peaches," he greeted her grandly, his arm sweeping into the office. "I am so glad to see you again so soon."

"So should I leave and come back?" she asked jokingly, turning to him in the middle of the sterile examination room.

He raised his eyebrows dramatically, leaving his eyeballs unprotected and vulnerable. "Oh no. No, no, no. It is good that you are here," he answered quickly, shutting the door and taking her far too seriously. He hustled to the wooden cabinet and pulled out a large, white envelope.

"What is this?" she asked, reaching to meet his extended hand. His whole face smiled to communicate his pleasure at being able to assist her.

"It is my cousin, Sun Yi." Peaches frowned mockingly, slipping the color brochure from its sleeve. "I have spoken with him about your business, and he says that you only need to give him the order and you will be good in business," Dr. Kim said with a smile. He brought his hands together as if to clap, but instead just held them together, awaiting her response.

Peaches concealed her excitement. There were pictures of previous clothing designs Sun Yi had manufactured. She was glad to see familiar names amongst his clientele. According to the quantity chart, the bigger the order, the smaller the cost. "This looks good," she whispered, nodding slightly as if to reserve room for doubt.

"And he also provides distribution company that may be interested. It is all inside." His explanation was accompanied by a sharp jab with his arm toward the brochure. Peaches turned the page. It was more than she could have expected. She slowly slid the brochure back into its sleeve.

She made her face mask her excitement. "I'll have to discuss this with my partners," she said with muted glee, hoping he would think she wasn't satisfied.

"Is this what you wanted?" he asked. His wrists clasped together, though his fingers reached for her.

She let out a gush of air and leaned against the examination table. The paper rustled under her. "No. I'm sorry. It's just that I'm going to miss you." She let her big, silver eyes go slack as she held his questioning gaze.

His smile struggled to stay afloat on the pale sea of his flat face. "You are going someplace else?"

"I love coming to spend time with you, but I need to start saving for a house. And..." she shrugged.

"And what?"

"Well, this is going to take up all of my time," she explained, flipping the offending envelope against her thigh.

Dr. Kim rubbed his small hand over his narrow chin.

His eyebrows had come together in thought. He looked around the room as if the shiny instruments on the silver tray by the door would give him an answer. "There must be some way..." he stammered.

Peaches cocked her head to the side, observing the workings of his mind.

He looked at her then, having decided what must be done. "Maybe I have not been fair with you?" His eyes pleaded. "Maybe I should make our arrangement more fair."

"You have been very nice. I don't see how..." she answered, allowing space for him to offer his unfinished decision.

"Yes. That is it. I have not been fair. I think twice the amount is more fair." Now he stood straight, where before his body seemed to have been in a sort of slump.

"You really don't have to. This clothing line is going to keep me very busy."

"More fair I will make for our arrangement." He was reaching for the cabinet to pull out the beige envelope. He lay it on the counter. Peaches knew it held her usual payment. She watched silently as he walked briskly to the blue blazer hanging on the coat rack. "More fair," he said, looking at her quickly with a small smile as he stepped back to the cabinet with a checkbook in hand.

Peaches thought to object but quickly reasoned that he would not have the nerve to write her a bad check. He concentrated without hesitation on the figures he scrawled onto the powder blue slip of paper. Then he grabbed up the thick envelope and handed both to Peaches.

"More fair," he said, and stood back to watch as she read the amount of the check. Peaches wanted to jump up from her semi-reclined position and kiss him. Instead, she smiled with one side of her mouth and calmly placed the envelope and check into her purse. She looked up at him slowly and motioned with her index finger for him to come near. She'd accepted his very generous offer, and she had a special treat for him.

Peaches slid the white frock from his shoulders and laid it softly onto the examination table behind her. She loosened his tie, slipped it from around his neck, and let it fall to the floor. Next, she unbuttoned the top three buttons of his crisp shirt and rubbed her fingers over his chest, twirling the soft hairs around her fingertips. She leaned in close, her face touching his, and whispered into his ear, "Thank you."

She felt him shiver at her touch as she trailed her hands down his body and stopped at the small tent in his pants. She rubbed him through the material as she looked into his eyes, which had clouded over with anticipation. Her fingers expertly worked the zipper and freed him to the air. He lay across her fingertips like a lounging housewife. Gently and tenderly, she massaged his flesh and brought him to a quiet stiffness. Kneeling before him, she took him into her mouth. She slid down the side of him with wet kisses. He shuddered over her, bracing himself with weak knees. Up around his uncircumcised tip she slid down the other side. She lifted him, took his nut sacks into her mouth and rolled them across her tongue. He let out a gasp and trembled, rolling to the balls of his feet and placing his hands on her shoulders for balance. She'd never done this to him before and he was shaken up. She smiled over his balls and hummed a soft vibration. His grip tightened on her shoulders as she stroked him softly. He moaned gruffly through clenched teeth.

"You like that?" she asked, rising to meet his smoky eyes.

He nodded shortly, his mouth working but no words coming through his lips. Peaches efficiently pulled her skirt up around her waist and slid onto the examination table. She slid the condom over his penis and spread her legs wide, giving him a good look at her shaved pussy.

Dr. Kim slid inside of her with a jerk. Peaches opened her blouse so he could suck on her breasts. He sucked her nipples in turn and then buried his face in her neck as he humped her with quick, short strokes. His breathing matched his effort. His pants were around his ankles as he jabbed shallow strokes into her. Peaches rubbed her hands through his hair, messing it up for effect and rubbed across his ears. It was the most attention she had ever paid to making him feel special. The result was a quick nut and a sharp gasp against her neck as he jerked into her with finality.

Peaches let him relax against her. He deserved it, she thought to herself, as she whispered in his ear how great he was and how good he made her feel. She was nearly halfway to recovering her bail money.

★ ★ ★

Viola Sparks worked in a high-rise, tinted glass office building. On the ground floor was a Gladstone's restaurant, a 24-hour Fitness (complete with a juice bar and a health food store), a flower shop, and a mini post office for sending important packages after hours. A Citicorp bank occupied the next two floors. Near the top of the thirteen-story building were the law offices of Lowenstein, Knight & Sparks. Viola was the only woman of color in the office besides her secretary. She'd been hired as an associate and quickly made partner after she won a huge tobacco case for the firm.

Her reward was a corner office and a six-figure salary. She was still in debt and had yet to find love because of her long hours in the steel and glass tower.

Dahji arrived just before noon. He carried a Louis Vuitton briefcase that matched the brown of his Hugo Boss suit. The wide collar on his beige shirt hung over his lapel, and his shirt sleeves jutted out fashionably over his wrists. His soft-bottomed Gators stepped with ease over the carpeted lobby of the law offices. A perky, blonde woman sitting behind a high desk directed him to the wing of the floor where he could find Viola Sparks. With a wire strapped to her ear and only her head visible, Dahji suspected that she would not make it to lunch today. She handled the numerous incoming calls efficiently, giving small instructions, apologies, and asking people to hold with a smile plastered across her thin lips.

There was an obvious switch in the décor the closer he got to Viola's office. African art adorned the walls and earth-tone couches were placed neatly in the waiting area. A beautiful, dark-skinned woman sat comfortably behind a desk at the far end of the room. Dark curls of hair framed her cherubic face tenderly. Her features were young and polished. She looked up when Dahji stepped through the glass doors that announced Viola Sparks as an attorney at law.

"Hi. You must be Dahji McBeth," she said, smiling up at him. She had transcripts in front of her.

"The one and only," he responded.

"Ms. Sparks is expecting you. Please go right in," she said, pointing with the yellow highlighter pen between her manicured fingers to the heavy mahogany door to her left. As Dahji stepped toward it, the secretary was announcing his arrival into an intercom. Viola's voice answered from two places as he opened the door. She was rising from the desk, her green eyes looking at him through gold-rimmed glasses.

Long hours, no sex, and fast food had transformed her curvaceous figure into a pudgy frame with soft, blunt curves hidden by her two-piece skirt suit. Thick thighs and ankles walked with measured grace around the desk. Her skin was still smooth, but with the roundness of weight to keep it young. The freckles dancing across the bridge of her button nose gave her added sex appeal.

"It's been so long, Dahji. How have you been?" she asked, allowing him to take her into his arms. She politely rubbed along his back before stepping away to look at him again. "You look good!" Her relaxed hair needed a touch-up. It hung loosely to her shoulders, the roots a reminder of her roots, growing in a darker brown than her red-tinted highlights.

Dahji grinned. "You look like you need to leave this office," he said, ignoring her playful tap on his shoulder.

"You're not afraid to tell the truth. That's what I've always loved about you." There was something in her eyes that spoke to a future situation. Dahji would wait until it revealed itself.

"The real is all I know," he responded as she stepped back behind her desk to assume her position of power. Her office was dimly lit. Shafts of light came in through the horizontal shades over the windows to illuminate the exact places it seemed most needed: desk, bookshelf lined with legal texts, and the mini-bar against the wall under a portrait of her in a frilly pink blouse. She smiled down from the wall over her accomplishments.

"I know that's right," she sighed with a warm smile, settling into her puffy leather chair. "So what's really going on with you?" Her eyes sparkled with meaning.

Dahji extended his legs in front of him and folded his

hands over his lap. "Same ol' same. Staying one step in front of the average. Breaking into this pro football thing, and I got a situation with a clothing line about to pop. So..." he said shrugging, hopeful about the possibilities.

Viola pulled a brown folder with leather strings from a vertical metal file holder. She lay it on her desk like a prize not ready to be opened yet. "I spoke with my partner and he was kind enough to draw up a basic client contract for your football player. It has enough blank spaces for you to insert your own numbers." She tapped the folder. "Also, I have some forms here for your special girlfriend to sign so that I can represent her. She'll have to come see me before we go to court."

Dahji listened intently, watching Viola's face assume its professional look while hinting at a personal objective. "I really appreciate you coming through on that for me," he said, watching her study him. "Guess who I saw recently?" he asked, making the green in her eyes turn dark.

"Who?" Her expression was impatient, but she didn't want to miss the gossip.

"Coretta."

"Coretta Coretta? The one who almost kept you from getting married?" she asked, her trimmed eyebrows rising. She wore too much makeup over her eyes. The blue paint clashed with her natural redbone. Working around white folks had a way of making a sistah change her ways, Dahji thought to himself as he nodded his head in agreement.

"She say her daughter is really mine." He stated this plainly, not giving away how he felt about it.

"Serious?" There was a hint of the lawyer in her voice, ready to pounce on the claim and prove it bogus.

"Yep. Her man locked in the bing, and she say she knew she was mine all along." He shrugged.

"So what do you think?" Viola leaned forward and put her elbows on the desk and her chin on the back of her interlocked fingers.

"Moms say she mine." Another shrug.

Viola smiled, leaning back into her chair. "Well, congratulations. Maybe that will settle you down. So what does Coretta want from you?"

"Nothing. We just really start communicating again. Frog don't leap if it ain't no pad to land on."

Viola grinned. "So this girl here," she said, patting on the folder. "She got you bailing her out of jail and hiring her a lawyer and everything. She must be something special. What's up with her?"

"Just a friend; caught up in a trap due to mismanagement."

Viola gave a hoot and clapped her hands in the air. "Mismanagement! You never cease to amaze me. You have been shouting about management since high school. Is that really working for you?"

"You got management?" he asked calmly, after waiting for her sarcasm to lose some of its bite.

"I manage myself," she answered indignantly.

"Naw. You just ain't met the man who's willing to invest the time. Believe me, every woman needs—no—wants to be managed. Just all depends on the brother."

Viola was curious. "What does it depend on?"

"If he strong enough. Like water, a woman rises, and if there's a brother strong enough to hold her, then she'll accept management."

" 'Cause we do the choosing," she cut in triumphantly.

Dahji nodded. "No doubt. Y'all do the choosing. And it's my job to get chose."

She grinned widely and let the silence grow pregnant

between them. For the first time, Dahji recognized the whir of the air conditioner just under a low jazz horn playing in the room. The room smelled of roses; electric roses like the ones that plugged into the wall. It was hidden somewhere. He looked around for the small wall deodorizer.

"Does she have a record?" Viola asked, bringing him back to her. He was thinking about how cool it would be to come into an office like hers and manage his clients. Maybe even work the clothing and modeling business out of something like this. Sell wallpaper, mugs, clocks, blankets, towels and whatever else he could fit the image of a beautiful woman on. He was privately excited, knowing that it was something that could be done.

"Who?" he asked, thinking about Coretta and what she could have been involved in to get arrested.

Viola widened her eyes and tapped the brown folder. "Your girlfriend who doesn't have proper management."

"Oh. Naw, this was her first time. But she shouldn't have to go to jail, right?"

"Well, all that depends on what the charges are and if there are any witnesses against her."

"I'ma have her come talk to you next week," Dahji assured her, knowing that Viola could get to the bottom of the situation. "How much damage is this going to do?" He grinned in an effort to soften her financial estimate.

She took off her glasses slowly and then pressed the intercom button on her phone console.

"Yes, Ms. Sparks?" came the young voice of her secretary.

"Please hold my calls," she said directly.

"Yes, Ms. Sparks."

"Have you gone to lunch yet, Tomika?"

"Well, I was highlighting the transcript for you."

"Go to lunch, Tomika. Pick me up a turkey sandwich, please."

"Okay. With Sun Chips?"

"Yes. Thank you. See you in thirty minutes."

"Yes, Ms. Sparks," Tomika replied.

Viola stood, came around to the front of her desk, and leaned against its shiny, wooden surface. She could have kicked Dahji's foot if she'd wanted to. "Dahji," she began, "you are right about something."

He looked up at her. Something had changed in her face; it was young and sensual. He'd seen glimpses of it during their talk. It reminded him of her in high school, when she was her more beautiful self. It was a time before responsibility and being a grown-up robbed her of her vitality. "What's that?" he asked.

"I do need management," she responded in a way that suggested a specific field of enterprise. "And I think you can help me."

Dahji let his fingers flip away from each other as they lay over his lap. "That's what I do. This gon' help my bottom line?"

She smiled. "Your money is no good with me," she said, lifting herself from the desk and standing over him. She rubbed a hand over his flowing mane. "Do you mind if I choose you to manage a situation for me?"

Dahji couldn't help but smile. It was no surprise to him that his friend would demand from him something that was famous for its stamina and size. This was her opportunity to experience the pleasure she knew he was capable of providing. He looked up at her with a steady gaze.

"My dick bin twitching since I walked in here," he lied.

She smiled appreciatively as she knelt before him and

reached for his zipper. Dahji opened his arms and let his hands rest on the cushioned ends of the chair. She grabbed his dick in the middle and pulled it through the opening in his slacks. It lay like a snake across her palm. She looked in his eyes excitedly as she gripped the heavy meat in her hand. She squeezed it to check its thickness. It pulsed, making her mouth open to gasp but there was no sound.

"It's so big," she whispered, shaking her head slightly before bowing to take the thick, bulbous helmet into her mouth. She groaned as she wrapped her lips around him and slid down its length. She hungrily licked across the base, then came up to the head and went down again. Her moans were guttural and primal. She was breathing hard through her nostrils as she sucked on him deftly.

Dahji gripped the armrests tightly, surprised at her aggressiveness. Her head bobbed and rotated as she gulped on his dick. It was as if she was unleashing long-denied desire and didn't want to disappoint. She moaned and groaned with each slurp around his dick.

Her lips popped off the head and worked at his alligator-skin belt. Quickly she undid it and unsnapped his slacks. After pulling them down to his ankles, she returned to relieve him of his silk boxers. Dahji was now naked from the waist down, and Viola gazed with wonder at the suspended meat before her. She dived onto it once again. She held it up, licked him from the base to the tip and swallowed him there. She gripped his thighs and sucked him up and down ferociously.

Dahji struggled to maintain his composure. Her hair fell into his lap as she worked and tickled his inner thighs, adding to the sensation her mouth was giving him.

"Shit," she whispered, coming up for air. While still on her knees she undid her skirt and let it drop around her knees. She stood then, so she could step out of her skirt and pull her panties off. "Come on, Dahji. Come on!" she urged him as she turned around and placed her hands on her desk.

Dahji stood up from the chair with Viola's wide ass before him. She swayed her hips from side to side in anticipation. He held her in place and sunk his dick inside of her.

"Oooohhhhhhh!" she groaned as he slid into her deeply. She was tight from inactivity. Her nameplate fell to the floor as she repositioned herself.

Dahji braced his feet on the carpet and moved in and out of her with tight strokes. Her moans sent shivers through his body. Her fresh ass cheeks were spread before him and the tension of her pussy made him squirm. He couldn't remember the last time he'd had pussy as tight as this. This tightness was different from a muscle trick done by an experienced woman, this tightness took him back to fucking a woman who'd never been fucked before. This tightness was common in high school but very rare in adulthood.

"Damn," he grumbled, gripping her fleshy waist tightly and smashing into her, his stomach muscles tight.

"I know. It's been a long time," she moaned, pressing back against him. She was growing wetter and his strokes found a tight rhythm. A pattern was developing. As she moved back into him, he shoved between her walls and his thick head pulsed sensitively.

No, he could not remember the last time he'd had good pussy like this. She was as tight as a fire hydrant and growing wetter by the stroke. The sound of him slapping into her ass echoed in the room. Her gasps followed each slap. When the first drop of sweat trickled down Dahji's face, he knew this would be no ordinary fuck session. She tossed her hair from side to side with each pounding, adding to the hypnotic rhythm they had developed.

She hissed with an intake of air and slammed back into him one good time so that his dick slid out of her. She turned around and hopped onto her desk. She spread her legs as Dahji stumbled forward, his pants still around his ankles, and nudged his meat into her once again. Viola gripped the edge of the desk as Dahji fit himself between her legs and slid into her. She raised her ankles high in the air and her pussy opened for him. They met with wet slapping sounds as he pummeled her with slick abandon. Sweat trickled down both sides of his face and his breathing was as hard as hers.

"Ahh! You got it!" she gasped, looking down her body at his thick dick going in and out of her fat, untended pussy.

"This what you want?" he asked, his face tight with passion. He slammed into her wet pussy with long strokes. He rubbed along her hot walls going in, and dipped his dick at a sharp angle on the way out. She cried out at his effort. He found her tender spot and stroked to this meaty space with precision. She bucked, hissed, and shuddered under his pounding. Like a dance, he swayed into her soft flesh, making a thudding beat as their bodies met. She shrieked in pleasure and huffed to maintain her end of the momentum.

Sweat trickled down Dahji's spine and Viola's flesh was hot and moist under his touch as he grunted, feeling himself grow hot in his center.

"Ooowwww!" Viola gasped, vibrating violently as she creamed over his meat. He came away from her with a fresh coat of her milky pleasure. With each continued thrust, her cum waxed and thinned over his swollen joint.

Dahji short stroked her with powerful thrusts, the tip of his dick hitting her bottom. He swelled inside of her and exploded deep within. She felt the hot juices flow from him and wrapped her legs around his waist to keep him close while she squeezed the pulsing organ.

"Shit," Dahji gasped as the last of his shudders escaped him. Viola smiled up at him as she lay on her back across her desk.

"That was incredible," she breathed out happily, her skin glowing, cheeks rosy and green eyes glittering. "Simply incredible," she added, exhausted, wiping damp strands of hair from her shining forehead.

"You got it good, V," he said, feeling her pulse around him. She smiled with heated satisfaction and breathed hotly with her mouth open, a soft sheen of sweat on her face.

Dahji pulled out of her slowly, tensing as she tightened her pussy around the tender meat until he was free. This was one of the rare times he found satisfaction from a woman. He knew at that moment that he would be back to manage her in the same way.

Chapter Twenty-Six

Sherrelle

Sherrelle was surrounded by colorful HoodSweet apparel. She basked in her newfound determination to make an impact in the clothing industry. Along with the shipment of boy shorts, wifebeaters, t-shirts, gym shorts, fleece jackets, nylon jogging suits, and cotton sweaters was the paperwork that would tie her to the HoodSweet enterprise. She'd received an allotment of business cards that named her Midwest vice president of sales and marketing. She stared at the cards for a long time. This made it all the more official. The feeling in her stomach was like large, exotic butterflies swimming in shallow water. She was both happy and nervous—happy that she was taking charge of her life and nervous about what it would mean for her marriage. She'd been Percy's wife for a long time, and now it was time to be her own woman.

She heard Peaches pull to the curb, her car struggling as it died in front of her house. When she looked out the window, Peaches was already running up the driveway ahead of the falling sun and away from the car that might blow up at any minute with anger.

"Why don't you get a rental?" Sherrelle asked in the doorway as Peaches climbed the stairs.

"I'm going to get every ounce of oil from that thing," she answered in a sweet exhalation of breath. She fell against Sherrelle as if she'd just been saved from certain torment. "Help me," she hissed against her neck.

"You are beyond help," Sherrelle responded around her laughter as she supported Peaches on her arm, pretending that she did indeed need help.

"We are so about to be major bitches!" Peaches said, flopping onto the couch and staring wide-eyed at the clothing strewn around the living room. In her purse was the manufacturing brochure.

Sherrelle was standing on the edges of the enterprise, looking at Peaches with a sense of wonder. "You think so?" she asked nervously.

"Hell, yeah, girl! Don't get scared now! Shit is going to get real right around this camp. Trust me," she said with her head held high and her arms flung across the couch to her sides. "And your husband is just going to have to be mad as a cat in the dog pound!"

Sherrelle laughed at this. She needed some humor to diffuse her nervousness. "You talk to Dahji?"

"I just got off the phone with him." She started to swivel her ass on the couch and wave her hands in the air. "That's my man, girl," she sang. "He went to see my lawyer and told me I gotta go see her on Wednesday. Ain't that sweet?" she asked Sherrelle.

Sherrelle slapped her hands to her thighs in a pout. "What did he say about Marlin?"

Peaches let her head slide back on her neck. "Have you forgotten that you're married? First you have a fight and pretend like it's nothing, and now you trying to play wifey. What's really going on?"

"I don't know. He's all inside of me," she answered, stepping over a box and sitting next to her friend on the couch. "I just want things to work out for him."

"If my man got anything to do with it, then it's already handled. Don't trip," Peaches assured her.

"What time he want us to come to his house tomorrow?"

"In the a.m." Peaches bent to lift a pink sweater from a box. HoodSweet was scrawled across its front in cursive letters. "I'ma wear this for the website." She held it to her chest and turned to Sherrelle.

"That's cute, but I was thinking you should wear something like this," she said, pulling a white, half-tee from a pile by her foot.

Peaches snatched the thin material from her. "I ain't trying to be all hoochiefied for our first photo shoot! We can have them other bitches do that."

"What other...?" Sherrelle questioned.

"Oh. I didn't tell you? Dahji got a whole plan worked out. He's going to have a bunch of women model for their own websites. He wants to put them on coffee mugs, wallpaper, screen-savers, and whatever else a bitch can get put on," she said, waving her fingers through the air. "It's way past what we thought. Now ain't my man a boss?"

Sherrelle was absorbing it all. She hadn't considered how big this could be.

"But he did say that he was on his way to handle some business for Marlin. I don't know what, though," Peaches added with a shrug before reaching for a blue nylon jogging suit.

★ ★ ★

Dahji watched the sun disappear behind the row of satellite dishes atop the Hyatt Regency Hotel. He'd arrived thirty minutes early and parked at the back of the parking lot. This was the last important business of the day. This would set him right as a sports agent and make Marlin a happy man. His dick lay between his legs, idling like a powerful sports car ready to roar when called upon.

Her name was Sasha Grand and all Gloria would say about her was that she was the wife of a wealthy man and had an unsatisfactory sex life. She'd also said with a wink in her voice that she was someone he might want to keep in contact with. He didn't have a problem with that, but what Gloria had failed to realize was that he was committed to using his other head to get ahead.

He'd just drank his second vial of ginseng when his cell phone rang.

"Coretta. What's up?" he answered.

"Hi." Her voice was laced with sweetness. "I was just thinking about you. How are you?"

"Straight as the board of health. Where's my daughter?" He liked the sound of that: his daughter.

"She just got through eating dinner. Her stomach hurts because she drank too much soda."

"Is that right? Why you let her do that?"

"I didn't," Coretta said in her defense. "She snuck into the icebox and did it herself. I'm not even going to whoop her because her stomach is doing it for me."

"We gon' have to get together so I can spend some time with her," he said, watching a sharply dressed white couple emerge from a Lincoln stretch limousine under the green canopy at the entrance of the hotel.

"How's this weekend for you? There's a park near my house."

"Sounds good."

Coretta let the quiet separate her thoughts. "I really enjoyed spending time with you," she said.

"You had that planned didn't you?" He had to admit that it was nice to make love to her once again. Now that he knew how cruel she could be for her own self interests, he would be able to manage her better.

"Did you like my plan?"

"For that once. We gon' have to chill on those impromptu pop-ups though." Traffic had suddenly grown heavy at the entrance. Two large, white vans had just deposited two loads of elderly men and women dressed for summer in Hawaii: tourists. Colts football hats bobbed above the crowd.

"Oh. You got a girlfriend or something?" Coretta wanted to know.

"Something like that," he answered vaguely. "Check it out—I'm 'bout to roll. Get at me later when my daughter's stomach stops hurting and she can talk to me."

"Okay. Where you got to go right now?"

"There you go. You know what happened to the dog who stuck his nose in the hole?"

"Let me guess—he got bit."

Dahji smiled. "Naw. Red ants crawled up his nose into his brain and drove him crazy. He never stopped barking and went hoarse."

"That's crazy," Coretta laughed out. "Well, I'ma keep my nose to myself. Talk to you later, boo." She laughed some more with a private joke.

Dahji checked himself in the mirror (shaking his flowing mane so that it sat just right over the collar of his leather coat) and put an Altoid on his tongue to kill the tart ginseng. He cupped his balls to awaken them before he stepped from his Range Rover.

Girbaud jeans over suede Phat Farm boots and a Calvin Klein white t-shirt set off his cool mod look. With a minimum of pieces (one carat diamond hanging from his ear and a diamond bezel Rolex on his wrist), he could have been a young entrepreneur or hip hop artist— or maybe even the comedian pimp Katt Williams. It wouldn't have been the first time he was mistaken for him.

Gloria had said that Sasha would be in room 369 at six thirty. He checked his watch: 6:40. She must have been here before six, he thought to himself, wondering how he could have missed an African woman who may or may not have been obese. Maybe it was because he had been looking for a very dark, purple black woman in kente cloth. The woman who answered the door only fit one of those criteria. She was obese but she wasn't purple black. She was a white woman with long, blonde hair and electric blue eyes that lay hidden in her pretty face like rare diamonds.

"Good evening, Mr. McBeth," she said with a bright smile. She spoke with an accent. Dahji let his hand slide into her soft palm, thinking that she must be filthy rich. Or royalty. The diamond ring wedged over her knuckle stood out from her pasty finger like a moment of sparkling wealth. Around her neck was a lady Rolex chain with a row of diamonds leading to a crown of diamonds in rose gold between two mounds of creamy breasts. These breasts heaved as she stepped to the side to let him pass. The purple negligee did nothing to hide the heavy, round limbs attached to her barrel-sized torso. She was layered in silk that looked like all it would take was one pull of a string to send it cascading to the floor like a dropping curtain.

"You must be Sasha Grand. Where are you from exactly?" Dahji asked as she closed the door behind him. A quick glance around the room proved her efficiency and thought-fulness. Near the foot of the bed was a cart of food: shrimp, raw oysters, and two silver buckets holding champagne bottles wrapped in fluffy towels. All of it was untouched. She had been waiting for him. He recognized the voice of the black African woman singing a tribal song (he came by this education in his youth, under his father's tutelage when he thought young Dahji might fancy a singing career) through speakers set high throughout the large suite.

"South Africa," she answered, moving tentatively toward him. "Ever traveled there?" she asked, her hands clasped in front of her. She was nervous. Dahji made up his mind to think of her as a woman he desired with all his heart.

"Not yet. But there's still time," he replied, slipping the leather coat from his shoulders and laying it across the corner of the cart.

"Sure there is," she said, relaxing. "You'll love the country." Her accent was nice, Dahji thought to himself as he lifted a glass toward her. She nodded. "Please. Thank you," she answered, taking the opportunity to have a seat on the bed.

Dahji poured a drink and handed it to her. Then he poured one for himself. "A toast to new friendships," he said, touching his glass to hers.

"Thank you," she said, bringing the glass to her lips. "I really didn't know what to expect. I've never done this before." Her smile was youthful and thankful.

"Gloria is a very special person. I don't usually do this myself." He grinned when her eyes studied him. "But I'm glad I agreed to meet you." Now she smiled, her rosy cheeks balling up under her eyes.

"She didn't mention that you were debonair."

He shrugged, plucking a raw oyster from the plate and dropping it into his mouth. "I don't know about that," he began, lifting another oyster from the silver tray and stepping toward her. "But it's easy with a woman as pretty as you." She let him place the oyster on her tongue. She chewed happily, her eyes flashing and her hands falling to her sides atop the bed. She was like a schoolgirl just discovering her womanhood.

"You are really nice," she said, her face widening into a generous smile. "I like your hair." Her eyes studied his mouth as he bit into a shrimp.

"Are those your real eyes?" he asked, lifting the tray and a bottle of champagne from the cart and sitting next to her on the bed. With his foot, he pushed the cart across the carpeted room until it bounced against the mirrored dresser. He blinked away the reflection of them as they sat on the bed. For one instant, he saw how small he was next to her, the way her arms bulged from her body. He briefly thought of a pale Barney the purple dinosaur. He smiled despite his best effort not to.

"Please share," she asked, her insecurity rearing its ugly head. Dahji faced her as he refilled her champagne flute.

"There was this man who came home from work to make love to his wife. He was a mechanic." Dahji refilled his own glass, aware of her attention on his Rolex watch. Her eyes scanned him further, looking to detect something she may have missed in her first character assessment. "He wouldn't take a shower. He'd jump on his wife the moment he got home."

She was smiling, taking a sip of champagne. Her hand brushed across his leg to urge him on.

"His wife complained to him that he was too rough. She wanted him to pamper her, and take a shower, and talk sweet to her." Dahji took another sip, giving Sasha time to digest his story. "So he says okay. Next day, he comes home and showers, puts on some good smelling lotion, caresses his wife. He asks her, 'Is this nice honey?' She says 'yes.' Then he asks her if he's being romantic, if he's showing enough finesse? She says 'yes' to all of this."

Sasha laid her palm on his leg. It was warm.

"Yes, he's being romantic. Yes, he's showing finesse. So then he says, 'Good. Now will you please pass the pussy?' "

The sound that came from Sasha's mouth sounded like air erupting from the end of an elephant's trunk. It was short and loud, then it dissolved into quiet laughter, her whole body bouncing and rolling, her eyes shut tight. Dahji was smiling at her and sipping his champagne when she opened one eye to see if he was still there. He smiled wider and placed his hand over hers as it squeezed his thigh.

Dahji took her champagne glass from her and stood to put the tray of food and bottle of hooch back on the cart. He turned and stood in front of her with his legs apart. She'd settled down and was looking at him with a calm expression, a hint of a smile playing at the corners of her full, red lips. He loosened his belt slowly and let his pants fall open to reveal a glimpse of the silk boxers beneath. She took a deep breath as he pulled his shirt over his head and dropped it to the floor.

"You have a beautiful skin tone," she said, her eyes moving over his bare chest.

Dahji stepped over to her and thrust his hips forward. "You want to help me out of this?"

Sasha gently pulled at his pants as he stepped out of his boots. She bowed her head as she followed the pants to his ankles, and held him steady so he could step out of them. When she raised up, the back of her head bumped against his protruding dick.

"Oh," she gasped, then widened her eyes when she saw the thick joint standing at attention. She raised her hand under it and let it weigh on her palm. "Oh," she repeated.

Dahji reached for his pants and pulled a Magnum condom from the pocket. He held her gaze as he ripped it open and slid the rubber over his dick. He then pulled the thin spaghetti strap that dropped the curtain over her shoulders. Her hanging breasts were tipped with large strawberry nipples.

"Very nice," he said, reaching for a breast with both hands and taking a thick nipple into his mouth. He sucked on it tenderly, feeling her breathe heavily. He laid it back against her body and repeated this with the other breast. She assisted by holding up the first one so he could switch easily from one to the other, letting his tongue drag across her soft, sun-scented flesh.

"That feels so good," she whispered as he pressed her nipple between his teeth. She worked her silk negligee from her body and scooted up on the bed, him following with her nipple between his lips. He rubbed down over her stomach and found the crease that would lead to her pussy. She was wet and he dipped his finger through the fleshy mound. She inhaled a strong gust of air and her body shuddered. *This is going to be easy*, Dahji thought to himself.

"Yesss," she whispered, grabbing at his swinging dick and spreading her legs wide on the bed. "Stick it in," she instructed. Her stomach spread out like a water balloon on cement. He arched his back to fit around the huge mound and poked his dick blindly into the spot between her legs. It was hit and miss until he decided to rub it along her legs like a track until he caught at her opening. He knew he'd hit her sweet spot when her mouth flew open and her eyes shut tight. She gasped when the head pushed through her wet folds. He couldn't get a full stride into the sopping wet pussy because her stomach was in the way. He reached below her navel and lifted up her gut, opening her up to him and allowing him to share more of his dick inside of her.

"Oooowweeee!" she moaned with satisfaction. Like a stuck pig, she squealed with each motion. Her legs rotated like propellers beside him as he struggled to keep her stomach lifted and out of the way, and position his body so he could maintain contact with her pussy.

She folded over his meat like a warm blanket. Squish, squash, squish, squash; her pussy spoke as he stroked the hot flesh. Warm like an oven and fitting like a squeaky glove, she tightened around him. Her breasts fell over her body like heavy sand bags. They bubbled and rocked as he humped into her. She hissed through clenched teeth, her hands finding his hips and rolling on the slim frame as a guide and an urge.

"Ooowee. Ooooohhhhweeee," she shrieked, her legs rocking beside him. Her body rolled as one while, under the skin, separate quakes shook her smoothly.

Slowly, she rolled to her side and hitched her leg up just under the knee. She opened up for him, giving him better access. As he sank into her, she squealed anew with muted pleasure, the breath escaping from her lips like air seeping through a hole in a tire.

Dahji grabbed her heavy leg and lifted it higher, her pink pussy winking at him as he disappeared inside the fleshy wound. It took all of his length to penetrate the obstacles of fat along her thighs and what fell from her waist and stomach. Yet she was hot and comforting, deep and tight. He stroked her long and slow, hitting every part of

her pussy, enjoying the odd sounds she made. Her blonde
hair lay matted around her forehead, her perspiration a glue
seeping from her pores. She shined, pink from pleasure as
Dahji sank into her deeply, increasing his motion and mar-
veling at how her body absorbed him. It was his challenge
to make her scream out. He jabbed into her roughly, making her lips part from the sudden intrusion. Hard stroke
after hard stroke, he sank into her.

"Ahhaaahhhahhhhaaa!" she finally screamed out, her
body rocking on its side and pushing her juices out of her
pussy and onto his swollen dick. She turned onto her stomach and spread her knees wide. Her ass shot up in the air.

He fit himself between her legs and gripped her wide
hips like two beach balls. His jutting joint found the wet
hole again and sank into it. She rotated her hips before him,
making him tremble. He climbed nearly on top of her ass
and stroked downward, hitting the spot that made her pant
heavily into the pillows. Side to side, front to back, he went
in and out, gripping her hot ass.

"Slap it. Slap it," she instructed, coming up for air.

Dahji gave her a soft slap on her ass.

"Harder!"

His hand sounded like an assault when it met her flesh.
She bucked and screamed out for more. He slapped her ass
again, leaving a red print. Again she screamed out, her ass
slamming back onto his pounding dick. He was beginning
to enjoy it as much as she was. He slapped her ass as he
pounded into her. Again and again, his open palm made
hard contact with her ass. She was red and huffing, moaning into the pillow as she quaked and rocked, creaming
thick pleasure down her legs and over his dick. He was slick
going into her.

"In my butt. In my butt," she gasped, wagging her hips

as an invitation.

Dahji spread her cheeks and found the pink hole. He squeezed past the tightness and explored a new feeling. Her cream disappeared from his dick as he slid into her ass. She lowered herself down on the bed and lay flat like a large sea animal. Her arms and legs were spread wide, hugging the mattress. Dahji felt her ass tighten around him, squeezing him and massaging him. He struggled to pull out, fearing that the rubber would slip off. She held him in place and worked her ass muscles around him until his head swelled and he exploded. He pumped against her ass and collapsed onto her back, feeling like he was on a raft out to sea.

Dahji was trapped inside of her. He could feel her body settling under him like a large radiator powering down from blazing all night through a fierce winter storm.

The deep, throaty voice of the African woman sang out in a ballad, surrounded by the heavy beating of drums. Then she lowered her voice to a whisper and the drums were replaced by flutes and the chirping of birds.

"Tell me another joke," Sasha requested in an exhausted, hot whisper.

"Master John's daughter was intent on sleeping with a slave. To punish her, Master John sought out the slave with the biggest dick. He was going to get the slave with sixteen inches of dick. He really wanted to show his little girl not to mess with the slaves." Sasha giggled under him, her body vibrating against his stomach.

"So the master went to the fields and asked for his head slave Bonifu. He said he was looking for a slave with sixteen inches and wanted Bonifu to fuck his daughter."

Sasha laughed some more. Dahji wasn't sure if she was laughing at the master or the daughter.

"Bonifu grabbed at his potato sack for pants and backed

away from Master John. He told Master John that he could-
n't do it. 'No, Master!' he shouted. 'I ain't gon' do none ah
dat! I ain't gon' cut off two inches of my dick for nobody!' "

Sasha roared out in laughter, her body heaving and
twisting. Dahji rocked with her, holding on for fear of
being rolled off the bed.

She calmed down and blew out a loud breath of air.
"You are so funny. I do hope I can see you again," she said,
one eye looking up past her shoulder.

"We might be able to hang out again," Dahji answered
as he worked his dick from her asshole.

"That would be so nice," she said, turning over onto
her back with a wide roll. "If there's anything that I can do
for you, please let me know. I'm going to give you my personal number. Okay?" she asked, coming to a sitting position.

Dahji nodded with a smile; he had another one in his
pocket. He was sure that she would come in handy. He felt
her eyes on him as he stepped into the bathroom. He
grinned into the mirror. Yeah, he would keep her on file.
She would definitely come in handy.

Chapter Twenty-Seven

Marlin

Marlin was high. When the coach called him into his office, he wasn't expecting what came next. He was told that he'd made the team and was handed some papers that detailed the terms of his agreement.

When he called Dahji to give him the news, he shouldn't have been surprised that Dahji had sounded so sure. Dahji simply instructed him to come by the house. When he asked Dahji if there was a party going on— what with the laughter and music playing in the background— Dahji responded that there was snow on the mountains that was about to melt and run down into the valley and make the grass green.

Marlin laughed, said that he was on his way, and jumped into his Escalade. The running back inside the glass ball stood firm as he shook up the snow inside and placed the gift back onto the dash. He still hadn't spoken to Sherrelle after their fiery exchange the previous day. It was amazing to him how she moved inside of him. But she was married. And he was married. These certainties seemed small against the passion he felt in his bones for her.

Marlin pulled into an empty space outside the high-rise building that Dahji called home. He wasn't surprised at the gleaming steel and tinted glass that rose to the sky like a monument to privilege and wealth.

The lobby was carpeted with a thick, royal blue shag, and dotted with large palm plants strategically placed by the stainless steel elevators and bookending the two sets of large leather sofas under vibrant watercolor landscape paintings. Directly in front of him sat a heavy black man behind a waist-high mahogany desk. He stood, revealing the large pistol on his waist when Marlin walked through the door. He was hanging up the phone and reaching for a folder hidden behind the ledge of the desk.

Marlin waited by the desk, aware of the musk cologne the man wore. He looked like he should be playing football.

"What's up, bro?" the guard asked, dropping the folder to the desk and reaching for the phone again. He was a busy man.

"Marlin Cassidy for Dahji McBeth."

Ron, as it was revealed by his gold-plated nametag, pressed on the phone console. "Mr. McBeth, I've got a Marlin Cassidy here for you," he said gruffly, looking down at the folder. Marlin knew he got the okay when Ron looked up at him and nodded his head.

"You got it," Ron said before replacing the phone. "Go on up. Elevator on the left will take you to the top."

"Right on," Marlin replied, giving the hefty man a small head nod.

The elevator opened onto a quiet hallway. At the far end, there was a deeply carved wooden door. In the middle was the word penthouse, stenciled inside of a square, gold plate. This was where Dahji lived, Marlin said to himself as the thick hall carpeting absorbed his steps.

Laughter. Shrieking giggles. Horns blaring. Jay-Z rapping over a hard-knocking beat. Marlin listened at the door, feeling the energy of what was on the other side seep into his soul. He was a new man running for the Indianapolis Colts. He never imagined that he would get back on the field by way of the little man he'd met in a Jacuzzi. He knocked on the door and gave himself a quick once-over—Jordan warm-ups over Jordan trainers, hair trimmed into a tight Caesar, face smooth with a generous smile of satisfaction and good news.

The door opened. Marlin wasn't expecting the beautiful, dark-haired Latina who stood before him. Her light brown eyes sparkled from a face with long lashes, generous lips, and deep dimples. "Hello," she said, her voluptuous body curving inside of a velour, HoodSweet tracksuit. The top was open halfway to reveal her creamy cleavage.

"Marly Marl!" Dahji's voice rang out before he stepped into the frame holding a camera. He handed it off to the beautiful woman who'd opened the door. "Penelope," he said as an introduction, "meet the new running back of the Colts." He nodded his head to urge Marlin inside. He was not prepared to see Sherrelle standing in a pair of boy shorts and a wifebeater by the large window overlooking the city. And by her stunned expression, she was not prepared to see him either. They held each other's gaze for two beats, then Dahji said, "Grab the camera, Penny. I got some business to handle real quick."

"Hey, Marlin," Peaches waved from a chair by the window.

"How y'all doing?" Marlin asked, his eyes sweeping around the room to include the pretty blonde woman standing next to Peaches.

"Hi," Sherrelle breathed out when his eyes stopped at her.

"Ebony, Maria," Dahji called to the cocoa-complexioned woman who stopped just short of reaching Sherrelle's beauty and the dark-haired Latina who stood next to her by the couch. They both wore matching HoodSweet v-necked t-shirts and pink boy shorts. "Y'all take some pictures with Sherrelle," he instructed while motioning Marlin to the kitchen.

"What you got going on?" Marlin asked from his seat at the edge of the counter. Dahji pulled a folder from a drawer.

"That's your girl's clothing line right there. We gon' take it to the next level—mugs, wallpaper, ringtones, image downloads, whatever else. Didn't I say the valley about to turn green from fresh water?" he asked, looking up at Marlin with a smile as he slid a short stack of paperwork across the counter.

Sherrelle stood between Ebony and Maria. Her eyes looked up at him as she posed for the camera. Marlin struggled to tear his gaze away as a smile crossed her lips that he knew was for him. "What's this?" he asked, picking up the paperwork.

"Contractual agreement," Dahji said slowly. "Basic. Twenty percent for me, eighty for you. Got incentives in there for everything from carries to how long you stay healthy. Got some stuff on substance abuse, which you ain't got no problem with, right?" Marlin didn't know Dahji had looked up at him until he realized he had stopped talking.

"Not me," Marlin answered, seeing a hint of seriousness in Dahji for the first time. "Stuff make me dizzy," he added with a small grin.

"Performance is everything, Marly Marl," Dahji said.

They were changing positions. Peaches joined Sherrelle in front of the window. They smiled for the camera and intertwined their bodies, as if to suggest that they were or had been lovers. Something in Dahji's voice made him look back at him.

"That's right, bru bru. It's all about performance," Dahji said. "That's what they want from us. Stud."

Marlin nodded his head though he knew not what Dahji was talking about.

Dahji smiled. "Want something to drink?" he asked, already moving to the refrigerator and grabbing a jug of cranberry juice. "See, Marly Marl," he began from the cabinet where he was grabbing two glasses, "white folks expect us to perform. They don't expect us to think. When we start thinking, then we a problem." He poured the dark red liquid. It swirled in the glasses like vibrant blood. Dahji handed Marlin a glass and toasted him in the air before taking a big gulp.

"Black man got a big dick. Black man can run the ball. Black man can't think," Dahji said in a low whisper, then pointed his finger to his head. "Black man got to think to get ahead, Marly Marl, without making a whole lotta noise. Quietly."

"I feel you," Marlin answered. "You look like you do alright for yourself." He nodded subtly, eyeing the man responsible for putting him back in the game.

"Got a man with a gun downstairs." He grinned broadly before going back to his point and the neutral expression he wore when making his observations. "That's why I love your coach. Black man who proved that we can think. You're lucky to be playing for him, Marly Marl."

"I'm lucky you're my agent," he answered, raising his glass for another toast. "To the thinking black man."

"Sho, you right!" Dahji smiled. He let Jay-Z's words flow through the luxurious space as they turned to watch Sherrelle move with sexual energy and smile for the camera. She attracted her equal in Peaches. "What you gon' do about her? I know love when I see it," Dahji asked, his head tilting toward the living room.

Marlin looked at Sherrelle. She'd slipped on some nylon track pants and a jacket. It only enhanced her beauty. "Ain't nothing I can do. We're both married." When the words left his mouth, there was no conviction in them. They were as light as cotton and could easily be blown away with the softest of suggestions.

"It's a new day and a new time, Marly Marl."

"What's up with you and Peaches? How'd that situation at the jailhouse go?" Marlin wanted to know.

Dahji lifted his palms to the ceiling. "It is what it is. She under new management."

Marlin smiled. *New management*, he thought to himself as Sherrelle caught him staring at her. There was a light around her. It seemed to cast a shadow over the pretty white girl who had joined her by the large, green plant next to the wicker chair. Sherrelle's long, dark hair hung in loose curls over the red nylon jacket.

"Let me tighten this up," Dahji said, walking into the living room and grabbing the camera from Penelope. He pulled Sherrelle from the scene and directed Maria and Penelope to model in front of the window.

Sherrelle was walking in Marlin's direction. Their eyes were locked on one another. Marlin turned to her as if pulled by an invisible string. His heart skipped a beat as she made that final step to him and her lips met his. She kissed him wholly, her tongue on fire as it moved over his.

"Woooo!" Peaches hooted from the living room. Her

cheer was echoed by the "You go, girl!" and "That's right!" and "Muy caliente!" chants of the other women.

Sherrelle let her lips explore his and her hunger grew more intense. Their arms found their way around each other and they embraced as if reuniting from a long absence. Tenderly and lovingly, they explored each other and relished in their common attraction. Words were not necessary as they spoke their intentions to each other. They were in their own space, finding one another outside of the constraints of their private lives. Hands lay over each other like water around raindrops.

He did not know whose lips moved first or who first threw their inhibition aside, but it was clear that they were locked together so closely, not even air could come between them. Still dressed, they were more than naked. Their skin pulsed—behind the ear, at the fingertips, above the eyes. A needle of excitement ran through them, coursing through his knees and traveling up her thigh. He held a hand across her throat. He wanted to vanish inside the heat of their bodies like a drop of dew in the sun, feel her breasts under his fingers, hear her call his name. It was true, the way he felt. It was safe. Like a net close to the surface, he could be caught, wanted to be caught, wanted to catch her. She felt good in his arms, like this was where she was meant to be. Her lips spoke of the same feeling. Indeed, it was a new day and time for a new love to be shared to compliment a new success. They were united in this.

— finito —

TRU LIFE PUBLISHING

NAME:_____

INSTITUTION: _____

ADDRESS: _____

_____

CITY: _____ STATE_____ ZIP_____

PHONE: (_____)_____ FAX: (_____)_____

E-mail: _____

Credit Card: Visa ☐ MC ☐ Amex ☐ Discover ☐ ecard ☐

Number _____

Exp Date: _____/____Signature:

TITLE	PRICE	QTY	TOTAL
1. The Streets Love No One	$14.95		
2. A Lovely Murder Down South	$14.95		
3. Gods, Earths and 85 ers	$9.95		
4. Consequences of Oppression	$9.95		
5. Juicy Moments	$15.00		
6. Mirror and The Reflection	$12.00		
7. Looking For Black Love	$9.95		
8. A Neighborly Affair	$15.00		
9.			
10.			
11.			
12.			
13.			
14.			
15.			
16.			
17.			
18.			
	Subtotal		
...SHIPPING CHARGES...	Tax		
First book..........................$3.50	Shipping		
each additional book...............$1.00	Total		

Make checks or money orders payable to:-
TRU LIFE PUBLISHING ·
P.O. Box 21224, Brooklyn, NY, 11201

TRU LIFE PUBLISHING

NAME: _____

INSTITUTION: _____

ADDRESS: _____

_____

CITY: _____ STATE _____ ZIP _____

PHONE: (_____) _____ FAX: (_____) _____

E-mail: _____

Credit Card: Visa ☐ MC ☐ Amex ☐ Discover ☐ ecard ☐

Number _____

Exp Date: _____/____ Signature:

TITLE	PRICE	QTY	TOTAL
1. The Streets Love No One	$14.95		
2. A Lovely Murder Down South	$14.95		
3. Gods, Earths and 85 ers	$9.95		
4. Consequences of Oppression	$9.95		
5. Juicy Moments	$15.00		
6. Mirror and The Reflection	$12.00		
7. Looking For Black Love	$9.95		
8. A Neighborly Affair	$15.00		
9.			
10.			
11.			
12.			
13.			
14.			
15.			
16.			
17.			
18.			
	Subtotal		
...SHIPPING CHARGES...	Tax		
First book.............................$3.50	Shipping		
each additional book...............$1.00	Total		

Make checks or money orders payable to:-
TRU LIFE PUBLISHING ·
P.O. Box 21224, Brooklyn, NY, 11201

Introducing **Hood Sweet Designs**

ITEM: T-Shirt
STYLE: Z

Sample order form

	ITEM	COLOR	SIZE	STYLE	PRICE	QTY	TOTAL
1.	T-Shirt	B	XL	Z	$14.95	1	$14.95

COLOR	STYLE	SIZE
W = White	Y =	S = Small
B = Black	Z =	M = Medium
		X = Large
		XL=X-tra Large

HOOD SWEET

NAME: _____

INSTITUTION _____

ADDRESS: _____

_____

CITY: _____ ST_____ ZIP_____ + _____

PHONE: (_____)_____ Fax: (_____)_____

E-mail: _____

Credit Card: Visa ☐ MC ☐ Amex ☐ Discover ☐ ecard ☐

Number _____

Exp Date: _____/____ **Signature:** _____

STYLE Y

STYLE Z

W = white   B = Black

	ITEM	COLOR	SIZE	STYLE	PRICE	QTY	TOTAL
1.	Tank top	W B	S M L XL	Y Z	$14.95		
2.	T-shirts				$14.95		
3.					$14.95		
4.					$14.95		
5.							
6.							
7.							
8.							

Subtotal _____

Shipping _____

NY Tax _____

Total

...SHIPPING CHARGES...
Ground first item...............$ 3.50
each additional item...........$ 1.00

Make checks or money orders payable to
TRU LIFE PUBLISHING ·
P.O. Box 21224, Brooklyn, NY, 11201

HOOD SWEET

NAME:_____

INSTITUTION _____

ADDRESS: _____
_____

CITY: _____ ST_____ ZIP_____ + _____

PHONE: (_____)_____ Fax: (_____)_____

E-mail: _____

Credit Card: Visa ☐ MC ☐ Amex ☐ Discover ☐ ecard ☐

Number _____

Exp Date: _____/____Signature: _____

HoodSweet

MORE THAN A DYME

HoodSweet

MORE THAN A DYME

STYLE Y　　　　　　　　　　　　**STYLE Z**

W = white B = Black

	ITEM	COLOR	SIZE	STYLE	PRICE	QTY	TOTAL
1.	Tank top	W B	S M L XL	Y Z	$14.95		
2.	T-shirts				$14.95		
3.					$14.95		
4.					$14.95		
5.							
6.							
7.							
8.							

...SHIPPING CHARGES...	
Ground first item	$ 3.50
each additional item	$ 1.00

Subtotal _____

Shipping _____

NY Tax _____

Total

Make checks or money orders payable to
TRU LIFE PUBLISHING ·
P.O. Box 21224, Brooklyn, NY, 11201

Signature Peter Mack Apparel SINCE 1889

Introducing Hood Sweet Designs

ITEM: Tank Top
STYLE: Y

ITEM: Tank Top
STYLE: Z